W9-BTB-544

BUT NOT FOR LONG

ALSO BY MICHELLE WILDGEN

You're Not You

BUT NOT FOR LONG

MICHELLE WILDGEN

Thomas Dunne Books ≋ New York
St. Martin's Press

This is a work of fiction. All of the characters, organizations, and events portrayed in this novel are either products of the author's imagination or are used fictitiously.

THOMAS DUNNE BOOKS.
An imprint of St. Martin's Press.

BUT NOT FOR LONG. Copyright © 2009 by Michelle Wildgen. All rights reserved. Printed in the United States of America. For information, address St. Martin's Press, 175 Fifth Avenue, New York, N.Y. 10010.

www.thomasdunnebooks.com
www.stmartins.com

Library of Congress Cataloging-in-Publication Data

Wildgen, Michelle.
    But not for long / Michelle Wildgen. — 1st ed.
        p.   cm.
    ISBN 978-0-312-57141-2
    1. Married people—Fiction.   2. Environmental degradation—Fiction.   3. Interpersonal relations—Fiction.   4. Madison (Wis.)—Fiction.   5. Psychological fiction.   I. Title.
    PS3623.I542B87   2009
    813'.6—dc22

                                        2009023456

First Edition: October 2009

10 9 8 7 6 5 4 3 2 1

FOR STEVE

ACKNOWLEDGMENTS

I owe heartfelt thanks and a pile of favors to numerous people, all of whom went way above and far beyond. Emilie Stewart is a warrior, and one I'm eternally grateful to have at my side. Katie Gilligan's enthusiastic support and insightful edits made this a much better book than it was when it came to her. Helen Chin's thorough copyediting smoothed the many oddities that pile up over three years of shoving words around. Claudia Zuluaga understood where the book was headed about two years before I did and was kind enough to repeat it to me, over and over. From the first to the final draft, brilliant readers Sarah Yaw, Rae Meadows, Albert Martinez, Sydney Long, Jon Raymond, Emily Dickmann, and Lucy Neave provided much-needed feedback and, in some cases, excellent therapy. I think every single family member, friend, neighbor, and acquaintance I have has done free publicity work for me, and I appreciate every single bit of it. Finally, Steve O'Brien's willingness to live his entire life as improv is creatively inspiring, generally hilarious, and deeply unhinged. His unwavering love and support are crucial, too. Thank you.

Weather forecast for tonight: dark. Continued dark overnight, with widely scattered light by morning. —GEORGE CARLIN

MONDAY

CHAPTER ONE

The loose dock drifted into view on a Monday morning at the end of May. Hal had stationed himself at the kitchen window at six A.M. with a cup of coffee. This way he could wake up slowly as he gazed over the short stretch of his backyard, with its fallow mud square that was supposed to be a garden, and out onto the calm water of Lake Monona. Upstairs, he heard Greta and Karin begin to stir: two alarms going off, two sets of footsteps moving back and forth from their respective bedrooms to the bathroom. He tried to distinguish one from the other: Greta's brisk staccato even in bare feet; Karin's heavier tread.

A flock of geese was moving from his neighbor's yard through Hal's yard, chomping grass. Periodically one would pop up its head and cast a watchful eye at its surroundings, making Hal wonder if the geese could sense him there behind the glass.

The geese were fat and smooth as eggs, their undulant necks a wonder of engineering and sensitivity. They were beautiful, Hal reflected, and they were plentiful—that flock alone might feed fifty people or more. Goose meat, even wild goose, was dark and filling. Not to mention that in the arboretum across town were gangs of turkeys that often fanned out over the roads, intimidating the joggers. How far would a few of those birds go, if they were roasted and stuffed? Hal figured he could manage some meager dressing from whatever frozen bread and bottled spices he had in the warehouse at work.

It was spring, the wrong time of year to be thinking about serving turkey or goose, but since winter Hal had had a growing list of food pantries, soup kitchens, and families asking for increasing help from his employer, the Southern Wisconsin Food Initiative. The letterhead said "SWFI," but the workers had nicknamed the organization "The Swiffies" instead. Meanwhile, all the Swiffies' usual donors of surplus lunch meat or frozen pizzas or white rice were suddenly models of efficiency. Hal, whose job depended on the wanton largesse of corporations, hated a recession even more than most people. He wanted every CEO smoking cigars and tossing brandy snifters into their fireplaces if it meant they'd keep up their donations, but they were all getting lean and efficient, the bastards. So each morning that spring, Hal had been getting up earlier and earlier, and drinking his coffee while he looked out the window and ran numbers in his head. Seven hundred pounds of potatoes. Twenty cases of pretzels. One thousand pounds of star-shaped noodles. Seven hundred pounds of cherry-flavored candies half-melted into possum-sized blocks of wax. It all sounded like a huge amount until he reviewed how many orders had been placed for that week, how many food pantries and church groups came in to shop and wandered through the shelves, increasingly pissed off and disheartened, leaving with only a few gallons of ice cream and boxes of bread.

Then Hal would head toward the Swiffies' own kitchens, where volunteers were stretching boxes of noodles and commodity ham into hot meals for delivery. His coworkers got a lot of mileage out of the daily spectacle of vegetarian Hal, who lived in a cooperative house devoted to sustainable eating and organic local food, being so relieved to get his hands on bins of dried veggies flavored with chicken solution and sodium chloride.

Thank God for the prison gardens. They were the Swiffies' best source of summer vegetables. If Hal could just hold out a couple months, there'd soon be truckloads of cucumbers and peppers and tomatoes, all carefully tended by hundreds of felonious hands. Amazing how quickly that aspect ceased to matter. The first year Hal had worked for Swiff and the prison veggies arrived, he'd been unable to stop himself from regarding the huge bins with suspicion, as if an inmate might be hidden among the zucchini. Now he was desperate for that donation, with inmate or without.

The thought of the prison gardens reminded him that he ought to have been planting his own garden. Even the prisoners were ahead of him.

Hal was still sipping, brooding in the direction of the lake, when the geese snapped to attention. The big one raised its head and issued an echoing call. There was a thunderous flapping of wings and alarmed cries as the gaggle rose into the cool May air and fled the bank of the lake.

Then Hal saw why they'd left. Out on the shimmering water was a raft of some sort, floating into his view from the northeast. On the raft sat an empty chair, beside which was a small rectangular shape that might have been a crate or a bucket. But what had startled the geese was a dog—a huge, toast-colored, heavy-shouldered thing even from a distance—that was standing by the chair, gazing searchingly into the water. Hal watched the dog's jaws snap, its ears flopping toward the surface of the lake and twitching in communication. The dog's weight tipped the structure slightly downward, exposing the pontoons beneath the wooden planks. The lake splashed against the wood and then smoothed out again.

After a few seconds, the images began to order themselves for Hal, causing him to set down his mug, spilling coffee onto the counter. The empty chair, the drifting raft, the dog barking fiercely into the lake. It was not a raft, Hal realized. The dog was standing on the dock that was supposed to be anchored to the bank of Lake Monona, in a park three houses east of Hal's house. Someone must have unfastened the dock and set it adrift.

The rising sun illuminated the edges of the dog's fur, so that the fuzz seemed to glow at its haunch and skull, its belly and tail. The dog's tail stuck straight out behind it. Its barking was harsh and rhythmic. The chair was dark against the white pools of light on the water. Its fabric was pinholed with sunlight, sagging at the seat and backrest with the lost weight of its inhabitant.

The park near Hal's home was tiny, just a square of grass with a few climbing toys, a sandbox, a picnic table, and a small dock. The dock, part of which was now drifting in Lake Monona, was meant to be a two-part object, a small section anchored on the bank plus a detachable length of wood. In the winter the city removed the long section from the water and let it rest on the snow-covered bank till the thaw. This year, overwhelmed by the rising lakes and streets buckling from weather shifts, the city had not returned the Morrison Street dock back into the water until only a month earlier, at the end of April.

It was the long, buoyant section of the dock that had been unsecured and was now floating in the lake. When Hal ran over to the park, he found the metal pole, which was supposed to fasten the two sections together, in the grass beneath a tree. He decided not to touch it.

The neighbors had begun to gather, standing with their arms crossed against the breeze, which was still crisp even in May. They saw Hal on his cell phone and nodded, content to let him do the calling, content to assume he knew whom to call for an event like this. He didn't know—he just called 911. Once he finished, he joined six or seven people clustered at the edge of the bank, their row of feet braced in the sloping mud. They watched the dock float gently away from them—perhaps fifty feet out? forty?—and speculated on the breed of the dog. How long could the dog have been out there, if the dock was now moving toward shore—all night, or only minutes? No one knew enough about the movement of lake water to guess; no one was even sure if lakes had tides—Hal thought maybe they didn't.

"Anyone recognize the dog?" asked one man. Hal turned to look at him: the man was huge, maybe six six, with rimless glasses and a giant's mouth. He barely knew his neighbors, Hal realized. He'd lived on this street for years, waving politely, but he didn't know the names of any of the people around him.

"I don't think so," Hal said. He never noticed dogs, which made him feel guilty, as if he were single-handedly contributing to their unspayed plight. His roommate Karin adored them; she kept a dish of treats on the front porch for passing canines. She also kept trying to vote in a pet, but to no avail.

"I might," said a woman. "Maybe from the other side of the Yahara River? I feel like I've seen it somewhere."

Hal waited for someone to speculate on how the dog had come to be out on the lake by itself. Because clearly someone had brought it here. When no one else mentioned this, he finally raised his voice and asked, "Do you see anyone else out there?" The group was silenced. Now all of them shaded their eyes and peered out toward the placid water beyond the dog.

"Its owner might have fallen in," said a young man, protecting his shaved head from the sun with a hand held above the crown. For some reason, this suggestion prompted the group to turn to Hal, startling him. Their faces all shifted inquisitively in his direction.

"I told the dispatcher there might be a person in the lake," Hal offered. "I'm sure they're sending a boat."

"Or someone could have just put it out there for a joke," said another person. No one answered immediately, but this possibility seemed to calm them all, and they returned to debating the breed. Just as they had settled on a mix of retriever and possibly some shepherd in its dark face and low haunches, the dog raised its head, twice patrolled the length of the dock, and leaped into the water.

Now they all leaned out over the lake, taking turns holding on to a tree trunk at the edge of the bank, and observed the dog's progress. It swam in eager jerking motions in the direction of the shore. Hal felt the crowd around him becoming almost jolly, cheered by the dog's smiling jaws and the happy look of its bobbing head. He even began to enjoy the crispness of the breeze and the time with his neighbors.

"It's moving awfully slowly," a female voice observed.

The group quieted; all its lightness fled. The dog was indeed slowing down. Hal turned and saw Karin in her running gear, her long maple-colored hair in a ponytail, the muscles at the tops of her thighs standing out flat and smooth below her yellow shorts. She was twenty-four, twelve years younger than Hal and fifteen years younger than Greta. Much of the time the age differences didn't matter.

Karin patted his shoulder in greeting, then observed the others: the huge man in glasses; the bald young man who was now wrapping an arm around a woman; two bearded graduate students from the crumbling house across the park; a tall silver-haired man in khakis and a polo shirt whom Hal had once helped ease a canoe onto a Volvo; a woman dressed for work in dark pants, heels, and a glinting silver ring; and two women in jeans, bright T-shirts, and leather sandals.

"It's having a hard time," one of the graduate students said. "It's farther away than I thought." The dog seemed to be treading water about twenty feet out, several houses down from where they stood. Now they began to move as a troop, heading through backyards, which they normally would not have done, to the spot on the bank closest to the dog.

As they moved through Hal and Karin's yard, Hal saw Greta's shape in the upstairs window; then she darted out of the frame. He saw Karin glance in Greta's direction as well and then turn back toward the dog. The dock, with its empty chair, was now heading toward the capitol.

"Was Greta on her way?" Hal asked.

Karin squinted at him in the sunlight. "What's she going to do?"

Hal shrugged. "I have no idea," he said. "But probably something we haven't thought of." Greta had an air of frightening efficiency.

At that, Karin frowned. "Did it have a leash?" she asked. She began to remove her running shoes, dropping them casually to the dirt. She peeled off one sock, then the other.

"I can't remember," Hal said. He closed his eyes and pictured the silhouette of the dog, the sun, the nimbus of fur standing on end. "I don't think so."

"Well," she said, "if anyone has one at home, they might run and get it." She peered into the water's edge to judge its depth and then hopped in and began to swim.

The two women in jeans and T-shirts ran off down the street, hopefully in search of a leash, and Hal watched Karin do a neat, strong crawl in the direction of the dog. As she neared it, she switched to a breaststroke. She didn't want to frighten it, Hal decided. Next to him the woman in heels murmured appreciatively.

Karin had reached the dog now and seemed to hook a hand inside its collar. The two began to move in rhythmic surges, powered by kicks, toward the shore. Karin was on her side, an arm wrapped beneath the dog's chest.

Hal was feeling relieved now. He had forgotten for the moment about whoever had brought the dog out there in the first place and was simply enjoying a satisfying rescue. He had often had the feeling his neighbors regarded their house with amusement or even suspicion; kids rarely came to the co-op to sell candy bars or cookies for the marching band, and after one unsuccessful block party to which Hal and his roommates had brought baba ghanoush and homemade pita chips and everyone else brought bratwurst, they'd given up on making friends on their street. But with Karin out there saving the day, his house might take on a new aura.

A tranquil silence occupied the group until the second the dog showed its teeth. The dog and Karin were a few feet from the shore when it seemed to recover itself: its head pivoted toward Karin and its jaws snapped at her face. Hal saw her flinch backward, splashing water. The dog broke away, jerking toward the edge of the dirt and clambering up the bank. The group drew back as the dog's head and shoulders appeared over the edge of the grass. Suddenly the dog was a real creature, huge and frantic. Its paws and belly were black with mud, its face darkened and golden-eyed. It darted in their direction and Hal, along with everyone else, feinted backward. Hal collided with the huge man he'd talked to earlier. He caught a whiff of coffee, cinnamon, and pine from his neighhor's chest.

Now Karin had reached the bank and had begun to climb out of the lake. Hal skirted the barking dog to lean down and offer a hand, hauling her up the muddy slope. Her clothes clung to her in streaming ripples and her legs and arms were cross-hatched vividly from the dog's claws.

The dog was darting in arcs, first away from the lake and then from the people, and now it bolted, disappearing between houses. No one followed. Most of the group was still scanning for a police boat, and so the arrival of two uniformed cops from the sidewalk behind them took them all by surprise. The cops strode toward them, boots shining and picking up grass. They looked each person over in turn. Their arrival only made Hal more nervous, their grave expressions confirming what they had all managed to forget while chatting about breeds and lake tides. Yet Hal noticed the police were relaxed. The park was now the cops': any place that experienced an upheaval immediately belonged to them.

Hal felt a cold wet hand on his shoulder. Karin was catching her breath next to him. The claw marks on her arms looked as purposeful as tribal scars. She smelled of algae and water, something vegetal and fermenting, and her bare feet seemed huge in the earth. She was breathing hard, wiping water from her face. Hal had lived with Karin for nearly a year, had watched her head out for her run each morning of the week, and somehow had never equated that discipline with practical physical strength. He wanted to get her a brandy and a towel, a giant breakfast, and watch her move furniture. He looked closely at her, relieved to see that the dog hadn't actually bitten her. Her face was unmarked, but reddened at the nostrils and cheeks, her pupils huge, her lips the color of clay.

Now Greta came jogging from around the corner, her hair still in a towel. She wore an elegant little silk skirt, blown against her legs by the breeze, and a huge Bucky Badger T-shirt. She must have just gotten out of the shower; wet patches showed at the small of her back and chest. She nodded at Hal but went straight for Karin, took the damp towel off her head, and wrapped it over Karin's shoulders. Then she took a quick step backward, as if the gesture had been too intimate, and folded her arms.

"What was in the lake?" Greta asked. She looked around at each of the spectators, pushing her hair off her face. She was so blond that, wet, her hair was transparent. Next to Karin she was miniscule, wiry and tense, her teeth bright white and too big for her mouth. The lines at her eyes and bracketing her lips deepened as she squinted in the sunlight.

"Just a dog." Karin began to towel off briskly, her teeth clattering. One of the cops spoke into a radio. The other neighbors took a step toward the street, keeping their bodies half-turned toward the threesome, in case they were beckoned.

"I guess it didn't belong to any of them," said Greta. "Whose was it?"

"Whoever took it out there," Hal said.

The three of them looked at one another, struck silent. Out on the lake Hal now saw a boat approaching the untethered dock, someone stepping up to secure it. The chair slid and stopped just before going into the water.

They stood in a half-circle, watching the people on the lake and half-blinded by the sun, and then the sense of nervousness and adrenaline left them all at once, so suddenly that Karin sat down in the dirt. Hal experienced a delayed shiver of revulsion at the thought of whatever Karin had been close to out there in the water, in the greenish light below the surface. He was imagining her hair rushing through fingers that reached up from the depths, something brushing against her legs as she swam toward shore.

Back in their house, Hal hovered about Karin as if she'd gone through the ice, draping a fresh towel over her shoulders, placing a cup of coffee with hot milk before her on the big weathered kitchen table, and toasting some homemade bread while he leaned against the counter with his arms crossed, mouth pressed tight.

The three of them lived just east of the capitol building on the central isthmus of Madison, Wisconsin, between two lakes: the larger Lake Mendota dwarfed the city from its northwest side and Lake Monona nestled to the southeast. The two were connected by the Yahara River, a small portion of which bisected the isthmus a few blocks from Hal's place. On a map, the tightly populated strip between the lakes looked a bit like the knot on a bow, or the body of a winged insect, with the rest of the city sprawled out on either side. The isthmus was the city's prime real estate, a stretch of land less than a mile wide that housed the state capitol and the university, the mile of State Street connecting the two, and the residential neighborhoods on either side.

The co-op's neighborhood was an older collection of aging and rehabbed Victorians and Tudors. The area was once wealthy, fell into disrepair, and then began to gentrify in patches, retaining its scruffier roots while the real estate prices near the water soared. One house might be an elegant turreted structure gone condo, while next door its peeling neighbor leaned perilously in a scrubby yard. Hal and his roommates lived in the Morrison Street Co-op, a narrow, three-story gabled pink Victorian with a small front porch. Its gingerbread trim was blistering slightly and the windowsills needed scraping and repainting, which the housemates kept meaning to vote on. If Hal weren't living in a communal house, he might still have been able to afford the neighborhood, but only as a renter, and certainly not on the lakefront.

The front room of their house was painted a dark fuchsia with ivory trim—meaty, but vibrant. The couch was a sagging, comfortable wheat-colored sectional with a blond oval coffee table. To the left of the front door, a set of dark mahogany stairs led up to the second and third floors. Opposite the stairs was a decorative fireplace, and on the wall above it were several pictures of people and livestock: someone laughing among a sea of goats; one of disembodied men's hairy legs, surrounded by chickens. One chicken cast a sidelong glance out of the photo, its bright amber eye fierce and clear.

The kitchen where Hal and Karin now sat was the best part of the house. Its walls were a yolk-yellow that at first appeared to be marbled, until one got close enough to see that someone had painted the marbling in a rosy orange. Occasionally the room would light up with a flash of reflection off the lake. The stove was an old black gas-powered model. Mottled carbon-steel knives hung by their blades from a magnet on the wall; cast-iron pans hung from hooks just above the knives. On the fridge was a poster-board chart titled, "Will it curdle?" According to the chart, milk—cow, soy, or almond—would not curdle in chai, but berry teas curdled nearly everything. Earl Grey was a toss-up.

Karin had begun to protest the special treatment but gave up almost immediately: the dry towel's warmth and roughness was a comfort, the heated milk an especially pleasant touch. Still, she felt silly letting Hal fuss over her. She hadn't exactly swum the English Channel, though her muscles were still aquiver with leftover adrenaline. She felt that everything was largely okay. They were back at home, the sun was out, and everyone was getting ready to go to work. The world went on, most of the city totally unaware that some woman on Morrison Street had taken an early swim.

Then again, out on the lake the cops had been talking gravely to one another when everyone else left, the walkie-talkies clicking and chattering at their belts. They weren't leaving. In fact, more were arriving.

Greta had established that Karin was healthy and calm, and that Hal was involved in breakfast, and had run back upstairs to finish dressing for work. She left for her office by seven most days, and sometimes stayed twelve hours. Twice in the two weeks she'd lived here, she'd arrived late to the dinner she herself was scheduled to prepare. The first time she seemed mortified and did the dishes with manic care. The second time she arrived with two large spinach and mushroom pizzas, taking care to point out that they were from a restaurant that specialized in local ingredients. The other two had been unsure how much to say: she was adhering to the letter of the co-op law, if not the spirit.

"How much did that dog weigh, do you think? Eighty, ninety pounds?" Hal asked. He set a plate before Karin and busied himself in the refrigerator with butter and honey.

"It was hard to tell in the water," Karin said. The dog had felt surprisingly small when she wrapped an arm around it, its ribs light and tapered at the center of its chest. Yet when she'd watched it tear up the bank from the water, the dog had suddenly appeared mammoth to her, all powerful hind legs and broad shoulders, a glistening brush of lake water flung from its tail.

"Did it break the skin?" Hal took her by the wrist, examining her arm for punctures. "Just some scratches," she said, shrugging. "It didn't mean to. It got frightened all of the sudden."

"Great. Lake water. Hold on." Hal disappeared into the bathroom. Over the year they had lived together she had turned over to him her cut finger, her oil-burned wrist, and her sprained ankle, the heel cupped gingerly in his palm. She usually found him comforting, though today he seemed more rattled than she. Hal returned with a tube of ointment, checking the expiration date, and crouched before her, dabbing gel at the scratches on her arm with a fingertip. Karin watched him work, his big hands, the way his thinning dark hair still stuck straight up from sleep. Above them, Greta dropped something heavy and gave a muffled cry.

"You okay up there?" Hal called. They both listened for Greta's faint reply, then Hal nodded and returned his attention to Karin. "What'd you say to Suzanne Leung?"

Suzanne Leung was a local newscaster who'd shown up as the three of them were leaving. The police on the shore were chatting with the ones in the boat who'd dragged in the dock. They greeted Suzanne Leung like an old friend.

"I told her my name," Karin said. "And that I didn't see where the dog went or why it was out there in the first place. She wanted to know if we saw anyone with him."

Hal shook his head. "I didn't," he said. "Listen—did you see anything this morning? Or last night?"

"No," she said. "I don't know if we would have heard anything anyway. People who actually do this sort of thing don't usually call for help. Wouldn't they isolate themselves instead?"

Hal looked startled. "Isolating yourself doesn't have to be— well, it doesn't have to be *isolating* yourself. Sometimes people go on a retreat just to regroup. They come back." He turned the tube of ointment over and over in his hands. "It makes you wonder," he began. "Maybe it was someone we knew. Maybe he chose that spot for a reason."

"*If* there was someone," said Karin. She changed the subject. "Apparently there's been a rash of abandoned pets lately. Did you know that? The shelters are bursting."

"People get frightened," said Hal.

Karin searched Hal's face. He looked suddenly pale. "Hey," she said. "Are you okay? It's too soon to get upset. There's no reason to worry until we know what happened."

"Right," Hal agreed. He glanced at the clock. "I'm sure you're right."

Now Karin stood, draping the towel over her arm. She needed to shower and get to work. She loved attending to the mundane and practical details of life, the satisfying ticking off of tasks on a list. Karin was an assistant editor at a dairy industry trade newspaper, which had a circulation of fifty thousand, though no one in the nondairy world had heard of it. She needed to get to work and sketch out her questions for an interview this week with an Elaine Rothberger at Drumlin Cheese, a two-year-old venture near Waupaca. They were a family operation, which wasn't terribly newsworthy. But they were also cave-aging their cheese, which was. Most people used temperature-regulated rooms, and for good reason, though the old-fashioned thing to do was to simply have a good open-air cave with shelves inside it. A cave was also potentially much cheaper, if you could work with conditions. No skyrocketing fuel and energy costs, no faltering electricity.

"Well, I've got a lot of work to do," she said. "Thanks, Hal."

He lifted an open hand and let it drop. As she left the kitchen, he called after her. "You haven't forgotten to give me any messages, have you? No calls?"

Karin poked her head back in. "No," she said softly. "Who are you worried about?"

"No one," Hal said. He waved her off toward the shower.

At the top of the stairs she collided with Greta, who was now fully dressed in strappy orange leather sandals, her flighty skirt, and two layered silk tops in fuchsia and pale green. Diamonds sparkled in her ears. Dressed for work, Greta served only to remind Karin how badly the rest of the house needed repair: her silk garments seemed forever about to snag on the peeling banister or the paint where it bubbled at the baseboards. The contrast was lessened on the weekends, when she wore cracked leather pants and T-shirts.

Greta was reaching into her bag for a pair of sunglasses. "Sorry I had to get ready—my whole week is about getting set for this prospective donor, you know. But I'll be home in time to go to the party tonight, I promise." She looked hard at Karin. "You shouldn't feel bad," she added. "For letting it get away. Whoever left that dog out there was probably out of his head. It should have had a leash on it or something. I mean, do it to your*self* but don't bring the *dog* into it."

Greta seemed to have well-formed beliefs about what had happened—as if she could somehow have more information than Karin did, but Karin hadn't thought to feel guilty about any of it. She couldn't be held responsible if someone had decided to swim for it and left their dog stranded. That was what she imagined: someone had gone out there, to relax or to fish, and suddenly the dock gave way. Next thing you know, a person had to swim, and maybe they weren't sure if the dog could. Maybe the person had swum ashore, phoned in the incident, and had gone to sleep and hoped the whole thing was over by the time he awoke. The dog had been seen and rescued. It might not be in a shelter yet, but it was at least somewhere on dry land.

The claw marks on Karin's skin throbbed sympathetically. Greta made a move to pat her shoulder, then drew back, blushed in embarrassment, and raced down the steps. Karin could smell her own skin, which still bore a fragrant layer of lake water, wet dog, and earth.

Hal needed to dress for work, too, but first he wanted to call his father. In his bedroom, he dialed and nudged the door shut with his toe. His father's phone, somewhere up in northern Wisconsin in a cabin Hal and his sisters had not yet seen, rang and rang. It was startling to think about just how long it had been since he'd heard his father's voice. A month, at least. More. Hal had had a busy spring, and he'd gotten in the habit of leaving his dad a message and forgetting he'd even done so until he tried again. Now he realized that the last time his father had left him a message in reply—on Hal's home phone during business hours—had been in March. His father had been a phone-talker, letter-writer, socializer, and a churchgoer while Hal's mother was alive. But since she'd died a few months earlier, he'd retreated.

Even the letters had stopped, and his father's letters had persisted since Hal's childhood, despite the arrival of e-mail. They were usually jotted down on sheets of notebook paper and popped in the mail along with a coupon for an oil change. He wrote about the animals in the yard, the progress of his squash, how to choose a mutual fund. Here was also where he'd often first broached health problems that perturbed him, or memories that had recently become vivid again. The last letter had come just before Hal's mother died. "I've been thinking about the buck you almost got the fall you were seventeen," his father had written. "I'm sorry I didn't let you shoot at it. It's an uncomfortable thing, to want to kill something not just for food but because you want its beauty, too. Now you must understand that more than I ever did, what with your eating habits, ha ha. Hunting is a necessity, not a theft, is what I'm trying to say. I suppose you know that, but it's something I've been pondering. I guess I'm not really sorry I didn't let you, just sorry I had to deny you something.

"The squirrels are all over the bird feeders again. The redwings won't ever come back if this keeps up. Your mother wants to know if you want those peanut clusters from church again this year. If so, we'll add to our order. Love, your father."

It was the lake that did it. Hal wouldn't be feeling this way if someone had jumped in front of a car. He'd be saddened, of course, but it wouldn't remind him of anything or anyone. Yet there was something about the idea of someone out in the park late last night, or this morning, silently moving about the grass and the water, and calming the dog to keep it quiet, someone who knew exactly how to dismantle a dock without a sound, that had made him very nervous.

Hal gave up on his father's ringing phone, finally, and tried one of his sisters. His niece picked up the phone. "Hey there, hyacinth," Hal said. "I need your mom, okay?"

The phone clunked to a floor or a tabletop and Hal waited, listening to the sounds of feet and hollering. After a moment, his sister's voice was audible, talking rapidly about something to do with shoes and mud. Her voice grew louder and louder until, with no transition, she spoke directly into the receiver:

"And knock the dried mud out; beat the *shit* out of it, Vivvy; Hal, hey."

"Hey, Rennie." He stopped, gazing out the window again. He couldn't see anything from here, not police or more bystanders or Suzanne Leung, if she were still there.

"I have to get the kids to school, Hal. What's up?" Rennie sniffled. She was plagued by allergies in the spring and by cracked skin in the winter. In his mind his sister was never still, always rubbing her nose with a tissue, massaging some cream into her hands. She'd been delicate as a child but went into a rage if anyone said so.

"I wondered if you'd talked to Dad lately," Hal said.

Rennie drew a quick liquid breath. "Nope," she said. "I guess not since—I don't know, maybe Vivvy's birthday in February? He sent her some cash and she phoned him. Or maybe she just wrote to him, actually. I guess it has been awhile. Why, how is he?"

"I don't know," Hal said. "I haven't heard from him, either. I just now started to wonder."

"Well, give him a call and tell him to call me, too," Rennie said.

"I can never get him at that stupid cabin. He won't put in voice mail."

Rennie laughed. "Voice mail!"

"A machine then. I just think it's ridiculous for a man his age to be off in the woods and unreachable."

"The orange one," Rennie said distantly. Then, her voice clear again: "I know. Don't you think he'll get lonely? He'll come back."

"I don't see how. He sold the house."

"But that little cabin, or cottage, or whatever it is, cost a lot less. He has savings if he needs it."

"Yeah. Maybe." Hal heard the front door slam and looked at the clock. Nearly eight o'clock now. "I might be on the news, by the way."

"That's great! Who're you taking down now?"

Hal smiled in the direction of the window. "Nothing like that. I'm a bystander this time. There was a dog . . . abandoned, I guess, in the lake by our house this morning. My roommate got it out of the water."

"I love your pinko house. Ha. Who's there these days?"

"One's new. Greta. Karin's the one who rescued the dog."

"How is she? Tell her we miss her. Vivvy has kind of a crush on her, I think."

"She'll be flattered."

"Well, don't let her give it away, Vivvy'd be mortified I told you. I think Karin gave her a few back copies of *Bitch* and now her eyes are opened. Listen, I'll come down soon and reacquaint myself with everyone, okay? Give Karin a hug for us." She was already pulling the phone away, her voice dimming.

"Yeah—but what about Dad?"

She returned in a rush of air. "Well, try Janey. She might know. And I guess we'll just keep calling. He has to pick up sometime. He's probably just deer-hunting a lot."

"Ren, it's spring. Where did you grow up?"

"Oh, yeah. Fishing. Or gardening. Don't worry, Hal. Try Jane."

He phoned his other sister while he changed into work clothes but she was already gone for the day. She lived near Milwaukee in Whitefish Bay, also known with varying degrees of affection by the locals as "White Folks Bay." Jane clerked for a Milwaukee judge; her husband, Kevin, was an ear, nose, and throat man. Hal liked to go there for the occasional weekend and drink Kevin's Belgian beer, eat shavings of cured meats of international origin on pricey crackers sprinkled with rosemary. Hal was supposed to be a vegetarian, but with his family such distinctions felt foolish and insincere. They knew him too well. They'd known him back when he ate a Whopper every day after school, when he hunted deer with his father every fall and rinsed the blood from the truck bed.

Jane's voice mail picked up. "Hey, guys." He poked his head through the neck of a T-shirt. "It's Hal. I'm just checking in to see if you've talked to Dad lately. Give me a call."

He tried his father one more time. Hal listened to the ringing while he tucked his wallet in his back pocket, while he left his room to check that the coffeemaker was off, while he went upstairs once more to be sure Karin had gone to work, and up until he locked the front door. At the doorway he hung up, took aim, and left the phone chucked onto Greta's beloved green silk chair.

CHAPTER TWO

Greta arrived at her office to discover a cluster of her colleagues bending over a computer monitor.

The fund-raising operation for Grinwall College was housed in a converted Tudor near the student dorms. The college was a little collection of older buildings, beautifully ornate on the outside and cinder block on the inside, on the far west side of Madison. Grinwall viewed itself as a kind of satellite due to its location on the edge of town, whereas its rival, Edgewood College, enjoyed a close-to-central location. The community college was on the far east side. In between, everything was dwarfed by the University of Wisconsin. Greta sometimes envied Edgewood, a fellow small, private institution, for its rolling green grounds visible from Monroe Street, the students strolling from shelter to shelter behind its fences like free-range chickens. Grinwall was the smallest of the local schools, and in the past had distinguished itself with its welcoming student health center and a strong religious studies department, but in the last several years it was plagued by restless students and changes of regime. This spring was worse than ever, and Greta entered the campus each morning, anticipating—even looking forward to—the newest signs of student discontent: the environmental demonstrations in the form of a seven-foot tower of unopened paper towels and napkins in the center of the quadrangle; a guerilla vegetable garden that had appeared one morning where a stretch of emerald grass had stood on the president's lawn the night before; endless viral flyers for sex-positive feminist caravans to the vibrator store on Willy Street.

The resurgence in student activism came at a difficult time for the development office. Five years earlier, someone had done the math on Grinwall's endowment and realized it was in trouble: other schools of similar size were operating on four or five times the endowment. It was as if the previous generations had all been too retiring and Midwestern to ask, assuming the students would flood the coffers a few years down the road. The old president, a fixture of forty years, was dispatched practically in the night, and a new one was hustled in from New England. Greta's job now involved not only overseeing several new hires, but also meeting with the president every month to compare numbers. The fundraising department brought in more people, issued four times the solicitations, and began to organize fund-raisers and reunions. (Where had all those students gone? How to find them?) The effort was working, but the response from the president remained tepid. The president was eyeing Vassar numbers and doing her best to sweep away the napkin tower before any prospects visited campus. But Greta was always pleased when the students won a point. With the right prospective donor, she even emphasized the clashing campus activism. For every PETA protest, she would tell the donors, there was a wild-venison chili cook-off.

For every circle of kids clasping hands and praying on the quad, there was a crew smudging the research laboratory with burning clumps of sage. She was good at figuring out which donors would be pleased by the constant conflicting conversation that ranged over the campus, as pleased by it as Greta herself was. She had missed out on that part of college life. She'd been busy looking at cheap drywalled town houses and framed Ansel Adams posters when she ought to have been dabbling in bisexuality and animist ritual.

Greta's coworkers were gathered in Charles's office, a little golden corner room on the second floor. Greta's office was its replica across the hall. Charles was leaning back in his chair, lanky and languorous, his whitening brown hair brushed straight back off his forehead. When she knocked at Charles's open door, Greta's colleagues looked up as one, precise as a drum corps. "What is it?" she asked, and for a moment she truly couldn't have guessed. Once she'd ascertained that Karin was fine, once it was clear there was nothing more for civilians to do about the runaway dog or the rogue dock or whoever had set it adrift, she'd focused on preparing for work and let the morning slip out of her mind. Plus it had all occurred so early. It might have been a dream.

"You're in the paper," Charles said, grinning.

Greta headed around to his side of the desk, neatly displacing an assistant and two grant writers. On the Web site for the local paper, there she was in profile: a color photo from barely an hour ago, walking in a tight phalanx with Karin and Hal on their way back to the co-op. Karin's head was bent downward, her hair a slick coating over her shoulders and arms. Her brows were knit, mouth downturned. Hal's hand was clutching her shoulder. Greta looked perturbed and seamy—her hair wet and expression peevish. Her naked face had a pallid sort of meth-lab drabness. She'd only been thinking of being on time for work, but the three of them—startled, insufficiently coffee'd, and distracted—looked like suspects from one of those houses that turns out to hide a cellar filled with animal bones.

Greta shrugged. "Oh, yeah," she said. For a moment she still didn't see the significance, why her coworkers were observing her with guardedness and confusion. "I wasn't the one who rescued the dog," she admitted. "And the dog might have been okay in any event. Though it was getting tired. Karin's just—"

And here she realized. She looked again at the photo. The caption referred to all three of them as housemates on Morrison Street. Greta had not yet told anyone at work about her move.

She straightened up and headed toward the door. "I should have you all over soon for a housewarming," she sang out, adding, "We love the neighborhood."

She darted into her office and closed the door, the second sweat of the day gathering fearfully in her armpits. That goddamn paper, she thought. She set up her laptop and opened the same local Web page. There they all were.

There was an overseas war on that just kept bleeding outward from its original eye; New York had flooded yet again, crippling the subway systems; odd chemical smells had been blowing in across the lakes all spring, leaving downtown Madison infused with a scent of bananas and petroleum that went unclaimed by any local factories or power plants. No one could cover any of that on the front page instead of a dog in a lake?

Greta clicked on a headline about the New York flood and up popped a photo of people on the Lower East Side, sloshing through flooded streets in short skirts and brightly colored rainboots. If she looked closely she thought she could see an expression of grim pleasure on one woman's face. They looked less perturbed than Greta, Hal, and Karin had.

Some clumsy fool had probably taken his dog and a case of beer out on the lake to fish. He'd slid into the water like a damp sack of beans—it wasn't news! Greta being at the lake on the east side of town when all her coworkers knew her to live on the west side, Greta strolling around with a crew of hippies on Morrison Street when she was well known to be living with her husband in University Heights—none of this was news.

Greta closed the Web browser after one last cringing glance at her photo and opened up a prospect file instead. She lined up a pad of paper and her favorite pen. She could do today what she did every day: work until she forgot the rest. No one bothered her while she was working.

Her best prospect at the moment was a novelist, thirty years ago a mechanical engineering undergrad. The rub was that she'd transferred to UW her senior year. Greta refused to let that stop her: for all she knew the woman had needed a break in tuition. Maybe she wished she could have graduated from Grinwall. Maybe this was her chance for an honorary degree.

Greta had never found herself wooing anyone in the arts before, though perhaps the designation was a bit off in this case. The woman, Julie Voltsheim, was more like a corporation: her daughter was her lawyer, her husband her accountant, her son did public relations. Every other year Julie Voltsheim turned out a new book, featuring either Macy "Mack" Guilford, reluctant Idaho female private investigator, or Henry Footling, honorable, lonely nineteenth-century New England police chief. Occasionally she broke out of the series altogether with stand-alone novels set in Hawaii or Cuba. Greta had read several from each category, taking notes along the way. The books became longer and denser as the two series progressed, becoming darker and more politically engaged. Slave trade, prostitution, corporate marauding, the mob—they all made an appearance. She noted the locations, too, because Julie Voltsheim might be writing from familiarity about Los Angeles, Boston, or Sugar City, Idaho.

Greta learned what she needed to learn. She had made herself conversant with biotech terms, with software development, with battery manufacturing, and with construction, but this was new. Here was a woman who'd dropped out of engineering, disappeared from alumni lists for years, and resurfaced on Long Island, writing mystery novels. Her books had no jacket photos. Greta pictured her being in her fifties, gray hair drawn back in a twist, with tweed trousers and driving loafers and a plain silver wedding band. Maybe Julie Voltsheim had left college a crank, lips pressed tight over some engineering theorem she couldn't shake loose, contact lenses crisping in her eyes, and then sometime that summer she threw it all off. Greta liked the idea that you went under one way and surfaced another, exchanging your failures for new material.

Toward the end of the morning, Charles knocked on Greta's office door. She'd been reading reviews of *Death in the Valley (A Sugar City Mystery)*, trying to familiarize herself with Julie Voltsheim's best-reviewed novels and the ones to avoid mentioning. She was also noting the sales figures: how much money might this woman be worth? It had to be millions: her books were all best sellers. She couldn't go in there spouting sales figures, though she would give Voltsheim the chance to tell her if the woman's ego demanded it. The delicate place lay in Voltsheim's change of direction, whether her time at Grinwall sent her down one avenue or running—screaming—up another. Maybe Julie Voltsheim wouldn't touch the School of Engineering; maybe she wanted to endow a chair in the Writing Department. It was Greta's job to find the human direction, to offer Julie Voltsheim an opportunity rather than to ask her for help. That was key: Greta made them feel as if *she* were helping *them*.

The knock drew her slowly out of the review ("raunchy and raucous, bracing as a shot of whiskey") and back to her office. Charles was standing in the doorway.

"You up for lunch?" he asked. "Nothing fancy. Maybe just the café?"

Greta eyed him. Charles seemed blameless, relaxed, and unconcerned. Why, he had once passionately asked during a training seminar, would you give money to someone who doesn't *care* enough to wear cuff links? He could have moved over to the UW Foundation in a heartbeat. Greta didn't understand why he hadn't. She herself was ensconced after so many years at the college, and, what was more, she had found she enjoyed the jumps in energy that rocked a small school like this. At UW, all that discussion and all those statements might just be absorbed into the mass. But here, the students were pissed, the school needed money, hounded faculty peered from their office windows before dashing to their cars: it was all very invigorating.

Maybe it was safe to go to lunch with Charles. Maybe he wouldn't start asking her a lot of questions. He was the reserved sort. It was likely he simply wanted her advice on a stalled prospect. That happened sometimes: you were within inches and then you lost your momentum; a prospect went on vacation and returned foggy and happy, no longer focused on why you kept buying her lunch.

"I think I can," Greta said. "What do you need?"

"Oh, nothing in particular," he said. "Just to catch up." He paused, then added with gentle emphasis, "See how you're doing."

Greta straightened in her chair and gave him a glossy, dismissive smile. "I'm so swamped," she said. "Now that I think of it, I couldn't possibly. This mystery writer has me terribly caught up in mayhem and murder." She gave a husky little laugh, and marveled inwardly at her own vapidity. She was relieved it was only Charles asking her to lunch. He was her equal and no closer to their department head than she was—Greta had made scrupulously certain of it. She could decline at least once without political ramifications.

Charles stuck his hands in his pockets and watched her for a second, then nodded. "Next time," he said. He turned, then paused. "All well?"

Greta busied herself neatening a file folder. "Of course," she said. "All is lovely. Next time."

CHAPTER THREE

Hal had moved to New York the summer he was twenty-two to take advantage of an empty room in the apartment of a girl from college. Andrea had had a room in a pale-blue vinyl-sided three-flat building in a section of Brooklyn that was not quite Park Slope and not quite Gowanus. It was a blend of brownstones and strollers and graffiti-covered brick cities nestled beneath the Brooklyn-Queens Expressway underpass, dotted by industrial graveyards. He and Andrea called their neighborhood Gowanus Slope, and the moniker seemed to get at the area's general feeling of a homely slide into the muck of the nearby canal.

Hal and his friend Wes and Andrea had hung around the same group at UW, though Andrea was generally at the opposite side of any given circle from Wes and Hal. She was short, rounded, and compact, with a figure like a voluptuous gymnast and, frequently, a stumpy brunette ponytail that was a refusal more than a hairstyle. They'd all met in the dorms freshman year. Andrea played volleyball and rowed, drove home for the occasional visit to Westerville, Ohio, and cheered for Ohio State when they played against the Badgers. Back then, Hal could never remember her major: he'd thought it was something too obscure or boring to sink into his head each time she told him. And anyway, they didn't talk that much. At parties he would see her in the kitchen, playing card games with a pile of coins and a can of High Life before her on the table. The light in the shitty houses was unkind to everyone: it sallowed her cheeks and deepened the shadows of her eyes and cheekbones. She never wore makeup but never looked unfinished, either; her round face was as smooth and golden as a little baked bun, her mouth an emphatic pink. Sometimes she wore tortoiseshell glasses, sometimes she didn't.

It had taken a good four years for Hal to notice even that much about Andrea. He hadn't paid attention; he and Wes had been engaged in a faintly hostile but enthralling involvement with a couple of Alpha Chi sorority girls during their junior and senior years. The girls possessed an endlessly swapped collection of high-heeled boots and vampy dark nail polish, and they seemed as likely to move back to Indiana and marry young as they did to obtain entry-level jobs at the Chicago Stock Exchange and forget they'd ever lived anywhere but Lincoln Park. Wes and Hal were both delighted and repelled by their girlfriends' assertive handling of finance classes, cigarettes, and small-town boys who hunted. At the time, Hal was still one of those boys. He was easy pickings for the Alpha Chis. Of course, Hal had made it his business to be easy pickings for the Alpha Chis.

He and Wes had lived on Regent Street their senior year, in one of the dilapidated houses carved up into rooms. It was walking distance from Camp Randall Stadium and Mickie's Dairy Bar, where every hungover student knew to go for a dish of scrambled eggs, ham, melted cheese, and sausage gravy. Only years later did Hal realize a dairy bar was supposed to be kosher.

Back then Wes had been all criminal-justice swagger and fake Rolexes, and Hal had admired his bluster. Hal was a math major with no clear idea of what to do for a job. He loved the elegance of numbers, of the systems that humans had not invented but had discovered, unveiled layer by layer to reveal the intimate patterns of the world. There was nothing that couldn't be understood through mathematics, or at least very little, and one night late in his senior year Hal had looked across the room to the mirror in Joe Hart's Tavern at the reflection of Wes and Lila and Jenny and Hal himself. Looking at Jenny and Lila, who glanced at each other after each joke and declaration, he began to think of game theory, players in decision trees, as he watched them evaluate one another and respond accordingly. They were fascinating, actually: they regulated each other without even realizing it. Hal noted that Wes's hair had grown out and lay curled on his forehead like a Roman emperor's, and that Wes's smile at Jenny was not one of fondness but of friendly animal detachment. Wes was always building, identifying, and incorporating the next wave. He set up patterns in everything he did, from the way he studied to the way he ordered a drink, and Hal believed that Wes would make his way anywhere, at anything. A man like Wes was ubiquitous, like a string of Fibonacci numbers, each number created by the set before it, patterns repeating, expanding, and widening in rings.

And Hal. In the mirror, Hal had watched himself talking and laughing, his red plaid hunter's jacket on the chair behind him, and he'd seen a boy who had no idea what he was doing, who would go along with the people around him until they moved to their next phase, and he would cast around for a new value against which to define himself. He was a variable, the unknown and unquantifiable. He was X.

Or maybe he was only drunk. He was still discombobulated and slightly hung over the next morning. He'd left the Alpha Chi house around eight A.M., and started walking across Library Mall toward his house on Regent. This was late in the year, near the end of April, and while the campus was quiet at this time he knew the rest of the city was moving. The farmers' market around the state capitol was starting up, and cars were streaming to the center of the isthmus. Hal had never been to the market at that point. He lived on pizza and tacos and thawed batches of venison sausage his mother had made.

There was a Catholic church on Library Mall, St. Paul's, that was letting out just as Hal headed past it. He was amazed anyone would go so early, but here they were, people strolling out into the sunshine and pausing to talk. The mall was usually filled with food carts and a fruit vendor and people preaching or selling newspaper subscriptions, and Hal had slowed to enjoy the relative emptiness of a Sunday morning, the untouched grass near the fountain in which there usually, though not this morning, floated some detritus from the night before. Some of the churchgoers had coffee, and the swirling steam from their cups in the clear morning light had struck him as unearthly, the way it rose into their faces and dissipated in a halo. Hal figured his parents were off at church themselves right now, or on their way. They were Lutherans who found the rituals of Catholicism and its predictable mass of always-equal length a bit of a cop-out—easier to check it off than truly live it, was the general prejudice.

Andrea was one of the last to emerge. A moss green skirt flared around her knees and she wore a lighter green sweater; she crossed her arms when she entered the cool air. Hal waved, and for moment he thought she wouldn't respond. Up close, her skin was velvety in the bright sun, her lashes gold around her hazel eyes. The sun seemed to illuminate her teeth and shade the clear pink line that marked the shape of her lips. Her earlobes weren't pierced, Hal suddenly noticed—they were downy and neat little crescents with faint horizontal folds in the center of the flesh. Hal wanted to take her earlobes between his thumb and forefinger.

"Hey, Hal," she'd said. "Coming back from the sorority house?" She gave an arch emphasis to "sorority house." Their friends were not Greeks but weekend athletes, business majors, English students, and small-town Wisconsin kids who had converted the out-of-staters to Friday fish fries. Hal's and Wes's dabbling was regarded as a dubious youthful experiment.

"Yup," Hal said. He felt an urge to tell her he didn't think he'd go back, but decided it would be too disloyal even to heartless, shiny Lila to say anything yet. The two of them began walking toward University Avenue, back in the direction of their houses. "You want some breakfast? We could go to Mickie's."

Andrea shrugged. "Sure," she said. "I could use a ham scrambler."

Hal was silent for a block, uncertain what to say. Andrea in a different context was a stranger to him. "Have you always been a churchgoer?" he finally said.

Andrea laughed. "Here and there," she said. "I like being up when no one else is. That's why I row, too, really."

"I like being up early, too, but that's not enough to get me to church," Hal said, and he laughed. Andrea smiled politely, but Hal realized he sounded lumpish and dismissive. He'd fallen back on that attitude out of habit.

"I grew up going to Lutheran church," he said after a moment, making amends. "My parents are probably there right now." He waited for her to ask why he wasn't, too.

Instead, she asked, "So, what will you be doing a month from now?"

"A month? Probably working and looking for a grown-up math job."

"What is a grown-up math job?" She cocked her head at him.

"I don't know," he said. "I could get certified to teach high school or something. I don't think I want to teach any younger than that. I don't even know if I want to teach."

"Did you do student teaching or anything?"

He shook his head. He'd only thought of this recently. He hadn't done anything except float it out there to his friends, who focused on summers off and hot teenage girls. Anxious to shift the subject from himself, he asked, "What about you?"

Andrea paused at a crosswalk, her hand briefly resting on his forearm while they both glanced up and down for traffic. As they began crossing the street she said, "I'll be in New York. I'm kind of scared of it, but I got a job, so I'm going. One of my cousins has a place in Brooklyn so I'm moving in with her."

"That sounds amazing. I never even thought of it. You'll be all fabulous and club-hoppy, right?"

He found it a little odd, and maybe a little sad, that straightforward, stolid Andrea would be pursuing the glittery big city dream. She'd lose weight and wear heels, he thought glumly. She'd talk a lot about the number 6 train, which she'd call "the Six," and would start wearing red lipstick to play poker.

Andrea laughed. "Hardly. I don't think I'll be able to afford a lot of clubs. Oh well, what else was I going to do with this major, right? No, I'm kidding. There's almost too much choice, actually."

Hal nodded, trying for the hundredth time to recall her major. Too much choice? Was she in computer science, maybe? Finance? Finally he stopped and turned to look at her, in embarrassment focusing on her feet. She was wearing low-heeled leather shoes with a covered pointy toe and straps at the back. Her ankles looked surprisingly nice.

Hal thought he could smell the scent of bacon and cooking cheddar on the breeze. Across the street from where they stood was Camp Randall. They'd both be in the stadium next month, part of one massive capped-and-gowned and sweating crew, filing up and down from folding chair to stage and back. Hal broke out in a sweat just thinking of it. Andrea was waiting for him to admit that after four years of being friends, or at least close acquaintances, he had no idea how she spent her time. He gave up and looked her in the eye.

"Education and psychology, with a minor in social justice," said Andrea. "I got a job at a housing nonprofit. Think Dorothy Day, not Jerry Falwell."

Hal wasn't sure who Dorothy Day was, but he was impressed nevertheless. Andrea had made a simple declaration, lacking even the muscle of a verb, but it filled him with admiration for her. In the egoless little shrug that accompanied this statement Hal saw Andrea's life in the city for the next several years, and he realized it was one he'd never pictured, for anyone. The whole idea of taking on the burdens of a big city was to beat it down and master it, to remake oneself in the city's most glittery image—not to dig into its underbelly and stay there, working.

Andrea was made of a thousand colors, Hal saw then, from ivory to rose to gold to chestnut to chocolate. She was a faultless ratio of curve to straight line, of yield to ceramic hardness. Hal stood squinting in the light, famished and slightly dizzy, wondering what astonishing formula had produced her.

When Hal informed his family he was moving to New York immediately following graduation, they were largely bemused. His sisters clearly had never thought him capable of such an adventure. His father seemed pleased and perplexed that a son of his would move to the toughest and filthiest city in the nation with the expressed plan of making no money. For weeks, Hal's mother told him, his father mentioned Hal's impending move to people at church, shaking his head in mock confusion and speculating how long it would last. Several letters had arrived in the mail from him in a single week, accompanied by newspaper clippings of crime statistics for various neighborhoods.

In June his mother drove in to help him pack. She arrived at the house on Regent Street in her faded jeans and tennis shoes, short red hair pushed back by a rolled bandanna. Hal jogged down the stairs and found her chatting with his roommates, four of whom were slumped on the couch over mixing bowls of cereal. True to form, Wes had set down his Tupperware of frosted wheat and risen to greet her.

"There he is," said Wes. "The most surprising man we thought we knew."

Hal hugged his mother, who had shrunk down to chin level within the last few years. Her shoulders were bony and fragile, which he found disconcerting and somewhat sad, this evidence of his mother's growing smaller and older, so he squeezed her until she made an exasperated sound of protest and pushed him away.

Up in Hal's room they began labeling boxes and sorting shirts.

"I'm not sure how many of these you should even take with you," she'd said. She held up a faded Wisconsin Badgers T-shirt. "Did you rub this on concrete?"

Hal eyed the shirt, which was frayed at the hems and flaking white lettering all over the carpet. "Let's toss it," he said. "Who knows when I'll wear it."

"Do you need suits for your job?" she asked, glancing up at him. "We can give you some money for suits to get you started."

"I don't need them," Hal said proudly. "Maybe one for special occasions. Andrea says it's business casual at the office and sometimes even casual in the field. If we're actually building, then obviously it's casual." He was enjoying being able to talk with some authority about his new job. Not long ago he'd thought he'd be applying to the PDQ gas station's night shift and reading *Jugs* alone by the tobacco rack.

His mother nodded. "Well, looking at these clothes I think you need a few new things even if it is casual. Let's budget some money ahead of time and when you get there, you let us know what you need. You know what they say, right? Dress for the position you want, not the one you have."

"Yeah, maybe," he'd said. His parents had been full of career advice, but Hal suspected they were out of their depth in trying to guide him into a job in New York City. Even Andrea, who had been there for only two weeks, said she'd recalculated almost every plan she'd made so far.

"I'm looking forward to visiting you there," his mother said. "And spending more time with Andrea." She paused. "This is a bit of a whirlwind, you know. Are you sure you should move in with her? Maybe find a roommate first."

Hal stuffed another pile of T-shirts in the trash bag. He'd looked terrible all along, obviously. Someone ought to have told him.

He realized his mother was waiting for a reply, so he said simply, "It is, but I'm sure."

He felt so confident about the whole decision that he couldn't even get worked up when his parents questioned him. There was a reason everything had knitted up so beautifully: the extra room that opened up in Andrea's apartment when her cousin moved in with a bond trader, the volunteer coordinator position at the Housing Trust, the way he and Andrea had come together as neatly as a mollusk closing its shell. It was as if they had only been waiting all this time.

Andrea was as unassuming in her determination as she was in everything. She would do exactly what she felt was right and nothing more, and she would never try to force anyone to agree with her. She simply did as she wanted. Hal had found out that she'd been peripheral to their social group because she was always off doing something concrete: off making phone calls for Planned Parenthood, off working at the campus health center. Calm though she was, however, it was a mistake to think she was malleable. She was not just determined, Hal had realized, but ferocious. In bed he'd found her to be a revelation of drive and openness, of sheer joy in the body and what it was there for. Her arms and back were taut from rowing, her thighs full and muscled. Her neck smelled of wind and biscuits. Her nipples were the color of apricots, her belly a curved silky plain. And Hal had never even guessed. No wonder she'd always won at poker.

Next to him, his mother sniffled. "Sorry, it's dusty," Hal said. She didn't answer, but sniffed again, and when Hal looked over at her, he saw his mother was crying. She was kneeling on his faded brown carpet over a box of old shirts and athletic socks, one hand idly thumbing the cardboard's edge. Her head was bent, the pale freckled skin folding beneath her chin. A tear streaked down her cheek and fell onto the socks, and Hal saw that her skin was downier than it had once been, illuminated by the clear shining track left by the tear.

Hal was baffled. When had he ever seen his mother cry? He must have, but watching her now he realized how rare this was. They were a hardy Wisconsin family who shot deer and gutted fish and went to church. No one cried.

"Mom?" His voice sounded warbly. Downstairs he heard his roommates hollering and slamming the front door as they left the house, and he was relieved they were going. He wanted to shut the door and shield her from the general loudness and clumsiness of his house and himself.

"I'm *fine*," she said, shaking her head. She swiped at her eyes and looked at him, laughing. Her smile twitched and crumpled slightly, but then she mastered it. "I'm proud of you. I thought it would take you a few years to find yourself, and there's nothing wrong with that."

"Thanks," he'd said.

She'd shaken her hair back and shrugged off any last emotion. "You *will* need some help budgeting, though. Trust me on this. There'll come a day when you'll have a week till your next pay-check and only a bag of lentils to last the whole time, and that's when you call me."

Hal had loved his job from the start. Maybe part of it had been falling in love with Andrea as well, riding the subway to and from their apartment each morning and night. They worked in different departments. Much of his job was scheduling and plan-ning, pairing volunteers with duties, and he'd found a well-matched worker and task as satisfying as a perfectly worked equation. The concrete nature of the goal—people needed shel-ter; the Housing Trust found ways to build it—appealed to the practical Midwestern heart of him. He enjoyed his job less for re-ligious or ethical reasons than for reasons of symmetry. He didn't like *surplus*, slopping around without usefulness, and he didn't like a vacuum where a pleasant fullness ought to be.

His mother was right about the lentils. He and Andrea were shockingly poor once they'd paid their rent, and they soon be-came devotees of all manner of dried legumes. They had liked to spin it as their young and poor romantic days, but really that first year gave them both a very close look at the lives of the people they were trying to help. To this day Hal could feel the relief he had felt back then, when he'd realized just how much a dried gar-banzo bean would swell when soaked.

Andrea was promoted within a year, and later left for a differ-ent nonprofit. Hal missed riding the subways with her, stopping off on a whim in Union Square to check out the market or a bookstore, but he found that being without her at work was free-ing. In some ways she still knew him as the college boy he'd been for a long time, the one who'd enjoyed melted cheese on every-thing and dropped the occasional thoughtless homophobic slur. No one else at the Housing Trust knew that boy, and he had no interest in introducing them.

He and Andrea lived in the same place for three years, then moved farther out in Brooklyn as the rents rose. They never talked about getting married, though their parents brought it up each Christmas. (Hal's father sent him a letter describing his own proposal to Hal's mother, plus an accompanying clipping detailing what to watch for in antique rings.) They simply as-sumed they would keep doing the same thing they had been do-ing, because for a long time they had loved it. They rode out to Avenue J and bought sublime pizza from an old man who moved at a glacial speed and never wrote anything down. When they could afford it they had food delivered and stayed in all weekend. When they had no money they camped out eight hours before the free plays in the park to get a seat. They fought about whether to go to Ohio or Wisconsin for the holidays. But everything was good until Hal had begun to notice how loud the trains were, how filthy the sidewalks. Wes had spent a year out west in Port-land and when they returned from visiting him Andrea ecstati-cally breathed in the scent of vendor peanuts and gasoline while Hal realized how much garbage was all over the streets, that the dominant color was brown. It had never occurred to Hal that after so many years together, in which they had left college and stepped into adulthood so smoothly and lovingly, they'd pull apart in their late twenties over something as random as the city they'd ended up in. Well, there was more—there always was—but moving was what they'd fought about until they had no other conversations.

He'd started putting out feelers to the people he still knew in Madison, which led him to the Swiffies, at that point still a small organization running several mobile pantries. The move from providing shelter to providing food was not only natural but un-expectedly gratifying. Both were elemental, of course, but people couldn't accomplish anything without food: kids couldn't con-centrate, adults couldn't get jobs. In housing nonprofits, so much time was spent on grants and with city and county government—sometimes all the satisfaction you got was from handing some-one a piece of paper to sign. He was rarely there to see them move in or enjoy their new shelter. There was nothing simpler than handing someone a plate of hot food and a place at a table to eat it. Nourishment was everything. An apple was everything. A glass of milk was everything. Hal's work brought him an almost Zen-like focus on the minute aspects of consumption: the pop of seeds that plumped a fig, the velvety starch of cooked legumes, the rhythmic work of the teeth.

He had so little savings from the years in New York City that when someone mentioned he could live in a co-op for a few hun-dred bucks a month, he'd leaped at it. That first co-op was an antiracist, pro-feminist, lesbian, gay, bisexual, transgender–supportive house, and that was fine. They all were, really. He liked his housemates, and he liked the association. But when he visited a friend at the sustainable-foods co-op on Morrison Street, the rightness was unavoidable. Even imperious. Talk about a group of people who understood that an egg could encapsulate the whole world! So he moved in. At work he tried to feed great numbers and at home he enjoyed the focus of feeding the people close to him. In one place he appreciated volume and richness and set aside too many questions about sustainability. And at home he dwelled on the candy-green striation in a German Stripe tomato or the particular flavor of a butter that resulted from one small field of clover out in Green County.

He missed Andrea, whom he spoke to once annually for the first few years. His relationships lasted a few months up to three years, but he hadn't lived with a woman other than the occasional roommate he slept with (there was a difference) in a very long time. Hal believed he got all the experience of working out differences and relationship issues in the course of living with so many people. When you had a group to occupy you, whoever thought to narrow your attention to just one person?

When the power flashed out Monday evening, Hal was slouched in his folding chair in a hot, sparsely populated yellow room, half-listening to the Monday night antiwar community action committee.

Next to him, a woman was speaking passionately. He usually enjoyed the careful framing of words at these meetings as people established their liberal credentials and then felt they could relax. The prickliness of community always interested him. It didn't matter where you found it—he knew from his father that church groups had the same problems. The issue was in figuring out what people wanted. It was never the obvious; there was always another layer.

He shifted uncomfortably in his seat while the woman ticked a series of points off her fingers. It was nearly six thirty, and though he wanted only to head home, the Neon Daisy Co-op was throwing a welcome party that night for the co-op community's newest members, which included Greta and a new mother and son who'd moved into the Womyn's Co-op. Twelve co-ops around town belonged to the local association that had banded together in the sixties. Several times a year they all gathered for formal meetings and informal parties. The meetings usually focused on questions of bicycle care, as well as solar-panel maintenance for the houses that had them and loan applications for the houses aiming to purchase them. The association had an advertising budget for the local weekly, a cookbook coordinator who had been gathering recipes for several years and currently had plans for a 500-page tome of vegetarian cooking, and a rotating officer who kept an eye on relevant topics in local government. They sent out a newsletter, brought in instructors for self-defense, nutrition, yoga, and conflict resolution workshops, and maintained a Web site delineating the various co-ops' philosophies and room openings. Membership remained fairly stable, but there were a few co-ops who had once been part of the association but had left it years earlier. Officially there was no ill will, but relations between the general association members and the ones who'd rejected it were cool at best. When Hal ran into the members of the Fauna Co-op, an animal activist house on Spaight Street that had departed over disagreements on veganism, for example, everyone exchanged nods and searching glances tinged with mutual disappointment.

He had to be home by seven to pick up drinks and his roommates, then go and be festive. He was trying not to admit that he felt hungry and sluggish. Sluggishness was what had left him standing idiotically on the grass that morning while his own roommate dove to the rescue, left him watching a helpless dog shake itself off and dash away toward traffic.

Tonight the talk of the war had stalled on a list of complaints over the buses chartered for the Memorial Day protests. Last time they'd been overcrowded and sweaty, apparently, and the lackluster feel of the march was blamed partially on this. But in fact everyone was feeling beaten down. At least you could choose a new charter bus. That was an easily remedied problem.

At first, there had been book drives for soldiers, and someone had found out where to buy body armor, and they had passed out lists of the basics the soldiers requested—and their needs had been desperately, pathetically basic, toothpaste-basic, new-socks-basic. Presumably they still were, but talk had since shifted to yet another round of elections, and as the war's boundaries expanded, its needs felt too daunting to fully address. Early on, Hal had been intrigued by the awkwardness of it—these were not people accustomed to discussing what soldiers needed, and some of them had probably thrown trash at the returning Vietnam vets back in the day, but last year there had been a growing sense of sympathy for the people in a bad position of such magnitude. He'd been proud of his community for managing the leap, but it seemed to have become too difficult to sustain. They were always qualifying their support—no one was supporting the torturers and the sadistic dog handlers—and after a time it was just too difficult to specify whom you supported and how, and the attempts to send supplies had petered out.

He had also perceived a general belief, largely unstated, that soldiers had families who were more likely to send these items. And perhaps there was a little bitterness in it as well, recrimination that said the people who'd supported the war, their bumper stickers insisting on it, could clean up their own mess. He'd tried to be a supporter of the soldier and a protester of the war, but it never worked. He'd spent all his time parsing the nuances of his beliefs and meanwhile the war continued, year by year by year.

"There are plenty of places you can go," someone was saying. "There's always Louisiana and Mississippi. Go to the Appalachians. Plenty of relief work to go around."

After the way his workday had gone, Hal just wanted to go to Sweden. Or Norway. Some country that showered its citizenry with medical care, all secular tranquillity and rivers of flashing fish, where even the booze was clear and made with fruit. He would have no work to do there—the way he imagined it, they'd be compact, fertile countries with plenty of food to go around. He could relax and meet tall milky women with gray eyes and glinting, serious eyebrows. He could bake saffron-currant buns glazed with egg, and educate himself in herring. He didn't even know the political systems of any of these countries: did they have a two-party system based on mutual loathing? No, they probably disagreed on issues like compulsory compost recycling—whether to do a lot, or maybe even more.

The head of the committee, Libby, a gorgeous woman in her sixties with long white hair, for whom Hal had nursed the occasional maternal crush, had stood and was wrapping things up. "Okay, on to miscellaneous topics. We have a local dairy that will remain nameless for now but apparently is willing to sell raw milk, if people are interested. Anyone?"

Hal's hand shot up. "Is it Sweet Heather?" he asked. Sweet Heather Farms raised a herd of twenty cows and made a rich soft-ripened cheese you had to eat with a spoon. Hal waited for it every year. There was no greater apex of principle and hedonism than a cheese like that.

Libby smiled. "It's a farm in Barneveld several of us are familiar with, suffice it to say." She paused. "Okay, yeah, it's Sweet Heather. Stop by their farm if you want any. You all know the drill, right? What you ask for, legally, is cat food. Keep it cold and drink it fast."

She was still talking when the lights went out. Immediately the exclamations began, the shaking of heads and muttered swearing. Atavistically, Hal was startled, even frightened by the first wave of blackness, as if someone had cut the power lines. Then his heart calmed down as he realized what it was.

"Great," Hal said, standing up. "Again. Well, the meeting's over anyway, right?" Might as well nip it in the bud or everyone would expect to stand around all night predicting the length of this latest power outage.

They all stood motionless for a moment, allowing their eyes to adjust to the darkened room and to the evening light still coming through the windows. After a second or two, the shapes of his fellow meeting-goers reasserted themselves in the dimness, and the group began to shuffle slowly out the door, hearing the occasional clank and hiss as people hit their toes on walls and chairs.

In the houses around them, people were poking their heads out at the sound of other voices, waving, and then disappearing again. The meeting attendees clustered around the door, shaking their heads, gesturing toward the dead street lamps. Hal debated joining them, but really he didn't want to. The start of the meeting had cut off the chatter about what he'd been doing in the lake this morning and why his female roommate had been the heroic one, and he didn't want to give them all an opportunity to return to the subject. He waited till he was far enough away that he wouldn't get drawn back in, and called out his good-byes.

These meetings often reminded Hal of leaving church. The childhood road from church to home, where the Packers were usually playing on TV if Hal could only get there to see it, had been littered with Herculean obstacles: the doughnuts and coffee (Hal invariably wolfed down a lemon-filled and waited hopefully near the door), his parents' promise to drive the elderly home, then the relentless chatter while again Hal waited near the potpourri basket in the foyer.

Earlier that day, his other sister Jane had phoned him at the office: she hadn't heard a word from their father, either. "Rennie isn't worried," Hal had told her, but Jane was unimpressed.

"Rennie never worries even when she should," she'd said. "I'll keep trying him."

"You realize we haven't seen him in months," said Hal. "I haven't had even an e-mail or a call from him. He's not answering his phone, either. He might have fallen and broken something. He might've cut himself."

"I know," Jane said, "I'm hoping he's just hibernating. Have you had a letter from him?"

"Not for months."

Jane said, "Me, neither." Hal had listened to her breathe. In the background he'd heard the sounds of office chatter, phones ringing. "Listen," Jane said. "Call Uncle Randy, he's only a little

ways away. Have him go by and knock on the door. And let me
know." Hal had spoken with his uncle next, who was busy repair-
ing some sort of engine part but promised to drive over later.

Hal walked along the Yahara River in the direction of Lake
Monona and took a right on Morrison Street. He wondered if his
house was stocked up on candles and flashlight batteries. They
had been on the list for weeks, but whose job was it to buy more?
They'd been stuffing one-dollar bills into a jar for expenses like
this, but now Hal pictured the full pottery vase sitting on its
table. He had a bad feeling it had been his job.

He was strolling, trying to enjoy the pleasant lingering heat in
the dusky night air. Another blackout. They had not been lasting
very long—in fact, he was surprised the street lamps weren't
flashing back on already.

Today had been the worst work day yet in a difficult spring.
He'd been on and off the phone all day with his sisters to no
avail, finally distracted by the group of college guys who'd shown
up to volunteer in the warehouse and break down bulk food into
individual packages. They were some kind of campus group doing community service, and twelve of them had milled about in
the entryway, energetic and well muscled, in sweatshirts and
baseball caps. Hal didn't usually handle this, but the warehouse
manager was out, so Hal had asked a couple workers to set the
boys up with a huge bin of brown rice to be separated into two-
pound bags and boxed in groups of six. "Or breakfast sausages,"
Hal had said, "we have those, too, right? Or those frozen enchila-
das." The workers had exchanged glances. "Not really," one said,
and Hal had been too rushed to get into it. "Great, brown rice it
is. Thanks," he said, and went to check on the meal delivery
preparations. He'd forgotten all about the warehouse volunteers.

Two hours later one of the volunteer boys came wandering
out to the front offices. "We're done," he'd said, adjusting his cap.
"We're here for another hour, you need more?"

"Always," Hal had said heartily. He often found himself slipping back into a manly loudness around boys like this, who reminded him of himself in college. He must seem aging and false to this kid, who smiled politely and said nothing. He'd gone back to the warehouse to see what else he could set up. As he passed the volunteer room he saw that the boys had lifted the Toyota-sized box that had contained brown rice, and were shaking it out over a bin to get the last few grains.

That pleased him. He was whistling as he flung open the door to the main cooler, the huge cold room where all their food was housed on tall metal shelves, and his whistle had echoed off the walls. Two of the warehouse workers, in sweatshirts and puffy jackets, were standing before a pallet of packaged rolls and loaves of bread. There was a shelf of frozen vegetables, and a few stacked pallets of canned soup. But the rest of the room, the great expanse of which was usually filled with food, was emptied. There were some bins of produce and a few gallons of milk that only looked paltrier against such emptiness.

They had enough to make scanty meals for home delivery for a few days, if that. He'd had to lean against the shelving to steady himself. Maybe the warehouse manager was off securing a massive delivery. But the workers shook their heads when he asked. "We've been asking and asking," they said. "We figured something would show."

He'd thanked the college boys and told them he'd mark them for the full three hours of service. He'd gone to speak with Diana, his boss, but she was on the phone, shaking her head at him when he peered in her doorway. Finally Hal just went to his office and tried calling grocery stores and Oscar Mayer to check on donations. He'd managed to get a delivery promised from one, but it was nothing compared to what they needed. He'd made more calls for another three hours and then left for the community action meeting, so preoccupied he almost rear-ended someone on the way.

As he neared home, he was still trying not to think about the next day at work. He had no idea what he was going to put together as a hot delivery meal. Brown rice. But what else? In the past, Hal enjoyed the frugality of figuring out how he could stretch his supplies, in his head dividing the pounds of bulk food into neat portions, knowing he could add volume with water and that good flavoring, even just onion, could create a sense of richness that wasn't precisely calculable. But right now his calculations were all out of whack. He had nothing to work with here. He had imaginary numbers.

At the park, Hal walked over to the dock. It was back in place; a teenage couple was sitting at the end with their feet dangling over the smooth, bright surface of the water. They glanced at him and then returned their attention to the view.

Out on the lake was a white boat with blue, official-looking lettering. People were moving about on the deck, but he couldn't tell what they were doing. He watched for several minutes, then walked back over the grass and down Morrison Street. It was seven o'clock. He had just enough time to put on a new shirt and head over to the Daisies' house.

A man was sitting on their porch swing. He did not seem menacing—not his posture, anyway, which seemed exhausted more than anything. He was leaning back in the swing, his head resting against the wood, both feet flat on the porch floor. He'd have been any other man, completely unnoticeable, if Hal had passed him on the street. It was just the proximity that was so unexpected, that he'd broken the unspoken boundary of the edge of a square of grass.

He didn't look very big. Five nine, five ten. Hal was six three. He was cautious, but he wasn't worried.

"Can I help you?" Hal said. He took his key away from the lock, suddenly remembering there were two women right on the other side of the door. He shifted his body so that he blocked the entrance.

The man raised his head and looked in Hal's direction. It was difficult to follow his eyes, which kept drifting. He wore a dark suit, a patterned tie half-knotted beneath his collar, and gleaming, expensive lace-up shoes. Even in the evening it was too warm for a full suit, yet he hadn't taken off the jacket. A layer of sweat veiled his face.

"I doubt it," the man said.

"Well, you're here," said Hal, "so I'm assuming you think we can help you with something. Why don't you tell me what?"

The man rummaged in his pockets, then put a stick of gum in his mouth. He held the package out as an offer to Hal, shrugged when Hal shook his head politely and automatically, and said, "I'm waiting for Greta."

"Oh," Hal said. "Oh, okay. Does she know you're here?" The man just shrugged again. Hal waited for more, then said, almost to himself, "You do know her, right?"

"I know her," the man said. A smile surfaced, then sank. "I thought I knew her better. But there she is in the paper this morning, in about the last place I expected. I decided to sit here and think it through first. I'm not sure she knows I'm out here." He didn't seem very worried about what Greta knew. He turned and glanced into the front window, seemed to see nothing, and resettled himself on the swing.

Whoever he was, Hal didn't want to be near him anymore. The man's voice was quiet and even. He seemed very tired. He might stay out here, but so what? Hal wasn't going to call the cops on a well-dressed man sitting on his porch, especially not when the police were called upon to do plenty else during these power outages. Hal thought briefly of stories of hoboes being fed soup in exchange for yard work. He had no yard work to offer the man. Karin had done it all over the weekend.

"I'm going inside," Hal said. "If she hasn't come out yet she may not want to see you, you know. You might want to get home before it's dark; the traffic lights will all be out." Hal wanted him gone before they left the house unoccupied, but he didn't think it was wise to admit they were leaving. You just never knew, and to him this was a stranger. "Why not just call her in the morning?"

The man nodded as if he ought to have had the same idea. He didn't move.

Hal slipped inside, locking the door behind him.

Karin was there in the living room, putting on lip gloss without looking. On the coffee table was a ring of unlit candles. They must have had some batteries, because next to her, a portable radio was playing. The flooding in New York had receded, but there'd been riots that day throughout Syria, the West Bank, and, strangely, Holland. It made Hal feel better to know some other, more civilized country was in disarray, too. From the sounds he could imagine it all: fire, people leaping, arms raised up in silhouette.

"Where's Greta?" A thought struck him and he turned back to Karin. "Have you seen her today? Did she come home from work?"

"Do you need to change, or can we head straight out?" Karin glanced at him and then returned to the mirror, wiping a fingertip beneath her eyes. "She knows her husband is out there. I'm sure if she wanted him in here she'd invite him."

Hal stood very still. There had been no talk of husbands, but given her age it only made sense that she had been married before. Yet he found it hard to imagine Greta, who seemed to find the daily interactions of life with housemates endlessly trying, with a spouse.

"How did you know?" he asked. He could see the husband's

feet propped up on the railing, the movement of his pant legs as he rocked the swing gently back and forth.

Karin joined him at the window, glancing back toward the stairs. They heard no sound from the second floor. "She told me when I saw a stranger on our porch," Karin said.

"It never occurred to me she was married," Hal said wonderingly.

"Still is," said Karin. She brushed her hair back off her face, her eyes gleaming. "What? You never care when I bring guys home."

Hal blinked. "I like the guys you go out with," he said absently. This was slightly true. Karin had a taste for crunchy Libertarians who showed up on bicycles and pontificated incessantly on local beers. She had never seemed terribly serious about any of them. Whenever one of them was holding up a glass of Bell's Oberon Ale and ensuring that Hal knew he knew who Oberon was besides a beverage, Karin was smiling coolly in their direction, amused and unimpressed. She took a man upstairs occasionally to spend the night, according to a system or whim that Hal had never once predicted correctly.

"Yeah, well, I don't think Greta needs you to be up in arms," Karin replied.

Hal stepped back, trying not to show how flustered he was by the whole scenario—himself belligerent and protective, Karin suddenly the repository of secrets, a desperate man after Greta.

Karin went on. "You don't think this thing will go too late, do you? I have a cheesemaker interview tomorrow morning." Neither needed to ask if the party would be canceled because of the blackout. The Daisies would never consider it. "I just hope the phones stay on."

He found Greta in the bathroom, the door open, smudging pencil around her eyes. A candle burned on the counter next to her. Hal thought about sneaking away before she knew he was there. Greta was not the kind of woman who collapsed in your arms. She would be the sort who struck out in frustration.

"Hey," he said. He leaned in the doorway. She glanced at him in the mirror and gave him a quick smile.

"Hi," she said. "What's up? I should be doing this at the window where there's light, I guess, so tell me if I look like a floozy."

"You look great."

"Thank you. The radio say anything about the blackout?" she asked.

"I didn't catch anything," said Hal.

She nodded and said nothing, blew out the candle and turned to face him. Greta's lashes framed her green eyes starkly; her blond hair was caught up at the back of her head in a twist. She was so pretty, in her way. She didn't have Karin's pure, sugary sex appeal, but her features were so firmly formed, her nose straight and slightly pointed, her mouth framed with smile brackets. Greta's lines added to her attractiveness. They didn't appear to be a sign of softening with age, but looked as carefully and symmetrically added as if she'd been sculpted and the artist had found her face too bland. She'd been a boring, pretty girl in her twenties, Hal guessed. He and Greta were not far apart in age. He wondered when she'd married the man on the porch.

"Well?" Greta whispered. She cast a covert—or was it flirtatious? It seemed flirtatious—glance toward the front of the house. "Should we ask him to come with us?"

He pretended to take her seriously. "Sure," he said. "I'm sure the Daisies won't mind. I was kind of a dick to him, though. I didn't know who he was."

He turned back toward the stairs, just to test her, he supposed, and sure enough as he took a step she was right there next to him, a hand on his arm. She wasn't kidding anymore.

"No," she said. "Let him stay there. And don't worry about being a dick to him. He can take it."

They looked at each other for a moment. Greta wiped her palms nervously on her skirt. "Is he crazy or something?" Hal finally asked. "Did he hurt you?"

Greta laughed a little, apparently to herself. "He's not crazy. He probably *is* drunk. And no. He never hurt me." She gave an almost imperceptible emphasis to *he* and *me*.

Now Karin came up the stairs and stood at the landing, arms crossed. "Greta, I think he may have lain down on the swing."

Greta seemed to take this in stride. "He'll be fine," she said shortly. "He'll probably leave when the lights come back on. Now, we're bringing wine and some vodka, right? May as well not leave it all for him."

"Are you comfortable just leaving him here?" Hal ventured. It was awkward not to know his name, but Greta hadn't said it, and Hal was too nervous to ask her.

Greta said, "We'll lock the doors."

"He looked awfully hot in that suit," Karin said. "He's just sitting there and it's going to be dark soon."

"Well then," said Greta. "Take him a change of clothes and a candle." She shut her bedroom door behind her rather savagely.

Hal and Karin looked at each other. Karin jerked her head in the direction of the living room, and he followed her down the stairs, moving slowly through the gathering dimness. The house was hot inside without air-conditioning.

"I think you should go talk to him."

"She obviously doesn't want me to," Hal said. "Since when do we all jump in to each other's marriages in here?"

"No one's ever been married here before. Anyway, you heard her say he's probably drunk," Karin whispered. "Do you want to come home and find some poor guy choking on his own vomit on our front porch?"

"He won't choke," Hal said. "He'll get bored and go home. It'll be better that way. He didn't seem too incapacitated to me."

"You're the community activist," she said.

"We should all be community activists," he replied. "It's supposed to be part of what we do."

"I know, but professionally speaking, you feed the downtrodden, and the downtrodden are on our porch. I think you should go out there."

"Oh, come on. His suit cost more than your car," he protested.

"It *is* the suit that gets you, isn't it?" Karin said. She was looking at him keenly. "But if he looked like one of your little hipster man-child buddies with messy hair and an army jacket you'd be out there now."

Hal was speechless. Karin smiled, knowing she had him.

Greta clattered down the stairs. She had changed clothes: her shirt was a bright flare of white, on her feet were flat bronze gladiator sandals that reached nearly to her knees. Their soles smacked on the wood floors. "You win, okay?"

"Huh?" they said innocently.

Greta stalked to the front door. She looked furious, but all she said was, "Come outside in five minutes and we'll leave."

"What are you doing?" Greta asked.

Will sat up and smiled at her, as if they'd bumped into each other over petit fours and tea. "Why do you ask?" She wondered if she could leave him out here, if he was really so bad off. A little power outage shouldn't keep him here forever.

"This is all very theatrical. Very junior-year-of-high-school," Greta informed him. She suddenly remembered Justin Konigsdorf, her high-school boyfriend, who had once thrown money at her. They had been having some sort of fight, about what she didn't even know, and Justin had accused her of wanting only money from him—he sold golf gear at a pro shop. He'd made his point by flinging about seventeen dollars on the floor. She'd always wondered what movies he'd been watching that week.

Will offered her a spot on the swing but she shook her head. She leaned against the banister instead, frowning.

"Your face looks swollen," she said.

"Oh, it isn't swollen," Will said. "I'm fine." Once she had come home from a business trip and that was the first thing she'd realized when she saw him after two weeks: his cheeks were bloated, and he bore a burgeoning double chin. He kept his graying dark hair short all over and brushed to one side, with neatly squared sideburns. His pale eyes were rimmed with lashes so dark they looked slightly fake, but he had a large nose with a forceful bridge that had been broken more than once. He'd never been cute; he'd been handsome, the kind of man who made you wish men still wore hats. He was still handsome, but he had begun to look rather beefy and unhealthy. A teetering-wreck kind of handsome. Greta tried not to soften her expression; she was angry to find she pitied him. Not because he was drunk, again, but because she could still see who he used to be. It hurt her that he was losing his good looks and his air of ease, even though she knew losing all these qualities might be best in the end. He could regain his looks; he could learn how to be humble and friendly again. She tried to think of what had happened to him as a kind of possession, because it allowed her to hope it could all be reversed.

"Why'd you move in with people?" he asked finally.

She sighed. "This just worked out, for some reason."

"That's good," he said. "I'm glad it's working out. Still, I'd have thought you'd prefer solitude at this point. Though I guess they're good people. Watchdogs. Dog-rescuers."

Greta watched him closely, to see if he would make eye contact. He did so briefly, in darts and glances. When he was drunk he would hold her gaze out of defiance, but he couldn't focus. Now he looked at her and then made a show of resettling himself, crossing his legs and pulling at his tie.

She and Will had never gotten a dog, though for years they'd formed a small informal cottage industry of babysitting dogs for friends and family. They'd watched rambunctious puppies, behaviorally challenged adoptees, twitchy hounds, and saintly, massive Bernese mountain dogs that liked to lean against their legs and cut off circulation to their feet. Will had been in law school then, wiry and bearded, home studying all the time and caring for the parade of dogs.

They'd even taken care of an ancient, weakened retriever when the owner was called out of town, mainly trying to keep the dog comfortable until its owner could return to have it put down. Will had carried the dog in and out of the house when it had to urinate, and each time afterward he'd settle down crosslegged next to the dog's bed and, with a damp towel, clean the fur beneath the dog's tail, meticulously and tenderly. Much of the fur had fallen out and Greta had been unable to bear the pinkness of the dog's skin, the sight of it so shocking on a furred animal. But Will had rested one hand on the dog's flank to calm it and dabbed at its tail with the towel until it was clean.

Now Will heaved a great sigh and rocked the swing creakily, and Greta returned her focus to him. These moments had been coming to her in the weeks since she'd moved. They were the accompaniments of a long marriage, all those little objects she'd forgotten. The strange part was that each one eased her way just a bit. She knew it was time to give up when she realized how different Will used to be: how funny and how generous, how naturally and how fearlessly he'd reached toward everyone else.

If Will had any idea what Greta was thinking, he wouldn't admit it. "My sister says hello."

Greta hadn't talked to Sarah in several weeks. She hadn't even passed on her new phone number. She nodded, refusing to ask about her. She'd call Sarah herself.

"I'm not drunk," he added. Greta shrugged. The fact that he denied it so believably meant nothing. She had heard him say, confronted with newly unearthed bottles of vodka, "It's not what you think."

It didn't matter anymore. It didn't matter anymore. She repeated it to herself a few more times.

"I have to go be welcomed at this party tonight," she said, "even though I have to get up early tomorrow and be prepared for a big lunch with an alum, and the president has made it clear we all need to meet our quotas or else. But I live in a community now, so I can't make them change the party just for me. Plus, now my whole office keeps staring at me and waiting for me to explain why I moved. I think Charles plans to ask me to lunch every day this week until I crack. So I need to be focused. I have things to do. I can't stay up all night reminiscing about old times with you."

"Our times aren't that old, Greta."

She interrupted. "Are you planning on driving home? I don't think you should." This was where she had always been tripped up on her plans to let him fall without cushioning the blow. What was she supposed to do, let him drive drunk and kill some child because she was making a point? He'd always known it, too. For a long time she'd stayed if only to keep him from driving, eventually settling on the best compromise she could: she dropped him off each morning at his office. He got home however he got home, but not by driving. If they'd lived in New York City or Chicago, without a car, she would have been long gone. That was what she told herself.

Will shrugged. He jingled the keys in his pocket. She sighed, looked out at the sky, which was full of clouds and streaks of pink and orange, and held out her hand. He set the keys in her palm. She looked down at them, thinking how she knew even his keys well, recognizing each and every piece of warm metal that lay in her hand.

"It just doesn't seem like you here," Will said. "At all."

"Sure it does," Greta said automatically.

She had to admit that the whole house gave off a feeling of waning energy, of effort not totally borne out. It was not refined but nor was it bravely bright and threadbare. The co-op reminded her of a person's first apartment out of school, about nine months in. The effort that had gone into painting and decorating was still paying off, but she sensed it might not be renewed. When it came time to repaint, she felt the house stood a very good chance of going beige. Yet the place had made her feel a little motherly, almost. She felt as if she could take them all in hand and get things into shape. They could chip in for a new couch. She could start cleaning out the two vacant rooms on the third floor and get them ready for more housemates. But she liked the kitchen. She liked knowing someone had so painstakingly painted the ir-regular lines on the wall.

"Don't tell me you're happier here," he said.

She put the keys in the front pocket of her skirt. Then she leaned down toward him, smelling the medicinal, pine-sap scent of gin and the conditioner he rubbed through his coarse dark hair each morning, and the smoke, from people standing outside the bar he must have gone to, that clung to his suit. Her mouth was so close to his ear she could almost feel on her lips the fine, tiny hairs on his skin.

"Well," she whispered. She felt bitter and fierce. She'd gotten some energy back. He was leaning into her now, into the warmth of her breath and into the thought that she must be giving in to him somehow, since he'd come all this way and waited so long. In the last weeks before she had moved out, Will had wrapped him-self around her like a vine each night, saying, *We can't be happy some other way. You don't want to leave me.*

Greta paused—perhaps it was kinder not to say anything—but then the words rushed forth. "Don't worry if I'm happy or not. I left. I'm gone."

She took a step back then, watching Will's face to see if he would react, or if he would only stare blankly at her. But Will was looking at Hal and Karin, who had just emerged from the house, holding a couple bottles to take to the party.

"We're going," Greta said briefly, and headed down the steps. The other two watched, eyebrows knit, and then began to follow her. Hal paused to lock the door behind him, glancing back apologetically.

On the sidewalk Greta strode ahead of them, but she stopped a few houses down, waiting at the park until the other two caught up to her. Above them the tree branches arched across the empty street, with an inordinate amount of birds gathered among the leaves. The air was heated and damp, and kept swelling with the flapping of wings, panicked bird conversation. Perhaps they fed here in the evenings, on the fish that drew near the surface of the lake. The dock was empty now, the white boat still far out in the water.

All Greta said was, "Are they diving?"

Hal shook his head. "I can't see what they've been doing. It's too far away to tell. That boat's been there since I got home. Maybe it's moved somewhat."

"Maybe there isn't anything to find down there," Karin said. "The dog could've been barking at a fish. Maybe it turned out to be a joke."

"I don't know," Hal sighed, checking his cell phone. "I think someone went out there on purpose."

"Could be accidental," said Greta. "It's like snowmobiles and ATVs—every year someone gets wasted and dies out there. Or they go through the ice. It could be just some guy who thought he'd watch the sunset."

"I'd think the police would be all over the place," Hal said. "Obviously someone's missing."

"Is the lake even very deep?" said Karin.

No one answered. All three began to walk again, this time more slowly. Greta cast one last glance in the direction of their house, her lips disappeared between her teeth, her chin lowered.

"Nice of the Daisies to throw a party," she said. "Isn't it?"

"They're good at that kind of thing," Karin agreed.

Obviously no one was going to press her about the husband, so Hal took up the thread as well. "We should have thrown our own," he said.

Now Hal watched Greta and Karin stroll along before him, Greta's feet in their bronze sandals, her brown skirt flipping around her knees. She wore a tank top that showed the pale muscled backs of her arms, the suede corrugation of her elbows, the sharp knob of her spine at the base of her neck. Not an outfit most women wore to join their suited husbands for dinner, but maybe that was the point. When he and Karin had gone outside, Greta's husband had been gazing up at her, half dazzled, half drunk, as if she'd grown wings.

Next to her, Karin seemed tall and healthy, her skin already lightly tanned, her hair a sleek fall down the back of her orange cotton T-shirt. As Hal watched, she examined one scratched arm and then the other.

Greta tried to force herself to relax, breathing deeply. She counted her steps, watching her feet flash beneath her on the sidewalk. She used to breathe this way, counting beats and concentrating on slowness, on nights when Will hadn't come home. The breathing helped sometimes, and now she felt her body calming down, the adrenaline dissipating, now that she knew he was at the house, and safe, and that she was moving farther and farther away from him.

She offered to take a bottle from Karin and cradled it in one arm, hoping it didn't slip on her sweaty skin. Moving out was supposed to remove this sort of thing from her life.

She did look back once or twice, but Will wasn't following. He wouldn't budge. He'd wait.

The problem with drunks was this: though so unpredictable, they were also crushingly boring. You never knew what they would not manage to follow through on, but you could guarantee why.

It was so monotonous in retrospect, yet at the time each incident was new and involving. What had first seemed like one odd aberration at a party or a misjudgment over the holidays had intensified slowly and decisively, and the whole time, Greta knew, she had been ten steps behind, waffling on the terminology. It took her a year to name it a "problem," another to call it by name. She was embarrassed now to think of it, as if she had been one of those old ladies still whispering the word "cancer" over the deathbed. And she really had no excuse; his family was peppered with alcoholism—an uncle, several cousins—but for years Will appeared to have dodged the bullet. She'd been gullible—benighted, even—though she'd always prided herself on sharpness. But somehow, up close, Greta had lost perspective again and again, taken in first by the half-hearted, deceptive attempts to sober up, then infuriated by the same old rhetoric about why he didn't need to.

Getting into any kind of discussion when Will was drunk was pointless, but sometimes she'd done it anyway. It had taken her the first two years of the major drinking period to realize that even their worst fights changed nothing at all, because although she said everything she'd been thinking, tore into Will with relish and sarcasm she'd known she possessed but hadn't thought she'd ever use, he never remembered.

So he never called her on whatever she had said the evening before, but the words had their effect anyway. The fact of saying such things at all loosened some coil inside Greta, and soon she said anything and everything she had ever fantasized. In her imagination there were no consequences. Greta could sit on the couch for hours, frozen, gloating about what she just might do when Will finally got home, her fantasies bright and hard and inconsequential in the best possible way. She felt no guilt for any of it. No one could be expected to deal with this and not be out of her mind with rage. She felt entitled to it all.

When he did arrive home, at midnight or three or seven A.M., she never did any of the things she'd thought about. He would fumble at the lock with the wrong key till it broke off and she finally stood and let him in. When the door swung open he usually offered her a huge fake grin. Sometimes she started in on him as soon as he walked in; mostly she learned not to bother, because often he simply could not process her response. But she gave herself the occasional release.

Once she hit him on the back with her fist, a hammer-blow just to see how it felt. She did it as he bent down woozily, hand gripping the closet door, to remove a shoe. Or, she would give him a hard shove as he was headed to bed. Whatever she did, it stunned him every time. He'd turn and look at her with genuine, hurt bafflement. *What are you doing?*

Maybe he remembered these moments, maybe he didn't. Greta did, and it frightened her. She felt how close she was to breaking through the middle-class veil into something tawdry and photographed, something irreversible. Their house had a short flight of steps at the front door, a concrete walk at the bottom. She tried very hard not to imagine pushing him down those steps when she heard him trudging her way. Or else she did the opposite, and she tried very hard to picture it, to remind herself what could happen if she let go. She knew exactly how it would look: Will falling with barely a sound, his arms outstretched, and she knew the exact expression on his face, because she'd called it up before, with that shove. He looked as hurt as a child who never thought you'd slap him.

So instead of violence she had talked, with a scorn that ought to have withered the wood frames of the doors, blighted the ficus, fermented the apple juice in the fridge. She believed she had two excuses: One, such viciousness was what his drinking had brought out in her. He would never stop drinking if he was not made to see the depth he'd sunk them to. Looked at this way, her diatribes were a favor, almost a medical responsibility. Two, he remembered nothing. The things she said to him would have leveled a better union, but between Greta and Will, her cruelest accusations simply fizzled and dissipated. Their marriage was as toxic and resilient as lye or nuclear waste, with a half-life of millions of years.

She had come to understand the couples you saw at parties, whose disgust was so palpable that they were genuinely frightening. You wondered how they had not yet slit each other's throats and knew not to get too close or you'd be there for the big day. She and Will used to discuss such people on the way home, letting a faint veneer of pity color their observations. Poor harpy. Poor blowhard. What had brought them to this? Perhaps they were lovely apart; she calm and funny, he sympathetic and expansive.

Greta had taken the pin from the grenade because only the faintest memories stayed in Will's head. She could accuse him of being an unshaven, pathetic, limp waste of space, and *he would never know.* It felt wonderful. How many times had she had to hold something back in front of friends or family or coworkers, while Will slurred whatever popped into his head? No more. Destroying wedding gifts, defacing calligraphied poems, dumping the vodka she'd unearthed from his closet on Will's inert form in their bed—as she did these things Greta had felt herself to be tremendous and supple, made magnificent by the sheer force of her anger. It was so much better to let it loose than to be the downtrodden wife whose husband barely recognized her.

By the time they reached the Daisies' house it was nearly eight o'clock. The sun was no longer visible, just the streaks in the sky behind the clouds. The house was an oddly assembled, pale yellow, green-trimmed structure studded with sun porches and strange little alcoves. A sculpture crouched in the front yard, hammered curls of rusty metal inside which crouched a wooden monkey with its arms around its knees. The whole effect was both evolutionary and uterine.

Greta averted her eyes from the sculpture and stood still on the front walk, just for a moment. She breathed deeply. Again. Again. She focused on the crowded porch, where all seven Daisies were standing in a row. The Daisies were twenty-five at most, and the collective feeling of youth and energy on the porch was palpable. Their flopping shorts, their baggy skirts, their skimpy tank tops and colorful creature tattoos! They waved their ropy arms in greeting, revealing the vulnerable, pale undersides of their biceps and vole-sized tufts of hair. Greta waved back. She thought she recognized one or two from Grinwall.

Behind her, Hal waved and murmured, "Man, the Daisies. They always have to do it big." Sure enough, they then threw out their arms and cried "Welcome!," and Greta realized they were aping the idea, acknowledging the hippie overtones by overdoing it completely. Nevertheless, their hosts hugged all three of them hello, startling Greta with the sensation of their furry underarms on her bare shoulders, their scent of musk and twine and candle wax. She hugged back, grateful and frazzled. She was being swept in, swept up. She could concentrate on this place all night. Will was gone; he wasn't here.

"Come in, come in!" a young man—Gregory—was saying. He ushered her in the door with an arm still slung around her shoulder.

"Wow," Greta said. She stopped in the doorway and looked around. The room was dim but filled with lit candles on every surface, plus a few heavy flashlights balanced on end and projecting cones of light toward the ceilings. The floor plan was almost entirely open but for a twisting iron staircase up the center like a corkscrew. It looked fantastic, though you had to wonder if it was remotely safe. With Gregory beside her, Greta moved slowly around the room in the flickering light, peering at the walls. The west wall was painted black and covered, top to bottom, in framed sketches. The back wall was painted in vertical stripes that swelled and then thinned to pins, the colors shifting from emerald to a silvery green. The east wall was hung with objects: mandolins and dulcimers, a tarnished old trumpet, clock gears and old-fashioned forceps, and rusty scissors and heavy leather buckles.

Greta turned to Gregory, only really seeing him now. A mop of gold curls hung in his face, and he was barely taller than she was, with warm brown eyes and a short stubby nose. "This is a crazy place," she told him.

He laughed. "It actually doesn't always look this way," he said. "We shake it up every six months. One person gets to direct each wall."

"You undo all this?" she said, appalled.

He shrugged. "We take photos," he said. "Monty keeps a catalog. And it doesn't always work out this well. It depends on who's living here. One year three people had abortions and someone went to rehab and every fucking wall ended up just muddy green. It was miserable. It looked like the Vietnam war in here."

"God. How long did you leave it up?"

He looked at her as if she'd asked an extraordinary question. "Six months," he said. "That's where the house was then, so we just let it be."

Hal went straight to the buffet table. There were three platters of fruit and crudités from the supermarket, which relieved him. Clearly not from a garden. At least he wasn't the only one.

The Morrison Street Co-op was still the only true sustainable-foods co-op, at least based on the evidence of the buffet table. Lately he got the unsettling feeling that the only difference between his co-op and anyone else's was that theirs did the out-reach that was mandated in the house charter—hosting tastings of local products, visiting schools to talk about how cheese was made or to show kids how to cook a vegetable. The whole local food thing had come into vogue, and now everyone was eyeing their dinner guests competitively, out-organicking each other and casually dropping the province of the cheese and coffee beans into conversation.

His co-op had been founded in 1970 by a group of poli-sci graduate students for the purpose of saving rent and pooling protest duties. Then it had floundered for several years, identity-wise, until somewhere in the mid-nineties the sustainable-foods moniker had taken hold, which was about the time Hal moved in. The Morrison Street Co-op didn't have the same feminist political urgency and startling bursts of fecundity of the Wo-myn's Co-op, the wary gravity of Muslims for Peace, or the youthful, tattooed zip of the Neon Daisies, whose graying drug connection remained allied with the house even as its members changed. The Two Lakes International Co-op in particular was enjoying a vogue at the moment—with the country at war, Two Lakes got to model a tiny vegan United Nations in a campus-area Victorian, talking grandly at the farmers' market about sanctions, ostentatiously modeling negotiation tactics in crowded parking lots at Badger football games.

Hal filled a plate with hummus and chips, opened a beer, and headed out to the back porch, where at least the darkness felt natural. The candlelit house was too disconcerting, all leaping shadows and furtive movement. He said hello to people but kept moving toward the folding chairs at the back of the yard, hoping to have a moment to eat, drink, and collect himself.

Hal pulled his cell phone from his pocket and checked it once again. No calls.

Their mother had died that winter, and Hal was still tallying the effects. He hadn't realized, for instance, that his relationship with his father had been so entirely routed through his mother. His sisters and mother had always held everyone's attention, because their relationship was deeply involved and contentious. For years, Hal and his father had watched the three females trade grievances, pleased that men didn't need to dissect every emotion. Hal had never understood what the women were all fighting about anyway: he and his mother had never been close in his childhood, until they connected suddenly and profoundly when he was an adult. It still shocked him to think he now knew as much as he might ever know about his mother. From here on out he would only begin to forget her.

The silence between him and his father had happened without any announcement or argument: only now did Hal understand that with his mother dead and his sisters having called a truce, his father was no longer standing beside him, offering a wry comment on the arguments among the women. He'd slipped away.

Their dad had moved to northern Wisconsin a month after their mother died. There he fished, hunted, observed his patch of land and the animals that lived on it. He no longer went to church, which saddened Hal unaccountably. His dad had enjoyed church life so much, the socializing, the community chitchat, the drives and petitions and fund-raising. His father was a community man, a social animal, just as Hal's mother had been.

Now Hal imagined his father rose at dawn each day, untethered his boat from the dock, and caught bass and crappie. He might tend a garden. He might read and listen to the radio, but obviously he never wrote letters anymore.

"Hey, Hal. I figured we'd run into each other." Hal took a moment to identify the voice, the glow of an orange leather bag and the pale vee of an arm in a sleeveless shirt. It was his boss, Diana, standing before him in the dark backyard with a plate of fruit and vegetables in one hand, her red ponytail draped over her shoulder. He'd forgotten how many of their friends overlapped.

"Well, hey, nice surprise. I need to talk to you." He gestured at the chair beside him and she nodded and sat down. Even seated, Diana seemed about eight feet tall. It was her deep voice, he thought, her golden eyes fastening on you like an eagle's. Hal was slightly afraid of Diana and also frequently fought the urge to touch her.

"I tried to catch you today," he said. "What's going on with the warehouse?"

Diana rubbed her forehead. "We can't get the amount of donations we were getting before. Nowhere near it. I'm trying to reach out to new places but it's slow going. Maybe I should have seen it coming but I've never experienced a drop like this, to be honest. It caught us all by surprise."

"What are we going to send out for the rest of the week?" Hal asked. "And we'll have to cancel the mobile pantry if something doesn't come through."

"I know." Diana looked at the carrot stick she was holding and set it back down on her plate. "I might be able to get some eggs. We'll have to candle and wash them all, but it's better than nothing. If I can get seed donations, we might be able to get some unused community garden space for free and that'll help us through the summer. I just don't know."

They sat in silence, watching the rest of the party.

"You think other countries are doing better with the power supply?" she said. "I had to run back to the warehouse to have them pack the few perishables we have in ice. We better come up with a generator if this keeps up." She jutted her chin in the direction of the flickering house.

"We're going to need more volunteers, is what we'll need. If were talking about gardens and more unprocessed food, I'd say we might need twice as many as we have now."

Diana was nodding. Then she took a sip of her beer and said, "We'll deal with it tomorrow, okay? How was your meeting?"

"Lot of talk about relief work. Now I wish I had something planned myself."

Diana reached into her tiny orange purse and found a quarter-sized tin of mulberry balm, which she rubbed onto her lips with a pinkie tip. Hal imagined Diana on a windy, sandy-blasted plain, her hair braided away from her face, forehead scorched, mouth moisturized and gleaming. "Yeah? Where to?"

"Sweden," Hal blurted.

"Sweden, huh. Hundred percent literacy and an HIV rate of something like one in one million." She eyed him knowingly. "What are you going to do, import religion and steal all their condoms?"

Hal laughed uncomfortably. "You would have the statistics on the tip of your tongue," he said. Diana lifted one shoulder and dropped it, acknowledging the compliment. "Maybe I should put a plane ticket on my Visa before the fares get even worse. Don't you think a decent respectful American qualifies as an ambassador these days? I might get a tax break."

"Yes, try that," she said dryly. She began to poke through her fruit, choosing a slice of apple. "Hal, you *can* just take a vacation. You have some time still. Why Sweden, anyway?"

Hal looked away from her and into the flickering windows of the Daisies' house.

"I think it would be very clean," he admitted. "And quiet. Sort of calm and hard-working and crisp and welcoming. Lots of candles everywhere, and those open-faced sandwiches . . . smorrebrod."

"Oh." Diana reached over and touched him between the shoulder blades. For a moment he felt the whole flat of her palm, her fingers, and then it was gone. "First of all, a lot of what you just described you can find in Minnesota. You're getting a little Brothers Grimm on me here. Listen to yourself: candles and hardworking peasants and forests. Be honest, Hal: is there a woodcutter anywhere in this fantasy?"

Hal was stricken. Over the past couple hours he'd begun viewing it as a serious possibility.

"I don't blame you," Diana was saying. "Really. A couple years ago I started drooling over the idea of learning glass blowing. I think I thought I would sort of accidentally start it as a career. But we're in a bad time." She paused, but Hal could tell by the knit of her eyebrows that she had more to say. "In fact," she said carefully, "this may not be the best time to get into it, but the fact is, I've been thinking about this, too."

"You're taking a vacation?" Hal said. Was it remotely possible she was thinking of a vacation together?

She glanced at him irritably, as if she perceived the thought. "I mean you," she said. "Maybe you need a good problem to throw yourself into. Get your head back in the game. I've been debating how to bring this up with you ever since the thing with Mrs. Bryant last week."

"Oh God," said Hal. "Are we still talking about that? Are we going to talk about it forever? All it was, was a schedule problem, when you think about it. It was like oversleeping."

"You wanted to do something for her, which is nice. I get that, obviously. But a schedule problem when we're talking about a bunch of housebound people waiting for their meals is pretty important. I thought seriously about taking you off home duty altogether, you know."

Hal managed to be quiet for a moment, then burst.

"Are you seriously questioning my commitment here, Diana? Seriously? I spent the whole afternoon calling every grocery store in town. Do you know what I make? I've been doing this job for eight years while the rest of the world builds up a fat IRA and a savings account, and I do this instead."

He would never, never get to Sweden, to Copenhagen, to Finland or even Los Angeles. The way fuel prices were heading they would all be stuck right where they happened to be, all but the very rich, landlocked not only on the continent but in their state, in their town. Suddenly Madison's marooned feeling, its cozy nuzzle in the shadow of larger cities on larger lakes, was claustrophobic. How was anyone supposed to get out? How was he supposed to have planned for this?

"I know," Diana said. "I do it, too."

"Then you should know! Did you see how much nicer Mrs. Bryant was after I just sat and talked with her for a while? Before that the evil came off her in waves. Now you go in there and she almost smiles." This was an exaggeration. "I thought we were supposed to be helping people, but if the idea is only to push a Salisbury steak underneath the door—"

"*Hal*. Stop it." He did. "You can go back in your own time and talk with Mrs. Bryant. I applaud it. But you do not leave a van full of meals for other people who are just as hungry and need as much help as Pearl Bryant while you drink tea."

Diana had twisted in her chair to face him, searching his eyes. She took a deep breath, then shrugged. "Okay, I've said my piece. You're a good guy, Hal, even though you make me nuts. I know you've had a rough time this winter, with your mom and all. But I really need you now. It's time to forget about all that right now, if only for a while. I know that sounds awful, but at the moment it's true."

She stood up and took a step toward the house. A vision descended upon Hal, of something that would never happen: Diana walking backward, beckoning him to follow. Hal had to be very careful about even imagining such a thing. That was a fireable thought, and he used to know that, back when he was active and impassioned and would not have hesitated to help an animal in distress, or have a conversation with the drunk guy sitting on his porch swing.

The real Diana was at the Daisies' door, hugging someone he couldn't recognize from here. She waved briefly in Hal's direction and stepped inside the dark house.

Hal knocked back the rest of his beer, feeling foolish. Diana wasn't the sort of woman who'd comfort someone with sex. Where were those women? You read about them but Hal had never come across one. He had even tried to *be* one but that failed too—the few times he had tried to comfort a woman with sex, it backfired. Sex seemed to refresh women, allowing them to view whatever problem he'd tried to obfuscate with icy new clarity. His last girlfriend would readjust the sheets and take a sip of water, then turn to him and say, "And you *are* being unreasonable."

Maybe Hal should have chosen to distribute something besides food, something less constant. You provided people with a warehouse of dried beans and powdered milk and canned vegetables, and for about twenty minutes it looked like a job well done, until someone made soup.

Food, the imperious requirement of it, now seemed to him as onerous as he imagined it must have to his mother, when he and his sisters were very young. The rounds of shopping and preparation and planning must have seemed endless: it was a fruited vine that ate itself, a need that was new and urgent every moment, and when your ability to meet it dried up, desperation filled your gut instead. In January, his first day back after his mother died, tasks he'd done by rote had baffled him. He'd spent several days going through file cabinets with his father, overwhelmed by the amount of paperwork his parents had generated. Hal had not generated anything close; he felt transient and irresponsible. He'd lost his faith that he was good at any of this, or that anything he did was really useful.

Perhaps he should have moved around among the organizations—then he might be dealing with some more surmountable problem. Hal was an anomaly, in that he had stayed with the Swiffies his entire time in Madison. The local community groups drew from the same informal network of people. The person you'd known from the Madison HIV/AIDS Foundation had moved over to the Community Housing Advocates, the Gay Lesbian Student Safety organizer was now a Rape Crisis volunteer. Perhaps that would have kept him fresh.

His mother had found rejuvenation in Hal's career. When Hal took his first job with the Housing Trust, he'd tried commiserating with his father, thinking that was what a son should do, but his dad relied on platitudes. They were well meant and generally true, but that was no help. But his mother, who had stretched their money and time to raise three children and who had been organizing the community gardens for years, understood just how grimy and Sisyphean such work could be. Her community garden delivered fresh produce to the sick, especially AIDS patients, during the growing season, and his mother had expanded it to include a massive canning drive to put up vegetables and pickles and tomatoes for the same people to consume in the winter. Every August and September she had become profoundly distracted, wiry and superhuman. "You wouldn't believe the drive this year," his mother once said. "Jean Henderstall swanned in and canned about three pints of her most subpar tomatoes and thinks it'll raise T-cell counts all over the state. Also, I don't know how to tell some of these women that their family recipe for beef tartare made with raw ground chuck from the Pick 'N' Save is going to kill the healthiest among us."

It was bad enough how often Hal still reached to call his mother. Without her to spar and commiserate, all of Hal's frustrations—the typical frustrations of any demanding job—mushroomed somewhere beneath his diaphragm. He thought about his near-empty co-op and wondered why other co-ops were so sprawling and crowded, their holiday parties like a gathering of nations. Maybe this was simple grief that made Hal feel as he did right now, a hundred years older than everyone else at the party. He felt like a mountain man, who only wanted some homemade corn liquor and to be left alone. Yet they had so much food right here; he could probably call them all together and get donations tonight—but what about the day after that? The situation couldn't get much more stark than this. He was supposed to be feeding thousands of people with a couple hundred pounds of food. The scales didn't, and wouldn't, balance.

Karin watched Greta be drawn beneath Gregory's arm and shown around the room. Greta didn't need her tonight after all. Karin always had a hard time judging these things: she steered people around at parties when it turned out they were comfortable introducing themselves; or she gave them a wide berth and later discovered they'd felt adrift. But Greta seemed happy enough, even delighted by the walls—the Daisies' main room was usually a source of delight, but it would have been better in full light—and Hal had gone right out the back door. Karin headed over to the bar on the right side of the room beneath the art wall. She thought maybe she shouldn't drink tonight:

periodically through the week she'd felt a grasping low in her belly, some barnacle clinging.

On the other hand, wine might loosen something. The whole sensation might just be her period, confused about timing. She was reaching through a sea of candles for the white wine when she felt a hand on her bicep.

"It's the rescuer!" the voice said. It was Helen, one of the women from Karin's old co-op. Helen was a couple years younger than Karin, willowy in a long flowered skirt and tank top that bared an expanse of smooth olive skin. She was balancing a baby on her hip, a dense little thing, round as a pumpkin, with startled green eyes.

"It's starting to seem crazier the more I think about it," Karin said. "I can't imagine why I thought it was a good idea. That dog might have been starved."

Helen hugged her, pressing the baby against Karin's arm. "I heard it was feral," she said.

"No, it was owned by someone," Karin said. "It had a collar. Someone pushed it out there."

They paused, each uncertain what to say to this.

Karin changed the subject. "I'd heard you were pregnant. This must be yours, huh?"

"You bet," Helen said dreamily. "Annicka. I was desperate to get out and see people, so I figured I'd swing by before she went down for the night."

"Kind of a spooky place for a baby."

"The party?"

"The earth."

Helen laughed, so Karin laughed, too, but she was thinking that Helen had always been reluctant to face up to certain necessary truths. She hoped for compassion from political candidates who had shown no sign of it in the past; she often forgot to wash fruit or check milk jugs for hormone-labeling and shrugged off any reminders. Still, maybe that was the only way anyone could steel themselves to have a kid, anyway. You didn't even know if you'd be able to feed them, much less send them to college. From what Greta said, colleges were on the endangered list, too.

They both gazed around the room and back at the baby before Helen abruptly placed Annicka in Karin's arms. She shook out her arms and then pushed her fuzzy dark hair away from her face.

"She's gorgeous," Karin said. "Heavy baby." Helen laughed joyously, as if her infant were weighted down with brilliance or pearls, and Karin shifted its weight and took a sip of her wine. The baby gazed at a candle flame.

"Well, you look lovely," Helen said. "I know I look rough at the moment—no, it's true, if there were light you'd see I can't even get my shit together enough to wear mascara—but I always love seeing how pretty you look. How's your house going?"

"Oh, it's great," Karin said. "It's good. You know, talking to schools about what they eat, cooking a lot, blah blah blah. We're supposed to host a tasting next month of local goat cheeses if you want to come. How about you guys?"

"Well, obviously you're holding the reason I've been so busy. But you know Kirsten and Holly had babies this year, too."

"That's insane," Karin said. "That house must be complete chaos now. Was everyone using the rhythm method or something?"

"Well, I was mainly using condoms but who can get it perfect every time, right? Sometimes that's how it goes. That said, Kirsten's boyfriend is a total pill. He was all delighted about it for a while, boring the shit out of everyone talking about prenatal vitamins as if we don't know our prenatal vitamins—I mean, come *on*, at this stage of the game everyone in our house could perform a C-section—then Henry's born and Jonathan is off camping near the Boundary Waters doing I don't even know what." The whole time Helen spoke, she was spearing olives from a little dish with a toothpick and chewing them around her words, as if she didn't know when she'd have a chance to eat again.

"What about yours, you?" Karin asked vaguely. She was on thin ice here, unable to recall whether Helen had purposely had a child alone or if there was a man in the picture.

"Oh, Tim," Helen said. "We're good. To be honest, I think a change in living arrangements is coming soon. This was a surprise"—she touched the baby's cheek—"but we've gotten used to the whole thing now. I think it's time."

"Maybe so," Karin murmured. She glanced around the room: Hal had come back inside and was in the kitchen, while Greta was up near the front window, now talking to Hal's friend Wes. Gregory was still hovering hopefully nearby, shaking a handful of peanuts into his mouth with one eye trained on Greta.

Helen nodded. "When are you going to take the plunge?"

"Me? No. I mean, I like babies. They seem like nice people. I don't know if I'll ever really go for it, though. My parents had me totally thoughtlessly, when they were like twenty, and I think it kind of ruined their lives."

Helen looked appalled. "I'm sure you didn't."

Karin shrugged. "Oh, I don't mean I did. Look, I don't feel guilty about it. It could have been any kid; they were just poor and young and they figured things worked out for other people, so why not them? But it didn't really. Anyway Hal and I have his nieces over a lot. And Greta, too, I guess. I should get used to including her."

Karin jostled the baby and a whiff of baby shampoo and powdery skin wafted toward her nose. Well, they were pleasing little creatures. She had to admit that.

"Ah, good old Hal," Helen said. "Is he good with them? I figured he'd be kind of rigid."

"I know, right? But he gets really goofy and affectionate."

Helen nodded sagely. "You can tell a lot by how a man deals with being vomited on."

Karin had moved into the Womyn's Co-op two years ago, at twenty-two, just out of college. Her classmate, Heather, already lived there, and Karin and Heather had had a sort of dalliance. That was how Karin now considered it—as refreshing as a sweep of her hand through a sparkling pond. At the time, of course, it had felt more profound. Heather had approached Karin with flawless confidence, and Karin was so startled and flattered and curious that she pretended she'd been dating women all along. She'd still been trying the relationship on for size when she began spending the night at the co-op, having breakfast with the other women, holding the babies. The other lovers, male and female, were there at times, too, for dinners and gatherings, and there seemed to be no difference between their relationships and those of couples who lived in separate apartments. The volume levels alone were exhilarating; Karin's house growing up hadn't exactly perked with conversation. She got drawn into the noise and energy of the Womyn's Co-op so fast that she moved in the first chance she got, not really noticing that Heather had not expressly invited her.

The spark left the moment they became roommates. Perhaps with women one required romance just as much as with men, and Karin should have made more effort to shower and put on mascara before she saw Heather every morning. But she'd felt so freed of constraints. Anything seemed possible in the embrace of that house: they could have community gardens, community money, community babies. In retrospect, she'd gone a bit overboard. Then Heather had noisily seduced a lean-haunched, black-haired thirty-seven-year-old weaver. After three months the two of them moved out and bought a cottage in Sun Prairie.

The painful part wasn't the romantic failure; it was the house failure. What had felt so inclusive, so familial, had become strained within months. Maybe Karin had made it that way. At dinner the first night after Heather and the weaver moved out, Karin had looked around the table at the others—who ranged from nineteen to forty-two, who wore T-shirts and earrings made of leather and silver—and realized they were unfamiliar. It was like being at a party of people you didn't know after your mutual friend had left.

Then the next wave of pregnancies had begun. Everyone had to sign up for child care; a bylaw that perhaps had not been as clearly articulated as it could have been when she had moved in. Karin actually did like children—sometimes they amused her. But they were all so soft-skinned and easily hurt—how did children make it through the day, much less through their teens? Karin had become obsessed by table corners and chokeable-sized coins. She winced and gasped when a child fell, while the mothers comforted them briskly and returned the children right back to the chaos.

Three more were born in the space of a year. The huge house became a colorful wonderland of toys and breast pumps and quarrels over the cloth-diaper service. Then the new little families began to move out. The pleasant chaos all got turned under, like earth in a garden, and a new batch of unburdened women moved in.

All those babies and children had had a strange effect on her own feelings: the ubiquity of them made any urge to procreate feel prosaic, maybe even foolish. Everything had probably *felt* all lovely and natural and harmonious to her parents, too, but next thing you knew you were still living in Ixonia, in a mud-bound mobile home with a half-built shed behind it. If Karin couldn't do a better job, she wasn't going to bother.

But Karin had no siblings, and there were times she looked at her aging parents, still in the same house, and realized her little tribe would be dying one by one, doomed as dinosaurs. What was that long-extinct fish scientists had discovered still living after all? The coelacanth. Karin feared she might someday be that coelacanth, lantern-jawed and creaky-spined. In another forty years, she might be haunting the perimeter of the city, eyeballs dangling hungrily before her like ping-pong balls, while only specialists recalled that she had ever been here, that she might be here still.

The baby grabbed at her hair and Karin let her shove a handful into her mouth, not much minding that now her hair would have a roughened, milky wet spot.

"Well," Helen said, swallowing another green olive, "you can come back anytime, you know. A lot of people stay. Kirsten's sure not going anywhere. And our new member, Marielle, has a little boy." Here she nodded toward a woman crouched in a corner with a weeping little boy, whispering fiercely. They seemed weary and frustrated, the boy's hair sticking up on one side of his head, a rock clutched in one filthy hand. A graying braid hung down the woman's back.

"I'm pretty settled," Karin said. She had learned to enjoy the particular relief of going home to Hal, to their quiet house with smoking incense and sophisticated music, its good wine and the occasional comforting, rhythmic sound of sex through the walls that reminded her they were all resolutely adult.

"Here," said Helen. She suddenly reached for her infant, almost elbowing Karin out of the way, as if she had just realized she couldn't stand another second without her. Behind her the sound of Marielle's voice carried.

"We miss you, anyway," Helen said. "No one's heard a word from Heather in years but we miss you."

Karin shrugged. Heather seemed so long ago, but of course that was how some of these women remembered her, bereft at the breakfast table, world music covering up the sounds from behind the closed door of Heather's room. Karin wasn't one to rethink the past. Being with Heather had gotten her down a different path from the one she'd been on, and that was enough reason for her to have been in Karin's life. It was more than what most people got out of sex at that age. "She was just an experiment, actually," she said honestly. "But you guys I haven't forgotten."

"Good," Helen said. "How is Hal, anyway? Still Swiffing?"

"Yeah. He'll Swiff till he dies. By the way, that's our new roommate, Greta, over by the window talking to Wes. The blonde in the fantastic sandals."

They paused, taking in the scene by the front window, next to a table filled with plates, candles, and flashlights. Gregory seemed to have given up on Greta for the time being and had disappeared. Wes was leaning slightly over Greta. His eye sockets were peaked half moons of light from the flashlights below. He was shaking his head. Greta's feet were planted wide, her back very straight, shoulders firm. She was talking quite seriously. Wes's grin faltered, and Greta flashed a grim little smile of her own. They watched as she toed one of the straps of her gladiator sandals neatly into place and tossed her hair out of her eyes.

"Hard to picture her diving into a lake," said Helen.

Greta had begun to move around the perimeter of the front room, staring at the instruments on the walls, sipping her glass of seltzer, when a hand weighted down her shoulder for a moment, and she turned to find behind her a man who introduced himself as Hal's old college friend Wes. He worked as a paralegal and had lived in the Sunflower Co-op for seven years, a juxtaposition she found strange. For a second, she wondered if he had ever crossed paths with Will's law firm. She wouldn't ask, of course. She was afraid of what other people thought of Will.

Wes was still chortling about something as he shook Greta's hand, shaking his dark matted curls out of his eyes.

Wes's mannerisms, his stance and approach, were those of a sixty-year-old banker in a slim, rattily clad, and silver-ringed body. "I hear you're crossing over to the other side for the first time," Wes said. A woman approached silently and stood beside him. Greta met her eyes; the woman did not smile.

"I'm new to it," Greta admitted.

"Good time to dive in," Wes informed her. "All this shit going on. Makes me glad I have some people around me. I mean, how long have the lights been out tonight?"

"Longer than usual," Greta said. People checked their watches surreptitiously; the power had been gone for over two hours. "The students at my school are really starting to get frantic. They're always energetic but it's starting to feel more frightened—the other day the administration had to coax an entire dorm out of its rooms. They were just holed up in there. I hate to think what they're doing now. I'll tell you what else, we can't drum up crap for career recruiters—no one's hiring—but the military's there every *day*."

"I thought the Army stuck to high schools, mainly," said the woman.

"I think they still do," Greta said. "The rationale I heard was that they're hoping students with the possibility of a lot of debt before them might look for a way to have a job, maybe pay some off. These kids are terrified they'll come out of school with a huge debt, no jobs, and thirty-dollar loaves of bread."

"They should be," said Wes. "At least we can fall back on each other! We can share expenses, share workload, while all the rest of suburbia hides in its little houses and cuts itself off." He took a deep drink of red wine from a squat, gilded Moroccan glass.

"Do we have to talk about this?" someone said. "It's a party."

"A dark party," Greta replied. She kept her voice pleasant and light, but she instantly disliked Wes's smugness. "I'm sure it'll come back on soon. Anyway, that's how it's done, right? You grow up, you become financially independent of your parents, you carve out your own patch."

"It's only been done for a few hundred years," Wes noted sagely. "The Dutch started it, as a matter of fact. Before that people lived in rowhouses and courtyard houses and apartments. Now we all want our patch of land."

Greta shrugged. "It's the American dream. Or part of it. I've never really thought we should tell people everyone has to share everything. Maybe our shades just shouldn't all be drawn, is all."

"You came from the *west* side, yes?" Wes inquired. He made a gesture as if he had expected no better from her. "There's a serious community over here, Greta. It takes some time to get used to, I imagine. It's more than just buying bulk at Whole Foods." He sipped his wine and swished it lightly around his mouth. "But you can see what's happening here, right? What did they call it on the news—a period of contraction? Try 'going back in time.' Have you looked at the roads around here lately? I hold my breath every time I drive over one of these rickety old bridges, I'm not kidding. This is just the beginning. Too far too fast, and we didn't have the infrastructure to sustain it beyond fifty years. Or no one budgeted for it, anyway. I really think it's that simple. The savings account is dry."

Greta was now sipping determinedly on her seltzer, feet planted apart and pelvis canted slightly forward as if for balance. She didn't want to do this. She hadn't set out for a party looking to argue—Wes had approached *her*. Will had come to *her* house. She was only trying to find a place to live.

"Here's my worry about the co-op model," Greta said. She didn't want to talk any more about the state of the world; it felt too large and frightening. She'd feel better if conversation remained concrete. "I've been thinking about it since I moved in. You have a bunch of people, who normally would be saving up money, investing, working jobs that allowed that kind of planning. Instead, though, they're living in cooperatives and working jobs that pay minimally."

She sipped. The room had grown very quiet. People appeared to be looking very intently at Greta's sandals. "The good part about that is the co-op lets you do that, right? It lets you carve out time to be an artist or a community activist who deserves more money, or whatever. But I wonder what happens in thirty years. Does the co-op keep ageing, does everyone stay? Do you end up with a house full of seventy-year-olds taking care of each other and sharing expenses then? Or do people just end up destitute once the cracks in the model show? Because I don't see anyone over, say, forty-five in this room."

Greta saw Karin turn away from a woman with whom she was in close conversation. Greta waited to see if Karin would come over and join the conversation, but Karin remained at the drink table, watching. Hal was over by the couch, opening a fresh beer and avoiding the eye of a redhead standing near the spiral staircase.

"So," asked the blond woman, "everyone is just being irresponsible?" The woman ran a finger along Wes's waistband, which Wes ignored. Greta would bet that Wes had a type and that this was it to a T: women with long necks and broad shoulders and at least one lightly radical stylish affectation. This one wore her hair shorn to an inch and dyed platinum. She wore no eye makeup, plum-colored lipstick, and earrings of some complicated copper-wire knots, tiny and glinting. She looked like a sculptor.

Greta shook her head. "It's not that so much," she said. "I know irresponsibility, believe me. I think it might be sort of a fantasy. I can't be the only one wondering," she said. "Look, this may not be sustainable, right? Whenever we have these blackouts I suddenly feel like we have all these things we've devoted ourselves to and they're useless! What if this whole model is the same way? What if the bottom just drops out and everyone was so busy arguing over what to plant that no one has an IRA?"

At this, Hal sat down rather heavily on the couch. The sum total of his current investments was five thousand dollars in a savings account and a box of coins from his father. Greta was correct that the idea was supposed to be living affordably and saving more of his meager Swiffie salary. It never worked out that way. He'd returned from New York at least partially to better his finances, but no one ever admitted how fucking expensive— how unsustainable!—it was to live sustainably, how much the organic food and the small-maker cheeses cost, and how quickly the fresh produce in the farm baskets went bad. He would have bought a hybrid car years ago if he could have afforded it.

"Wow," Wes said. He shook his head. "Just . . . wow. Welcome to the co-op community!" He turned toward Hal and said, "Hey Hal, what is this now, the boojie co-op?"

"Don't be scared to hear another point of view," Hal said. A false smile eased over his face. Greta appeared bleakly satisfied, as if sparring with Wes and terrifying Hal by mentioning his financial unreadiness was just what she'd been gearing up for.

Greta had too much money to live in their co-op, that was the problem. Well, her own income was reasonable, or she wouldn't have been able to move in. The co-op association required an income statement, meant to ensure the community was of low to moderate income. Now that they'd let Greta in, any other new members would have to be on the low side, to keep the average in range. (Hal's secret fear was that the board had pitied the Morrison Street Co-op for its empty rooms and let in someone just above the moderate cut-off anyway.) But Greta had arrived with the trappings of her husband's larger income, and here was part of the problem. She dealt with money differently than the rest of them did: Hal had already seen this in her passing comments over the newspaper and the financial statements she pored over in her mail. Greta saw money as an entity to be moved and ma-nipulated and coaxed into growth. She thought about money not as a perpetual dilemma of stretching what was lacking but as a generous puzzle she could ponder and then rework to her own advantage. Hal could forget all about money without Greta around—or at least he could budget and pay his membership to the housing cooperative and feel even, if not winning. But now he had to think about money all the time. With Greta had come statements from Fidelity money markets and financial manag-ers, with her had come her swirling skirts and sumptuous leather accessories, and it was spiritually ruinous, Hal now saw, to have such items at such close range. Greta's clothes were of finely knit cashmere and silk, their seams stitched as tightly and carefully as if she were employing a convent of nuns to do little else. She had butter-soft toffee-colored riding boots and a jacket of leather so fine and tender-skinned it was slightly obscene. Faced with such exquisiteness, even Hal was hard pressed to argue in favor of the calf.

"Who are you, Abbie Hoffman?" Greta asked. "I never even understood why 'boojie' is such an insult. 'Oooohhhh, I'm middle class. Stop me before I send my kid to an excellent state school and donate to Planned Parenthood.'"

Karin and Helen snorted with laughter at this, and a moment later Wes chose to join them. The music volume swelled drown-ingly and purposefully; the Daisies hated arguments. Then some-one bore a vat of veggie chili and a platter of cornbread to the table, and the room surged forward to eat.

CHAPTER FOUR

The power was still out at nine thirty, when they'd finished dinner. The darkness didn't seem so bad anymore, however, because the children had all gone home and now it was just a candlelit party. Everyone seemed to feel close to normal. With the children gone the Daisies circled the dark room, offering joints and cigarettes. The joints could be smoked indoors, cigarettes were taken out. Karin watched Greta eye the joints. She wondered if Greta had some kind of extreme antidrug stance. She might. She certainly seemed startled by their appearance.

Suddenly Karin realized Greta's husband might still be on their porch. She'd forgotten all about him. She wondered if he'd had dinner.

Greta, Hal, and Karin were clustered around a little end table. Near them were Wes and his girlfriend, Karin's friend Marit, Hal's boss Diana, and a few Daisies, includ-

ing Gregory, sprawled out on the floor. Wes had become charming and relaxed. Maybe, Karin thought, he felt he had made his
point, challenged the challenger, and was willing to let it lie now.
She could never tell with him. She'd slept with Wes once, shortly
after moving in with Hal, though she hoped Hal didn't know.
She'd never worried about the encounter again until now. Greta
had stared him down and Karin had fucked him. For some reason having had sex with Wes now felt as if she'd given up ground
to him. She'd never worried about it before, but Greta seemed to
bring this insecurity out in her. She glanced over at Marit, wondering if she could find time to talk with her alone. The two of
them had been friends since high school, Karin's one relationship that had left Ixonia with her. Marit had lived in a co-op
around the same time Karin first moved into Helen's, but she'd
left after a few months, telling Karin she liked her solitude too
much to live with anyone until she was forced, by falling in love,
to try it again. Some nights Karin went over to Marit's house
with a bottle of wine, a wedge of hard cheese, and some bread.
Marit always kept a fig jam to serve with it, which Karin adored
but never bought for herself. She counted on having it at her
friend's house, in her cozy living room that was filled with plants
and art from the classes she taught. It was enough to captivate
Karin for an evening, but at the end she was always grateful to
be back in a busier house, the sounds of other people moving
through the walls.

"I can't figure out why some have gas and some don't," Marit
was saying. "Like the really big chains, shouldn't they have
plenty? But that BP on Willy Street has been out, off and on, for
weeks."

"I think it's going under," Hal said. This appeared to cheer
the others, who were happy to think the closed gas pumps were a
single corporate aberration.

"Maybe," said Marit. She twisted her long brown hair into a

bun and secured it with a rubber band from around her wrist. Her earrings, silver wire hoops, shivered as she laughed. "I have a perverse urge to drive everywhere now. I keep forcing myself not to." She laughed slightly, but the response was muted. People nodded sheepishly.

"Sometimes I can't take it, though," someone else said, "and I just get in my damn car and go for a drive."

"Really? I never liked driving," Hal was saying. "I mean I did as a kid, when you first get your license, but I got out of the habit. When I came back here and got a car I felt like I'd had a stroke. I barely remembered how to do it."

"Dude, you looked like you'd had a stroke," said Wes. "Remember? Mr. Mysterious."

Hal shook his head ruefully. "I looked like I'd been beaten," he said, and drained his wine.

"Which you had," Greta said. Karin turned to look at her, perplexed. Greta nodded and shrugged, lifting one palm to indicate that she'd thought Karin already knew.

"Beaten?" Karin said. "When? Did I miss a house meeting?"

"Years ago. It was stupid," Hal said. "I never hid it from you or anything, it was just a long time ago." He looked at Greta. "How did we even get on the subject?"

"We were talking about living in cities," she said, "and I said I never had any problem in Chicago. It was just the other night, Karin. You were out playing pool, and Hal and I went for a walk."

"Oh," said Karin.

Hal was nodding. "Right." He glanced around, looked at Diana, and said, "Well, you'll remember. I was doing a phone interview while I was getting ready to move. I was walking while I talked to Diana here, on my way over to my friend's place in Chelsea. And I was right in the middle of answering some question about—I don't know, tax breaks—and this kid clocked me in the back of the head. Right there on Ninth Avenue." Diana was nodding.

"But why?" Karin said.

"Why do you think?" Hal said irritably. "He wanted my phone and he wanted my wallet. It's not brain surgery. Well, it could have been, but luckily not."

"So what'd you do?" Marit asked.

Hal and Greta exchanged a glance, and Hal leaned back against the couch cushions, suddenly seeming relaxed. "I called her back to finish the interview."

At this there was a raucous burst of laughter. Wes's girlfriend clapped her ringed hands. Hal allowed himself to laugh as well, because the laughter was flattering to him, but he met Karin's eyes—she was not laughing—and shrugged slightly.

It sounded funny now, years later, because he was sitting there, healthy and unmarked, telling the story, but it had been a harrowing and vertiginous moment—the sidewalk that rushed up to bite his palms, the startling clarity of all the shoes around him. A cataclysm had clapped at the back of his head and whiteness flared at the edges of his vision. He'd been faintly aware of the hands that had reached into his back pocket, and into the pocket of his jacket, and, confused, he had leaned back into them, grabbing an arm and trying to pull himself up, as if the person was trying to help him. Then he was shoved back toward the sidewalk again.

He didn't like to think of it. He'd been on all fours on a crowded city street, confused and disoriented, and had watched the shoes of his mugger sprint away. The mugger had worn white tennis shoes, the soles spotted with pink wads of gum.

But Hal had clutched his phone. He hadn't realized he was doing this; his knuckles were scraped where they had hit the pavement. If he hadn't already been planning to move, he might have toughened up and accepted the incident as the price of living there. Andrea had been mugged once in their crappy Brooklyn neighborhood and took it in stride. She'd handed over her wallet, pepper-sprayed the guy, and ran.

"Too bad you didn't have Karin with you," Wes was saying. "She'd've kept you safe."

Laughter surged at this, then died away as people paused to think about that morning.

"No more news?"

"We haven't heard any," Karin said. "I would start with the dog, personally. But I don't even know if they found it."

"You know something wild?" Gregory interjected. "I think I saw that dock last night. I just thought it was a raft out on the water, some guy hanging out with his dog."

"When?" Greta asked. "What was he doing? Just drinking a few beers and sitting?"

Gregory shrugged. "Right around dusk. I figured they watched the sunset and were heading in. But this was over here, not by you guys. The guy was just sitting there in the chair while the dog walked around."

A silence fell as they all considered this. "Would you stay out there all night," Hal said, "just hoping someone will see you?"

"Or he came back in and headed out again later," said Karin. "Trying to decide what to do."

"He probably passed out," said Greta heartlessly. She got to her feet, brushing her skirt, and turned to Gregory. "How about that yard?" she asked. "Can I see your sculptures?"

Gregory was up instantly, his curls settling around his face. "Come on," he said. "I'll give you the tour." The others watched them go. Hal and Karin looked at one another.

"Those sculptures aren't even his," said Wes, and the others seized upon the change in subject, the volume of their voices rising in relief.

Outside Gregory took her hand and led her down the steps off the back porch. "First, the monkey," he said.

They headed out front to the first sculpture Greta had seen. Gregory was going on about some kind of metal-forging, something about crucibles, but Greta wasn't listening. How easy it was. She'd never fully gotten the hang of the signals—she'd paired off too young to have had a few adult years of being put through the paces. There were phrases that functioned like magic: all you had to do was give the code and everyone understood. She hadn't thought it would work so well.

"Nice job with Wes back there, by the way," Gregory was saying.

Greta shrugged. "Men like that make me crazy," she admitted. "They love to nod, have you noticed? To be absolutely certain my smooth rat-brain takes it all in."

"Huh." Gregory laughed, clearly confused. "You were smooth," he said.

She looked at him. "You know, the less intelligent the animal, the smoother the brain?" she said. "A human's gets more wrinkled as it grows. A rat's is practically smooth. That's what I meant."

"I wonder about a pig?" said Gregory. "They're extremely smart."

For a moment Greta went taut with regret and emptiness. Will was probably still sitting on her porch, if she wanted to have this kind of clueless conversation. She eyed Gregory distastefully, then took another look. His eyes were dark pools, the tips of his hair frizzier than an hour ago.

"Are you high?"

"I took some mushrooms," he said. "Come here."

Now he pulled her over to a secluded spot around the dark corner of the porch. From his pocket he drew a plastic baggy, a lighter, and a cigarette pack. "Welcome," he said, and pressed upon her a damp, loosely packed joint he'd wriggled out of the pack.

She took it with barely a protest, feeling reckless and pleasantly rebellious. She wasn't an addict. She could do as she pleased. It was only a joint. She lit and inhaled, and let the tingling in her fingertips spread further into her body. Her body—she'd forgotten all about it.

"I still have some 'shrooms, too," Gregory said. "If you're amenable."

Greta hesitated, eyeing him through the smoke, surprised to find herself very amenable indeed. She had already knocked over the first domino. She gazed around at the other people, up on the porch, through the windows. They were laughing and chatting pleasantly, pausing to look at the candles or to pick up a flashlight and shine it at the clock on the wall. No one was angry with her. At dinner Wes had been perfectly charming. Perhaps such discussions were average around here, and everyone debated quite passionately and then let it slide off their backs.

She saw that no one was terrified about having drugs and alcohol around, nor did anyone overdo it, not even the Daisies themselves. Healthy people! People who could venture outside themselves, a little sidestep to the left rather than an obliterating crash.

Greta was embarrassed to have behaved so combatively at the party, her first party over here, and filled with gratitude that anyone had even tried to speak to her. Here was this young man— this boy, really, he might have been twenty-one—talking about something she was not remotely listening to but doing it so cheerfully and generously as he sucked in smoke, chatted through clenched teeth, and handed the soggy little paper back to her. Greta inhaled the joint fiercely, wanting to throw herself in, to say thank you, to share.

In the end she accepted one leathery, foul-smelling mushroom the size of a cricket and gulped it down, Gregory laughed delightedly. He touched her cheek, her earlobes. His fingers smelled like a boy's: iron, dirt, rust, like bicycle chains.

"What did he look like?" she asked. "The guy out there on the lake. Was he big, maybe?"

"Don't," Gregory said tenderly. He kissed her forehead, his mouth fringed with dry skin. "The first few minutes of a mushroom are crucial. We go straight to the good place."

A short time later Karin appeared from around the side of the house and approached the porch steps where Greta sat perched at the top, staring into a water glass and listening to the music. She had been there for some time, woozy and taut with laughter and possibility. The sides of her eyeballs, of her very vision, were aglow with violets, lime green, and fiery coal-ember oranges. The music kept vibrating, swelling forward to touch her and retreating coyly. The wine, now gone, had been pale and light as water. Karin's rising head appeared to Greta as a sphere of fire, her long hair alight, and the image of a fireball dampened the nervy high of it all.

Karin bent down to take Greta's wrist and draw her to her feet. Hal's darkened shape loomed behind her, broad and benign, his smile faintly visible in the gloom. "Am I the only one?" she asked. The others shrugged and said, "We had a little," but she couldn't tell if they were comforting her. "You have to get up early," they said softly.

"Everything okay?" another voice said. Greta peered around her roommates and saw Wes approaching. Gregory patted him on the shoulder and Wes brushed the hand away, frowning. He turned to say something inaudible to Gregory, the two of them glancing her way, and Greta decided woozily that she hated Wes, not just for thinking she was a boojie dabbler, which she was, but for the satisfaction he no doubt felt upon seeing her prove it.

Karin held her hand as they made their way toward the door, waving at the leftover Daisies. Greta clasped the hand tightly, enjoying its dry warmth and softness. Karin's streaky hair fell down her back and over her shoulders; a satiny patch of pale tan skin showed between the waistband of her army-green pants and her orange shirt. The scratches on her arms had faded, or else the darkness simply covered them. Karin seemed to be all texture and light. A lovely human. Greta was very fond of both her housemates.

Hal was talking—Greta tried to listen more closely to him until she looked up from the sidewalk and saw that he and Karin were speaking to Wes, who now reached for Greta's arm and clasped her wrist. She gazed at the fingers wrapped above her hand, and then followed the arm up to the shoulder and the face. To her surprise, he looked sincere instead of sardonic. It was a trap, of course. Here it came. Wes said, "I'm sorry. Gregory was trying to be welcoming. You'll be fine tomorrow." Stymied, Greta nodded and let Karin lead her down the sidewalk.

The walk home took far longer than the walk there, perhaps a natural phenomenon. Greta trudged next to the other two, who appeared to be quite sober. She saw geometric patterns in the grass and felt a rising tide of shame at her own frivolousness. She was hoping Will would still be at the house; Will would understand the urge to throw it all off and forget. He used to be good at that; he would perceive the moment when a family gathering had grown too tense and make the joke that leavened the mood. She almost understood him now, his need to chase that feeling of social ease and joy, even if he lost control of it. She ought to have known better. She was too old for all of this.

The moon drew the clouds around itself, small lights moved about behind the windows of the houses. Greta realized it was darker than ever.

"It never did come back," she said.

"I know," said Karin.

As they neared their house the sounds of the lake were clear, a lapping and a hollow slap against a hull. The last of the psychogenic effects departed, the electric connections fizzling out, her brain once more an ordinary jelly. As they turned up their front walk, Greta slowed, and the other two slowed with her. Of course, Will had not left. He was still reclining on the swing, his head was tipped to one side, mouth open. He stirred as they walked up the steps, opened an eye, and let it close again.

"We can't leave him out here," Hal said. "It's almost eleven."

"You do whatever you need to," said Greta. "I have to try to sleep. I can't help you."

Karin couldn't think of anything else to do but read by flashlight and wait to fall asleep. She'd set up her interview with Drumlin Cheese for mid-morning tomorrow, despite the woman's insistence that they had very little to share yet. "I can tell you what I *want* to do," she'd said. "What I hope to do. What I've actually achieved is a different story." Heartlessly, Karin wheedled her way into the interview anyway, explaining that often what seemed humdrum to the producer was in fact news.

She set her cell-phone alarm, figuring the electricity would return while she was asleep. The power outages this spring had only lasted a couple hours, and already it had been five.

At her office that morning, Karin's boss had greeted her with a bagel and lox, and pressed her for every detail on the dog rescue, just in case there was some way for them to report on it. After a few minutes, it was clear there was no way to shoehorn dairy into the incident, and Karin had called Elaine Rothberger at Drumlin. Then she'd called Animal Control.

"I just needed to know if you've had any missing dogs picked up," Karin had said nonchalantly. "I'm looking for a big dog, a mutt, I guess, probably a mix of German Shepherd and lab. Or maybe even some husky."

"Uh-huh. When did you lose the dog?"

Karin had paused—had it only been a couple hours? It had. "This morning. He has a red collar."

There had been a long pause while the clerk clicked away at something. "Nothing here. Sorry."

"What about his registration?" Karin asked. "Can you cross reference, say, dog registration against recently missing dogs? Do you have, like, a database?"

"The City Treasurer has a database of licensed pets, sure. But I don't have some CSI way of searching for breeds and paw prints, ma'am."

"Well, now I feel stupid," Karin said.

"I'm sorry, ma'am, but all the shelters are swamped right now and so are we. If you want to come down and look for your dog, you certainly may."

For a moment, Karin thought she might. But what would it get her? Even if they had the dog, they didn't seem to have a way of finding who owned it without tags. Maybe she could get someone at the City Treasurer to tell her who had licenses by neighborhood. Unless the person didn't live in their neighborhood—she'd drooped under the weight of the unknowns. That hadn't even occurred to her before: this person could have come to their part of town from anywhere in the city, or the state, or the whole country.

In the room next to Karin's, Greta was making a great deal of noise, opening drawers and moving furniture. There was a third floor, with two more vacant rooms that Greta could have chosen, which made it rather odd for her to choose the room beside Karin's. But Greta had only peered up the stairs to the third floor and then turned back, shaking her head, and, as far as Karin knew, had never explored the rest of the house.

During the first eight or nine months Karin had lived with Hal, the house group had been a foursome, a woman next to Karin on the second floor, a man upstairs beside the last empty room, and Hal on the ground floor. Karin had been the newest one. Then the group reformed as a nascent couple and a pair of onlookers, and she and Hal had begun to find themselves alone before the news in the evenings after dinner, their roommates strolling out for long walks and frozen custard. In their absence, Hal and Karin had fallen into a routine of dessert on the front porch, and jaunts to the pastry shop and the bar down the street. They didn't even mind when the other two moved out in February, or when so few calls came in about the extra rooms. By then it was spring, and they were walking to the farmers' market and filling the house wagon with produce, going to the park to throw the Frisbee around. They'd been resigned to waiting till fall, when the next batch of students might bring some nice Southeast Asian Religion Ph.D. candidate, and then Greta had finally seen an ad and phoned. Now Hal apparently told her things he'd never bothered to mention before.

The noise in Greta's room had quieted. Karin got up as silently as she could and peered out the window and into the darkness. She had the odd sensation that she would see Greta's husband down there, stretched out on the grass, but the lawn was empty.

Hal paused in the doorway to the living room, sipping his water and peering toward the front window. There was Greta's husband, the shape of his head clearly visible in the moonlight. He was moving slightly, the swing rocking back and forth. He took a sip from something. A tremor moved through him, and then his shoulders rose and fell again, as if with a deep breath.

Hal tiptoed to the couch and sat down with excruciating slowness. The evening was dead silent, and he didn't want the man to realize he was watching. He just wasn't quite ready to wave or make eye contact.

The house gave out a creak, a slight pop somewhere in the basement. A car went by on the street, a snatch of music and voices trailing behind it, and Hal watched Greta's husband turn his head along with the sound. He seemed to look in that direction for a long time. Hal saw him rub his nose, run a hand over his head and through his hair. Greta's husband leaned his head back against the window, his hair flattening against the dirty glass.

This man didn't look as if he had the wherewithal to stand, much less whip a machete out of his briefcase. He looked exhausted and probably dehydrated from alcohol and sweat.

Hal sighed and stood up, no longer moving stealthily, and went to the front door. He leaned out into the warm night air. "Come on," he said. Greta's husband looked at him, startled, but before he began to speak Hal interrupted, waving a hand toward the door. "Come in."

Her husband nodded slowly, his lips pursed tendentiously, and Hal immediately regretted asking him in. It was a ponderous nod, fake and badly acted. He was very, very drunk. Hal was about to go back in when the man got to his feet, leaving his briefcase on the swing. He took a step, then went down on one knee as he misjudged his weight. Hal sighed again. The man took his hand when Hal offered it—the man's was sweaty and very hot—and pulled himself, very heavily, back to his feet. He followed Hal into the living room, and when Hal gestured to the couch, Greta's husband all but fell on it. He seemed to be unconscious before he even made it to the cushion. It was much too warm for a blanket, but Hal debated removing the man's tie or shoes.

The guy seemed to have been waiting for the right opportunity to lose consciousness. He hadn't even stopped to ask who Hal was or feign a politeness at the invitation. It was clear he was unable to. In fact, when he'd gotten close enough, the husband had tried to look Hal in the eye but his irises were jumpy, practically vibrating with the attempt to focus. The whole thing made Hal feel foolish. He must have been riding a wave of altruism and machismo; he'd briefly felt as if he were Christlike but decisive, a doer and a helper, but this husband—Jesus, Greta, *nice husband*— he was like meat, he was mud in a sack. It didn't seem to matter where you threw him. He'd spent his entire adult life reaching out toward people, but it did less and less good. This, too, was a pebble dropped in a pond.

Hal brought in the briefcase and locked the front door behind him. He was about to go back to his room, but then he paused. He untied the laces of the man's shoes, dark brown leather wing-tips that shone in the darkness. It took a little wrenching but he got them off the man's feet and set them next to the couch. A puffing sound escaped the man's lips, one long breath. Hal caught a whiff of gin, something sharp and a little metallic. He felt, suddenly, like a pushover. The guy was drunk; he wasn't homeless.

Still. They shouldn't have left him out there so long.

TUESDAY

CHAPTER FIVE

The co-op was the first place Greta had visited when she'd decided to move out. She knew she was supposed to keep looking. For one thing, she had severe reservations about the idea of roommates beyond college age. Not to mention the whole atmosphere of community life, its neat piles of mail in separate baskets, the job board—it struck her as more wishful than realistic. The smart thing would have been to check out ten different, more expensive apartments, and, only then, cowed by bathtub mold and intruder-inviting outdoor lighting, return and rent this one.

But she was already so tired of the whole idea. As she had picked up the phone to make the first call, she'd realized she was operating on a fleeting burst of adrenaline. Having forced herself to close her office door at lunch one day and call the first number she saw in the classifieds, she had found a clean room in a nice old house on a densely

packed lakeside street. Morrison Street—she'd never even heard
of it. She had found people who asked her to dinner to see how
they got along, who set the table with neatly folded napkins and
matching flatware (she had been expecting torn paper towel and
lumpy handmade plates from someone's pottery class) and Greta
had felt like crying with relief.

She didn't cry, of course—Greta was not a crier. She had offered
to help with that first dinner and concentrated on chopping the
cauliflower perfectly, thinking it might impress the other two to
see that she was a fine, conscientious cook. Maybe she could skip
the whole process of calling and trudging through a dozen soulless
white lofts on the far west side. So what if the man was clearly an
aging hippie and the woman seemed so young and blithe, the sort
who maddeningly assumed anything at all would be just fine. The
two of them had been waiting for her on the porch, which didn't
even give Greta the walk up to the door to put on her game face.
They'd been sitting on either side of the porch steps, Karin's long
legs stretched out and crossed before her, her feet bare despite the
crisp spring air. She was leaning back, weight braced on her palms.
Hal was hunched over his knees, elbows resting on his thighs and
hands clasped. As Greta parked her car, she'd seen the two of them
turn to one another and confer. Hal was nodding as Karin spoke
to him. Her profile was striking, her nose long and tipped down,
her mouth generous. One shoulder peeked through a fall of long
chestnut hair. Hal seemed to be wearing an array of layers, potato-
colored pants and a couple of long-sleeved T-shirts in gray and
oatmeal. He was clean shaven and shaggy-haired, his deep-set eyes
impossible to see until she got much closer, when she saw his gaze
was dark and watchful. Greta found them both unexpectedly intimidating; Hal so serious and Karin so self-assured. For a moment Greta thought she had the wrong house—these two did not
seem to need a roommate at all.

The meal was a vegetarian curry, fragrant with coconut milk, turmeric, and lots of ginger. Karin was in charge of the night's dinner, and she spoke little while she minced garlic and ginger, humming lightly under her breath. She sniffed the curry deeply as its steam rose from the pan, and mentioned that she had made ice cream with salted caramel for dessert—"And I can tell you where it came from right down to the cow," she'd added. "Sophie."

As they sat down, Hal and Karin set out a dish of rice and several bottles of Indian pickle and chili paste. Greta had stared at the bottles, taking several minutes just to settle on mango chutney. Her brain was befogged right then, and for months she had had a bad habit of procrastinating on the smallest decision and then reaching blindly for the first solution that presented itself. She had felt Hal and Karin watching her surreptitiously while she observed the condiment bottles, as if the choice were a test of some sort. She realized she was acting oddly. When she'd reached for the chutney she had the distinct impression her hand had lurched forward crazily.

"So, have you always lived in Madison?" Hal asked.

He spoke softly, as if she were a nervous rodent. The fact that she had elicited—and was briefly comforted by—such careful treatment had only annoyed Greta, particularly in front of Karin, who had cast a magnanimous look Hal's way when he spoke, as if to praise him for his kindness.

Greta shook herself out of it, straightened up, and said clearly, "I grew up in Illinois and came here for undergrad. But we—I lived in Chicago for a few years, too, and then came back."

Hal was nodding delightedly. "I lived in New York!" he said. "What brought you back?"

Greta had shrugged. There were several reasons: jobs after law school for Will, the brief time in which they had thought they might have children. She didn't want to say any of that now. "Just time for a change. I miss it, though. I miss the restaurants and the museums, mostly."

"Sure, sure," Hal said, and Karin broke in.

"Not too bad here, though, right? I read somewhere we have more restaurants per capita here than anywhere in the country."

Greta nodded and took a bite of her curry. "Yeah, but you can't ask it to compare. It just can't. You can't do the same stuff with two hundred thousand people that you can with a few million." She regretted it as soon as she said it: Karin had looked away and concentrated on adding more pickle to her plate. "Of course," she added, "there's nothing like our farmers' market for accessibility and variety."

"Still," Hal said, oblivious, "I used to get *bahn mi* in the back of a jewelry shop on Mott Street and they were amazing. A whole meal for about five bucks. The ones here can't even come close."

Greta conceded this with a brisk nod, trying to drop the subject. "This is delicious," she told Karin, who gave her a grateful smile.

"It really is. So. Greta. Tell me again what you do?" Hal had said.

"I do fund-raising for the Grinwall College Foundation." She took an enormous bite of tempeh, its firm bulk tasting of nothing but a faint pastelike tang, and chewed furiously. People often had heard of Grinwall but knew nothing of it: it was compact, Jesuit, and pricey. Depending on the department, faculty were either proud to be in a smaller, more nimble institution, or else they resented the nearby behemoth. Despite the Grinwall administration's attempts to foster singularity and school pride, the Grinwall students mingled with the UW students as if nothing separated them: drinking from the same fishbowls of blue booze, trooping in blocs to the same house parties at the edges of the UW campus.

A look of surprise flitted over Hal's face, quickly replaced by studied calm. "That sounds kind of like what I do," he said. Karin had shot him a look of confusion, which he shrugged off, adding,

"Well, you know, volunteer-y, community service kind of stuff. I work for SWFI. The food organization."

"It's sort of like Meals-on-Wheels," Karin said. She was the youngest of them all, mid to late twenties in Greta's estimation. Her hands were unadorned and short-nailed, with long, capable fingers and smooth skin. A girl's hands.

"Sort of," Hal said. "Anyway, do you work with corporate donors, or more individual stuff?"

"Depends," Greta said. Her voice croaked slightly on the first syllable. The other two politely averted their eyes while she paused, sipped her water, and began again. "I, uh, started off directing the student volunteers who do the alumni drives. And I spent a lot of time with prospective donors in the local industries. At the moment, I'm working with a lot of prominent alums. Though we're too small to have very many, actually. UW takes them all first, I guess."

Karin looked pleased. "I give to UW," she said. "I'm not prominent! But I still give fifty bucks here and there to Letters and Science," she said. "I was an English major there. Though I always feel a little stupid, you know, wondering if fifty bucks really matters." She salted her curry and set the shaker wordlessly in front of Hal, who did the same.

"Oh, it definitely does," Greta said. Her rice fell off her fork. She gave up and ate the three grains still on it. "Those add up, for one thing, and usually they're loyal, reliable gifts. Plus, the number of alums who give gets factored into the school's ranking. But best of all, they're unrestricted. We don't have to earmark it for someone's whim, you know, we can use it where it's needed." Greta felt slightly calmer. Even among far-left co-op dwellers she believed her profession was close to unimpeachable. Who could fault her for supporting education at the expense of the businesses that polluted water and mercilessly cut health benefits? She was practically Robin Hood.

Karin had looked pleased. She was spooning some oily orange pickle onto the edge of her plate. She nibbled a piece of lime, and then, impressively, ate a whole chili pepper. "I told you so, Hal. He's always going into his televangelist mode and telling me to give till it hurts. It hurts right away."

Hal laughed. "I just like to annoy you. If you'd had brothers you'd be familiar with this dynamic." Karin smiled into her plate.

During dessert a businesslike air took hold of them. Karin, the first to finish, set her spoon beside her bowl and folded her hands. Greta, her spoonful of vanilla ice cream still in her mouth, became the object of two gazes.

"We should talk a little about how we live here," Karin said, "what we try to do. It's a little more than just cheap housing and roommates, it's only fair to say."

Hal had nodded sagely and leaned his elbows on the table.

"We try to eat together at least three times a week. Every other Sunday is the only one that's basically nonnegotiable, because that's when we have a state-of-the-house discussion and bring up whatever might be going on, make new rules, revise old ones, discuss upkeep on the house, that kind of thing. We don't really rent so much as buy into the housing cooperative overall. And we try to cook all our food from scratch," he said. "It's part of the whole local, sustainable-food thing we try to do. So a house rule is to rotate cooking duties, and whoever is on it that night is expected to use actual ingredients, not a jar of Prego, or mac and cheese, or what have you. We should probably be more vigilant about condiments"—here Hal furrowed his eyebrows in the direction of the lime pickle—"but that might get more onerous than necessary."

"Not even organic macaroni and cheese?" Greta asked, feeling skittish. Every other Sunday? What if she couldn't stand to talk to people that day? What if she had to go visit some client? That couldn't count against her.

"No one's keeping track of what you cook on your nights"—Greta fought to prevent the doubt from registering on her face—"but of course we notice if someone's relying too heavily on premade food."

"And in season we belong to a CSA," Karin added. "The deliveries should be starting soon."

They waited for Greta to indicate she knew what "CSA" meant.

"The boxes?" she said. "Vegetables from local farmers?"

Both looked relieved. "Exactly," Karin said. "Community-supported agriculture. We get used to using what's in season, relying on the local growers when we can, that kind of thing."

"Other co-ops have other philosophies," Hal said, shrugging as if to say he couldn't account for them, "although most of them are following our lead these days, I notice. But we were the first. And anyway, the idea is to take a fairly simple approach but one with real impact. The food co-op's right nearby, the farmers' market is in walking distance, it's really not too hard to stay with it. We eat really well, actually."

For a minute or so the three busied themselves with their napkins; then Greta cleared her throat. "What about meat?" she asked. "Are you both vegetarian?"

"I am," Hal said. "Karin eats meat sometimes. It's not a meat-free kitchen per se. But you'd have to think about where any meat comes from. There are plenty of local farmers to buy from. Definitely no commercial feedlot meat."

"The truth is we really never eat meat here," Karin said. "Maybe every once in a while. But it's just easier to avoid it."

"Oh, and there's outreach," Hal added. "We take turns doing outreach in the schools, connecting kids and farmers, showing them where their food comes from, et cetera, et cetera."

"A lot may not need it, depending on the school and the age, but some really do," said Karin. "Some don't care, at least not at first. We try. I don't know how successful we are, but we try."

Greta was nodding. Not really meaning to, but nodding nevertheless. She had a feeling the standards were higher than she
ought to agree to. However, she was feeling desperate, and eager
to take on a minor challenge if it meant she could relax from the
bigger ones. If these people wanted her to cook, she could cook.
She was a great cook. But she needed to make a change as soon as
possible: she was always tired and overly sensitive to light and
loud sounds; her daily fear and tension had made her as delicate as
a preemie or a tropical flower. The muscles in Greta's neck and
back ached; she slept in the guest room or on the couch and sometimes even on the floor, because nowhere felt quite comfortable.
She wanted to go to sleep right now. The co-op philosophy could
have been centered on volleyball or leather for all she cared.

She had to say something good, and what came to her was the
kind of electricity that had often nailed several thousand extra
dollars for Grinwall.

She had matched Hal's and Karin's posture, leaned forward
on the table and clasped her hands. "This is just what I've been
looking for," she said intently, holding each of their gazes for a
moment. "For one thing, I think the need for community is particularly significant right now. I kind of want more people around,
do you know what I mean? You know what else? I grew up watching my mom can tomatoes and pickles and fruit every summer,
and I've been wanting to get back to that." She was building energy now. What good fortune! She hadn't thought about her
mother's canning in years but there it was, the memory waiting
for her to make use of it. She let her gaze wander out the window
and then delivered her best effort. "I can't *wait* to see your garden," she said ardently.

Hal and Karin had gone as taut as if Greta had expressed a
wish to see their genitals. "Maybe that's where you can help!"
Karin cried. "We don't have a garden yet this year! It's so ridiculous, I know, and we have been talking about this for months."

"Are you a gardener?" Hal asked.

"I would love to be one," Greta intoned. Just then, she really did. Hal and Karin settled into an extended bout of nods. Greta took her moment and offered to do the dishes, but the other two waved her away.

There was a brief pause. Then Greta said, "Well, I should be going." She stood up; Hal and Karin joined her. As Greta preceded them down the hallway, she let herself relax. That moment of not being looked at gave her deep relief, the cozy wrap of anonymity. She realized that no one knew her in this part of town. You could start completely fresh, even in a small city like this. She didn't have to explain a thing to anyone.

Greta had driven west to her house, thinking she would hear from Hal and Karin in the morning. She passed the capitol and drove through the campus to the neighborhood where she had lived for eight years. Tonight she was relieved to be back on familiar turf after her evening on the near east side, where the houses were shabby as often as charming, and which to Greta's eye bore a general aura of Victorian kookiness she could really do without. It was all so self-consciously funky.

She'd never realized she liked things to be orderly, but here she was, glad to see these neat yards, with their gardens carefully planned out and pink-blossomed, the houses as sturdily bricked as a cottage in a fairy tale. The buildings she had just left seemed to loom in her memory, rickety and unreliable. But still, the co-op, the whole block, had great bones. No wonder they were building condos over there, no wonder almost all the old houses had already been purchased and rehabbed. Maybe every single person who'd migrated to the near east side was also starting afresh and concentrating on the work of building, sanding, planning, smoothing.

As she turned onto her street, Greta's heart had begun to race. She was looking for Will's car in their driveway, wanting to see it yet hoping she didn't. She wanted him safe at home, shut away in their room but maybe unconscious, or at least mute, wanted him accounted for but that was about all.

She had had no idea how she would manage to move out and not loiter over here after work each day, calling repetitiously, pointlessly, into the night, just to be sure he was alive.

That night, his car was not in the driveway. She'd breathed deeply, both relieved and worried anew. Who knew where he was? He might be home by ten, or he might not come home till the morning. There was no longer anything she could do, and there never really had been. She would have to get used to not knowing.

Greta woke up at six thirty, when the light came through her window and reached the bed. She was still tired, but luckily mushrooms and pot wouldn't give her a hangover. She'd shown restraint in spite of herself.

Her clock was still dead; she saw the time on her cell phone. She reached over and flipped the clock power switch on and off, but no. She felt a complex wave of foreboding and disbelief: the power should be back by now, but in the morning light it was hard to believe it mattered. It was hard to believe it wasn't on somewhere and just not in her room. She had always thought of places like Los Angeles and New York as so foolish and over-taxed that it was amazing their structures held in place at all. But how hard could it be to keep little Madison running smoothly?

Will was probably still downstairs. She didn't even get a moment of fog before the previous day came rushing back: it was right there waiting for her. She should at least have a split second to herself.

She gave herself five minutes to lie like a slug, and then got up and put on her socks to go downstairs. Her silk nightgowns, so beautifully bias-cut they could have been dresses, lay in a gleaming, surprisingly diminutive puddle of sage and chocolate brown and hot pink, shoved in the back of one drawer. Greta had seen no evidence of anyone having sex in the house—were they keeping it outside the house, or were they just in a dry spell? She'd assumed the attitude toward sex would be fairly earthy and open, in a thin-walls kind of way. But Greta had been feeling astoundingly unsexual. It was hard to recall a time when sex seemed like a worthwhile pursuit. Her skin felt muddy and indistinct, her blood thick and slow.

But she had been feeling better in other ways. She'd begun wearing T-shirts some mornings with nothing beneath, and she let the hair beneath her arms grow out a bit on weekends. Of course, then she was relieved to shave it off on Monday, but it was a step toward ease, Greta thought, and toward relaxing. Karin apparently regarded a bra as only an occasional option, and she was unguarded about baring the chestnut curls beneath her arms. Greta was more relaxed among near-strangers than she had been at home.

After years of affectionate intimacy, Greta had ceased to assume that Will was the loving friend who looked at her body and saw her youth and her history and her current self all in sum. Instead, Greta had become hyperaware of each flaw, and of her own figure as a loosening thing. By the time she moved out she had thought of her body as an uncontrolled and unlovely object with smatterings of hair and wobbling flesh, and she had felt an unbearable need to be reined in and sleek, to be armored. She'd begun to wear a bra at all times, and to shower and put on mascara before she sat down at the table with her own husband. Will never mentioned the lily-shaped burst of veins on her calf or the angle of her breasts, but she tensed, waiting for it, because who knew anymore what he'd say?

But with Will here even that minimal comfort level was destroyed. So she dressed, undergarments and all, and went down the stairs as silently as she could. He was there on the couch, fully dressed but for his shoes, which were untied and set carefully next to the couch and next to his briefcase. He was on his stomach, one arm flung down toward the floor, the tie slung over the edge of the couch. She must have watched him for a good minute before she was sure he was breathing.

In the kitchen she flipped the light switch. Nothing happened. She boiled water on the stove to make coffee and got started on her oatmeal. Thank God the gas worked. She checked the front porch for a newspaper, uncertain one would be even be there, but it was.

She poured the boiling water over fresh coffee grounds, straight into the glass carafe, and waited a minute to strain it. Perhaps they should buy a French press if this was how it was going to be.

As she reached into the refrigerator for milk, her hand registered the tepidness of the air inside. This was a problem. These little flickers had never lasted so long, but it had already been over twelve hours. Maybe the seal would hold in some cold air. She shut the door and pictured the contents of the refrigerator, unwilling to open it again. Luckily, it was largely empty; they were due to get their first farm-share delivery in the next day or two. Hopefully the power would be back by then. Impossible that it wouldn't be. In the meantime, one of them would have to get some ice and group all the food on the bottom shelves where the cold would linger.

She peered back at the couch, where there was no movement from Will, and sat down with her cooling coffee and opened the newspaper. The newspaper printer must have a generator, but the paper was much thinner than usual; only the front section and a local section. A tiny black-bordered box on the lower front page informed readers that the newspaper would be a limited edition today, but after today, any publication would depend on how long the generators could power computers and printers before they, too, ran out of juice.

Greta gnawed on her lip. This was new. The notice had a warning tone, a distinct "Don't count on us" feel to it.

The power company offered little help. An official referred to the outage as "a massive power fluctuation, due at least in part to the unseasonable heat in the region.

"Our initial estimates of power outage in the Madison area," the official continued, "have been expanded to include today's outages in large swaths of southern Wisconsin, northern Iowa, and possibly spreading eastward toward Milwaukee and the Chicagoland area, though all efforts are being made to arrest that spread. Our transmission circuit protective devices, usually successful, have unfortunately not fully contained the blackout."

Greta paused to imagine the blackout reaching Chicago and Milwaukee, cities so much wider and more densely packed. Hopefully they'd stop it before then; maybe larger cities had better ways of addressing such things. But how naïve—someone wise and competent must be in charge! She could just imagine how Hal's friend Wes would have responded if she'd actually said such a thing—how frustrating that she was even thinking of him. Greta figured anyone else would spend twenty minutes quasi-arguing at a party and then just shrug it off, but she knew herself. She would be having arguments with Wes in her head for weeks, and by the time she crossed paths with him again she'd have built up an entire plan of reasoning. Meanwhile he was no doubt patting his solar panels contentedly. She was sipping her coffee and ruminating on this image when she remembered Wes touching her arm, the light warmth of his hand around her wrist. He had been kind. She'd been so busy arguing in her head that she'd forgotten it.

Shamed, Greta returned to the paper, where the mayor was quoted:

> *While I am confident that our back-up generators are up to the task, at the moment it is imperative to use only the*

*most necessary energy. Many essential services should be
back in force in the very near future. In the meantime, we
ask that people remain calm. However, as the city may
lose water pressure during this brief incident, we suggest
citizens boil water before consuming it. It's regrettable we
couldn't forestall this state of affairs, but we're working
together to restore power. I'm not worried.*

From there the paper covered the latest insurgent bombings
and the accidental shootings of civilians at a checkpoint. Greta
skimmed it all, absorbing little. She drank half a pot of well-
boiled coffee and ate her oatmeal, and still no one had gotten up
by seven fifteen.

Having Will here was strangely comforting, or maybe it was
just one familiar thing in an unfamiliar place. She thought he
would get to work by nine; he somehow always did. Not missing
work allowed him to think he was doing better than he was. Yet
his mere presence out there in the other room, his lumpish form
on the couch, seemed to radiate submerged hostility and outright need. It begged for her to go in there, poke him or touch
him or do something. As long as she engaged with him in some
way, he might not care how.

Why wasn't Karin up and going for a jog? Shouldn't Hal be
awake by now? Just as she was thinking she ought to knock on
doors since no one's alarm would be working, she heard the ringing of cell phones in the lower hallway and upstairs, the sounds of
people moving and bed springs creaking. Of course. They had
both set their phones to wake them up.

That was how functioning people worked: faced with a
change, they changed. They didn't drag themselves over to someone's house and wait to be dealt with. Greta still felt unable to
get the balance right: she either did too little for everyone out of
sheer pissiness, or she did more than anyone needed. Earlier that

week she'd warned Karin and Hal numerous times that they needed to pay the bills. It was several days before they even needed to send them in, but still she couldn't stop herself. She was so used to saying things over and over, and she had heard the wheedling, aggrieved tone in her voice even as she spoke. It was humiliating to let other people see her behaving like this, humiliating to have brought Will in here like a rash of bedbugs.

She ran up the stairs—passing Will, who had not moved—and nabbed a spot in the shower. There were no windows in the bathroom, so she showered and shaved her legs by candlelight, a bizarrely erotic start to the morning.

When she opened the bathroom door, Karin was waiting in the hall, leaning against the wall with a fraying blue towel draped over her shoulder and a meditative expression. Greta flushed, embarrassed to recall herself from the night before, holding Karin's hand like a child. Who knew what she had said? Karin straightened up and gave her a quick smile.

"Morning," Greta said. She stepped out of the way of the bathroom, but paused, then added in a rush, "I'm sorry about last night. It was out of line."

Karin shook her head. "No big thing," she said. "People eat a 'shroom now and again. No one cared."

"Oh. Well, that's good, I guess." She looked down at her damp feet, glistening with drops of water across the instep, and forced herself to stay. "You were nice," she admitted. "Thanks."

"Well, what else would I be, right?" Again that smile flashed and disappeared. Karin readjusted her towel, folding over the bleached spots. Greta tightened her own towel around her rib cage.

"Right," she said. This was going badly. Once or twice in the weeks she had lived here, Greta had seen Karin get this way: light and crisp and untouchable, and it was unsettling. "Well, okay. See you later."

Karin opened the door and then turned back to Greta. "Is your husband still here?"

Greta nodded. "He's on the couch."

"Is he okay?"

"He's still asleep, but he looked okay," Greta said. "Listen, if he did anything on it I'll buy a new one, I promise. Maybe time for a new one anyway, right?"

But this, too, went over badly, and Karin frowned. "I wasn't really thinking about that so much, but if you think we need new furniture maybe we can discuss a budget."

"I wasn't thinking that," Greta backtracked. "I like the couch. Where did you get it?"

"Hal and I bought it on Craigslist," said Karin, "with our last housemates."

"Ah," said Greta.

They were both moving backward, one step at a time, until finally they were far enough away that they could stop talking. Greta had just turned when Karin called, "Good luck out there today," and Greta managed to call out a "You, too" before the door closed.

She was out the door at eight, while Karin was still in the bathroom and Hal seemed to be moving about in his room. Before she left she dropped Will's keys with an unceremonious jangle on his suited back.

Outside, the light was bright and golden and normal. Out on the lake there were two white boats. Surrounding them were rows of blue and white flags with a notch in one side, rising from buoys bobbing on the waves. From one of the boats, two divers dropped feet-first and disappeared beneath the surface of the water.

CHAPTER SIX

Hal awoke to his still-dead clock with a distinct sense of failure. He was reviewing his conduct of the night before and finding it wanting on every level. He'd been rude to a guy who was clearly in a bad way, his one attempt to help had been half-assed and tinged with hostility, and then he'd simply gone to bed. And now Diana wanted him to stock a warehouse and feed all these people and none of them knew how they'd make that happen.

And he had never reached his father, either. Maybe his uncle had managed to.

Hal peered out the doorway before he went to the kitchen. He saw stockinged feet hanging over the couch arm. Greta's husband was still asleep on the couch, a set of keys on the small of his back, rising and falling with his breath. Hal liked to think he had a decent understanding of addiction. This wasn't the fifties; he knew better than to think an alcoholic was just lazy, with a taste for martinis. This man had a major illness. Greta's husband might not be able to help how irritating he was. And what help was Greta? That part bothered him. Hal liked Greta; he admired her intelligence and her brusque manner, because he thought of her as too honorable to sugarcoat. This was what stopped him from getting annoyed even when she turned that honesty in his direction.

It made you wonder what kind of help Greta would be over the next few months. Why he was worried about that time frame in particular, he wasn't certain. It was just that feeling of foreboding brought on by these blackouts, by the empty gas stations, and strangenesses, and the way officials offered less explanation with each incident instead of more. A sensation of slippage, of gaps in the grid.

Greta must have made coffee somehow, but by now it was cool in its glass pitcher. He poured it into a pan and set it over a low flame. A paltry little newspaper was unfolded on the table.

Now Hal began to ponder his day. If they had phones, they could keep trying to raise donations. They could stretch out what little they had to deliver meals. Plans would have to be made, for now and maybe for the future as well. They needed a generator. Maybe Diana could get through to someone at the city and argue that they fell under essential services, if the city was truly managing to maintain any of those. But then again, the upside was that they had few perishables to chill. What they really had right now was space, empty space.

The coffee was steaming. He poured himself a cup, heavy on the milk before it could go bad, and read what little the newspaper had to offer. School was closed today, and was supposed to be closed for the duration of a blackout, but the district had already used up all its snow days. The school year would have to be extended once the power returned.

After another cup of coffee and a banana, the sunlight pouring into the kitchen, Hal's day felt as if it could almost be normal. That was what was so frustrating about it. For some people, the blackout and the food costs and the shortages were probably no big deal. The rest of the world was a well-insulated place, its enormous engines all geared toward keeping it moving, and those people were so accustomed to their way of life that Hal felt reassured they would marshal immense will to get it all back—the power, the fuel. Most people would be fine. It was Hal's people who wouldn't be. It made him wish he didn't know anything about the people who weren't going to get anything from the mobile pantries this week, or who would show up for a meal and get only a snack. It was tempting to retreat and forget all about it. Get drunk and let it be someone else's problem, or flee all the way up north and never answer the phone.

Hal had not yet seen photos of his father's new house, nor had he visited. Now he began to worry that what he had been imagining as a simple cabin with a couple extra rooms and a shed might really be a decrepit shack. His father had told them he planned to move in February, mentioned it casually over the Super Bowl relish tray. Hal's mouth had been full of braunschweiger. His sisters were on either side of him on Rennie's couch. He remembered looking down at Rennie's blue-jeaned knees, faded at the kneecaps, the gleam of her leather boots, and at the faint sparkle of Jane's stockings below her heather gray skirt. His own knees were covered in dark green corduroy. They'd all looked up at their father, who sat by the fireplace in a cracking leather chair. He looked the same as he always did. His pants were neatly pressed, his silver hair brushed, his button-down shirt blue and green plaid. He had gotten up that morning, just as he did the morning after Hal's mother's stroke a month before, pressed his clothing, shaved, drank coffee, and ate wheat toast and grapefruit and high-fiber cereal. He seemed regretful when his children were upset and baffled by his announcement, but it was clear there was no changing his mind, either. The kids' regret seemed to be a side effect over which he had no control. "I see your point, I really do," their father had noted. "But it's done. I accepted an offer on the house, and my offer up north has been accepted, too. There's not a thing I can do about it now. I'll write."

Hal had listened to his dad and his sisters in the first phase of discussion, Rennie's voice pitching higher and higher. He had been suffering through the indignity of chewing an unwanted mouthful of braunschweiger and knowing he was missing his chance to calmly and logically persuade his father. By the time he'd swallowed and taken a sip of water, Rennie and Jane were in full, bewildered argument. None of it made a difference. Their father was no less affectionate than he'd ever been. When he left—before dessert—he called the grandchildren to him and lifted each in the air as handily as ever, and then he beeped the car horn twice upon pulling out of the driveway.

Any man would think of selling the house he'd lived in for forty years when his wife died. He might not actually go through with it, but it was natural to consider it. What knocked Hal and his sisters for a loop was how swiftly and wisely their father had accomplished the business of dissolution in the weeks after their mother had died.

Hal had finished the second cup of coffee. He headed into the living room to wake Greta's husband.

He removed the keys and put them inside the shoes, which were soft leather, thin soled. Hal had never bought shoes like this, but he guessed they were several hundred dollars. The suit, too, was some kind of summer-weight wool, a charcoal gray with near-invisible seams and a pinstripe so richly, quietly muted Hal thought it probably required access to a certain tax bracket just to see it. You could pay rent with this man's outfit, though it was softened and rumpled from the heat and sleep.

He seated himself on the coffee table across from the husband. "Wake up, man," Hal said. He stared at the man's face, its shadows of whiskers poking through, the mouth pushed out in a pout against the couch cushion. He reached over and jostled a shoulder. "Come on."

One eye opened, revealing itself to be a brilliant green Hal hadn't noticed the night before, and focused directly on him. It was startling, as if he'd awakened a serpent. Hal drew back slightly.

"You okay?" he asked.

The man was very still for a moment, then he said, "Yes." His diction was formal—waking up on a stranger's couch and he didn't even give in to a *Yeah*. Hal chalked up a point for wherever this guy had gone to law school. Or for his MBA, whichever.

"Good," Hal said. He stood up. "Come on in the kitchen. Greta made—coffee's made."

There was a pause that seemed to last several minutes, in which the man's green eye stared at Hal unmovingly. Hal watched it for that vibration he'd seen the night before, when the man couldn't focus. It occurred to Hal that he was very likely still drunk. Hal sighed and reached down to pocket the keys.

He went back to the kitchen and had finished his cereal before Greta's husband appeared in the doorway, hands at his sides, his shoes on but not laced or tied. His dark hair was threaded with silver and stuck, coarse and thick, in the direction it must have laid against the couch cushion. Hal watched his face for expression but there wasn't any. Finally he got up, gesturing toward a chair, and poured a cup of coffee from the saucepan.

"Milk? Sugar?" The man shook his head, but Hal poured in milk anyway. He suspected the man needed some form of food, even just a slug of it. He set it down in front of him, and the man took a long sip, the cup trembling slightly.

"I'm Hal," Hal said.

"Will," said the man. The word croaked a little and he coughed richly and repeated himself. "Will Perrin."

"Perrin. So did Greta keep 'Ohlin' all along or change it back when she moved in here?" Hal asked. He couldn't quite tell why he felt all right asking such a question: pique, most likely. At both of them. Who were these *people*, in his house, with their flaky marriage and their sleeping on porch swings? But it felt good to concentrate on something small, so Hal latched on. He could insist that the worst thing he dealt with today would be only this.

"I'm sorry," Hal corrected himself. He didn't really mean it but he wasn't going to be an asshole this morning, he'd decided. He looked at his watch. He was going to be late if he didn't get moving; it was eight fifteen. The walk to Swiff took fifteen minutes, five to bicycle, but he still needed to shower. And he should get some ice for the refrigerator. And batteries, matches, and candles. He felt better, having a list of needs he could actually accomplish.

"Don't worry about it," Will said. "I deserve it, I assume. And she kept the same name all along." He sipped his coffee. "Are you guys Luddite or something?"

Hal stared at him, confused, until Will lifted his coffee cup in the direction of the saucepan. "Sorry," he said, "I just don't see a lot of people making coffee this way anymore. Ever."

"There's no power," Hal said slowly. "There's been no power since last night around six thirty."

Will stared at him, then looked around the kitchen, up at the dead lamp, at the light from the sun, and down at his coffee. "Right," he said.

"You don't remember?"

"Sure. Of course."

Hal let it drop. It was possible Will didn't know even where in town he was, how he had gotten here, and how long he had been here, yet he seemed reasonably content to sit and drink his coffee and stare at the table. Hal had a flash of himself the night before at the community meeting, staring at his shoes.

"Well," he said. "You probably have a job to get to." He paused. The coffee cup in Will's hand was not steady. "Are you okay?" he asked. "Can you make it home?"

"Of course," said Will. He shook his head loosely at the folly of the question, his eyes shut tight, his lips pursed. So he was still drunk. There was no way he could drive home, coffee or no.

"You can't drive," Hal said, shrugging. He hoped if he presented it as a foregone conclusion there'd be no argument.

"No," Will said. "I don't drive drunk anymore."

"Big of you," said Hal. "How'd you get here then?"

"I wasn't drunk when I got here," said Will. He met Hal's gaze, his eyes reddened and shadowed underneath. There were deep lines from nose to mouth, deeper than Greta's. The situation struck Hal as tragic all of the sudden, this couple who must be forty, doing this. They were only a few years older than Hal, but Hal imagined more stability in anyone past their thirties. Though he had taken few steps to ensure it, he imagined it for himself as well.

How old was this man? A sheepish frat-boy aura clung to him, but his eyes were dead. Bright green, yes, but hooded and expressionless.

"Did you sit in your car and drink?" Hal asked. He really wanted to know how someone approached the decision and action of sitting on his estranged wife's porch swing all night long. He looked at the clock: eight twenty. Why wasn't Karin down here yet?

Will rubbed his face, the flesh of his cheeks moving a little too loosely, and said into his palms, "I sat in the park." He straightened suddenly, as if recalling something, and darted a glance toward the living room.

"Do you need something?" Hal asked.

Will met his eyes, shook his head, and tried to settle himself into his chair. "No, I'm fine."

Hal drank some coffee, ruminating. Probably there was still a bottle out front somewhere, maybe in the living room in the briefcase, maybe beneath the swing on the porch. He thought Will had had a reflex to hide something just now, before realizing how pointless it might be. But then Will stood, muttered something about checking his cell phone, and went into the other room. Hal listened to the sound of the briefcase opening, but when he peered around the corner he saw that Will had moved over to the far side of the room and turned his back. He swallowed a drink of something.

This man could have had alcohol poisoning last night and no one would have known. People overdosed on booze, it could be done. They could have walked into the living room to find a corpse. Hal didn't really believe the man sitting in front of him was in immediate danger of anything more than a vicious hangover, until he drank more gin, most likely, but someone had to drive him home. Basic calculations indicated that he could not be sober yet. Would you leave a person woozy with hypoglycemia to find his way home during a blackout? You would not. He could take care of this quite easily, and he knew how to do it. Hal wanted to see only as far as each individual task before him. He had not the slightest idea how he would fill an empty warehouse—Diana had reasonable plans for the future, but for now, they were fucked, plain and simple. There was nothing they could truly do about it. But drive a man home, buy batteries, buy ice? Yes, yes, yes.

Will returned from the living room. He seemed to be looking a little better.

"Well, you'd better eat," Hal said. "Then I'll drive you home. I don't know if you want to call your office and tell them you'll be late, or absent, or what, but you can't go in like this, trust me."

Will just nodded. Being with someone who had no plans to be anywhere made Hal feel almost as untethered. Like back in college, when if Wes had another beer at four A.M., Hal felt he could, too. If someone else was blowing off work it felt as if you, too, might skip work with impunity. Will might very well sit at their table for hours, eating and drinking what was put in front of him, until he needed another drink. Fine. Let that work in his favor, let him eat something. Hal began to slice up fruit. Then he got to work making pancakes. He dug into the warming freezer for blueberries and added them, too.

For the moment, as he poured a perfect disk of batter onto the skillet, it felt like a Sunday or some minor holiday. It didn't feel like a crisis at all.

CHAPTER SEVEN

Karin had slipped out of the house just after Greta, but before Hal was up and moving. On her way out the front door, she'd seen a gray-suited bulk stretched out on the couch. He was handsome, she decided, but barely holding on to it. She wondered whether it had been Greta or Hal who had let him in. She decided on Hal.

She gave the couch itself a once-over as well. The morning light did it no favors. The wheat color of the upholstery was paler along the back and top seams, worn by years of heads and outstretched arms, probably. The cushions sagged in the center beneath Greta's husband. She and Hal had been delighted to find it online for a hundred dollars, but maybe even that had been ridiculous. She left the house thinking that Greta was right, the couch was terrible, and yet they'd had people over and invited them to sit as if it were perfectly nice. Maybe to their friends, it was—but if Greta had a friend over (Did Greta have friends? Where were they?) they would probably glance wordlessly at their surroundings and dash for a restaurant.

Outside the sun was well up and the heat was already settling on the earth. Karin looked up and down the street for signs of electricity, listening for blow driers or televisions. The yards were so quiet she could hear the sound of the lake slapping on its shores, the conversation that carried from two boats on the water. Three people were moving about on one of the boats, face masks on top of their heads.

In the car she flipped through the radio, not caring about the blackout explanations. What did it matter what the explanation was this time? Her lights didn't work when they said the transformer equipment was outdated, and they didn't work when they said the new equipment had introduced some glitches. She was listening for a mention of the stray dock, the lost dog and its lost owner. There was a clip about yesterday's incident, but it didn't use Karin's name. She was downgraded to a bystander. The dog had not been found, and police weren't saying yet whether they had an idea who its owner was, or how long she would be watching people dive into the lake outside her house.

Where was the dog? Yesterday morning it had headed in the direction of East Washington, a huge six-lane avenue that ran like an artery down the central length of the isthmus. A year ago a dog on that road would have met certain death, but gas prices had been fluctuating and right now they were high and traffic was down. The dog might have made it across East Wash and kept going in a straight line across the isthmus, only to have found itself at the other lakeshore.

The radio announcer's tone didn't sound as if the police regarded it as a prank. What had been in that bucket, next to the chair? That could have been a clue. Why hadn't she asked? It might have contained a magazine, some cigarettes, a novel. A bottle of gin. One of her aunts had killed herself when Karin was in high school by sitting in her running car in the garage. Karin's cousin had told her that on the front seat had been a book, an ashtray with numerous cigarette butts in it, and a bottle of wine and a plastic cup. Something to pass the time while she waited.

The Madison police might never say a word about the unmoored dock if they could help it, and it would be lost in the shuffle of the blackout and the gas shortages. Over the course of a day the unmoored dock and its inhabitant had become miscellany. Karin was relieved that anyone cared enough to be out on the lake at all.

As she drove, she scanned the sidewalks for a flash of golden fur, a dark canine face. Nothing felt right. There were few other cars on the road and the houses were still quiet. It was early, true, but not so early she couldn't expect anyone else to be out. As Karin approached the BP she saw that not only were the pumps out of gas, but the store appeared to be shut down as well.

She decided to go and look. It was ridiculous that no one seemed to know what was going on—maybe no one was asking the right questions. She'd just go see if there was a sign on the door. Karin turned around and then headed back to the gas station, pulled in and got out of her car, peering through the glass into the dark store. All of the products were gone; the shelves empty, the coolers in the back dark and bare. Without brightly colored packages obscuring everything, she saw how shabby the place was, how filthy its linoleum and battered its countertops were. She thought she glimpsed a motion: maybe just a flapping of paper, some leftover plastic banner.

Karin touched the door handle, out of curiosity. She pulled, ever so slightly, to see if it would give. The door swung open, unlocked. Inside, the store smelled of cleanser and something sweet—the leftover odor of packaged pastries, a smell of sugar suspended in cooked shortening and vanilla.

She moved slowly through the little space. Her feet crunched over a stray corn chip. The clean-out had been complete but sloppy, magazine subscription forms still littered the floor, a few receipts on the tile behind the counter. A dead mouse, looking oddly flattened, lay beneath the cash register.

A shiver of revulsion jogged up her spine. Karin bolted back to the fresh air, to the safe cleanliness of the car that waited for her like a patient beast.

The decision was obvious; she just wanted to get out of town. Elaine Rothberger was two and half hours north. She'd been planning to profile Drumlin briefly, just to acknowledge the new business and their cave aging, but now she was thinking how rural this farm must be, how isolated from Madison, Milwaukee, and Chicago. Why not just drive to a better place? That instinct had guided Karin out of the decrepit mobile home she'd grown up in, it had gotten her to college and it had gotten her out of a house noisy with children to a calm and pleasant grown-up one. She had her notebook, her tape recorder, and a past issue of *Dairy Now* already in the car. Instead of heading west to her office, she took a left on Williamson Street and went east.

When she was outside town she took out her cell phone, relieved to see it had a signal, and called Elaine Rothberger.

She presented it as a prize: "I usually don't do this," she said. "I usually just talk to people on the phone, but you guys are doing such amazing work, and I'm dying to see your cheese caves. There aren't that many in use, you know. You're a pioneer." She didn't say anything about the power outages and neither did the cheesemaker, which confirmed what Karin had suspected. Her instinct must be right; everything must still be normal up there.

The cheesemaker seemed flustered and hesitant, but eventually gave in. "We're not that interesting out here," she said. She gave a choking little laugh. "But if you want to write about the cheese I can't pass it up," she said finally. "I need the exposure. Come on up."

Once it was settled, Karin leaned back a bit—she'd been hunched over the steering wheel all this time. It was only a simple power outage, a lost dog and its lost owner, and a garden-variety alcoholic. It was almost funny to think of everyone relentlessly flipping dead light switches and kicking at gas pumps, those things reduced to object instead of tool.

Just to be on the safe side, Karin called her parents. "I'm staying home," her father said. In the background Karin heard the sounds of a radio listing school closings. "Hard to run the plant with no electricity. Your mother thinks the grocery store should still be open so she's already headed in. What about you?"

"I'm taking the opportunity to visit a farm," Karin said. "Madison's totally blacked out and no one even knows why."

Her father laughed. "Well, *Mad*ison," he said, as if he expected no better. And Karin knew he didn't; her parents viewed Madison as the free-love liberal cancer in the old-fashioned American heart of Wisconsin. They still didn't understand why she lived there. Her father seemed to believe there was a lot of public nudity.

She hung up and drove, concentrating on work. She and her boss, Francine, were part gadflies, part insiders. The industry people who read the paper barely knew what the staff looked like—from the photo that accompanied her occasional editorials one could see that Francine had a wedge of short, light hair, bright dark eyes, and a wide slice of a grin. Karin had had one such photo taken for her first column and she still meant to replace it: the picture was badly focused, her head looming out larger than it should be, her eyes pixilated and stoned-looking. Francine had insisted she wear a suit jacket and pull her hair back, which made her look as if she were in costume. Karin's beat was the cheese artisan, the small operation that won awards and mentions in the food magazines but sometimes barely eked out a living. Francine handled the industrial people, never betraying a hint of distaste at the press releases announcing yogurt in tubes or the latest spice-powdered shred. She knew a lot of folks at Kraft. She had started the newspaper ten years earlier, after a career at a regional dairy marketing organization. Francine was the descendant of a long line of chemists and scientists, and to her the industry of fabricating cheese-like products was no more than a puzzle, a particularly grown-up game of blocks. Karin liked her farmers' hands filthy, her cows named, and her cheese wrapped in limp chestnut leaves. Anything else was unnatural.

Karin had taken the job around the same time she moved out of the Womyn's Co-op. Before that, she was working at a local food store, writing their newsletter and ordering the stock. The move to profiling cheesemakers seemed fairly natural, and in some ways the cheese newspaper changed Karin's life by showing her what she very much wanted to avoid. She'd had her first dinner with Hal and their former roommates after a day of soundbites from the state Dairy Boosters. They had made her organic spaghetti with artichokes and tomato, talked about community and the Swiffies and sustainable agriculture and the wonders of the legume.

The dairy industry seemed to her a culture of fear. They saw how the one-two punch of bagel-shop overproliferation and Atkins had decimated the carb industry, and so began an assault of preemptive, slightly hysterical marketing. Wisconsin cheese was the ultimate convenience food, they insisted, as if everywhere people strolled along nibbling bars of cheddar out of hand. California, they grudgingly conceded, might surpass Wisconsin in cheese production, but the *spirit* of the West Coast enterprise was wholly lacking. Yogurt fought bacteria, calcium built bones, and *milk would never let you die.* The strain showed in every press release. Karin was okay with boosting the privately owned farms making beautiful cheese by hand. It was when the monoliths started talking about wholesomeness and goodness that she got disgusted. She never said this to Francine, who on any given day could be heard in her office, chuckling on the phone with a research and development contact who was perfecting aerosol jalapeño cheese spread in some Illinois bunker.

Karin drove through the flat fields that surrounded the city. The first miles of Madison's east side and just beyond it were the worst: a combination of new sprawl and seventies prefab buildings, age showing in the dated bubble-lettered signs above them. By July the fields would be a sere, urinous gold; in the winter the brown grass often showed through the patches of blowing snow like a dirty bandage. Right now the fields were as inoffensive as they would ever be: bare, flat, pale green. Karin regarded the city, its beauty centered carefully around the white wedding cake of its capitol, as a sort of tide pool of people and energy: silvery, quickened, collared by blandness till you reached into the rural sections of the state, where natural beauty reasserted itself.

She reviewed what she knew of Drumlin Cheese. They grew a few crops, produced honey, and of course dairy. They had won a rural development grant from the state for raising a certain percentage of sheep—the state, fearing bovine obsolescence, was encouraging sheep and goat husbandry. Drumlin was family-run, two years old, and they made four kinds of cheese: soft-ripened, some goat cheeses of a few different ages, and Gruyère and Gouda-style cow- and sheep-milk blends.

Their cheese was very good, especially for beginners. The soft-ripened one had an appalling name, though, one from which Karin planned to subtly dissuade them during this visit, if possible: "U.P. Brie." U.P. was for Upper Peninsula, the section of Michigan north of the cheesemakers. Apparently a family member had been born there, which was really no excuse. But the cheese itself was lovely: encased in ivory-velvet rind, its satiny yellow insides slumping lazily. It started off tasting like creamy, concentrated butter, and then the stronger flavors kicked in, mouth-filling and strong, faintly mushroomy, earthy.

Now Karin tried brainstorming more names for them, but then let herself zone out. She'd be fresher if she didn't overthink things.

Instead Karin found herself picturing something—someone—else. She pictured a person of about forty, wandering around in a little bungalow not far from Karin's own house. A person with brown hair streaked by gray, making one last cup of coffee and calling the dog in for its breakfast. The only sounds in that house would be the dog's toenails clicking on the linoleum, the lake forever swishing in the background, and the click of the leash being snapped in place.

Karin could no longer recall the moment of jumping into the water. She'd done it so thoughtlessly, certain the mud lay only a foot or so beneath the dark reflective surface, but now it seemed possible that the lake would harbor unexpected depths, a treacherous, invisible geography. But she refused to dwell on it. What else would she have done? Watch the dog drown? She'd done it thoughtlessly because there was no sound alternative. That dog had not been close to the shore. It was not swimming strongly. And no one else had been about to jump in, certainly not the owner who had put it out there. For all Karin knew that owner had walked right past them while they all had their backs to the street. Had they only turned, maybe they would have seen the person Karin now imagined. Maybe a woman in her forties, hair brown and gray and hanging in wet strings, leaving a damp trail of footprints on the sidewalk.

. . .

Karin arrived at ten thirty, pulling up a long unpaved drive and finally parking in the shadow of a massive dark-stained wood house. She couldn't tell if there was any electricity available, and it frankly didn't seem to matter. Madison, its weird empty stores and quiet roads and murky rooms, felt as far away as the Middle East.

She gathered her notebook and pens and recorder, looked briefly in the mirror, and poked at the inner corners of her eyes with a pinky. She looked a little tired but natural. She never wore makeup for visiting farmers. It was bad enough that she was young and inexperienced. If she wore lip gloss they might not even bother.

Outside the air was grassy-smelling, warm and heavy but cooler this far north. She stretched and shook out her legs, listening for sounds of machinery or voices. She heard nothing at all. Before her the house loomed, windowpanes shining and inscrutable. Her shoes were loud in the gravel. The trees arched over her; fields stretched into woods on either side.

There was motion farther up the driveway. She looked up and saw a huge animal regarding her. Some kind of hound, iron gray and wiry-haired, a long-legged creature that approached her so lightly its paws barely skimmed the ground. It never barked. As it neared, Karin slowed and then froze, realizing the dog's jaws were easily as high as her waist.

The silence—the dog's silence, the silence of the landscape around them—was deeply unnerving. The breeze moved through the branches of the trees, the surrounding grass was uncut and lissome, bending in one direction and then another as if in pleasant indecision, and at the end of the pathway rose the farmhouse, its window boxes filled with fire-colored petunias. The gray dog trotted toward her, caramel eyes agleam beneath a rakish flop of fur. Karin had the feeling she had entered a fairy tale at the wrong time. The scent of grass and manure drifted by.

She put out a hand to the dog, palm out, as if to stop it, but the dog simply kept coming and let its great head collide with her hand. She felt the knob at the back of its skull, its coarse fur. The arch of the dog's back rose almost to her chest. Yet its warm, wiry fur beneath her fingers was a relief, breaking the peculiar spell of the silence of the hilltop, its soundless guard. It was just a dog. A dog on a farm was hardly a shock. They were everywhere.

"Miss Phillips?"

"Ms.," she said automatically. As she looked up from the dog she saw a woman approaching her, wearing old jeans and lug-soled boots, hands in her pockets. The boots were brown and scuffed at the toe, grass clinging to the leather, and the jeans were bleached and faded in oblong patches over the muscle of the thigh. A frizz of black curly hair stood out around the woman's face, illuminated by the sun. The rest was pulled back in a pony-tail. She was startlingly young, younger than Karin. Her cheeks were round and lightly freckled, her eyes deep-set and elongated, the lids hidden.

"This is Carl," the woman said. She gestured at the dog, who bestowed an affectionate head butt to Karin's rib cage. "Carl!" The woman's voice went low and menacing, and Carl trotted over to her side. "I'm Elaine. I'm assuming you're from *Dairy Now*, right?"

Karin laughed. "Oh, sorry, right." They shook hands, Elaine's palms callused and hard. "Thanks for letting me come up here at such short notice. Sometimes I think it just makes sense to really see what I'm writing about instead of doing everything by phone. It's impersonal."

Elaine nodded. "I hear you guys have another blackout," she said.

Karin felt caught; perhaps Elaine knew she'd just wanted to get out of town, knew she liked Drumlin cheese but wasn't quite as fired up about their cheese caves and U.P. Brie as she'd indicated.

"Yeah," Karin said nonchalantly. "Seems to be holding on for a while, too, I guess, but I imagine it'll all be back to normal by the time I get home. I didn't really look at whatever excuses the mayor was peddling, so I could be wrong."

Elaine smiled briefly at her, and Karin knew she understood why Karin was here. She smiled back, blandly and boldly, and admitted nothing.

"Well, our electricity is still here," Elaine said. "The local power plant took us off the grid so it couldn't spread to us. Whatever else goes on, we've still hung on to that."

"What else?" But Elaine just shook her head and waved a hand. They were both silent for a moment.

Karin changed the subject. "I was having the oddest sensation before you came out." They began to walk up the driveway. "It's so beautiful and silent up here and I felt like this gigantic creature was sort of guarding it and I'd trespassed. Now that I know his name is Carl I don't think the impact will ever be the same."

Elaine chuckled. "My brother named him," she said. "You'll meet him, too. Come on into the house. We'll have a snack and then take a tour around the place, okay?" She looked worried suddenly. "If you want to, I mean. I don't know, how do other people do it? Do you usually get straight to work? I don't want to waste your time."

"No, that's great," Karin said. She was feeling stupid about admitting the fairy-tale thing. Farmers weren't usually into a lot of esoteric chitchat about weird sensations. "I'd love a snack. We can talk a little about your operation, too."

Carl disappeared behind the house. Elaine led Karin around the back, up a staircase to a deck. A grill sat to one end, next to a long picnic table, with two shaded tables on the other end. They could have sat twelve people. "Have a seat," Elaine said. "We're having cheese, if that's okay. What would you like to drink?"

"Anything with caffeine."

Elaine nodded and disappeared inside.

Over the deck's railings the land was visible for miles: undulant, green, the nearby trees giving off the fecund, yeasty fragrance of pollen. Karin could see two barns about a half mile off, the yellowed-ivory shapes of sheep against the fields. Sheep were better from a distance. Up close their oily, strong-smelling fleece took on a dirty polar-bear color, or else resembled the damp-patched gray of an old sweater of dubious origin. Karin preferred cows, whose barny scent of hay and manure was somehow inoffensive, their bristled skin smooth over their massive bodies. The Rothbergers raised both, plus goats. Goats were easy. A lot of people started with goats. They ate well and gave a lot of milk, and good goat cheese was always as chic as a little black dress.

Elaine returned through the sliding door bearing a tray of iced tea, a wedge of white cheese, and a plate of crackers and sliced apples. "I should really have baked bread for you, too," she said. "Complete the picture, you know." She set down the tray and rearranged the cheese on its plate.

"This looks great," Karin said. She added, "My roommate is always going on about baking bread. He buys fresh yeast, like every weekend, and then procrastinates and procrastinates until the yeast goes bad. Then the next week he buys more."

"Why doesn't he buy dried?" Elaine went back to the sliding door and closed it.

Karin smiled. "For numerous reasons, having to do with the earth and agriculture and nutrition, but chiefly so he'll never have to bake unless the stars align." For a moment she felt a wave of warmth for Hal, vexing though he was.

Elaine sat down opposite Karin and crossed her legs primly. She reached up and adjusted the umbrella on the table to give Karin more shade. Then she resettled herself and smiled, shrugging as if to say, *Well, you know what to do.*

So far in Karin's brief career, these profiles had proceeded in jerks and stops, aided by long pauses, questions the farmers often found extremely obvious, and Karin's wildly enthusiastic response to their products. Media-wise, you hit the sweet spot at either end of the industrial spectrum, either very big or very small: the artisans were usually people who had left some other career and come to cheese out of love of food and various political leanings, and they understood why and how to work the press at every level. People in big corporations knew it, too; they were employed to know it, coming out of marketing razors or crackers or whatever their last gig had been. Trouble came in the laconic form of the cheesemaker who'd been doing this for enough years that it was old hat, an operation neither new nor venerable, products neither earth-shattering nor appalling. They had a job to do and never really understood Karin's interest in it. She often had to hope for an upstart heir who'd been to business school and planned on taking it all over someday. She couldn't tell where Elaine, who looked to be twenty-two at most, would fall.

"So," Karin said, "who all is in on this operation?"

Elaine ticked them off on her fingers. "My brother Kenneth and his wife Janine. My parents. This is actually their land. We used to visit here when I was little and my dad's parents owned it, but Kenny and I grew up in Appleton. Anyway, you don't care where we grew up. My mom keeps the books, my dad keeps the livestock. I make the cheese. Kenneth oversees the crops. Janine meanders the landscape. Kenny used to help my husband."

Karin was writing furiously. "And did your husband move to another part of the operation?"

"He died," said Elaine.

Now Karin looked up. "I'm so sorry," she blurted. She glanced at the cheese Elaine had sliced for her, the hopeful ivory square of it. This didn't seem the right time to snack.

Elaine unbound her ponytail and shook it out, raking her fingers through it. A mass of near-black curls fell below her shoulders, the sun showing its dark-copper streaks. Her hair was a wild thing, a puffy cushion Karin longed to pat. "Yeah," Elaine sighed. "The funny part is that he wanted the farm in the first place." She gestured toward the land, the sheep in the far distance. "Like I said, we lived in Appleton. I was working in the office of a box manufacturer. My parents owned a gift store, my brother was working in construction. Janine was wandering the Appleton landscape. But Jack and I had this idea that it was time to get back to the land, you know, that we'd beat the rush he was sure was coming. My grandparents had left this to my dad, and Jack was the one who made up the business plan and everything. He sort of sat us all down at Thanksgiving one year and pitched it over pie."

"Wow." Karin was at a loss for words. Was it really such a sad story, or was it only that this poor boy had died? She saw him as fresh out of college, shaggy-haired and talking too fast, pacing before a living room of baffled family holding plates of dessert on their laps. "Was he the one who named it Drumlin?" Karin asked. She allowed her pen to touch the paper again.

Elaine nodded briskly. "Yeah. He wanted something to reflect the Wisconsin geography. You know what they are, right? You can put it in there if you want. Kind of whale-shaped mounds glaciers left around Wisconsin, if anyone's asking." She paused. "Try the cheese, tell me what you think."

Karin gazed down at the cracker on its blue square napkin. A line of ash ran through the cheese's center, the square banded by a soft rind. She took a bite and chewed thoughtfully. She stopped chewing. Then she bravely continued. The mouthful was so sharp it gave an impression of actual heat on the palate, followed by a bitter whiff that rose into her sinuses.

"Shit," Elaine sighed, watching her. "That's what I thought." She tasted a wedge of the cheese herself, while Karin sipped her iced tea determinedly. "Yeah, it's a nightmare. I tried something new. That sure didn't work." She pulled a wastebasket over to the table with one foot, plucked the cheese off its tray, and chucked it into the basket. "I was never really supposed to be the cheese-maker," she told Karin. "I just fell into it after Jack died. It was a car wreck, by the way, before you waste any energy wondering if it was at all mysterious or if he was a soldier or something. He wanted to make aged Gruyère-style cheeses. I like soft ones but we're doing both to keep the income through the year, you know. People always forget you need babies to get milk and that it doesn't go year round, so I try to stagger the aging. But I keep trying to invent new cheeses and brush them with this and that, and it's a lot harder than you'd think. I wanted to do a partner-ship with a local beer company, you know, to brush on the cheese during the aging? Like the Belgians and the Germans do. And I'm still experimenting with the beer."

"I had the, uh, the U.P. Brie at the Midwest dairy show," Karin said. "It was really very good."

Elaine seemed relieved. "Was it? I like that one. It's selling okay, too. The name, I feel compelled to mention, is Kenneth's idea. I'm looking for a way to gently tell him it's unspeakably bad. Janine thinks it's cute." She rolled her eyes. "Listen, let's take a walk, okay? You can meet the rest of my family and some of the livestock. I have my favorites." She rose and brushed off her jeans. Carl's iron-gray head appeared above the stairs of the deck, waiting.

"Great. And the caves, too," Karin said.

Elaine looked away. "Sure," she said after a moment. "They're not that special really, but of course you can, if you want. I should go by the henhouse, too, if you want to come." She turned away and down the steps.

"You were really nice about the cheese," Elaine called over her shoulder. She walked backward, giving Karin time to catch up.

"Don't write about it, okay? I don't need the whole industry knowing we're just a bunch of hacks up here."

Karin protested but Elaine was already walking across the grass, Carl preceding her. "It's okay," Elaine said. She shoved her hands into the pockets of her coat as they headed toward the barns. Her face, with its pointed chin and slanted eyes, the wide, thin mouth, was softer in profile. "There's a long tradition in my family of trying totally new careers now and again. My dad alone's been through, like, five already. I don't even know what the next one will be. Jack was the one kind of spearheading it. He dies, what, a year into the whole deal, and we're all still wandering around up here, frankly pretty baffled by it all."

CHAPTER EIGHT

At the very least, the crisis with the Swiff supplies had shifted Diana's attention away from Hal's incident with Mrs. Bryant the week before. The Southern Wisconsin Food Initiative had built a largely unsullied reputation since the sixties, gathering donations and delivering food to the elderly and otherwise housebound. According to Diana, that reputation was now imperiled single-handedly by Hal. He *had* been late for the rest of his home visits the day he overvisited with Mrs. Bryant. But Diana made it sound as if he were an EMT who'd stopped for a milkshake. Frankly, Hal had thought Diana's sense of proportion was a bit off.

Mrs. Bryant's house fell about halfway through Hal's delivery run last Thursday. He had paused to visit with her six or seven times over the previous weeks and heard a bit about the deceased husband, the sister's daughter who was

Mrs. Bryant's closest relative and the only one in the area. He often accepted a cup of tea (and made it, and served it, but the *idea* of hospitality lurked in the ritual somewhere). Mrs. Bryant stocked tea in odd, remaindered flavors: orange-clove, peach-clementine, licorice. Hal would sip politely for a few minutes and later pour it out in the kitchen while Mrs. Bryant remained in her chair, neatly and doggedly devouring her meal.

Last Thursday had been decent enough to start off, with gorgeous May weather: sunny, mild, the sky pillowed with sheepy clouds. As Hal had offered his usual sprightly knock and entered the Bryant house, he'd been struck as always by the darkness inside, the gloom that so often enveloped the houses of people he visited. He thought it came from too few doors opening, too few bodies moving in and out. The continuation of such an atmosphere seemed pointlessly cruel. Why didn't he and his coworkers all just take a day and open the window for these people, clean the panes, and clear out the overgrown trees that blocked the light? Before he'd considered the idea fully he'd blurted, "You'd get so much sun in here if the bushes out front were trimmed."

From her chair in the living room corner, Mrs. Bryant had nodded. "You could set your watch to Mr. Bryant's hedges," she informed him. She held out a hand for the tray and sniffed at it as she lifted the foil. That day it was turkey meat loaf, heavily laced with bulgur and carrot. Her expression suggested she'd seen worse. "Sit," she instructed Hal.

"I can't stay long," he said. He unfolded her TV tray before her and set the meal on top of it. Then he went to the kitchen for a cloth napkin and a fork and knife.

"I know, I know, the other shut-ins call," she said. She enjoyed referring to the other shut-ins, among whom she did not number herself.

"The lilac bush is a problem," she continued. She took a bite of carrot and chewed thoughtfully. Mrs. Bryant had not lost a single tooth. "When Mr. Bryant was alive those flowers were perfection, and we could have set a tray of iced tea right on the hedges, they were so even. That was one of his beliefs."

Hal had nodded, glancing at his watch. He was already fairly well acquainted with Mr. Bryant's beliefs, which included the importance of personal vegetable gardens and varying one's tithes between 9 and 14 percent, so the church didn't coast on assumptions.

She patted at her lips with the cloth napkin. Mrs. Bryant had what Hal thought of as good Yankee manners, deeply frugal and straightforward, yet with a real sense of propriety. The cloth napkins may have been the tip-off.

"Nice job on the egg noodles today."

"I'll let them know," said Hal. He sometimes invented compliments for the kitchen staff; it would be a relief to have a sincere one.

"How's your new girl?" Mrs. Bryant asked. Hal had told her a bit about his living arrangements and his new housemate. Even in the telling, Greta had presence. He'd enjoyed describing her: her flossy corn-silk hair; the deeply traced lines around her green eyes; the way her lips were usually set in a serious line; her hands short-nailed and ruched with veins.

Mrs. Bryant seemed to think Hal lived in more of a harem than a co-op, a misapprehension Hal was reluctant to correct. She took obvious pleasure in the idea of Hal ruling a roost. His mother had felt much the same way, befriending the people he lived with and casting significant glances at certain women when they weren't looking.

"She's not really a girl, she's probably forty," Hal had said. "She's fine. She does her thing."

"Good cook?"

"I guess." He shrugged. "Long as she cooks on her nights and it's edible and mostly organic that's all I can ask." Mrs. Bryant also appeared to think it was a boardinghouse.

"I was a fine cook," she said. "When I arrived here no one ever ate hot dishes. I made them and they looked at me like I was a madwoman. No hot dishes. Can you imagine?"

"Really?" Hal asked. "They ate everything cold? Well, maybe Cornish pasties you could have in the fields . . ."

She cut him off. "It wasn't Cornwall, for God's sake. Pasties, my God. Hot dishes! Tuna noodle, chicken and rice with bread crumbs. Those hot dishes."

"Oh," he said. "Casseroles."

"If that's what you call them out here." Mrs. Bryant had lived in the Midwest for fifty years but still frequently referred to her surroundings with the surprise of a new transplant. She took another dainty bite of meat loaf and looked at the branch-blocked window. "I don't know how you set it up these days with all your women but of course back then the division of labor was quite distinct. Indoor, outdoor. I never even touched Mr. Bryant's garden. If I needed herbs he insisted on cutting them himself."

"I'd like an herb garden," Hal said sincerely. They had barely even begun composting—he and Karin had put aside some coffee grounds in a bucket, planning to get a worm box going, but when he was about to show Greta on her first day he'd realized they'd neglected to buy worms and add soil. They'd only gotten as far as a bucket of garbage.

"There might be some mint out there yet." She nodded toward the window. "Or sage. Been so long I can't quite recall. You should take a look, Hal. Take a cutting home to these girls of yours. You're a good young man. They must appreciate you."

She eyed him as she said this, and Hal sipped his tea and kept his expression bland and pleasant. He knew Mrs. Bryant's intention was not the sweet compliment she wanted him to notice first. He had talked to her enough to know she didn't value sweetness very much.

The truth was that Hal wasn't very fond of Mrs. Bryant. He had found that she simply expected a certain sort of obeisance, often presenting as fact her need for the armchair to be shifted, the television antenna to be adjusted more carefully this time, a little nub of Parmesan to be grated over her dinner. If she didn't get whatever she'd requested she began to talk and just kept going, chatting about how you might have pleased her but instead had failed, things you had the opportunity to do but missed, details you might have thought she did not notice but which in fact she perceived minutely. She did this to everyone—the others entered and left her house at a dead run. Hal once asked Diana how she managed not to let Mrs. Bryant interrupt her, and Diana said, "She does. I just keep talking and the two of us yell away at each other about totally different things the whole time and when I leave she's still talking."

The problem was that Hal had earned a certain cachet by being on Mrs. Bryant's good side. He understood how to deal with people like this, and secretly found it easier than dealing with people who were polite and soft-spoken but still had no intention of accommodating you. He'd spent his whole childhood learning how to deal with intractable politeness: no one was calmer than his parents, no one more reasonable than his father over doughnuts after church. It was enough to make a kid jab himself with a fork. Better to face animosity outright.

Even Mrs. Bryant's niece had called and thanked them for the personal attention. She did this just as Hal was getting ready to toughen up on Mrs. Bryant and stick only to his Swiffie-designated duties. Everyone at work was deeply impressed by the achievement of pleasantries with the Bryants, patting his back and chuckling to themselves about Hal's magic touch.

It had been some time since people made a big deal about

Hal's magic touch. He'd once been known as the fund-raiser who could talk an extra 10 percent out of anyone and could please the meanest old farmer. But in the last few months something had shifted inside him: he no longer wanted to go out and bring around new people or maintain his relationships with the ones he already knew. He preferred working in his office, checking through orders and invoice sheets, and tracking the quantities that entered and left the warehouse. He could fix the mistakes when people accidentally ordered in pounds instead of cases; he enjoyed the satisfaction of the numbers adding up. People had begun to puzzle him. He no longer understood why some clients refused to master the Swiff procedures, and he became vexed by the sounds of his coworkers milling around outside his door. He noticed in particular that the director of communications peppered every half sentence with a gasping laugh that seemed to startle even her. As Hal tracked the smaller amounts of donations against the projected needs of his region, he thought he could understand why his coworkers were always chatting and strolling slowly through the building, touching door jambs as if for guidance, why the director of communications needed to force that breath out every thirty seconds. They were failing. Alone, at least, he did not have to gloss it over and talk about the good fight; he could try to accept the slow death. In Mrs. Bryant's dark house the list of needs were finite and achievable: more food, less dust, more light. There was relief in that.

Mrs. Bryant had moved to Wisconsin from New Hampshire in the 1950s, accompanied by a husband who'd had dreams of farming until he got a job on a dairy farm and quit after six months. The couple bought a house on the far east side of Madison and settled in for good, he a factory worker at Oscar Mayer and she a school secretary. When Hal looked at photos of the late Mr. Bryant he saw a feckless, floppy-haired young man turned toward the camera with a startled look over his shoulder, as if he'd just been poked with a stick. Hal imagined married life with Mrs. Bryant as a pugnacious, needling affair.

And yet she had shed the husband and the extraneous relations and she seemed content. No wonder Hal had found it so difficult to leave that day, even as the sun grew lower and he knew the other dinners were cooling in his car. He simply could not rouse himself, could not face the rounds yet again of bright conversation and false pleasantries. She was alone, Hal had been thinking, but for the first time he didn't pity her. Mrs. Bryant had her house, a warm shelter, and she had some food and entertainment. She seemed to need no one else. Hal sipped anise tea and realized he could hear almost nothing from the outside. No cars seemed to drive down this street. No children hollered or wept. Hal and Mrs. Bryant were alone in their cave, protected from the carnival of bizarre and destructive human behavior. It was rather wonderful.

He'd remained there for an extra hour, watching the time tick by from an antique horsehair couch that was at least half as comfortable as an actual horse. He was scarcely able to believe time was really passing, until the shaded living room grew so dim Mrs. Bryant's white hair and the gleam of her glasses were its only illumination.

Finally Hal had moved with a jerking motion that startled both of them. "Jesus Christ," he'd said, "it must be five thirty." He stood up, brushing his hands and looking around for a light switch. "I have got to go, Mrs. Bryant, I'm sorry. But I really have to go."

She remained unbothered. "Hal," she'd said, gesturing with one lumpy hand. "Calm down and reach into that little curio by the couch. You see the jade box? Open it up."

Inside was a little roll of bills.

"This isn't the remains of a stash, is it?" he joked.

"Ha! I wouldn't keep it there, no interest. It's just a little something to keep handy. This neighborhood is not what it once was. This way if a hoodlum breaks in I can tell him to take the box, take the box, and he'll think he's getting it all and leave me alone. One hopes. But you take one. Take a twenty, Hal. For all your time today."

"I couldn't possibly," he said. "It's very kind of you. But the Swiffies would never let me take a tip."

"The Swiffies would never let you sit and listen to an old woman as you have. This is between you and me, Hal. I won't tell my niece and you won't tell your boss. It's a little something, that's all. Buy your girls some flowers."

He needed gas. He needed his share of the electric bill. He needed to pay the principal on his credit card. But then again it would be nice to bring something unexpected home to Greta and Karin. A tiny ficus. A box of handmade chocolates.

"Thank you," he said finally. He worked an aged, velvety twenty-dollar bill out of the roll and held it up as if for inspection, to show he had taken only one. The rest of the roll was tightly wedged in the cool green space.

"Very good," she said. "Don't tell your do-gooder friends I have it; they'll hit me up for a donation for Greenpeace."

"It's an excellent organization," Hal said, but she waved him away and he folded the twenty into his pocket.

As he'd stepped out of her house Hal began to panic in earnest. The sun was nowhere near the same position as when he'd arrived: it was lower, bloated and dulled. He didn't want to touch one of the trays on the racks in the back of the van, knowing they would be stone cold. So he ran the rest of his rounds in high gear, apologizing quickly and darting back out of the houses again, refusing to look at the screen of his cell phone, which he knew would register missed calls from Diana. Many missed calls.

The discussion that awaited him at the office was everything you'd expect. Yet even knowing he was wrong, Hal couldn't make himself apologize. Plus, the twenty had somehow separated things for him: he had taken a side job. They couldn't very well blame him, given what they paid. He found himself digging in his heels and believing it as he insisted he had had no option, that they were missing the forest for the trees if they were so caught up in details that they couldn't make an old woman happy.

It was this position, maintained with unwavering passion, plus the artfully evoked image of tiny Mrs. Bryant with her clock-print dress and swollen diabetic leg, that kept his job. Diana allowed Hal to convince her that the day had been a case of compassion run slightly amok, of the charitable impulse they should all have, but should perhaps schedule more efficiently. She was probably picturing a brief détente with a crusty old soul, achieved through Hal's relentless kindness. A little teary learning across generations. Hal never mentioned that in fact he thought Mrs. Bryant might be slightly evil, nor that she gave him money.

He spent the money on a bottle of Ribera del Duero. At dinner that evening he plucked the wine rather showily from his shopping bag, and his housemates—his girls, he thought wryly, handing over the bottle—were delighted.

On the other side of campus, Hal and Will drove into the neighborhood of older, well-kept houses. It wasn't as rough around the edges as Hal's neighborhood, but neatly maintained, the architecture varied, the yards quiet. They had finished some pancakes, and then while Will lay back on the couch for a half hour, Hal had gone out and bought as much melting ice as he could and stocked the refrigerator with it. He offered to drive Will home.

Hal was directed to stop before a gabled brick house with a flagstone walk and a pile of newspapers on the front porch. That pile depressed Hal. How long had Will been gone? Or maybe he simply walked past them every day.

Will was hauling himself out of the car. Hal knew he ought to hand over the keys and say good-bye, but he didn't. Will didn't seem to find it strange when Hal accompanied him to the front door. He sat back against the porch post and waited while Hal tried two or three keys in the front lock. When Hal got one that worked, he opened the door and stepped back for Will to go in first, as if he himself were the host.

As Will passed by, Hal glanced up at the dim porch light. Off, of course. Had anyone ever changed the bulb in Mrs. Bryant's front-porch light? He'd looked up the last time he was there, through the web of spider silk and mummified insects to the dead bulb. He didn't think it was safe for an old woman not to have a well-lit porch. Then again, she probably rarely opened her locked front door to anyone. Plus, with no electricity, her front room must be as dark as a cave. The lilacs, the stupid lilacs. She'd been hinting for him to trim them for weeks and he'd been playing dumb, refusing to be cajoled into it but sitting and talking and accepting a twenty anyway. For the first time he began to worry about her, sitting in that gloomy house with no sunlight getting through. He'd never really thought of her in terms of worry. She loomed in his consciousness as a worthy adversary.

Hal followed Will inside the house, simply because he wasn't stopped. He was curious to see where Greta had lived before she moved in with them. The front room was a formal living room, done in pale colors. He saw a little grid of four circular depressions in the carpet next to the window where a pale-green silk ottoman sat, looking strange without Greta's beloved chair. At the co-op, she always managed to sit in it before anyone else could get to it. Hal had tried it out a few times and remained nonplussed. It was a chair. A perfectly comfortable, expensive chair with no ottoman.

Will set his briefcase down on the floor and proceeded down the hall. Hal heard a faucet run and the sound of drinking. Will must have been desperately thirsty all morning. He still wasn't in any shape to realize Hal didn't even belong here. Hal was about to call out a good-bye and leave the keys when he glanced out at the car and paused.

There was a muffled thump in the kitchen, then the hiss of a pop-top can. Hal debated going to see if it was a beer or a soda. What business was it of his? He stood there for a second, then put the keys in his pocket again and went down the hallway. He passed photos of Greta and a thinner, livelier-looking Will, all thick dark hair and pale eyes made silvery by the black-and-white film.

The kitchen was lit by bright sun. Will was at the table, two cans of seltzer before him. One appeared empty; the other he was downing with his head tipped back.

"I thought maybe you'd cracked open a beer," Hal said. He didn't really know how to do an intervention. Were there Alcoholics Anonymous meetings at this time of day?

Will sat back in his chair and stared at him. It appeared to be hitting him now that Hal had no reason to be there, certainly no reason to care if he had opened a beer or a seltzer. "Well," Will said, "thanks for the ride in my car."

Hal said nothing for a moment. "Can I call someone for you? Maybe you know some people from AA you should be in touch with. I could drop you at a meeting."

"Have you ever been to an AA meeting?" Will asked. He got up, opened yet another can of seltzer, thought better of it, and grabbed two before returning to the table.

"No," said Hal. He sat down across from Will. "I thought about going to an open one once or twice, sort of as research."

"Why would you need to do research?" Will's expression had focused on him carefully for a second, and Hal realized Will might be suspecting a fellow alcoholic.

It was almost with regret that he said, "For my job. Some of the people I work with are in twelve-step programs. I thought I could find out what they're about."

"Well," Will drawled, "I'm sure we can find you one. You must need a twelve-step program for something. Try this: What's the thing you most enjoy, and that no one wants to let you do anymore?"

"Do you enjoy it?" Hal asked.

Will shrugged, a loose-muscled lurch that spilled a little seltzer. "Everyone enjoys a drink."

Hal took a paper napkin from a basket and set it on the spill.

"It looks like fun," he said conversationally. He had come to hate this man just on the drive over, for his deadness, for the way he could radiate despair without admitting it. Yet nevertheless Hal had tried to help, and this was what he got. Hal was reminded of the people who, when you gave them a bag of dried garbanzos, looked at you as if you had handed them sand. The filthy secret in Hal's work was that at times you hated the people you helped. Sometimes you came so close to saying, as they scorned your offering, *I'm sorry, had you already bought lobster?* Hal would never say such a thing to the people Swiff worked with. He might think it, but he would never say it. Which was why it felt briefly satisfying to say such things to Will.

Hal took the other can of seltzer and opened it. "I mean, it looked like fun at my house. You know, my house. Where your wife lives." As soon as he said it, he felt a little thrill of fear and shame and exhilaration. Will must bring this out in people, but still Hal wished almost immediately to take it back.

Will stared at him, his mouth slightly open and his eyes hooded. Then he chuckled thickly, apparently to himself, and shook his head. "Everything's fine," he told Hal infuriatingly. "It's all good. You don't have to be here, Greta doesn't have to be here, it's fine."

Hal imagined throwing his can of seltzer at Will, not really overhanding it at his face, just a flip, something to shake him up. The two men looked at each other, and as Hal counted to three, he realized the answer was simple. Will was right. He had no reason to be here. He pushed his chair out from the table.

"So what do you do again?" Will said. Hal paused. Will wasn't looking at him, just gazing out the window toward a maple tree.

"I give people food," Hal said.

Will nodded. He seemed about to say something of interest but added only, "Oh."

"Yeah," Hal sighed. "What do you do?"

"I give people advice," Will said. "Taxes, law, that kind of thing."

"You're a lawyer?" Hal ventured.

"Sure," Will said, as if Hal had just offered him the chance to try it.

They sat in silence. Hal was thinking about getting up again when Will said, "Those pancakes you made were good. You ever eat them with jam? My grandmother served them with raspberry jam."

During this statement Will observed Hal with a startling intensity. Hal looked back uncomfortably. Was this an obscure cry for help? Maybe pancakes held a deeper meaning. Finally he registered from the silence that Will had exhausted himself on this topic.

"I make them on weekends a lot," Hal said. "Karin's big into cornmeal and blueberry pancakes."

"Greta likes buckwheat."

"I'll try them next," Hal said.

"You have to start them the day before or something. Greta always likes shit you have to work for twice as hard."

Hal rubbed his eyes. "Well," he said. "I guess I should go. I have to see a friend."

"On a workday?" Will said.

Hal looked at him, surprised to realize Will was more alert than he might have chosen to appear. "She's really old," Hal said. "She doesn't work, I mean. I'm not really scheduled to go but her house needs some work and it's been nagging me. Plus she's pretty isolated and I'm worried how she's getting along without power. I thought I'd swing by."

Here he may have been feeling a little proud, a little smug. It was true he wanted to look in on Mrs. Bryant, but now he was also itching to get that place fully cleaned and neatened. All week he'd kept thinking about the dust on the upper fixtures only he was tall enough to see, the yard that could so easily be reined in.

Now something else occurred to him. How much food would be coming her way? How much did she have at home? Mrs. Bryant was no self-sufficient island like Hal's father, capable of shooting and catching and growing what was needed. "I want to bring her a few groceries, too," he added.

And maybe he was trying to let Will know he was a helpful person, in case Will needed him. But so far Will, though clearly doing badly, wasn't reaching out for help. And maybe Will wasn't really so bad off: he had a house, he had some money. This could be just one bender. Maybe Will and Mrs. Bryant had the right idea. Just do for oneself and forget the rest of the world.

"You're kind of an all-around good guy," Will said. "Do you spend all your time showing up, driving drunks places, and then visiting shut-ins and feeling good about it?"

"I wouldn't call her a shut-in so much as a loner," Hal said. "Actually, you might have a lot in common." He savored a brief vision of the three of them, relaxing around Mrs. Bryant's coffee table and comparing notes on the people they were all better off without.

"Fine," Will said, draining off the rest of his seltzer. "I'll come along. Let me shower real quick."

Will suggested they bring a snack instead of groceries. "You can't just show up at someone's house with a bag of groceries," he said. "It's insulting. It's like you think she can't take care of herself."

"She can't," Hal argued.

Will sighed deeply. "Well, okay. But I think it's more polite to bring a snack, too, like a regular social visit. We can get her some muffins or something."

"I don't know if she likes those," Hal said. He was driving Will's car again, getting used to the tight clutch and smoothing out the braking. He was used to cars you had to pummel into submission; this one leaped to respond like a 1950s secretary. Even better, it wasn't Hal's gasoline. He had no intention of offering gas money, either. Will, he felt certain, could afford it.

Will snorted. "Everyone likes muffins." His hair was still wet. He'd dressed in dark gray pants, and a white cotton button down. He looked as if he should be popping out for flowers before a dinner party. Hal pulled up to a grocery store.

Will was already half out of the car. "Anyway, you just park and I'll go in and stock up. I know what the basics are. No. Wait here, it's fine."

He was suddenly quite chipper. Hal watched Will walk through the store's automatic doors, which were held open by two concrete blocks. He adjusted his seat and flipped around the radio to see if anyone was broadcasting. They were, though no one had anything more intelligent to say about the situation than what the skimpy paper had held that morning. The heat caused power lines to sag. Too much air-conditioning or maybe not enough. None of it really made sense, and the officials got off the air as fast as possible, sensing that people were realizing it. Toward the end of the report the back car door swung open and Will deposited two bags on the backseat. He got into the front seat, still holding a third.

"Okay," Will said, settling in. "Let's go see this person you supposedly enjoy visiting so much on your day off."

"It's not really my day off," Hal said. "I'm just not there."

"Even I called my office," Will said. "They're going to can me soon anyway but I did call. They'll let you slide if you just don't show?"

"I don't know," Hal snapped. He didn't want to think about it. Who knew what was going to happen? Pretty soon they wouldn't have any food to distribute anyway. He'd better get serious about planting the garden. "They might let me slide," he said after a moment. "I don't know how much help I could be to them today, anyway. It's kind of *Titanic* over there right now."

Will glanced at him. "Too pragmatic to go down with it, huh," he said.

Hal frowned. "No," he said. "Not that at all. I'm just trying to address a problem I can actually solve." Before Will could answer, he said, "So how much do I owe? What'd you buy?" Hal heard his tone becoming a little lofty but he couldn't help it.

"Don't worry about it. Flour, sugar, oatmeal, powdered milk since it won't go bad, olive oil, same reason, bread. Some broccoli and onions and a lemon. Apples and cheese for a snack. A manners snack."

Hal nodded. Will had done a better job than he'd expected. "Anything else?"

Will watched him for a long time. Hal kept his eyes on the road. "Why do you think I bought anything else?"

Hal laughed and shook his head. "Jesus, I'm not your wife," he said. "Who knows you're a drunk anyway, obviously. Don't insult me with the same crap, okay?"

Will didn't respond. He stared at Hal a little while longer and then turned toward the windshield again. He shifted the grocery bag on his lap. They drove the rest of the way without speaking.

"Well, well, well," said Mrs. Bryant. "Your pals aren't supposed to be here for a few hours, you know." She eyed Will closely. "New recruit? What's in the bags?"

Will held out a hand to her. Mrs. Bryant pretended not to notice.

"It's a snack," said Hal. "And a few things to get you through the blackout. I just wanted to be sure you were getting along okay without electricity. But you can't just show up without a little something." Out of the corner of his eye he saw Will smile to himself.

"Well, that's gracious of you, Hal. Let me know how much I owe you, and tell your friend to go fix it up. There's some light in the kitchen from the window but try not to cut off a finger." Mrs. Bryant waved a hand in the direction of the kitchen. Will went off with his grocery bag and Hal seated himself on the horsehair couch. The two of them sat in the dimness and listened to opening drawers and cupboards. Hal had no intention of telling Mrs. Bryant how much the groceries had been, but he liked it that she made the gesture. He found it dignified.

"How are you today?" Hal asked finally. "We had a good talk last week."

"One of your failings, Hal, is your need for acknowledgment at every turn. I know you stayed longer than anticipated. It was very nice of you. Let's not sit here in this black little room where sunlight dares not tread and keep jawing about it."

"I got a pretty serious reprimand for that," Hal told her. He was trying not to take the bait about the lilac but enjoying the chance to engage in some sparring. "If I'm going to get canned for something, I *want* acknowledgment."

She waved a hand. Today, despite the heat, she wore stretchy black pants and a massive powder-blue sweater with a cowl neck like a burka. "Oh, I can barely see you anyway. Your friend works for the do-gooders, too?"

"No," Hal said. In the kitchen he heard the sound of a knife cutting something and striking a surface. "He knows my roommate Greta. He came over last night to check on her and wasn't feeling well, so he stayed. I drove him home, and I don't know . . . He wanted to meet you."

"He knows one of your girls?" she said. "Romantically, I would wager. Interesting. I bet you're keeping an eye on him then." She overrode his protest. "He looks semi-healthy to me," she said. "Smells like a drunk, but looks functional enough."

"Does he?" Hal asked softly. "You can smell it? I think he bought something at the store on the way over here."

Will came back into the living room, carrying a plate of sliced dark bread, apples, and cheese. He set this down on the coffee table, moving aside a photo of Mr. Bryant, and returned to the kitchen for plates, which he then doled out to each of them.

Mrs. Bryant eyed her empty plate.

Will smiled at her. He wasn't going to fill her plate, Hal saw, though it was clear she expected him to. Hal took a brief liking to him.

"Well, Will," Mrs. Bryant said. "I gather you're something of a drunk."

Will took a small bite of apple. "What makes you say that?" he asked calmly.

"You smell like it," she said. "It's morning, and I can smell it from here."

Will shrugged, chewing his apple. "I'm fine," he said.

"I ask because I am not one of those people who sits around asking others to lie to them to make me more comfortable. Hal tells me you probably bought something at the store. Why don't you just drink it?"

"I don't want to," Will said. He had finished his slice of apple and was now sitting back against the couch next to Hal, watching Mrs. Bryant. That blank face was what was most infuriating. You felt as if you could hit him and Will would do nothing. He seemed to shut down and shrink into himself, as blank and sulky as a child.

"Hand me a slice of bread, Hal," Mrs. Bryant said. Then, turning back to Will, "I believe you don't want to. But you will."

"Hey," Hal protested, leaning forward on the couch. The folly of the whole visit had presented itself all at once.

"I'm being frank," she said, chewing. "You know I'm always frank. In the east we didn't sit around jabbering about how things were fine if they weren't. You either say something or you don't speak at all. Midwesterners have such a strain of *sap* through them." Her mouth, its fine drawstring lines radiating outward, was an odd grapefruit pink. The pouches beneath her eyes gave her stare a baleful power.

"I'm sure you're used to people begging you not to drink and making all sorts of promises if you'll stop," she went on. "It matters not a whit to me if you drink. But I don't have a house in which people dash off and guzzle in the bathrooms and kitchens. If you're going to drink you'll do it in a civilized manner."

"You don't know me," Will said. "You know nothing about me."

"No," she agreed, sounding fairly cheery. "Nevertheless, you do remind me of my husband, Mr. Bryant. Strong-willed. He looked like a bit of a sap, that was the humorous part. But he never gave an inch. Not one God-fearing inch." She chuckled proudly.

Will gave a polite smile.

"I bet you were never bored," he said.

Mrs. Bryant chewed her lip thoughtfully, nodding toward the dusty window. Was she about to tell them one of those bits of homespun wisdom and fond memory that was really pure domestic abuse? This was a pitfall with the elderly, who were wont to tell you stories of grandmothers who whipped them horrifically for sneezing in church or going near the old well. They all seemed to have lived long enough that their stories of striped hides and paddlings struck them now as amusing, as toughening and memorable, and they never realized that to Hal they sounded like the last members of a particularly vicious tribe.

"Well," she began, "you can't go hoping marriage isn't boring." She looked sharply at both of them. She seemed to enjoy catching people in moments of unrealistic optimism. This was not one of them; Hal assumed marriage could not be anything but monotonous. "Because it is boring. Of course it is! Same person, day in, day out! Same foibles, same jokes, same everything! But every once in a while you'd have a good knock-down, drag-out, and learn something new about a man. Yes, you did." She selected a piece of cheese and sat back in her chair, nodding.

Hal was uncomfortable discussing marriage with Will here. He both wanted to know about him and Greta and feared hearing any details. Marriage was such a private thing. He didn't want to know anything unsavory or pitiable about Greta. He liked her prickly dignity. "How so?" he finally asked, keeping his voice neutral.

"Oh, it's not for young men like you, I suppose," she said. "Not that 'young' is what it used to be. By the time I was your age, Mr. Bryant and I had been married for ten years and had already moved out here from New Hampshire. Anyway, I can tell you that when Mr. Bryant decided he didn't want to buy his own farm after all, wanted in fact to quit the job he had on Snedgar's dairy farm, I was simply livid, livid as can be. He had dragged me out here to nowhere, away from our people back east, and we still barely knew a soul except for the church ladies who liked to show up and nose around.

"I remember he came home late one night, smelling of manure, of course, and he chooses that moment to say he might have made a mistake. He was thinking about a factory job, he says. A nice steady thing.

"And, of course, in most ways a factory job was better. That wasn't the point. Mr. Bryant had bent my ear for months, before we even were married, about this great nation and becoming what you wanted and the freedom of being one's own boss. I felt that to have bored a girl silly for so long with all this, and then to give up so quickly, was bad form.

"And I told him so. Oh, I told him everything I thought. It may surprise you to hear that I thought of myself as a girl who should have been more straightforward at times, you know. I bottled things up, I always felt, though others didn't agree. Well, they didn't know. You have to realize, too, that Mr. Bryant was a few years younger than I was. It was a bit of scandal in Hanover, where we came from. I just knew they'd be saying I'd dragged him out and bet all wrong, bet on the wrong horse. They thought I pushed him around a bit, you see, which I did not. I come from women who know their minds, that's all."

Hal thought, rather proudly, that he could say much the same thing. His sisters were both capable and unflappable, his mother had grown more firm and direct the older she became. His housemates, too, come to think of it. He loved a capable woman— here he thought of Andrea, wondering suddenly if she had seen any news about their blackout and wondered how he was doing. What had Andrea done during the East Coast blackouts of the last few years? She'd probably served dinner to her neighbors before her food went bad, Hal thought, ashamed. Even worse, it occurred to him that at the time he'd read about those power outages, Hal hadn't even thought of Andrea, after all that time together. Everything fell away.

"And it may have been that I went a bit far. A bit. I informed Mr. Bryant of a few of his habits I wasn't fond of, and I let him know that others back home had commented on the same. I had worked myself into a fair lather, and I was finishing dinner and putting it on the table—it was salmon loaf; I used to put a touch of pickle in it to make it mine—and Mr. Bryant was sitting at the table the whole time, just watching me get upset. And finally I said, 'You lack imagination, pure and simple, James Bryant. You don't have that spark you wanted me to think you had.'

"Mr. Bryant had hardly said a word till then, but that stirred him. He was up and at me like a flash—had my wrist up behind my back and was right there up against me, pressing me to the counter. I can smell him still, those coveralls he wore. His breath, too. He'd just taken a drink of beer, and I think I even smelled the beans and cornbread they'd served him at the farm. And he told me I would think twice before speaking to him that way."

"It's a shock," Will said suddenly. "Seeing someone that way. It's like another face." Hal looked over at him. Will glanced at him and looked away, reaching for an apple slice.

Mrs. Bryant was nodding. "You're not wrong," she said. "I certainly didn't see it coming. He reminded me that I had him and only him out here, and he'd like to know how I planned to get back to Hanover if I were so inclined. Because I could go.

"He, of course, was assuming I wouldn't go. He was so upset he forgot I knew about the passbook account he had to save up for that farm he was never going to buy anyway. He hid the passbook in his drawer with his razors and things, underneath a little shelf paper, as if I wouldn't find it. Men are simple at times, Hal. I hope you never allow yourself to be so simple.

"Well, I apologized and was even rather sincere about it, since I did feel bad for saying he lacked imagination. It was true but you have to handle truth judiciously in marriage. And we sat down and ate our dinner and kissed good night and went to bed. And as soon as he was gone the next morning I got the passbook and talked them into letting me withdraw the money at the bank—it was in his name. I had begun to see that Mr. Bryant was not a trusting man. But I had my identification and even my marriage certificate. All that turned out not to be necessary with the account number and such. And I withdrew seven thousand four hundred thirty-nine dollars. I left exactly five dollars in that account."

She smiled and took the last bite of cheese. Hal was silent, but Will said, "So you won." The other two turned to look at him, and Will shrugged and said, "What? She did, and he deserved it. What'd you do with it? Did you go back to Hanover?"

She chuckled and shook her head. "I was gone for a time. I haven't told anyone ever where I was then, but all you need to know, and certainly all Mr. Bryant needed to know, is that I was gone for three months and so was his money." She smiled and shook her head. "Gone to him, anyway. For all you know, you two, I still have it somewhere, simply on principle."

Hal turned this over. Seven thousand dollars over roughly fifty years. He glanced covertly around the room, as if he'd detect a door in the wall or a little treasure chest. He stopped himself; of course he did. That wasn't why they were here.

"I came back eventually. I remember being a little nervous coming up the driveway but feeling good, too. He hadn't expected me to do any of that, and that's the key in this life, you two. People think less of you than you think they do."

She had finished her cheese. Hal watched her close her eyes briefly as if in pure satisfaction at a good story, a good snack. Next to him Will was glancing back toward the kitchen as if he had forgotten something and was shifting uncomfortably.

Hal was trying to picture a young Mrs. Bryant, with sixties bouffant and ballet shoes. "How much longer were you married?" he finally asked. He was beginning to think he had just heard of the youthful marriage before the long-lasting one, despite the names—perhaps there had been a Bryant brother.

"Another thirty years or so. Till Mr. Bryant had his coronary in 1991." She opened her eyes.

"Ah. So you did come back," Will said. "You were happy together in the end, after everything."

"Well, that was what people did then. 'Happy' is a strong word, Will." She paused, then said, "I hear you know Hal's girl Greta."

Will looked genuinely startled; in spite of his embarrassment, Hal found Will's response—any kind of response at all—deeply satisfying. "She's my wife," Will said softly.

"Ah," said Mrs. Bryant, as though it were all clear now. "In my day men in your position didn't try to be friends. They'd simply try to kill one another. It was quite straightforward."

"We're not in any position," Hal said. "Greta's just my housemate. You're way off base."

"I will have to meet this girl," Mrs. Bryant said. "She must be quite a looker. No children?" Absurdly, both men shook their heads. "Probably just as well.

"Now, Hal," she said, all business again, "I can't see a thing in here. I always thought it was old age but now that you've pointed it out I suspect it's that old lilac blocking everything. And with this blackout it's very hazardous." She raised one hand, palm up. "I know you've been avoiding the question of the lilacs. And I thought you were just being difficult, Hal, but I think I may have been inconsiderate, not to realize you may be worried about your landscaping skills. It doesn't sound like you really grew up working in the yard the way Mr. Bryant did. Things have changed, no doubt. Your parents probably sent you off to the library instead of out to the yard with a mower, am I right? Different times."

Hal met her gaze, which seemed benign, if you weren't looking closely. Their eyes were locked, and Hal began to see the familiar steely glint in hers. He could accomplish that task handily. The light would have a tremendous effect on the house, and Will would see that his wife now lived with a perfectly acceptable man. Mrs. Bryant was a woman alone—a spunky, independent, strong-willed woman who had made her fearless way through life. The three of them were like sailors in a rowboat, trading tales while they waited for the final squall.

Next to him, Will reached for a slice of apple, his hand showing the tiniest tremor, and as Hal looked at that hand, its uncertain palsy and its silver wedding ring, Hal realized that in this string of adjectives—spunky, strong-willed—he'd been thinking of Greta.

Hal flushed deeply, hoping Will had not somehow read his expression.

Mrs. Bryant saved him by clapping her palms down on her knees and lifting a hand, knotted with blue veins and swollen joints, in Hal's direction. A brittle straw of light cut its way into the living room, illuminating the hand rather terribly: the yellow ridged fingernails, the looseness of the knobby skin. Hal felt a wave of generalized panic; his retirement savings were never what they should be. He didn't even own a house he could sell when he got old.

"Help me up, Hal," she commanded.

"I need to get to work on that lilac," he said.

"In a minute."

He took her by the wrist, the soft skin sliding over her flesh and the bones eerily present as he pulled her up. That revelation of the inner workings of the body—this was the brutal nature of old people. Everything inside them announced itself: digestion, rotting muscle, the synapses sizzling fruitlessly in the dark. Hal held her elbow and walked her to the bathroom, at the door of which she swatted him efficiently away.

"I can do that myself," she said. "My niece's loutish husband installed some bars in the walls, for God's sake. Still, you did bring those groceries, which was very simpatico of you. Pay yourself back with a twenty from the cabinet, Hal. Just one, please." Hal hoped Will hadn't heard that, and he was about to refuse at least for form's sake, but then he didn't. Frankly Hal was tired now. A twenty wasn't so much. It was hardly soul-imperiling. He nodded and thanked her.

Hal turned toward the living room but Mrs. Bryant's fingers clamped down on his arm. "Give him a second," she said. She shook her head and grasped the doorjamb as she took a step into the bathroom, which was tiled with aging coral squares in need of a grout. "That's the very sad thing about drunks. That shame they feel. Just give him a moment to do whatever he needs to."

CHAPTER NINE

Karin's shoes were crusted with mud. The muscles in her legs had begun to burn. The Rothbergers' farm seemed enormous, spread out like a quilt over the whole valley. She and Elaine had been strolling for an hour, up and down the hills, stopping to meet the herds of livestock. Carl trotted along next to them, unless they passed a herd, in which case he galloped off in the direction of the livestock, ran a few rings around them to satisfy himself that they were in order, then returned.

Elaine had been rather quiet since they'd left the henhouse a few minutes earlier. It was a compact little wooden structure with several brown and white chickens wandering the fenced yard and one rooster keeping order, a lumpy scarlet comb flopping over one eye. Elaine had pointed out a few chickens with dark navy feet.

"You know those fancy French chickens?" she'd said.

"We're going to try a few. There's an Asian black chicken, too, that's supposed to be tasty. Poor feathered bastards. I thought maybe I could find a market in the restaurants for it."

Inside the henhouse they had both paused, blinking to adjust to the shade. Elaine had moved from nest to nest, a lined flat basket slung over one arm. Karin followed close behind. It was a disappointing yield, a couple runty mottled eggs. One seemed to have a few extra layers of shell at one end, like a callus. Elaine stood still for several seconds, her thumb stroking the misshapen shell.

"Not as many as you hoped?" Karin said. She knew nothing about chickens. Maybe they laid eggs later in the day. It was difficult to feel much worry out here, and she was congratulating herself for coming out to the farm and getting away from everything else. By now Madison must be back to normal, anyway. That gas station had simply been sold. The traffic lights would be blinking rhythmically again, her couch would be empty of husbands, all would be well.

"No . . . ," Elaine murmured, "not really." She drew a breath as if to speak, then shook her head. She put the eggs back in the nests, set the basket by the door. Karin thought she could feel the chickens observing them as they left the yard.

Neither of them spoke further about the eggs. Karin didn't want Elaine to fear she would write about whatever failures were gripping that portion of the operation. She was always reluctant to discuss any problem unless the affected person brought it up. When she was a teenager her parents had been the sort who would let her sob in her room for an hour before they called her to dinner, which would then be her favorite dish. They'd tried, in their way, even if they were generally exhausted by unemployment or the kind of draining work they managed to obtain. Her mother still thought tuna casserole was her favorite dish; she made it the three or four times a year Karin visited.

Karin followed Elaine toward the milking parlor. Elaine was saying, "Now, normally, obviously, our milking is automated. We have this new system and it's kind of beautiful how well it works. We had to get a grant to pay for it." She looked at Karin with a mischievous light in her eye. "But when we talked the other day you said you'd never really milked by hand before, so I thought we'd bring in one of the cows and I'll show you how. Sound fun?"

"Sadly, yes," Karin said.

Elaine laughed. She glanced at her watch, a weighty disc strapped on cracked brown leather. "Great. I actually don't think you'll find it overly fascinating, but it's worth seeing how it's done. You can't be a dairy reporter without knowing about milking, right? We can milk, check on the beehives if you want, and hit the cheese caves. Save the best for last. You're welcome to stay for a late lunch. I won't serve that awful cheese I was working on."

"Great," said Karin. "I've never really seen a beehive."

"They're not as picturesque as you think they'll be," said Elaine. "I was really disappointed when my husband first brought these home. I was imagining those rounded things, you know? But the professional ones are like boxes with frames inside them. You'll see."

Karin began to fantasize about lunch with homemade bread and freshly churned butter, a rhubarb crisp to finish. It was the sort of meal they ought to have more of at home, cooked by more than just Karin. Last week Karin had made an Italian torta filled with Swiss chard, potato, egg, and feta. She'd rolled out her own pasta sheets with local eggs for lasagna with fresh tomatoes and basil. And the other two certainly seemed to enjoy it, but when their turns rolled around Hal made the hundredth fritatta of that spring and Greta served an indifferent veggie chili to which, inexplicably, she had added nutmeg.

Yet Hal seemed to regard Greta's cooking as some exciting

new venture. If Karin dared to enjoy the occasional hanger steak, Hal hovered around opening windows and pointedly asked her to scrub the pan well. But when Greta sautéed a skirt steak for fajitas (she'd made black beans for Hal), the second the fragrance hit the living room, Hal's head had popped up like a gopher's. He'd stood just behind Greta as she turned the meat, inquisitive and eager and craning his neck to peer over her shoulder. "It smells pretty great," he'd admitted. "And I haven't been tempted in *years*." It was only a skirt steak, Karin had wanted to tell him. The whole world ate them.

Karin was looking for an opportunity to tell Elaine about the whole sustainable core of their co-op, but she wasn't sure why. She could invite her to a dinner, to host a tasting of local cheeses. She could trot her out at a school visit. Or maybe Karin simply wanted to establish that rapport with her, let Elaine know that Karin, too, could live this way, so low to the ground and to real growing things. Next to Francine, next to people in her hometown, Karin was a mild iconoclast for living in a co-op, but here, among an entire family who lived and worked and *produced* together, she was just a poseur.

"I wish I'd grown up here," Karin said. "It's so pretty. Kids must love it." The moment she spoke, she regretted it. She'd forgotten about Elaine's dead husband.

"I loved coming here when I was growing up," was all Elaine replied.

Elaine puffed slightly as they rounded a hill. They both stopped as they crested the rise, and Karin took another sharp breath at the view of the land, as if to try and absorb the sight of the patches of emerald leaves, the rushing water churning over rocks in a stream that threaded through the bottom of the valley before them. Elaine had pointed out three lakes already, adding that there were two more nearby. Now, as they stood and surveyed the valley, Carl darted forward. He was moving toward a figure approaching them and leading a cow behind him, a man with a baseball cap shielding his face. Elaine's hands moved to rest on her hips.

Karin decided this must be Kenneth. As he neared them she saw that he was not much taller than Elaine, but about Karin's own height. His dark hair was cropped close beneath his red cap, but seemed to be the same fuzzy curls as his sister's. His eyes were hooded and dark. The lines that fanned out at the corners were white-skinned inside the grooves. Next to him the cow's hipbones undulated beneath its skin, rising and falling hypnotically.

"The others are still in the pasture," he said, coming to a stop. "We milked them hours ago. But Angie calved pretty late in the season and she's been milking like a champ, so you should still get something. Actually," he peered at her udder, which looked rather warm and full to Karin, "maybe more than I thought. She's really producing these days. She's pretty docile, too. You shouldn't have a problem. You're Karin Phillips, obviously." It was not a question. He extended a grease-streaked hand and Karin shook it. His skin was uncomfortably warm to the touch.

"Good memory," she said.

He shrugged. "We're in the industry now, so I read your articles. Hannah Koch is a good friend of our family."

Karin mentally scanned through her recent columns, trying to recall what she'd written about Hannah. "Oh, Fig Tree," she said. "They do those phenomenal little crottins. I like them a lot. I thought you were going to be angry about something."

He nodded, smiling. "Nah, I was just curious what you thought of her. Hard to tell from your paper."

Karin wiped her hands on her jeans. The cow lowered its head and took a mouthful of grass. "Well, we have to be objective, unless it's an editorial. I can't really say whose work I love the most or don't think much of. Even if I want to."

He nodded. "Fair enough."

Elaine took off her jean jacket and tied it around her waist. "Jesus, Kenneth, quit grilling her." She turned to Karin. "Don't take him seriously."

"Hey, Elaine, how's that new beer cheese going?"

"It has real potential," Karin heard herself say. Elaine and Kenneth both turned to her in surprise. Beside one another their resemblance was suddenly strong. Karin realized she had over-reacted. After life with Hal, who took a brotherly pleasure in needling people, she ought to be better at handling this. She frowned. Actually, it had been awhile since Hal had teased her, grinning and daring her to stop him. Lately he seemed more formal, kinder, as if he suspected her feelings might be hurt. But he sometimes became almost goofy with Greta, jostling her with an elbow, trying to rile her into debate.

"It really doesn't," said Elaine. "Kenneth's an annoying little brother but he's right."

"The *idea* has great potential," Karin said. "Marketing, regional, tasty." She listened to herself stringing random words together.

"Of course it does," he said. "Elaine's going to be good at this. We'll figure it out."

Karin nodded, jotting it down on her notepad.

"Why don't you take her?" Kenneth said. "Head on in."

Elaine opened the barn door and the scent of hay and manure engulfed them; it smelled somehow warm, brown, and gold all at once. The barn was not the old-fashioned wooden structure she'd imagined, but long and clean and white, the sun coming through its roof, which must have been some durable plastic designed to let in light. Twenty pens were marked off by metal rails, the floor of each strewn with hay.

Elaine led in the cow, and as she did Karin saw that the udder was more swollen than she'd thought. The udder seemed all too human, so close to a breast Karin wasn't sure she would even try to touch it. "Ready to milk?" Elaine said. "I have to remind myself how."

Before them the barn stretched out, huge, quiet, and rich with scents. Elaine backed the cow into a corner against the rails and tied her securely to one.

"I'm pretty sure she won't kick you," she said. "Still, keep an eye out for that back hoof. Maybe I should tie it up, for safety's sake."

"Sure," Karin said faintly. She hadn't considered kicking.

"But you know," Elaine went on, roping the cow's leg, "she'll be so glad to have this big old udder relieved that I can't see how she'd mind. Now. We clean it first—nothing as important in a dairy as cleanliness. You wrap your hand around the teat and you squeeze—you're not rubbing and chafing, you know. Just a gentle squeeze, to mimic the motion of a calf's mouth." She swung a stool and a clean metal bucket before Karin.

Milking: the shocking phallic warmth of the teats, that smooth skin, lumped here and there with pink warts and fuzzy with white hair. As her fingers curled around the organ, Karin couldn't suppress the sensation that she was doing something obscene and private, something bestial. Elaine stood and watched.

Eventually Elaine said, "Jesus, this would take forever. Thank God we don't do it this way."

Karin blushed. "I know," she said. "I just wanted to see what it was like. If the blackouts hit you guys you'll need to know, too, right?" She meant it as a joke but Elaine looked worried, turning away from her and saying nothing.

Karin squeezed the teat, its heated flesh turgid and substantial in her hand as the milk streamed into the bottom of the bucket. Karin thought about breasts and udders, about nursing, about stealing fluid from an animal. It was all so freakish. Who the hell had thought this up? Yet she wrapped her hand around the teat of an unfazed cow and pinged away, the sound of the milk sizzling against the tin.

Her leg brushed against the half-full bucket, finding its surface startlingly warm. How had she never before realized what she was writing about, what all these people were doing? Living among the animals, encouraging the growth of liquid inside them, squeezing it out, and mashing and aging it into a cake. It was repulsive; it was genius. She felt a little sick, a little hungry, a little enamored of the whole enterprise. Humans were insane, and maybe wonderful, Karin thought wildly. She gave a delighted, frantic little laugh. Next to her, Elaine started to chuckle.

"I know!" Elaine said. Milk zinged on metal, the cow shifted her massive weight on her hooves. "What the fuck are we all doing? I worked with *boxes*."

The path down to the beehives went past a small shed. Carl ran up ahead of them and seated himself outside the door. Elaine laughed. "He knows the drill," she said, scruffing up his ears and laying a kiss on the dog's head. Inside the shed, a beige jumpsuit of heavy canvas hung from a nail next to several hats. They'd left Kenneth to untie the cow and take her back to pasture. Both of them were still a little punchy. Karin had bounded down the trail, barely able to stop herself from running. Up here the early summer heat was gentle and encompassing, a velvety warmth. She didn't think she would ever get tired.

"You have on jeans," Elaine said thoughtfully. "You probably don't need the whole suit, plus it's hot. Then again, if you get stung, it's on me." She looked Karin over apologetically. "You'll wear the suit, right?"

"Sure," Karin said. "I don't mind."

Elaine nodded. "Be careful anyway," she said. "The suit's protection but they can technically get through it if they really want to; it just helps. This is right in the middle of their work year. I'll get the smoker."

The two of them tucked their hair into the hats, which were essentially cloth helmets with mesh netting across the face and weighted edges to let the barrier lay flat against the shoulders and chest. The suits were heavy, tough cotton and nylon. Karin climbed into the one Elaine gave her—she suspected it might have been the husband's—the extra fabric pooling around her ankles. The gloves were heavy leather and slightly too large in the fingers. They came up to her elbows. She was sweating heavily, her breath uncomfortably present behind the screen. Elaine reappeared from the shed with the smoker, which was an odd-looking contraption similar to a bellows grafted onto a metal pitcher. The top was open and she was shoving shredded paper into the can. Then she closed it, held up a pack of matches and a handful of wood chips to show Karin she was prepared, and said, "Okay, here we go."

She cast a smile at Karin as she started down the path, her teeth flashing behind the gray mesh mask. "It's been so fun having you here," she said suddenly. "I think I need to get more people out here or something. It seems special to everybody else but sometimes it just feels like a grind. Anyway, I know you probably didn't plan to spend the whole day looking at every possible aspect of this operation but it's nice of you to show the interest."

Karin jogged to catch up. Her suit rose and settled awkwardly over her body, sweat dripping into her eyes. "I guess I didn't plan to," she admitted. "But I'm used to seeing a lot of very industrialized places, you know. This is a pleasure. I'm just being selfish."

"You do seem selfish," Elaine said, deadpan. "All your helping and interest. City people."

Karin laughed. "Do you think of yourself as a country person now? Am I a city person?"

"More than I am," Elaine said. They rounded a bend in the trees and suddenly a field was before them, a wide expanse of tall grasses, edged by trees in full leaf. "You should have seen it even a month ago. All the flowers. This is the clover field, which means for the most part the honey's clear and light and sweet. The hives are smack in the middle of the field. Hard to see them from here." She gestured to the trees at one edge of the field. "Those are chestnut and acacia. The bees hit them, too. I want to put a hive or two within the trees to compare. It's supposed to be darker and richer that way, or so I'm told. This is only my second year."

"So, your honey's kind of a blend," said Karin.

"Sure. I don't know how reliably you could isolate it. I mean, people do, of course, but your bees are still going to range around three miles. It's more that you go for the dominant characteristic by sticking them in citrus groves, or clover fields, or chestnut groves, or whatever. Anyway, I don't want to get into some big artisanal varietal honey-for-twenty-dollars thing." She shook her head. "I should, the money would be good. But I just like the beekeeping and the honey. We sell it at the market, but I'm a little selfish with it. It's like the cheese; it's such a weird little gift. And it's really beautiful, you know. When you hold it up to the light. It seems so biblical and constant."

She chuckled, rolled her eyes in Karin's direction, as if to say to ignore her, and then began to walk into the field to where the hives were, brushing the tall stems out of her way. Karin peered before them, looking for the boxes Elaine had described. The only sound in the field was the crunch of their footsteps, the snap of the occasional stem, and the leaves rushing back into place behind them. Karin tried not to breathe too loudly, listening for the buzz of the hives. After a minute or so, she could see the hives about thirty feet away, three large pale blue boxes among the grasses.

Elaine stopped to light the smoker. Karin crouched down for a moment while she waited, stretching out her stiff muscles. Elaine lit the kindling with a match poked into the smoker, waiting for it to take the flame before she added the wood chips. While they waited, Elaine peered around the field, eyebrows drawn together. Karin wasn't sure what she was looking for—she didn't see any bees nearby. Maybe they were clustered by the hives and not visible from here. Finally, Elaine added a handful of wood chips to the lit kindling inside the smoker. Slightly heavier smoke began to puff from its spout. Elaine gave the bellows a testing squeeze, releasing a scent of smoke and leather. She began to walk again. "Okay. We've got our smoke. Let's go see our bees."

The air smelled sweet and green and grassy, plus the occasional whiff of soil and manure. Karin breathed deeply. Out here the manure smell was not unpleasant. It was natural and right; it gave her a sensation of having stepped into the cycle, the revolving shifts of the land and the animals. Her cow, she thought idly, had liked her. She'd only milked the one, but the cow's dark eyes had ranged over her forgivingly and then glanced away, as if not to make her uncomfortable.

She was starving. Maybe Elaine would gather some honey and bring it back for dinner. It would be presumptuous to ask, she decided; she didn't work for *Honey Now*, but she desperately wanted to taste it.

"I thought we'd see a few sentries or something by now," Karin said. She risked opening up her netting to wipe sweat off her forehead and cheeks. "Maybe they had a rager last night."

Elaine didn't respond. She strode ahead of Karin toward the hives. The row of boxes reached Elaine's waist, each with removable tops and handled drawers. Elaine looked carefully at the hives, around their bases in the grass and in the field behind them. She straightened up and turned slowly, surveying the surrounding field. Karin looked around as well: the breeze strengthened, blowing Elaine's mask against her face. She swatted at it, still gazing up at the sky. A cloud passed before the sun and dulled the leaves and the shine on the beehives.

Elaine paid no attention to Karin, concentrating only on lifting the top of one box and looking inside. She was moving more quickly now, the smoke dribbling out of the can in her hand. Karin tried to get a glimpse inside the hives as well, and saw mainly a series of wooden bars. Elaine crouched and drew open one of the drawers, which was filled with the same group of frames. She lifted one out, causing Karin to take a quick, involuntary step back, but nothing came buzzing out of the hive. The frame was a rectangle of screened wood filled with honeycomb, dripping slightly when Elaine raised it toward the sun and inspected it. It looked fine to Karin, but Elaine's face was grim.

She eased the frame back into place and gently closed the top of the hive. Then she checked the other two. All three were the same: the frames dark and filled with honeycomb. All were empty of honeybees. When Elaine closed the last hive she reached beneath her netting and touched the sides of her nose, pinching the bridge.

"It's kind of amazing that they all just head out and then know where to come back to," Karin ventured. But her voice was far too loud in the emptiness. There was no drone of mosquitoes, no moths alighting in the tall grass.

Elaine held up one gloved hand, palm in Karin's direction, and shook her head brusquely. Karin shut up. Elaine was turning slowly in a circle, looking through the silent field.

"That's not what they do," Elaine said finally. "They should be here. They should still be guarding the hive, guarding the queen. Their major production is only just tailing off." Their eyes met, and suddenly the hot, protective suits seemed ludicrous. Karin reached up and carefully removed her hat. She hesitated partway through, but Elaine pulled hers off as well. Her brows were drawn together. Her silvery eyes seemed startlingly light against her skin. She rubbed her face with her gloved hands.

"They never just leave and then come back?" Karin said.

"Not all at once. They go off, gather pollen, come back, and store it. But the queen just stays and breeds, and the drones stay with her. They should be here still." Elaine turned toward the trees and began moving slowly through the grass again. She kept glancing back at the empty hives. "I didn't see the queen," she said.

"What does that mean?"

"I'm not sure," Elaine sighed. "Nothing good. But if they don't come back it's more than me not having honey to sell. Wisconsin's been doing fine, except for the occasional isolated collapse. They pollinate the trees, you realize. I mean, I can order new bees and a new queen and try to start over. If I really feel I have the money, which I don't. But you can feel the silence out here. It doesn't feel right. It isn't right for them to completely disappear like this. I'd feel better if I'd found them all dead."

They trudged away from the empty hives. As they neared the shed, Elaine reached over and wordlessly took Karin's hat from her hand, opened the shed door, and chucked both hats into the dark. Then she closed the door and turned to leave. Karin didn't know what to say, so she simply stood quietly as Elaine glanced at her, then paused, and went back in. Inside the shed she picked up the hats and brushed them off. Then she hung them neatly on the wall where they'd come from.

The cheese caves resided near one of the property's five lakes. When they glimpsed the door in the distance, Elaine seemed to perk up. She began explaining its structure and location. Karin clicked her recorder back on.

"I like to think the breezes kind of bring the whole landscape with them, you know? Pollen, molds, bacteria, all that crap in the air. . . ." Elaine was saying.

And there it was, a wood-lined door set right into the hillside, a tree stump just outside it with two flashlights and a bucket of wood-handled tools on top. Elaine picked up the flashlights and the bucket, handing a light to Karin. She stepped back to allow Karin in first.

Karin stepped inside, the door closing behind her. She stood in the dark cave air, which did indeed smell faintly of mold and tanginess, of the cool stone walls' scent of iron, or some clean cold mineral. The cave smelled like a strange combination of fresh and ferment, of unseen growth and life. Standing there, she had no clue how large it might be. Was that a sound of water moving, toward the back of the cave? It sounded farther away than she could have guessed was possible. She stood stock still in the blackness, listening, suddenly unable to feel the boundaries of her own skin. Karin's hands reached out of their own accord; dizzyingly, her fingertips brushed nothing but air. Were her eyes open or closed? A faint breeze moved through the cave, lifting the ends of her hair so they brushed her mouth. Beneath her feet she felt the graveled earth, its slant becoming more pronounced even as she stood. Her shoes were too smooth, Karin realized; the ground could shift and her shoes would skate along the loose pebbles, hurtling her into the blackness.

A cone of white light now stretched into the black air, casting a moon on the wall.

"Sorry," Elaine's voice said. "I stopped to get that little doo-hickey thing to test some cheese." She was right next to Karin now. Karin smelled the breeze in Elaine's hair, a scent of rosemary, or maybe sage, and the smell of water, like the edge of a lake. Elaine's voice continued, "Why didn't you turn on your flashlight?"

But it was hard to speak; Karin drew a breath and it seemed to dissipate uselessly in her mouth before she could derive any oxygen from it. She tried again, the sound echoing in the cave. Where was her body, its edges? She had an image of her flesh as some spongy substance, stretching outward and outward, her consciousness growing porous at the edges. Elaine's hand was on Karin's shoulder. Above the beam of light her face was shadowed with concern, her pale irises flattened and gold-backed like an animal's. "Sit down," she said, actually pushing Karin by the shoulder. Karin gave; she landed hard on her butt. Elaine was still tugging at her shoulder. What was Elaine's problem? Karin started to brush her off, still trying to concentrate on getting some of that air in to her lungs. It was strange, ancient air, thick and dense, and her body seemed unable to take it in. The cave echoed with a rhythmic rushing sound she couldn't identify. It really might be water. No one had mentioned water, which sounded closer, rising. No one had mentioned the cave was set so treacherously deep in the hillside.

"Karin, turn around, for God's sake," Elaine was saying. Karin felt hands on her skull, flat against her hair, and she batted at them without thinking, until the hands managed to turn her face a few inches to the left—and there it was, the mouth of the cave, its open door and elongated slant of light, right there in the corner of her eye. It was only three feet away. Karin scrambled toward it, getting to her feet clumsily, and then she was out in the sun and its sudden heat, pacing in the grass just outside. Carl gamboled around her, his jaws hanging open playfully, delighted with the game.

Elaine walked out then, clutching her flashlight.

"What the hell," Karin gasped. She breathed in a massive gulp and felt the ends of her limbs, her skin, and her fingertips, rush with blood. She could see it: corpuscles swollen with oxygen, everything plumped up again, thank God. She paced in ovals, watching her feet. Her skin felt strange, raw and hot.

Elaine gripped her by the shoulders. "Karin!" she barked. It was not unlike her Carl voice. Karin stopped moving and stared back at Elaine. "You hyperventilated," Elaine said. "That's all. Are you claustrophobic? Sit down for a second." She cleared off the stump and Karin sat down on top of it.

"I don't remember ever feeling like that in my life. There's nothing weird about that cave, is there?"

"I don't think so," Elaine said. "It's really nothing major; it's a hole in the hill with shelves and cheese and bamboo mats. I think you just needed your flashlight. You can lose your bearings in there if you aren't quite ready. I should have told you to leave the door open."

Karin rubbed her face. "I feel like a moron."

"Don't," Elaine told her. "That happened to me once, actually, right after Jack died. I went in there to see how he'd left things, you know, and for some dumb reason, I didn't turn on my light or prop the door, and I just walked in and stood there. It hit me like it did you. I think we're not used to blackness like that anymore."

"Maybe," Karin said. She leaned back on the tree stump. The sun on her cheeks felt soothing; she could feel bark against the backs of her calves. "I just lost the sense of myself, of having skin or being separate." She laughed a little foolishly. "You must think I'm an unspeakable twit. I come here to see what you do and then I act like I found Narnia." She stood up, looked around for her flashlight, and saw the gleam of its lens on the ground just inside the cave. "Jeez. I'm ready."

Elaine led the way this time, pausing to pick up Karin's dropped flashlight and turn it on before handing it to her. "Thanks," said Karin, embarrassed.

"So much nicer than one of those basement rooms, you know?" Elaine's voice came to her from a corner of the cave, where her flashlight cast a telescope of brightness on the dirt floor. Karin swung her light in that direction. Elaine was gazing at a shelf filled with rounds of Brie, her face alight.

"Those do seem more sterile in comparison to this," Karin said.

"Anyway, don't be embarrassed," Elaine said. "Really, don't. I told you the same thing happened to me. It's just the way the sun hits the hillside sometimes, or when it doesn't, I should say. When you have a little light at your back it's totally relaxed but sometimes something kicks in if you forget about that. When I did it I crawled out on my hands and knees, and threw up."

Karin shone her flashlight around the edges of the cave, establishing its dimensions before she did anything else. The walls were about eight or nine feet high, and the top of the cave came to a point. Shelves lined the whole thing, the lips of bamboo mats hanging over the edges, stacked with ivory and golden cheeses of various sizes. Karin touched an herbed one with her fingertip. Thyme leaves clung to her skin.

Some were wrapped in ragged cloths, stained with islands of dark mold, their bandages as stiff as the kiln-dried lace on a porcelain doll. On the next shelf was a landscape of little flat-topped ivory pyramids, gray at the corners. There were rounds a foot across, little discs an inch or so tall, and cylinders and squares coated with ash, prickled with a blanket of herbs, and bound in tattered linens like a mummy. Karin counted at least ten different types of cheese before her, more than twice as many as Drumlin advertised. She breathed in the air deeply—herbal, grassy, and then that wild, tangy mold scent.

Elaine reached up and gently lifted a wide golden cylinder off a mat. She set it on an empty shelf and worked a wooden-handled tool with a hollow cylindrical steel blade about six inches long through the side of its rind, rotating it into the center. When the blade came out it held a neat little cylinder of ivory cheese, which Elaine broke in two. She handed one to Karin and tasted some herself, chewing thoughtfully.

"What do you think?" she asked. Karin took her time responding, chewing and pondering. She felt it was a test of some sort, that after the debacle of her first entry into the cave she must be absolutely correct in her assessment. She needed something to concentrate on anyway, a place to focus her mind and remain calm. She guessed the cheese was cow's milk, and fairly young. Its rind was pliant, and the flavor and texture shifted along its length, from mild and tangy, its pâte soft and sticky, to firmer at its core, where it tasted of the beginnings of a whole mix of things: hazelnuts, and beer, and steak, and maybe some tart fruit or the reminiscence of it; it tasted like the memory of a dining hall in a Tyrolean monastery.

"It's going to be beautiful," she said honestly. "It's not there yet, but toward the center you can start to get at it. What is it? And how long have you had this, anyway?"

"It's been aging for about five weeks," Elaine said. "I planted a field with all kinds of stuff—you know, clover and rosemary and a shitload of lavender—and I turned the cows loose on it as soon as it was ready. The big rounds are from that field. I wanted to see how clearly it would come through."

"It does somehow," Karin said. "What are you going to call it?"

"I don't know yet," Elaine said. "I hadn't quite gotten that far. I'm doing a lot of experimenting, and so many fail that I don't want to name anything till it hatches, you know? But I think I'll have to come up with something for this one. She's going to be big." She brushed off her hands, shoved the tool into her back pocket, and replaced the rind on the shelf. She brought out another one, a littler one which she tested with a fresh cylinder, and again broke the sample in two. This, a chalky-textured blue, tasted muttonish. "Sheep's milk blue? Kind of Roqueforty?" Karin ventured.

"Sheep's milk, yes." Elaine's voice floated over from a darker section of the cave. Karin could hear the clicking of the mats on the shelves as Elaine moved something around. "I really don't like sheep," she said. "I'm starting to think the little wool balls know it. Maybe I should keep them out of cheese and just raise them for wool. They're so insistent. They make their presence known more than I like. I guess that's true of all the milk, but I feel like sheep-milk cheese can have this old-lady, musty, oily aspect to it, you know?"

"It's not my favorite," Karin admitted. She hadn't liked the sheep, either: they were startlingly toothy and direct of gaze, their eyes a bright gold, their tails fleshy and flopping. "I like it sometimes, though. And I do like a blend." She took another small bite of the unfinished blue.

"Why do you think you got so upset in the cave that one time?" Karin asked. She was trying to get the time line. It seemed to her the story in this farm was the family trying to keep going without the motor of its own business. "Maybe it was too soon, or something?"

"After he died, you mean?" Elaine said. Her voice was light and cool, unaffected. "Maybe so. But it was either let his work rot or keep it going. So when the troopers came to the house and told us, I came down here and I checked on his work. It's not so odd."

"Oh, I didn't mean that it was odd," Karin backtracked. But she was imagining Elaine walking past the state troopers and straight out to the cave. "Just that it must have been difficult. The whole thing is really—"

But now Elaine was next to her again, holding up the round to the light and examining it. Karin decided not to finish her sentence. She shone her flashlight helpfully at the cheese before Elaine shrugged and put it back.

"So anyway," Elaine said. "I come in here every day, flip the cheeses, smell them, get a feel for where they are, test the ones I need to test, and basically try to figure out when the next batch comes out and if it goes for sale. Of course, I know about how long it takes but there are variables, with weather and milk and whatnot. So I keep notes in my little book, and just eat and smell and poke them and see where we are. I'm trying out some new ones. I don't think four cheeses are enough for us to keep growing on. I want a whole bunch, rotating through the year."

Karin followed suit and let her voice go brisk and professional as well.

"Jack did all this before? Did he build the cave?" She fumbled for her tape recorder.

"He had contractors carve it out. He wanted the caves to sit downwind of the lake. When it was done he had us all traipse down here and check it out. Janine stayed outside."

"How about the rest of you? What did you think?"

"My mom was the one who really got it. And my dad after a bit, and Kenny. It doesn't exactly announce itself, you know? It's a damp dark hole in the ground, pretty much, and you have to be able to envision things. My mom used to serve us Brie when we were kids and forbade us to cut the rind off, so she was receptive."

Elaine paused, brushing her hands, and then said, "Let's go check out the livestock, shall we?" She started toward the door. "You can look around a little more if you like, as long as you don't poke the cheese too much or anything."

"Thanks," said Karin. "I *am* feeling better. I'll just peer a little."

She cast her light around the cave again and began inspecting the cheese closely. The fragrance changed with every inch she moved. She reached back through the shelves and touched the walls, a cool rough concrete, brushed into swirls. It dismayed her a little to find the walls were so clearly handmade. It was silly, she knew, as if it were inauthentic to build the cave and make it useful and secure instead of falsely primitive. What did she want? Crumbling earth walls and the bones of a dinosaur? She snorted a little at herself and glanced over her shoulder toward the door. She felt fine now. She didn't know why she'd felt so lost before. As she touched the walls with the flat of her hand, leaned in to inhale the scent of the mats and the ripening milk, the harsh fragrance of brandy brushed on some of the cheeses, and a footy little whiff of blue, she thought about Elaine, crawling out of the cave and vomiting. A terrible but understandable sensation—the reassertion of the body, maybe, refusing to let its molecules bleed into the air, as the mind feared it might. Karin knew the story would sound foolish if she went home and told Marit about that feeling, both towering and miniscule, that came upon you when you were in an unfamiliar and absolute darkness. The two of them prided themselves on their pragmatism; it was too embarrassing for Karin to admit that she was delighted to have the weight of the flashlight in her hand, its sunny circle of light on the walls.

Beyond the doorway of the cave she saw Elaine tossing a tennis ball past Carl, who loped over the grass—slightly above it, it seemed—and out of sight. Karin turned back to the wall for one last look, and her eye lit upon a shape on the concrete, a little reddish shadow largely hidden behind the vertical bar of a shelf. She eased her way carefully in, moving cheese aside and shining her light on the wall. It was a drawing, a little less than a foot tall. A woman, etched in broad strokes of porous ochre-colored paint, filled in with light blue or gray. She stood upright, her arms lifted and hands outstretched. The woman was nude, her breasts indicated by two simple curved lines, circles marking the nipples, the thighs meeting in a curving seagull of a V. The hands and feet were elongated and elegant, suggested in sweeping lines that looked effortless but Karin knew took great care to get right. Two curving crescents marked her cheekbones, and a half-moon marked the navel, curled in the center of an orblike pregnant belly. The little face gazed out from amid a cloud of curly, black hair—exaggerated a bit from the real woman outside the cave, Karin saw, but not by much.

CHAPTER TEN

Will was strolling back into the living room from the kitchen when Hal and Mrs. Bryant returned from the bathroom. He bent carefully over the plate of apples before sitting down on the couch again, selected a slice, and examined it. He took a bite, but then leaned back on the couch and let the apple slice rest on his thigh.

"What's up?" Hal asked. The fake nonchalance got under his skin. He just wanted to hear Will say he'd gone to the kitchen and retrieved a bottle. He resented being lied to.

"Just waiting for you," Will replied. His consonants were loopy and faded at the ends. Hal helped Mrs. Bryant settle herself back in her chair. All at once the visit had lost its one weak puff of steam.

"Well," Hal said. "Maybe it's time to head out." He cast a doubtful eye on Will, trying to see a change in him. Will saw him watching and took another bite of apple. He leaned his head back against the cushion and chewed. Hal watched the slow movement of his jaw and Adam's apple. Will's legs were splayed out, his feet at odd angles. One hand lay on the couch next to him, the other rested on his thigh. The apple was at best loosely held. Hal realized there was also a slice of cheese on the upholstery beside him.

"This was a dumb idea," Hal said.

Mrs. Bryant nodded. "He's going to be very little help in the yard," she said. "Where did you find this young man, anyway? You'll have to do better next time. Are your girls energetic?

"You know," she added casually, after a pause, "I do have some hedge trimmers out in the garage. Old rusty things I don't think a soul has touched for ten years. Who knows if they would even work. Of course, my fear is that the power will be out for several more days and this room will be in darkness the entire time. I don't know if you're up on such things, Hal, but in places like Sweden, where the light disappears for so long during the winter, the suicide rate simply skyrockets. Humans aren't meant to be hostage to such forces, you know. We're meant to take some control."

"Do you still want me to trim those branches?" Hal asked, rubbing his face. "I don't want to just leave him in here with you."

"He's not going to do anything to me," she replied. "He's not going to do much at all." She took a few more slices of apple and cheese from the plate Hal offered before he carried it into the kitchen, wrapped it in plastic, and put it in the refrigerator. The brown grocery bag was still on the counter. He peered in, saw two empty pint bottles of gin, and placed them in the trash before going out to the garage to find the hedge trimmers.

Once he actually stood before the lilac, Hal realized he had no idea how to proceed. The lilac bush was a loosely knit fabric of tough little branches, its blossoms just beginning to drop and the green leaves still obscuring everything. At first he had the notion of trimming only the dead-looking twigs, but after twenty minutes and no discernable change he knew he had to get bold. He never thought it would take so long to do a little pruning.

His father would have imagined a shape and started cutting the edges to find it, Hal decided. He had watched his father do yard work his entire life; how had nothing seeped through? He stood back and chose a shape for the bush, arbitrarily. Boldly he cut straight through a swath of branches at windowsill-level. Through the dingy windows he could make out the shape of Mrs. Bryant's white head.

Lilac trimming turned out to be unexpectedly satisfying, the scrape of the blades as the branches fell, the visual improvement so complete. He stood back, rather proud, until he let the new shape of the bush settle and he saw it as it really looked. The bush seemed rather spindly and stunted, the ground littered with blossoms. The window, with its peeling sills and dust-spotted panes, seemed to blanch beneath the sunlight. Hal's sense of accomplishment departed. This work was not some innate masculine skill, after all. He'd known it all along: he should have spent more time with his father.

There might have been a time when he would have trimmed the lilac into a pleasing, careful shape. There was definitely a time, it occurred to him now, when Hal used to be able to do so much more. As a teenager he had mown lawns and trimmed trees. He had fished for trout and gutted them in a flicker with a knife he'd kept singing sharp. He had killed deer and pheasant humanely, with one well-placed shot, and he had understood and respected the bloody work of converting their bodies to food. But then he'd moved far from hunting country and was rarely home for the season. Once he stopped eating meat, it made no sense to hunt solely for the sake of killing. Now Hal had no idea if he would remember what to do to dress an animal. The first time he watched his father do it, Hal had been eleven, stunned by the heated mingling of organ and muscles, the taut muscular bindings of the body that had expected to continue its work. His sisters had hunted as well—could it be they both remembered everything he'd forgotten? Not Jane, perhaps, but Hal wondered if Rennie, sniffling with her fall allergies all the while, could walk her daughter through gutting a wild turkey as easily as turning on the television. Hal could barely remember what the inside of an animal looked like, much less how to clean it and butcher it, how to make use of it. He had lost all of those skills—he no longer knew how to *provide*—but now they might be needed again.

He toed the lost branches beneath the lilac bush and returned the hedge trimmers to their shelf in the garage. When he returned to the living room, Mrs. Bryant was finished with her snack. Will hadn't moved. He was still sitting on the couch as if he'd been dropped from above, legs apart, arms slopped to either side. His head was tipped back against the couch cushion, and he seemed less sleepy than unconscious. Could someone incapacitate himself like this with just alcohol? It seemed more like heroin on top of tranquilizers.

Mrs. Bryant had a set of knitting needles in her lap and a basket of orange yarn beside her. Without looking up, she said, needles clicking, "Well, be careful out there, Hal. I worry about you, though you have a bit more to work with than some." She looked at him above the rims of her glasses. "There was some incident in your part of Lake Monona, correct?"

Hal paused. "It was just a dog," he said.

She rolled her eyes. "And some young woman apparently waded in after it." She shook her head. "Say what you will, but the young are eternally confused about where to focus their energies. A dog."

"Well, maybe not just a dog," Hal corrected her. "The dog isn't really the point. And some kind of activity is going on out on the lake. At least it was this morning. If the police are saying anything, the newspapers aren't being printed properly anyway."

"Well, many people had to turn their energies to the blackout. They may not have time to comment on it." Mrs. Bryant hitched a shoulder dismissively. Will stirred slightly on the couch, and the two of them turned to observe him. "And whoever went out there on the lake is unlikely to be in need of help now."

Hal shuddered. He'd managed not to think about the dock incident all day: it helped to focus your attention on someone like Will, someone who presented you with a whole new set of problems to solve. But now he just felt frustrated. He'd only hauled Will around for a while. He'd accomplished nothing.

"Don't get depressed, now," Mrs. Bryant was saying. "These things happen even when times are easy. What about your family? Aren't they around?"

"Sort of," he said. "My sisters and their families are. My father's up north. My mother is dead, though." He stopped, listening to the words. He hadn't said this in a long time—maybe he never had. He had told people, "My mother died," but somehow that had been less final—an active, finite task his mother had undertaken, like saying his mother had golfed. But now he heard "my mother is dead" as the irreparable state it was.

"Sad to hear. How long?" The knitting needles never stopped moving, but Mrs. Bryant looked up and made sure she caught his eye. When she did, she nodded slightly and returned to looking to her knitting. She seemed to mean this as acknowledgment, just to be certain he knew she'd paused over the statement.

"About six months," Hal said. He added, "She was only seventy."

She nodded. "Not so much younger than me, then."

Hal began to protest, but then he did the math. Good God, was Mrs. Bryant only eighty, or even younger? She seemed far older to him, but then Hal's perceptions were skewed. He'd barely begun to think of his mother as middle-aged when she had died. And yet each time he'd seen her in that last year or so, he'd been startled by the loss of pigment in her eyebrows and skin, the way the sag of her eyelids hid her lashes. Her death had been brisk and unstoppable: the stroke must have felt like a great cataclysmic release into the soft meat of the brain. Hal was closer to middle-aged than she had been.

"You're right, I guess," he said wonderingly.

"When my mother died I just wanted to stay home and let Mr. Bryant take care of everything," Mrs. Bryant said. "I was about forty at the time. Cancer, you know. No one said that back then. We spoke about growths instead. I stayed in the house for days, in my room, and Mr. Bryant had to do everything as best he could. His efforts weren't terribly impressive but I appreciated it just the same." She held up her knitting and eyed it, then shook it out a bit and resettled the yarn on her lap, saying, as she did, "But I think what you've chosen to do is wiser. Or maybe just kinder."

It took him a second to follow. Was this what Hal had chosen to do? Maybe so, whether he'd realized it or not. But here they were.

Mrs. Bryant turned her attention to Will. She looked him over and shook her head. Then she raised her chin in the direction of the curio cabinet. "Take one for your trouble, Hal."

Hal moved slowly, observing the little cabinet as he got his twenty. He'd never much looked at it before; he'd been too embarrassed, too busy taking his pathetic little tip, to see what else it held. The cabinet held a few polished gemstones, mounds of coins that seemed Russian, maybe, or bore some Cyrillic text, a rusty antique ice pick, and a miniature eggbeater. What was such a collection meant to convey—what was an observer to take from it? His father's cabin was probably filled with glazed hard fish and marble-eyed deer. Hal's own room held piles of T-shirts from fund-raisers, packets of heirloom seeds for squash and tomatoes and beets, half-burned candles, and CDs, none newer than three years old.

He was trying to imagine a domicile for the person out there in the lake: his countertops would hold cans and boxes of noodles and soup, great piles of out-of-date magazines, a bin of dog food. Pills in a daily divider, and a new leather leash.

Hal took his twenty and folded it carefully, to show he didn't accept it lightly. Then he roused Will, whose head simply lolled. A sort of barrier seemed to have dropped inside him; he might be sleeping with his eyes open. Hal jiggled him again. He'd only wanted to remove Will from Hal's own house, from Greta, and then along the way something else had wormed its way in. He'd acted out of annoyance and the desire to show him up—but how hard was it to show up someone in such a condition? It was dread-fully easy.

"Will, get up," he said. "Get *up*." Luckily Hal was bigger. He got him upright, with one arm beneath Will's armpit and wrapped around his back. Hal dragged him out to the car, letting Will hang on him, a damp hot flopping weight. Hal opened the passenger door and Will managed to get in, where he immediately murmured something and then let his head fall back again. Hal stood there by the open car door, feeling he had done something shameful and abusive.

As Hal was walking around the driver's side, the big white Swiffie van pulled into the driveway. He could see Diana's sleek head through the window, her ponytail swinging as she turned to climb out. He had never called in to work. As she emerged from the van a few feet away, their eyes met. Then she went around the back of the van and he heard the doors open and the clatter of the foil-wrapped trays.

It was later in the day than he'd thought; the sun was at its highest peak. He realized he had forgotten to clear away the branches, which remained scattered on the earth below the window. The lilac itself looked mutilated and stumpy.

Diana came to stand next to him, toting a tray. "Hello, Hal," she said. "Very interesting to find you here."

"Hi, Di," Hal said. He couldn't think of anything to say.

She shook her head. "I would have thought you might do me the courtesy of actually calling out, and maybe not on a day when we're scrambling to work around a blackout and get our stocks up."

"How's that going?" Hal asked.

Diana shook her head. "How do you think it's going? No one's giving anything. I'd tell you we need you except I don't need *this*." She gestured at the car, bending down to peer in at Will. "What have you been doing? Taking a nap? Doing yard work? I don't even know what to say, but this meal is getting cold."

"Hey—what did you make?" he asked. Suddenly Hal truly wanted to know. He might have made lentil soup. He would have told them to add finely diced ham for heft and to serve the bread on the side.

"Don't worry about it," Diana said. "Who is that, anyway? Never mind." She shook her head and turned to go up Mrs. Bryant's walk. When she looked at the lilac bush, she glanced back over her shoulder at Hal one more time.

Hal debated waiting for her to return. If he waited, he stood a good chance of being fired. But maybe not—now was not the moment anyone would want to let an extra hand go. But maybe he had made such an egregious error that Diana would decide to fire him anyway. He couldn't decide which he wanted. He was unable to get the Swiffies or their clients what they needed; maybe he had outlived his usefulness.

Hal squinted for some movement in the car and saw none. He suddenly wanted to be certain Will had a pulse.

Hal got in and pulled out of the driveway, anxious to get away. He pulled around the corner and put the car in park. Will's body shifted with the motion of the car and tipped toward the window as the car came to rest. His mouth was slack, the full lower lip dry. His deep-set eyes were closed, the lids purplish and seamed with sea-green veins. His nose was long, slim, with evidence of a healed break in the knob at the center. As Hal reached gingerly over to touch Will's neck—he really wanted to feel that pulse—he noted with surprise how perfectly groomed Will's hair was: the ears trimmed carefully, the hairline so smooth it might have just been cut that morning. It gave him a little hope: Will was managing some bit of upkeep.

Hal pressed his fingertips to the soft orbs of gland and muscle beneath Will's jawbone, whiskers prickling into his skin. There was a long moment there in the car, the glare coming off the car's hood, the radio silent, the scent of gin rising off Will's skin, while Hal waited to feel that beat. When he finally did, he let out a breath of relief. He hadn't truly thought Will had poisoned himself—not yet—but still he kept his fingertips pressed firmly into the cool skin, just to be certain it was really there, that sullen, steady throb.

Hal sat back and watched his passenger sleep. He had the sinking feeling that Will agreeing to accompany him to Mrs. Bryant's represented some effort on Will's part, a vague attempt at outreach. At reaching Greta? Or perhaps Will had had a brief moment of energy and lost it along the way. Either way, it made the whole day worse, to suspect that Will might have received Hal's half-assed, high-school-student version of community outreach with any sincerity or hope at all.

On the way back to Will's house they passed the same store they had shopped at earlier. Hal glanced over; Will was still asleep. He didn't wake up when Hal took Mrs. Bryant's twenty out of his pocket, or when he reached across the seat to tuck the bill in the breast pocket of Will's shirt.

CHAPTER ELEVEN

The first thing Greta did at her office was to check the telephone, which worked the first time but not the second. She tried her light switch, which did not work at all. She could run her laptop on its battery, but who knew when she could charge it again? She had left her cell phone off for the same reason.

At least the students were no longer barricaded in their dorms. They were all over the campus, standing in groups and eating from rustling plastic bags. They spoke in whispers and seemed given to pockets of nervous excitement, followed by breathless wandering. In Greta's office, everyone had come to work but seemed to have little idea what to do. There was a lot of office-supply organizing going on, and a great deal of peering out the window.

Greta was supposed to meet Julie Voltsheim, of Mack and Footling series fame, for lunch, assuming all bets weren't off. Maybe they were. Greta planned to go regardless. Everyone was too easily frightened by this blackout, or at least they showed it too much. She just wanted to do her job, to throw herself beneath its surface as she would any other day, so she planned to busy herself until lunchtime and then head downtown.

Julie Voltsheim had chosen the restaurant. Greta had offered up a whole range of places: a sushi restaurant where the gleaming silver chopsticks balanced on carved stones; an upscale little Italian nook that served individual dark chocolates and miniscule hazelnut tarts on square white plates; a Brazilian churrascaria Hal referred to as "the meatery"; and finally a simple French-American place that specialized in local ingredients. Greta had been careful not to give away the fact that she was craving the last one: she wanted ramps and asparagus; she was holding out for the possibility of morels. More than this, she wanted the smooth pale surfaces of such a place, its Provençal yellow walls and the slickness of its silver and glass. The co-op lacked silkiness sometimes, with its porous earthenware and handmade wall hangings, its lumpy honey-smelling candles—all the rough edges that proved how close you were to the source.

So, Julie Voltsheim, responding either to wishes of her own or sensing Greta's hope for spring vegetables and pâté, had chosen the French place. Julie Voltsheim might not show up; the restaurant might not even be open. Greta could keep trying the phones, but she wanted the excuse to go, so she would go. One shouldn't get thrown off track so easily: Greta planned to be there just as if nothing at all were different that day. She'd be as smiling and charming or as grave and watchful as the situation demanded.

This blackout had the feeling of the main event after a series of quick trial runs. In believing this, Greta feared she was being too pessimistic and, at the same time, that she was completely out of touch with the severity of the situation. Hal and Karin seemed to have had a contingency plan in the backs of their heads all along; last night Karin had informed them that they would turn off their cell phones in rotation, and briskly assigned Hal to buy ice before it all disappeared. Greta suspected they had been privy to some information she had missed. What had she been doing all these months? They'd passed with terrible slowness, but then she looked up and the seasons stretched out behind her. Nothing had changed; nothing had been accomplished.

Greta stood in the center of her office, eyeing her filing cabinet. It was the only thing she could think of to attack at the moment. She pulled her recycling bin and her trash can over to the cabinet and began sifting. She had files of old clippings on particularly generous donations, an extremely out-of-date file on lapsed donors, and several back issues of the alumni magazine. It turned out a French major alum had developed a software for retailers and made a fortune. She'd had no idea.

Greta made her lists of what to do that day, listed the donors she hadn't seen in a while, and wrote up notes on what they'd given in the past, who they were giving to now, and where their interests lay. She stepped out of her office midmorning for a bottle of water and a banana, waving briskly into her coworkers' open office doors but not stopping. No one else was getting anything done that she could see. They were still crowding into the offices with the most natural light and wandering confusedly about the kitchen, which had been emptied of perishables by the office manager. They all seemed to be wondering what to do in the absence of a microwave.

Greta wanted to join them. There was an air of almost festive frustration, as though all of them were freed from the requirements of adulthood as long as the power was gone, and she wanted to take part in it, but somehow she could not bring herself to do it. All of her social interactions were awkward lately. Mid-sentence, she would realize she was barely coherent, that people were looking at her with faint pity or concern. If she poked her head into another office she'd probably say something outlandish, or start to cry, within ten minutes.

She wasn't sure when this shift had happened. She had distinct memories of being able to walk into a party and find the fun people, be the fun person, but now she found that prospect terrifying.

So she returned to organizing her desk and catching up on trade publications. She acted like a professional. She had never come in to the office downtrodden after a bad night with Will, or wept at hopeful volume in the ladies room. She hadn't even told anyone at work that she had a new address. They didn't need it. They had her cell phone and her checks were direct deposit.

How to manage the same effect at home? This was the current question. The same detachment that worked so well at the office would seem unsocial at the co-op, even ungracious, given that Hal and Karin had been fairly accommodating. But now Greta was feeling a twist of apprehension somewhere in her abdomen. It wasn't fear—Will wasn't going to hurt her. But he knew where she lived, and it was possible he would show up like this again. Maybe this was a whole new reason never to leave a drunk: at home with them, you confined your embarrassment to yourself and a few familiar walls. You understood that you could not socialize with him, so you cut him out, found him waiting for you at home on the needy emotional end of a binge if you were unlucky, unconscious if you were lucky. Greta had learned to push Will toward unconsciousness instead of watching him feign clarity. *Go to bed*, she'd learned to say. *I won't try to talk to you. Go to bed.*

Just before noon, Charles knocked on her door and strolled into her office, whistling. Greta tensed, but she nodded when he raised his eyebrows in the direction of her extra chair. "Are you just realizing you don't need electricity for anything anymore?" he asked.

Greta relaxed. "It's just been holding me down all along," she said.

Charles sat down and crossed his legs, plucking at the knees of his trousers to straighten them. "I was just walking behind a couple students who were insisting they were happier without it. I went a couple buildings out of my way to eavesdrop."

Greta sat back in her chair. "Remember the group last fall who challenged people to a week without modern amenities? No washers, no laptops, no microwaves?"

"They turned in all their papers handwritten, right?" Charles said. "And they all grew up typing and so their handwriting was basically illegible."

"Yeah. So they all got terrible grades, which they then protested on religious grounds." She leaned back in her chair and grinned at Charles. "This is why I kind of love them. They almost never think the logic all the way through, but they make such an effort."

Charles stretched his long arms back and rested his head in his laced fingers. "They really do. You can't fault them for energy."

Greta opened her desk drawer and pulled out two pieces of chocolate. She tossed one to Charles, who caught it one-handed. She smiled at him. Today Charles's shirt was a dark-slate blue that set off the gray in his hair, his cuff links silver circles. He looked very handsome and untroubled by the blackout. For a moment, she felt the same way.

"How's your side of town?" Charles asked, and Greta tensed up instantaneously. This only angered her. What would she do, lose control every time someone alluded to where she lived?

She took a breath and cocked her head. "It's dicey," she admitted. "Last night people decided to party through it, or some people did, but the search boats out on the lake make it hard to relax."

"That's not related," Charles pointed out reasonably.

"No, but it feels all of a piece," Greta said slowly. She wondered if Will was out on the dock right now, gazing into the water, and for a moment regretted leaving him by the lake alone. "What about your neighborhood?"

"There's a lot of righteous indignation. Most of our neighbors are used to getting answers on anything they want, but none of their tree-shaking is doing them any good. If any city officials really do know what's causing this or how to fix it, they're keeping it closer than I've ever seen. I don't want to be an alarmist, but I don't see any indication the power's coming back any time soon."

Greta frowned. "I figured you'd know something," she said. "You always do."

Charles made an elegant gesture of acknowledgment with one hand. "Not this time. I can tell you that about ten stores were broken into last night. The cops cleared State Street by eleven to keep the students safe, but then a bunch of places on State and over on Monroe Street got hit. Windows smashed, stuff grabbed. More looting than anything else." He stood. "I'm going to get to work for a while. Are you still meeting your writer?"

"I'm showing up," Greta said. "She hasn't canceled."

Charles nodded. "I think pretty soon our esteemed president is going to come through campus and tell us all to go home, anyway. I'll be sure to let her know you were soldiering through. Listen. Be careful out there tonight. Head home after work and stay in. That's what Vera and I are doing. And check your locks."

She got up to see him out. At the door he paused and turned to her. Their eyes met, and Greta tried not to look away, out of pride, or perversity. Charles's cool gray eyes softened almost imperceptibly and he asked, "Would you like me to stop by and look in on Will?"

Greta stood very still, taken by surprise that he would broach it so directly. Then she said, "Yes. Please."

At twelve thirty she left the office and drove through campus. The stoplights were all out, and the UW students seemed no better off than the Grinwall ones. They were mainly standing around the sidewalks, gazing at the buildings. Every now and again one would toe the concrete just below the curb, before stepping all the way into the street. No exams? No dorm meetings? Were they all really so quickly thrown off? She beeped her horn at a few and edged past them, sending an encouraging wave in the direction of one standing in the bike lane.

The downtown parking garages had disabled the entry gates. Instead, a stocky woman in a reflective city vest wrote out a little white ticket, handed it through Greta's window, and lifted the gate by hand.

"This is just pencil. I could change the time to whatever I wanted on here," Greta noted.

"But you won't, will you?" said the woman. "You'll work with our fair city in its time of difficulty and pay for services like a grown-up."

"Indeed," Greta said. She tucked the ticket into her purse.

The local government buildings looked dead and dark. Greta squinted into them in search of human shapes. She supposed workers could use the stairs, work on paper for the day, catch up on meetings, but it was hard to tell if anyone was present. Greta was at work, her roommates had all appeared to plan on working today. Why not the government?

Greta poked a head into the restaurant and found the place dim but bustling, a host standing out in front of his station.

"You're open!" she said. "I wasn't sure you would be. Ohlin, party of two."

The host gave an approximation of a Gallic shrug. "We can write down orders, and we cook with gas," he said. His hand touched the center of her back lightly as he guided her toward a table. "We can give you candles if you find it too dark for your liking."

Greta took in the restaurant and her table at the window. Sunlight poured through the glass. She touched the leather banquette; it was hot already. Julie Voltsheim would feel sweated for cash.

"Do you have anything cooler, in the shade, perhaps?" she asked. "I do appreciate the window, normally I would love it, but without air-conditioning. . . ." And here she felt herself give a Gallic shrug of her own as they moved back to a shady banquette.

She was settled in and sipping water, trying to put her finger on what felt odd, when Julie Voltsheim entered the restaurant. Greta had managed to turn up a photo from an awards dinner a few years earlier, so she recognized her.

Greta waved and stood, deciding how best to greet her. They hadn't met before; a handshake seemed wise. Sometimes you developed enough rapport over the phone and e-mail that a warmer greeting seemed in order. East Coasters preferred a cheek-kiss; Midwesterners a hug. It was one of the first things Charles had told her when she started at the college, and Greta had found it one of the most helpful bits of information anyone had ever given her. She could read body language from a step away and adjust accordingly, lifting and turning her face, shoulders forward. It was a move as practiced as a curtsy, and one she did without thinking. That was what made you good at it: you didn't even pause to wonder.

Julie Voltsheim approached the table and held out a hand.

Greta reached out and clasped it briefly, noting that the hand in hers was long and firm and very warm.

The photo didn't quite do Julie Voltsheim justice. Her hair was short, floppy, and the stark, silver-tipped white of a sled dog or an arctic fox. Her eyes were a warm, melancholy raisin, and when she glanced at the still-empty window table that Greta had vacated, her profile was revealed to be Roman-nosed and firm-chinned. She wore white linen pants, lime-green flat shoes, and a pale-lemon silk shell. Nestled against her abdomen was the gleaming silver knot of a belt buckle. When Greta had shaken Julie's hand she'd felt the coolness of several wide, thick rings.

"I so appreciate your meeting me," Greta began. "And on such a strange day—I would have understood if you'd preferred to reschedule, but I'm certainly glad to see you."

"What's a little blackout between prospects?" said Julie Voltsheim. Her dark eyes gleamed pleasantly, smilingly. "We still have work to do, right?" She thanked the waiter who'd poured water, and took a sip. Her silver brows knit slightly. "Are we worried about refrigeration?" she said conspiratorially. "I can't imagine they'd be open if they couldn't keep their ingredients safe. . . ."

"Ah!" Greta said. That was what had felt odd while she waited: her warm, iceless water.

They both looked around at the people near them, who were eating in the dimness. No one was drinking wine from an iced bucket, Greta noted, but then wine at lunch wasn't so common anymore, anyway. "I've been coming here for years," said Greta. "I have the utmost faith."

But now she did begin to fret, the smallest burn of worry that she, if she had a business to run and coolers full of perishable food, would sell that food as fast as she could. She would sell it before she had to throw it away. Hal had told her the Swiffies gladly took donations from the local grocery stores of food a day or two past its sell-by date. "It usually doesn't matter," he'd said, shrugging. "We don't take bad *clams*, or something, but a lot of produce, if you use it fast enough—no problem at all. Rice, soup, sugar, noodles? Of course."

Greta wondered how he'd gotten rid of Will. It might have been easy. You never knew what direction Will would take: sometimes he was as docile as a retriever, other times he sank stubbornly into the couch and refused to hear a word you said. Sometimes she thought he drank just so he could have that privilege, of ignoring what everyone else had to address, sitting where everyone else had to stand, pissing in the open when the rest of the world had to find a private place.

She realized there had been a long pause, and now Greta met Julie Voltsheim's curious gaze and said, "I see morels! Have you had them yet this season? Otherworldly."

"Henry Footling is my alter ego," Julie was saying. Greta watched her cut a tiny bite of wine-poached trout and chew discreetly. "Everyone thinks it would be Mack, just because she's a woman. But I identify with Henry. I identify with his loneliness, his frustrations. His wife is a society girl who shouldn't have married him, his son is too weak to count on, his police assistants are of almost no use. I started writing about him when I was in Oyster Bay, and there was something about going out to the beach, in the winter, you know, that felt so bleak and cold and lonely, and it made me imagine this man, this man in his forties, stopping into a pub, eating peanuts and tossing the shells on the floor, asking for a mug of gin before he goes home. He came to me clear as day. Which is especially odd because I was only in my early twenties."

Greta smiled. "Why, do you suppose?" she asked.

She had been eating while she listened to Julie; now she was nearly finished and Julie's trout still gazed upward, startled by its sprinkling of almonds and chervil. Greta had worried about ordering fish, unable to shake the fear that the restaurant was simply getting rid of what it could, and had pulled aside the host when she excused herself to the restroom. The host had looked appalled. "But how are you keeping it all *chilled*? There isn't even ice for the water," Greta had asked. The coolers hold their temperature for some time, the host assured her. And they had immediately stocked up on as much ice as possible, almost all of which was used for storage. The host had bent over to speak to her, his hands clasped before him like a butler. *You're probably from Wausau*, Greta was thinking. "Madam, we are very careful. Had you ordered wine we would have chilled it, of course. But water that is too chilled only dulls the palate."

"Oh, for Pete's sake," Greta had said. "You don't want to waste ice, fine. Let's not make it a learning session." The host blinked, and Greta drew a deep breath and glanced back toward the dining room. She took a moment before speaking, thinking, *You come here all the time, you do business here, get a hold of yourself.* "I'm sorry," she said. "I'm sorry, really. I'm a little freaked out by this whole thing, this blackout thing. I'm just glad you're open! Truly!" And then she'd skittered back to her table to find Julie Voltsheim enjoying a glass of Sancerre, the globe of her wineglass tantalizingly filmed with moisture.

"Why did I feel that way?" Julie mused now. "I was single, in my twenties, miserable in my job, and sensually stifled. I don't mean sexually, really, though that, too"—Greta kept her face absolutely the same as it had just been; never change expression when the conversation goes somewhere you don't expect—"but it was as if I had extra layers of skin, or something, do you see? I *felt* so little, I enjoyed so little. I used to eat bread for dinner, looking at a wall, before I went to my night job. I only had the night job because I couldn't bear coming home to my apartment. It may as well have been a hundred years earlier. I may as well have been in a nineteenth-century Boston winter every day of my life back then." She finished off another morsel of trout and gazed thoughtfully at the ceiling as she chewed. "How were your mushrooms?"

Greta blushed, startled to find Julie's gaze back on her. She found herself thinking of the fungal taste of the mushrooms Gregory had given her. In college, people used to try mushroom tea, sprinkle them on pizza, or try to hide them and make them palatable at once. Greta never saw the point: shove them down fast, she'd said. Will used to get them sometimes, in the summers between semesters, and they'd drive to Devil's Lake and watch the water change colors, think they saw prehistoric fish flashing in the clouded depths.

"They were lovely," she said. "I ought to have offered you some."

Julie waved a hand. "They grow on our property," she whispered. "Keep that to yourself, of course. My husband makes risotto with them."

"What does your husband do?" Greta inquired. As soon as she said it she regretted it—of course she knew what Julie's husband did, and Julie would expect her to know. Greta covered her nerves by taking a slice of bread from a silver basket. She tore off a tiny piece, helped herself to the butter shining dewily in its little white crock. She sat up straighter, trying to remind herself that she was here not just to chitchat but to direct the conversation. Julie Voltsheim seemed to be the sort of person who had grown so accustomed to discoursing on herself, to the press, to audiences, to publishers, that she did so engagingly, and relentlessly. Greta felt a bit steamrolled by her. The restaurant was warm and still pleasantly clinking with silver and porcelain and steel pans toward the back. Somewhere Julie's husband was probably strolling through a field with a basket of chanterelles and morels, not even noticing the blackout.

"He was a math teacher," said Julie. "Now he tutors a bit, but for the most part he runs the business side of the books. The taxes alone are practically a full-time job. And you may know my son and daughter are involved as well. Do you have children?"

Greta shook her head; her mouth was full. She swallowed quickly. "I don't," she said. "It never seemed to be the right thing for us."

Julie Voltsheim caught the pronoun like a lynx seeing movement in the grass. "Husband?"

"Not so much," said Greta.

Julie nodded. "I wonder sometimes what it would be like, you know, if I'd kept on the same path as I was on back in Long Island: I was alone, and I would have had to learn to enjoy myself regardless, of course—but I do wonder. I married after I'd begun publishing the Footling series, and started with Mack when the children were young. I wonder if that sense of order you get from a mystery would have been so necessary to me if my life had been less hectic! It all seems like mayhem but not compared to life with two toddlers." She gave a husky laugh, and Greta joined her compulsively, too loudly, then silenced herself with another bite of bread.

"I was just at a party," she said, "with a whole houseful of people who raise their children together, sort of."

"Like a commune?" Julie's eyebrows rose with interest.

"More like a co-op. I forget the difference." Greta was hot; her teeth sticky with a paste of bread and butter. How did this woman do it every time—just as Greta hooked into the conversation, Julie plucked it from her again. At this rate Greta would be writing her a check. "Anyway," she said, "I'm curious: What brought you here? You were on the East Coast for some time, correct?"

Julie nodded and sipped her wine. "Correct. But we're from the Midwest, and we always had thoughts of coming back again. We'd look at real estate just to see, and then one day we found a place we loved, and things just seemed to come together. Finding morels in the woods out back just confirmed it. You should come mushroom-hunting with us sometime. I have a stand of elms they seem to like."

Greta was nodding silently, crumpling her napkin beneath the table. She barely acknowledged the invitation, which was probably mere politeness in any case. Something was wrong with her: she was off her game, forgetting information she'd taken care to learn, unable to find the thread to keep it going. They were nearly done with the main course, Julie Voltsheim might not even want dessert, and Greta still hadn't established the kind of rapport she needed. There was the gentle build and then there was fear. You had to pull the trigger at some point or else the prospect felt baffled and deceived. But Julie Voltsheim made Greta defensive; her trousers were probably not even creased yet. Her rings were made not of silver, Greta had detected, but of platinum. Greta felt wispy and flyaway next to her, sweaty and low rent.

"Anyway, we love it so far, other than these power problems and whatnot. And the other little hiccups I'm hoping are just temporary. I never thought of this as an odd place, but you seem to have some occurrences, yes? That, uh . . . that rogue dock?"

Greta froze, holding her bread crust. She began to butter it automatically, prompted by something—her amygdala, maybe, or some new function of her brain stem well developed over the years with Will—to feign calm. The photo of her had only been on the front page of the Web site, and only for a few hours. Now, with the power out, the whole page was likely down. The photo had been small, and without knowing Greta herself, who would connect the two?

She heard herself murmur something dismissive about the dock incident and took a bite of bread, a large one. She wanted the excuse not to speak for a second, but as she chewed she saw Julie Voltsheim gazing at her with interest, shutters clicking behind those plum-colored eyes. She would end up in a novel, Greta thought, downwardly mobile and desperate, the Lily Bart of Sugar City, Idaho. That was the folly of it—she'd moved out, trying to salvage some dignity from Will, trying not to be the couple they'd already become: the drunken couple, the couple in the bar or at the party whose facades start to show the unraveling seams and chipped yellow teeth. But she'd acted impulsively, and here she was: out there in the early mornings watching her roommate slosh out from a lake—having a roommate at all! Having *two*.

She swallowed her bread, eager to say something to once again redirect the lunch and regain a little dignity. She opened her mouth—she could begin with the lake, the lake would lead her to the campus, the campus to Julie Voltsheim's undergraduate years, Julie Voltsheim's undergraduate years to her wish to make changes for the better, and from there to the money to accomplish it.

The bread had not gone down. Greta swallowed again and said, "That was—" but her voice got clotted, tamped down in her throat. She held up a finger and shifted her chin, swallowing again. The bread crust moved, rose like a fish lifted by the tide, but settled back down in her throat once more. It seemed to have grown, to have become leathery and wide as a mitt.

Greta lifted her warm water glass and took a cautious sip, then kept sipping, as much as she dared. The water trickled down, the bread rising to let it pass but not dissolving. Greta felt the work of her throat in great detail: its glottal effort, the pulse of muscle and the wet contractions, like a python's, trying to ease the burden along. She felt the ragged edges of the crust against her flesh.

So this was choking. She made a fist and tapped it to her sternum. Julie Voltsheim looked mildly concerned. She pushed her water glass toward her. Greta took the water—her own glass was still half full—and tried once more, but the bread merely floated and resettled. She had never understood how this happened to people, but it turned out to be so simple and so complete, like the crust of bread that capped the stuffing in a turkey. Greta tapped and tapped, smiling, shaking her head, trying to convey that she needed help, but just a bit of it, the gentlest and most nuanced of Heimlich maneuvers.

"Better now?" said Julie. Her hands were braced on the table. Greta shook her head regretfully. A sense of inevitability descended: she might break a rib today. It had to happen.

"Ah," said Julie. She got to her feet, flapped her fingers at Greta to indicate she should stand as well. Obediently, Greta rose. Julie placed two warm hands on Greta's shoulders and turned her around toward the wall. Faces smeared in her peripheral vision but Greta focused on the yellow paint and a faint film of dust in the seams of the banquette.

Now she gave in to the urge to take a breath. Just as she'd feared, the sound that came from her throat was a desperate wordless heave.

The restaurant quieted and people began to stand. Greta was about to wave them off when she felt Julie Voltsheim wrap her arms around her, the long hands knotted below Greta's ribs, and squeeze. Greta hunched limply against her, feeling the warmed, damp length of this woman, leg to shoulder, the walnut of a belt buckle pressed into the small of her back, the softness of Julie Voltsheim's breasts against her scapulae, the startling, twinned thump of Julie's pelvic bones. Greta thought distantly that Julie was taller than she had realized. Julie squeezed again, and Greta's body—oh, she loved her body just then, how it recalled just what to do—gave it right up. The bread leaped daintily into her mouth, as if it had only awaited a *please*.

Greta was careful not to let her mouth open. Instead she held the soggy bread behind her lips, picked up her napkin, and spat the food into it as neatly as she could. She would not make any further spectacle of herself.

How hot this restaurant was, not even a fan to cool the sweat on her face. They were still standing there, Julie's arms wrapped tightly around her ribs. The other patrons had sat down again, turning toward one another but looking at their table through the corners of their eyes. Julie Voltsheim must feel how damp Greta was, wet armpits probably repulsing her. Greta was unaccustomed to such closeness. Julie loosened her arms and stepped back.

Greta sat down, and Julie did as well. The only indication that she was shaken was that she sat down beside Greta, on her side of the booth. They were breathing hard. Greta gulped at her water. Her throat was raw and abraded. Julie's hand was on her back, and Greta could feel every ridge of skin through her shirt. Around them the restaurant was buzzing again, and Greta wondered if it had ever quite stopped. They'd moved so swiftly that maybe only the people nearest them had even noticed that awful sound she'd made.

The women next to them gave Greta careful, probing smiles. One silently proffered her cell phone, but Greta shook her head.

"Are you okay?" Julie asked.

She nodded. "Thank you." Her voice was toneless and carrying. Julie rubbed her back and Greta let herself slump a bit, exhausted. Could it really be only one thirty? The women next to them had gone back to their meals, dredging their forks through the food and peering at Greta through their eyelashes. She could smell the woodsy scent of the mushrooms from here.

"I'm going to get you something to drink," Julie said, getting up.

Greta drank the rest of the water on the table. She drew deep breaths through her mouth, feeling each one rush against the sore ring inside of her throat.

Greta was trembling. She ran her hands over her thighs to dry them, then touched the ridges of cartilage at her throat. From reading Julie's mysteries she had learned about the hyoid bone, which was supported by the muscles of the neck. When a corpse had a broken hyoid bone, police suspected strangulation. She rubbed the skin over her voice box, trying to soothe it from outside. At the briefest glimpse of suffocation, her whole body had reacted with frantic disbelief.

The sensation of airlessness was taking longer to depart than it should. Not in her body—she kept drawing deep breaths to prove she could—but in her mind. Greta was realizing she had experienced this before. She grasped at it, rubbing her throat, feeling the hot skin. What was she recalling? She sat very still, searching, and when she realized what she was thinking of, the realization returned to her physically, like an immersion in warm water.

It had happened months ago, in March, or April. Before she'd left Will, just before she'd quite accepted that she needed to. She'd forgotten all about it until now.

She'd been at home one evening, waiting for Will. Already she'd cooked, eaten, read a book, all the ways she tried to pass the evening until the time when he might be home, then should be home, then was egregiously late. Still she'd heard nothing. He wasn't answering his cell. By nine she was unable to concentrate on an article and turned on the TV. That was how she did it, the shows passing time, a magazine flapping in her lap as an additional distraction, all something to look at until the phone rang or she heard him at the door. She could do several activities at once, Will's absence running through her mind concurrently, as if it were a stream she was forever walking beside.

By that point in their marriage, she hoped for a phone call, but not from Will. From the hospital or the police. If it was the hospital, she'd pick up the phone. But she wouldn't go and get him. The relief of knowing where he was, that he was alive and being taken care of, would be enough to let her sleep. He'd ended up in the hospital a few times after passing out somewhere. They couldn't move him or wake him, so the bartenders called the ambulance. Will never admitted this. She found out when the hospital phoned. Later on he just refused to discuss it.

If the police called, she wasn't so sure she would pick up. Maybe he could spend a night in jail if she didn't. She didn't think the police would tell her really bad news on the phone, so she counted those calls as safe. And if she picked up the phone, they might make her come get him. She didn't want to. She didn't want him *there* with her; she only wanted him alive.

But all of this was background to almost any evening, and none of it was new. This night was typical in its stretch of silence, its slow movement. As the hour got later, Greta knew she had to try to sleep. She synced her breathing to her own counting. She forced herself into it. Every now and again she could will herself to sleep, for a few minutes, in this way. But usually she lay on the couch and only splashes of sleep would come. That night she hadn't thought she'd dropped off at all: she had thought she was awake.

And maybe she had been awake. Maybe her eyes were open. She knew she could see the white flashing light of the television. Across the room, on the celadon chair, lay several library books and the packaging from a mail-order skirt. She'd put away the skirt but the large, heavy silver plastic bag it was shipped in had been on the chair across the room all evening.

The plastic bag was not close at hand. It was merely present. All night it had been in her line of vision.

She didn't feel herself falling asleep, but Greta had begun to see a moving image in her head, a dream she was aware of having. The dream felt like a story told by someone else, someone who knew her very well. Perhaps someone who had been observing Greta's life for years, and was sick of what it saw.

She'd dreamed of herself dressed as she was that night, in the process of settling herself on the couch. In this vision, Greta was just as she would appear to someone peering in the window: clear and sharp-edged, her sweatshirt too big and pouching at her hips, her pale hair slightly rumpled. One leg stretched on the couch; the other foot—it was sheathed in a faded argyle sock— touched the floor.

Greta lay there, dreaming but not quite dreaming, and watched her doppelgänger. She saw the plastic bag in her double's hands as she spread the silver plastic over her head and face.

Just then Greta had opened her eyes—certain only then that they must have been closed—and jerked up. She had bent chest-over-knees, pulse racing, just as she was sitting now in the booth at the restaurant. She had looked around frantically and saw the plastic bag where it had been all night, still across the room, but she was terrified nevertheless. Was it sleepwalking if you knew what you were about to do but could not quite control it?

In the moment before she fully awoke, Greta had been very close to getting up and reaching for the bag. She could hardly believe she wasn't already holding it in her lap.

Julie had returned to the table now, seating herself decorously across from her, bearing more water and a small glass half filled with white wine.

"I thought you might need a sip of something," she said, pushing it toward her. Greta drank the water down but shook her head at the wine. She wanted it, but she was afraid to become someone reaching for alcohol any time she was stressed.

"Thank you," she said. She looked up at Julie and found her smiling strangely: Julie's eyes were damp and her face flushed. She looked as if she might be on the verge of tears, but then she laughed instead. Julie seemed to have lost a layer of polish; the declaiming author had disappeared. Her cheeks shone.

"They hardly noticed," she said. "Oh my God, you could have died. They're all just eating."

Greta laughed a little hysterically. It was true that the other diners were quietly chatting and fanning themselves with menus and plucking morsels off one another's plates. The memory of the food filling her throat, of the other Greta carefully smothering herself, faded just a little.

"Have you ever done that before?" she asked. She breathed deeply, felt the air moving into her lungs, her blood rushing with oxygen.

"No! I learned it when the kids were small. My husband and I both did."

"Thank God," Greta said. She drew another deep and rattling breath. "Well. I guess you already knew lunch is on me."

Outside the restaurant they stopped and looked at one another. Here on the sidewalk the city seemed close to normal: sunny, busy, cars passing by. Both were seized by nervous laughter, caught in a flurry of conversation, as if the two of them had pulled off some kind of con. They talked over each other, only half-listening, gripped hands and let them fall again.

Greta laid a hand on her throat. She didn't know how to proceed, where to leave things. She couldn't tell if she should acknowledge the original purpose of the lunch or not—should she simply say she would call again? Should she tell Julie that she, Greta, was now inspired to make a donation to a choking victims society? Was there such a thing? Greta heard a strange little twitter of a laugh escape her. Her eyes smeared, teary.

Julie Voltsheim did something that startled her: she hugged her, kissed both Greta's cheeks, their damp hot faces sliding against one another.

Greta's throat was sore. She felt cornered, too sweaty to be touched, but the hug was comforting, too: there was something mammalian and primitive in being swept up and embraced, jostled into place like a kitten. It used to be that she'd think she was holding it together quite nicely, getting through her days, until she'd, say, go to the grocery store, and a clerk would eye her and say softly, "Are you okay?" And Greta would snap her expression back into place, spark up like a fuse.

"You're all right?" Julie asked, gripping Greta's shoulders and searching her face. "We'll talk again soon, but I just want to be sure before I turn you loose. You're okay?"

Greta nodded. "I am," she said. She wasn't, but it was imperative that she end the encounter with the teaspoon of dignity she had left.

She tried to proffer a bright expression, but the impulses went awry: her smile halved, her eyes darted off. She strung a few senseless words together and turned, running away from Julie Voltsheim at a trot.

But she had run only a few feet when Julie called her name. Greta heard her shoes clapping down the sidewalk, and when she turned, Julie was frantically churning through her purse as she ran, and holding up a palm to stall Greta. "One sec, just one more sec," Julie was saying. She fished out a little camel-colored leather notebook and a silver pen from her bag and began scrawling in the book. Greta glimpsed several long curving lines, Xs, and arrows. Finally Julie tore out the page and folded it into Greta's palm. "Directions," she said. "Come anytime, Greta, honestly. The morels are everywhere."

. . .

Greta drove back toward her office, choosing Lakeshore Drive because it took longer. Where was Will now? Was he still at her house, sleeping on the couch, or had he made it to work? She almost called his cell phone to tell him about this, to tell him she'd nearly killed herself at lunch, and maybe once last winter, too. She was having a hard time delineating whether she wanted to call her husband to hurt him or just to tell him, as she had for years, about something important that had happened.

Last year she had told him about a coworker of hers, an executive assistant who'd been at the college longer than all of them, and who had left the office on sick leave with what turned out to be pancreatic cancer. Greta had told Will rather calmly after work, still amazed by the swiftness of the diagnosis but not quite believing anything would really happen. Will had come home late, had quietly listened to her about the assistant, and then hugged her and went to bed. Three weeks later the assistant was dead, and when she told Will this as well, he was as surprised as if the assistant had walked in front of a bus. He didn't remember being told, Greta had realized. He'd come home drunk, faking it as always, and the whole conversation had slipped his mind.

That was why she hadn't told him about that vision with the heavy silver bag. It was like unburdening oneself to an operator— you were misreading the politeness as engagement. Will was unable to get to the surface often enough, for sustained periods, to do anything other than gesture at being a husband.

But she didn't tell anyone else, either. She didn't want to hear what anyone would say. Charles would tell her to go to a shrink—anyone would tell her to go to a shrink—and Greta didn't disagree. She hadn't realized that she was so distraught; she'd thought, for years, that she was managing. But obviously something else inside Greta disagreed, and it had stepped out from behind the curtain to lead her along—maybe to warn her, but maybe to make an offer. And the bag had seemed to her a reasonable suggestion, one she might well need someday. It might be time for this, the dream seemed to say. And you can have it any time you need to, with something as simple as a plastic bag.

Greta phoned her boss. She was about to say she must be coming down with something when her boss said, "Oh, everyone's going home. The students are all refusing to go back in—they're pitching tents on the quad lawn. Let's see how this stupid blackout goes tomorrow."

Greta had used maybe half her sick days in the last three years. She loved going to work, loved thinking only about how to solve the puzzle of this potential donor or that. Even her performances for the donors were dear to her. They reminded her how competent she was at everything that wasn't at home. But better yet, it gave her power. She'd never let herself be some woman stuck at home with a shitty part-time job and a couple kids, clinging to some asshole of a husband. She had clung, it was true, but she felt that was a decision she had made, and at least she had the means to change her course. And she had. She may not always have wanted her job but she never allowed herself to consider leaving it. She was self-sufficient. Her main worry was that Will would somehow soak her for money, not how to achieve the reverse. She didn't see how he could keep his job much longer. She didn't see how he could do anything much longer: he did not pay bills, he did not buy food, he did not change the oil in the car or file their receipts or balance their accounts.

But then again, she would not have guessed he would come to see her, either. She hadn't thought he retained even that much wherewithal.

She drove toward her old house. She wanted that ottoman.

She wanted the little end table, and the bench, and she wanted bed frames and bookcases she couldn't take with her today.

When she got out of her car, the neighbor waved at her. Greta waved back but kept walking. She and Will had spent all last summer spying on those neighbors after they moved in and immediately set about devoting two-thirds of their lawn to garden. By the time they finished, it was a trellised landscape roped with grapevines and squash and tomatoes, little jungles of chili peppers. The neighbors were out there every night, talking well after dark, the smell of charcoal smoke filtering in through Greta and Will's window.

Her key still worked; she knew he wouldn't have managed to change the locks. She would have.

Inside the front room there was a stack of newspapers on the floor. Her ottoman sat marooned without a chair. The little rounded bench was on its side. In the kitchen there were several seltzer cans on the table, but no rotting fruit on the counters, no flies buzzing around trash. It was better than she'd thought it would be, but also warm and silent and dead-aired.

She propped open the front door and picked up the ottoman. It would fit in the backseat of her car. She tested the bench; it was heavy but she could drag it across the grass to keep from scratching it. The end table was easier; it wasn't a solid carved block. She chose the end table for now. She felt in some vague way that the furniture—the simple mass of it—would be useful. It could be repurposed, sold, carved, burned, stacked into walls. She didn't know what she'd do with it—she simply craved the things she'd earned.

She was wedging the table behind the driver's seat when a car pulled up in the driveway behind her. When she saw Will's car she felt a strange rush of fear and nerves, but then she saw Will's head lolling in the passenger seat, and in the driver's seat was Hal.

Hal glanced at the form next to him and got out to meet her. Hal out of context was a whole other man. He seemed so scruffy over here, huge and faintly intimidating. "Fancy meeting you here," he said.

"You, too," Greta said. "Are you just coming from home?"

Hal shook his head and pushed his hair away from his face. He pulled out a cell phone, flipped it open, glanced at it, and flipped it shut. "We had a full day," he said, like the parent of a toddler. "I'll tell you all about it once we get him in there."

Greta was about to say, "We?" but Hal was looking at her steadily, ready for an argument. "Okay," she said. She closed the door on her furniture and the two of them went over to the car and opened Will's door.

He was breathing slowly and heavily. "Should we take him somewhere?" Hal said.

"Like where?" she asked. Will's shirt was wrinkled, a wisp of hair showing beneath the collar, but his neck was shaved clean and his sideburns were neatly edged as hedges. He managed this, of course. He managed one spectacularly useless bit of vanity. She reached in and patted his cheek. He stirred. She patted it harder, the slack skin jiggling slightly.

"All right, then," said Hal. He pulled her aside and reached in, looping his arm behind Will, and putting Will's arm over his shoulder. "Get the doors, please."

Somehow Hal managed it. He got Will to wake up enough to rest weight on his feet, to move forward enough to get him inside. Near the front door Will seemed to be gripped by a return to dignity, for he shook off Hal and walked ahead into the house.

Greta looked inside the door but didn't go in. Will had sat down in the living-room armchair, crossed his legs, and seemed to have gone under yet again. She and Hal watched him for a moment, during which he didn't move.

"I'm still not sure we should leave him," said Hal. He came out onto the front porch and pulled the door behind him, holding it open a crack.

Greta felt tears of frustration and exhaustion filling her eyes. "I can't stay here," she said. "I don't know what to do with him, anyway."

"Watch him?" said Hal. "Just be sure he breathes?"

"I'm going," she said. "I've watched this plenty of times: you watch him do nothing while you go nuts. Please don't stay here with him. Just come home."

She began walking toward her car, willing him to follow. Hal paused inside the front door before closing it behind him. For a second he stood on the porch, arms crossed, and looked around him. Greta saw the neighborhood through Hal's eyes: each house neatly closed away, the windows blinded by the afternoon sun. Hal shut his eyes and shook his head, and then shoved his hands in his pockets and walked back to Greta's car. They watched each other. His eyes were so hard Greta thought he might hit her. Just then she would welcome it; she thought she could tear apart anyone, even him.

But he said nothing until they reached campus. Then, finally, he said, "I drove him home this morning, actually, and then for some reason I took him with me on a visit."

"You took him to work?"

"It wasn't exactly work. He's pretty sick, Greta," Hal said. "I really don't think we should have left."

"I can't drag him anywhere," she told him. "Maybe you're big enough, but I'm not. He doesn't want to go somewhere. He doesn't want anything. I don't even know why he was there last night." They were both silent for a few blocks. "I'm sorry about that," she added. "Thank you for driving him back."

Hal smiled thinly. "I had a very stupid plan," he said. "I brought him over to see this woman on my route. I didn't know if they'd get her enough food today and I had no idea how she'd do with this power outage. She's all alone; she's completely isolated. I brought him along."

Greta eyed him. "You willingly took him somewhere?"

He nodded. "It didn't go all that well. He passed out on the couch for a lot of it."

She imagined Will leaning back on their own couch, the silver bag magically resurrected from whatever landfill she'd sent it to. Will would have that sort of power, malevolent and self-destructive.

She pulled to a stop at an intersection where a policewoman was directing traffic. A stream of cars moved before them.

"I need a lawyer," Greta said to the cars. "He didn't go to work today, obviously. For all I know he's already lost his job."

"I don't think he's lost it yet. He said they were going to can him but they hadn't yet."

"They are," she agreed. "I don't think he even told me about all the warnings. I heard about one from someone at his firm. They're lawyers; he could walk in there covered in blood and brain matter and if he did the job they wouldn't care, but you do have to get there." She wiped her hands over her face, peering above her fingers at the policewoman.

"He's on my insurance," she noted, "not me on his. That's something, I guess."

"If he does get fired maybe he'll go to rehab."

"It doesn't matter," Greta said.

"Of course it does. Rehab is a big step. If he dries out for a few days he might be able to think clearly enough to make some decisions."

The policewoman stopped the other line of traffic and waved an arm at Greta. Greta moved forward into the intersection.

"He went to rehab," she said after a few blocks. "He went last fall for four weeks, and I was so happy I told my whole family about it, and I trooped up there every weekend to see him, and I took part in their stupid round-table discussions with all the other families, and we played Frisbee on the lawn with all the other addicts, and they gave him a little coin and everyone was all supportive and delighted and hopeful. It's like summer camp. The food is bad and they get dessert and snacks every night and a set time to play and visit. He was like a counselor there; they all just loved him." She met Hal's eyes. "He's charming when he's himself," she explained. "He's very funny and very smart, and he gives off this confidence, and people want to listen to him. They want to hear what he says because he says it with such certitude they're sure he must be right."

Hal nodded. He'd seen no evidence of this but he believed her. It was the first time he'd been able to imagine Greta and Will together.

"And?" he asked.

"Three months," she said. "Through the holidays."

"I guess you had a nice Christmas at least."

Greta could tell he was looking at her closely. She braked at a hand signal from yet another cop—she hated driving through campus even when the lights worked—and turned to face Hal. "We had the best Christmas we'd had in five years," she said. "We were with my family, and we made a lot of toasts with apple cider because no one would drink alcohol. We went to midnight mass. I thanked God, and I don't really believe in God, but I was so relieved and happy that it spilled over. I would have thanked Santa. I felt my whole life being handed back to me, you know? And I stopped separating all our money—I didn't merge it back again but I stopped systematically putting new things in my name—and I booked a trip for us to Montreal for the spring. I was a total idiot, in short."

Hal said nothing. Greta took in his high forehead, the thick brows and dark lashes that framed his eyes. His eyebrows angled down slightly at the outer edges, and there was a hazel sunburst at the center of his irises. He was not quite handsome, but she had an inkling, suddenly, of Hal as charismatic, the gently prodding way he would humor you into volunteering, into donating, into taking your vitamins and eschewing meat. He had a low smooth voice and big hands. He was not as young as Karin. He was close to Greta's own age.

The cop waved her on and Greta began driving again. "What do you want to do?" she said. "It's what, three o'clock? We're not at work, you've earned some fun time by spending the morning with Will. What do you want? Can I take you to a movie? Well, there aren't any now, I guess. But I can buy you a drink. We can go for a walk."

She was gesturing as she listed the options—all felt inappropriately romantic and datelike but she didn't know what else to offer—and Hal caught her hand in his and held on to it, squeezing the bones. Greta stared fiercely at the road before her, refusing to look his way. She let her hand be hoisted like a trophy between them. Why was everyone grabbing and manhandling her today? Sometimes Greta felt herself to be a raw-skinned little doll, calcified under a few layers of shell and bone.

"I wasn't good to him today," Hal said softly. "I didn't do your husband any favors."

Greta wrenched her hand away. "This is what he does! He gets you to think that if you haven't bent over backward to help him enough then it's all your failing, and it's *not*. It's his. His own family never calls him anymore, Hal. And it's not because they're cruel and cold, it's because they can barely stand to talk to him. Mine stopped calling so they didn't have to talk to him; they e-mail. I don't even know if he has a personality anymore. I think he's curdled. Just don't fucking talk to me about how you failed him. You didn't beat the shit out of him; he should be grateful."

Hal's expression was somewhere between amazement, realization, and disgust. "Of course I didn't beat the shit out of him," he said. "I know I'm a little burned out but I'm not so far gone I seek out sick people and beat on them. What do you *think* of me?"

Greta's cheeks flared with heat. "No, that's not—I didn't mean that."

"I'm not where I need to be," Hal was saying, shaking his head. "I'm aware of that, you know. I know I'm completely useless at my job, I know I let my family just disappear, but I'm not some fucking thug, Greta. I thought I was at least getting most of the motions down."

He said into his hands, "Your husband is really, really sick. I feel like he might poison himself today, or tonight, or whatever, and I *still* couldn't wait to get away. This is why we're failing. We don't mean anything we say we do."

"Yes, you do," Greta said. "You tried. Thank you for trying. But I really can't. I can't deal with him anymore. I didn't leave for some nebulous reason. I left because I was nuts. I was violent. I hit him more than once. He didn't seem to feel anything, or respond to anything, so it didn't seem to matter, and it felt really good to go after him like that. To just *hit* him. Nothing else gets through. Nothing was enough."

She felt Hal watching her. Her face was red with shame.

"He's a big guy," he said uncertainly.

"He was sick and completely helpless," she said. "You can't make him respond no matter what you do. I felt like I was so small, comparatively, that he couldn't even feel it, but you'll notice I didn't hit him in the face, or anywhere someone would see it." She rubbed her forehead with an arm. "Think how filled a house is, with heavy things and sharp things. I came so close."

CHAPTER TWELVE

The first CSA box of the season was on the porch. Hal hoisted it up and took it back to the kitchen. Greta fought the impulse to go to her room and read a novel. It was only three fifteen. She wanted to do something with the next few hours. She didn't want to waste it staring at a book or draining the radio's batteries.

Hal was calling Karin's name, but no one was home. He came back to the living room, where Greta was straightening throw pillows.

"Did Karin tell you what she was doing today?" Hal asked. "I was assuming she'd come back early, too."

Greta shook her head. "She didn't tell me anything," she said. He frowned. "I'll call her." Greta dug out her cell phone, but Karin's phone was either off or out of range. She tried again, just in case, and got a busy-circuits message.

Greta flipped her phone closed and shrugged. "She's fine, I'm sure of it." Hal returned to the kitchen.

The blanket that usually lay heaped on the couch had been folded and draped over the back. She could see Will doing this in the morning, bleary and confused, but retaining enough sensibility to recall that you made such gestures in another person's house. She glanced toward the kitchen to see if Hal was visible. He was not. Greta bent down and breathed in the scent of the upholstery; its woolly mild warm smell that bore no hint of anything acrid.

She wasn't going to read; she could not turn on the TV. Nothing much was left to concentrate on and be distracted by: the food was tainted, the music was bland. She feared even their box of farm-fresh produce was some kind of marketing stunt, just some old Guatemalan fruit shipped out by Wal-Mart in a carefully dilapidated box.

In the kitchen Hal had spread the box's contents onto the table and was standing over the scattered objects, arms crossed, staring hard at two Japanese eggplants, a couple flappy heads of butter lettuce, some spring onions, and a bundle of spinach. He was tossing parsley from hand to hand.

Greta leaned against the door jamb. "Is that sparse or am I just new to this?"

Hal shrugged. "It's a little sparse," he said. "Of course, it's early in the season. Anyway, it's my night to cook."

"I know. I thought I might help anyway." She moved closer and pulled up a chair. "I could make pasta with spinach."

Hal sighed. "Usually it makes me feel better to plan dinner."

"Well, I said it before," Greta exclaimed. "Let's go do something! What do you want to do? We're grown-ups, we can do what we want. There must be something to do."

Their eyes met, and Greta was embarrassed at herself. That they didn't know each other very well was clear. She'd only been

alone with Hal once or twice. Karin was always nearby. She
forced herself to continue. "I don't know what you like to do,"
she admitted. Hal smiled slightly. "You have no idea what I like
to do, either," she added, "so don't get all smug."

"You walk by the lake and throw stale bread at the ducks," he
said. "Not to them, at them. You buy expensive chocolates and
keep them in your room."

"Good guesses," Greta murmured. And they were.

Hal leaned against the table next to her, his thighs about
three inches away. "You alternate between Tolstoy and old Ju-
dith Krantz paperbacks," he said softly. "You want to call your
husband but you won't. You look at real estate listings and read
books on home repair. You force yourself to stay downstairs when
Karin and I get home but you really want to go up to your room
and shut the door. You eat a lot of dried fruit, Greta. A freakish
amount of dried fruit. Sometimes I see you packing your lunch
and I think you're getting ready to hike the Appalachian Trail.
And after the night I met you, when you displayed a passionate
point of view on billboard legislation, you've never said another
word about it. Not one."

"Very nice," she said. "I'm pleased you're observing." So this
was Hal in his seductive mode; he wore it lightly, with a faint
smirk that said he knew it was a bit funny, too, but he looked her
in the eye the entire time. He really hit those notes. She'd been
waiting for this and dreading it, too. Did every woman who moved
in here get the treatment after a few weeks? Had Karin? Greta
missed Karin suddenly, wanting to sit her down and quiz her.

Hal was gazing down at her. She ran a hand over the ruffled
edges of the spinach on the table.

"You seem to be feeling better now," she said. Hal's expression faltered slightly, and Greta regretted it instantly. She was
always talking when she didn't want to, redirecting the conversation to some place she didn't want to go. But she had the sensa-

tion that this was a distraction for him, that Hal was able to ward off whatever he was upset about by shifting gears and moving his focus a crucial few inches to the left, and there she was, sitting in his line of vision.

"I feel a little better," Hal admitted cautiously. "Can't spend the whole free dark afternoon dwelling on it."

"All we do is cook around here," Greta said, standing up. She leaned a hip against the table. They weren't quite touching. "Have you noticed that? We cook, and we talk about what we're going to cook, and what we just ate, and what we'd like to eat. I thought I was a big food person but you guys really have me beat." She glanced at her watch. "The day is wasting," she told him. "Give me something. Give me something not food-related and we'll head off and do that, no questions asked."

"What do people do all day?" Hal said. "Everything seems so trifling. They knit and cook and go fishing and hunting and let the phone ring. It doesn't mean anything."

"You have no idea what to do," Greta said, disappointed. He made all their options feel foolish—sex or movies or baking or puzzles did all seem equally pointless.

She didn't know what to do, either. Hal took a deep breath and shook his head at nothing in particular. He took the spinach from her and leaned past her to turn on the oven. As he moved behind her, she felt him there, and they both listened for the spark of the oven turning on. He was close and warm and sullen and familiar, unwilling and desirous all at once. It was not unlike being with Will. Hal laid a hand lightly at her neck, cupped the edge of her jaw, then drew away and patted her shoulder.

The oven wasn't catching. It clicked and clicked but nothing sparked. Greta heard Hal sigh, then heard a jingling sound: Hal set a bunch of keys, Will's keys, on the table before her. He turned away from her and headed into the living room, where he picked up the phone and checked for a dial tone.

"Anything?" she said. He shook his head and sat down on the couch, tossing the phone onto the coffee table, where it skidded and shoved aside the candles.

Greta sat down next to him. He wasn't looking at her; he had freed himself of the moment in the kitchen as simply as slipping out of a jacket. She had to remember how this was done. She'd forgotten how to run the drill. It seemed imperative that she get these skills back, because it was ridiculous to think Will would ever get better. She'd been an unforgivable fool for hoping he would. The only thing she could think of to do was to force herself forward. Her clothes felt grimy, her armpits itchy with dried sweat, and her throat was still sore. The thought made her laugh; she hadn't told him about lunch. She nearly died and still the day was all about Will.

"What?"

"Nothing," she said. Greta leaned in close to him; she breathed in the scent of sweat and pine and the lemony enviro-detergent they all used. His mouth seemed hard to get to; his chin in the way and the angle treacherous. She pressed her mouth to his neck instead; it was soft but prickled with his beard. He flinched when she touched him. She stayed where she was, eyes closed, mortified, and waited him out.

CHAPTER THIRTEEN

Karin had disengaged herself from the Rothbergers with some difficulty in the late afternoon. After the cheese cave, a perplexing kind of current had run between her and Elaine. One would relax while the other was preoccupied, one would chuckle over the milking while the other frowned over the bees, that terrifying cave. The magic of the day had dissipated for Karin by then, and she agreed to lunch only because she had no other choice. So they sat down to pasta salad with olives and cottony-textured supermarket tomato and ate some cheese—thank God the cheese was good. She could still write a profile of them without obfuscating.

Then she remembered she was only there to write about the cheese—not the quiet honeycombs, the distressed poultry, the downward cast to Elaine's posture as the day continued. Just the cheese, and the cheese was still excellent. Grateful for the narrow scope of her job, grateful no one expected or wanted her to write an exposé, Karin had served herself a large wedge of Brie. She ate a little of it but stopped when she felt slightly ill: not nauseated but full, as if she'd eaten already.

Everything she'd tried lately, everything that felt right and brave, had turned out to be ridiculous, even dangerous. Her city was a mess, but she was hours from it, yet still in the shambles anyway.

Karin had wanted to sleep, to sit in the sun like a gecko. She concentrated on the cheese rind as it softened on her tongue, tried not to look out at the mirage of the verdant hills, the crumpled white lace of the rushing creek in the distance.

After lunch Elaine walked her to the door and stood there, waving, as Karin started up the car. In a burst of officiousness, Carl had charged after the car, loping over the gravel and woofing hoarsely. Startled, Karin accelerated and raced off down the driveway toward the dirt road.

She'd felt a strange sadness as she pulled away, the sense that she was leaving something momentous. It made no sense to feel this way, but the sensation of a mistake had filled her little car, and she drove with the window partially down to the hot dimming air, feeling nervous. On the seat next to her, where the air-conditioning would keep them cool, was a little box of newspaper and eggs from the henhouse.

When they had passed the henhouse on the way back to the farmhouse, Karin suddenly wanted to take some souvenir—she wanted *evidence*—to show Hal and Greta. Or perhaps she wanted to show Francine. She could write about them, she could document what was happening, but she had forgotten her camera.

She had gone the whole day not thinking about the person from the lake, too. She'd shirked every responsibility she had today, and where had it gotten her?

"May I take a couple of those eggs?" she'd asked. "I'll buy them."

Elaine had grimaced, saying, "You think I could sell these to someone else?" Then she'd paused. "Why do you want them?"

Karin shrugged, uncertain. "I bet they're still good," she said. Skeptically, but still wanting a reporter on her good side, Elaine had agreed.

By six Karin was close to Madison again. For the first time since she pulled out of the driveway that morning, she wondered about Greta's husband. It was possible he was still there on their couch. Maybe he had moved in. Maybe he was sitting with Hal and listening to the news, Hal's nightly self-torture. Karin often joined him out of solidarity. She thought watching the news alone was more frightening than watching it with someone.

Karin drove, feeling older and emptied. She checked her cellphone messages. One from Francine, checking in on her travels. Francine worried about Karin driving around in her old car on rural roads, but when faced with the idea of a company car, she steeled herself. Nevertheless Francine liked to have some communiqué at the end of a trip. Karin would text-message her when she got home and charge the paper for it. She was paid by the mile for her drives and reimbursed for text messages if they were work related. It used to be forty-two cents a mile, but when gas prices skyrocketed Karin had recalculated and presented Francine with a new plan, to which, all things considered, Francine had little choice but to acquiesce.

Karin's cell phone crackled and then Francine's voice dropped away mid-sentence. How would the Midwest manage if fuel became too scarce to use this way? When, Karin corrected herself: *when* it became too scarce. She could hear Hal already. A city like New York could take it. New York seemed to adapt at every turn anyway, to floods and collapse and odd toxic smells. They were either intrepid there, or dumb as gerbils. But they would weather the changes in gas, Karin was certain, because the city was made for life without cars. If you had a car in New York you were lily-gilding anyway. But out here, towns and houses spread throughout the prairies and roads, and Karin could imagine the delays of it all: would they go back to horses? Was such a backward step really possible? Anything was possible. Hal would say that as a species they were on their way already, beating each other in the streets for a few bits of money and a phone.

The key was to use fuel for mass transit and hauling, and horses and bikes for other things, Karin decided, sailing past a slow-moving Volkswagen. Also to market the horse idea as a back-to-land sort of thing, make it chic enough that people could pretend it wasn't necessary. They might not have to give up cars altogether. There would be more car pools, if people still had cars.

Karin imagined taking this same drive a few years in the future. She might post her trip on a Web site and let interested parties jump on. They could get to know one another, tell jokes, compare reading lists. But it would be terribly dangerous, of course. If no one hitchhiked anymore, who the hell would carpool with strangers? She might end up dead. This part of the highway was surrounded by empty fields; any callbox would be miles away. She could be robbed and raped and strangled, and abandoned in a field.

Karin peered down the road ahead for several miles, growing increasingly uneasy. She hadn't spoken to anyone in so long. She hadn't called home to say she was on her way. Why live with other people if you didn't use them as safety backup in that way? She could see Hal talking to the police a few days later, holding Greta's hand and saying, "I tried to discuss the safety basics, like calling and checking in, a thousand times. You can talk all you want, Officer, but recalcitrance is a disease these days. And the carpool Web site she used was accredited, which surprises me." In her mind, she saw Greta nodding.

Now the gloomy city appeared before her, looking smaller and shabbier. She was glad she'd made it back before dark. The city was supposed to be beautiful. Normally spotlights festooned the dome of the capitol and the round pale cylinder of Monona Terrace, reflected in the glittering surface of the lake. She knew that once dark came, the lack of light would leave the skyline looking dull. The lakes would be expanses of tar, absorbent and treacherous, drawing the city downward. The shapes of buildings hulked before the pink sky. The road before her lay empty. An airplane flew over the city, heading toward her, and Karin was briefly reassured until she heard its roar and realized it was not a passenger jet. It was a military plane. In a second it was upon her and gone.

Karin looked behind herself, in the northwest direction from which she'd come. Back in the distance she saw a little carnival of lights but she could not determine where it was—on the highway? They must be on the highway. Where else would they be? She was seized with the disorienting sensation that the lights were coming from across a field, a convoy rushing over grass and dirt.

They were moving quickly, or else she was slowing down (she was; her speedometer said only forty-five) and behind her flashed a cluster of swirling reds, blues, and whites. She saw them rushing toward her, and was so intent on staring at her rearview mirror that the first rumble of her tires on the shoulder made her bark a startled exclamation. She gripped the steering wheel and let her car pull over to the side and stop.

Now she could turn all the way around and look at the rings of flipping lights on the empty horizon behind her. Gradually she saw that it was a fleet of police cars. Of course, it was the police. But why were there were so many, and why were they all silent? They were rushing toward the darkened city with reckless velocity, so fast that as the vehicles raced past, her car shivered, buffeted by the force of the light and the wind.

CHAPTER FOURTEEN

Hal was sitting next to Greta on the front porch when Karin pulled up. As soon as he saw her car Hal stood. He moved so quickly Greta had to reach out and steady a candle. The two of them were surrounded by several thick pillar candles in wide dishes, ready to be lit when the light fell.

Karin got out of her car and began to trudge up the drive, her white shirt glowing in the evening light. She was holding a small box and turning her head back and forth, looking at the darkened houses. Her silhouette looked shorter and slighter than Hal recalled, more vulnerable and feminine than he usually thought of her. At least she was home safe. Who knew where she was driving half the time on these cheese-reporting ventures, what strangers she was stopping to chat with under the guise of research?

In the surrounding houses on Morrison Street, people

stood on the porches, their shapes visible against the pale siding. When Karin approached, they were drawn to the edge of their porches to observe her. When she looked in their direction, they waved. She turned back to Hal, who met her on the front walk. Karin raised her eyebrows uncertainly.

On impulse Hal hugged her. She looked awful: her eyes sunk into her skull like jewels in a mask above the dark cavern of her mouth. Where had she gone today that left her looking this way? Comparatively, the rest of them all looked healthy.

It was only six thirty, but it did feel later. They would have the sun for another hour or so. Now people were coming over, trotting down their steps and into their yards. This had been happening all evening—someone arrived and everyone came over to that yard to see what they knew. They were all a little awkward and sheepish about it, but no one seemed able to stop themselves. Their neighbors gathered at the edge of the co-op yard, and Karin and Hal and Greta went down to meet them.

Hal said, "You remember everyone, right? From yesterday morning." He laid a hand on Greta's shoulder blade as he gestured around the circle, then saw that Karin was watching where his hand had gone. He removed his hand, broke eye contact, and cleared his throat. "I guess we didn't really get a chance to talk then, but we've all been talking since this afternoon." Now he looked down into the box she was holding. It was filled with shredded paper and eggs.

"What's going on?" Karin said. Her voice was raspy. The hug seemed only to have upset her. "The lights are still out?" She looked down at the eggs. "I need to get these to a cool spot."

"Why do you have eggs?" Greta asked, and Karin looked at the eggs as if she were wondering, too. She shook her head and said, "They gave them to me."

Greta peered into the box and then held one up. The egg looked pathetic and pebblelike perched between Greta's thumb and forefinger. "What do they grow there? Soylent Green?" she asked. Hal laughed and Karin frowned. She nearly snatched the egg back and put it carelessly into the box again.

"It's a perfectly nice little farm that's just getting going," she said. "It's having some issues, that's all."

"What?" Greta said. "I didn't mean to—" She reached forward to touch Karin's arm but Karin took a step back.

Hal was about to say something to placate Karin before he realized he wasn't sure what he'd be placating her for. Luckily, the neighbors began to introduce themselves. "So, Gary is our next-door neighbor," Hal said, falling into line. "You know the twins, the little redheaded boys? He's their dad."

Someone else touched Karin's arm to check her scratches— this time it was the woman who'd been so nicely dressed already at six thirty in the morning: Hal recognized her shining brown hair and the silver ring. Hal saw Karin's eyes moving around too quickly, from person to person, from bearded grad students to the bald young man and his wife, baffled by the greeting. Now Karin was a known person in the neighborhood, the girl who'd hopped into the lake as casually as if it were a mud puddle.

The couple from the other side of the co-op were in their early twenties, the woman with hair to her waist and a stocky build, the man bald and lanky. She wore a short-sleeved shirt, an odd crocheted vest over it, and shorts creased at the crotch. Her husband—their names were Marianne and Benjamin, Hal had to remind himself—had pointed features and pale eyes, eyebrows lightly sketched. He didn't seem to require hair.

Greta and Hal had come outside and met them all two hours earlier. It had seemed foolish to sit in dim hot houses when there was no discernible difference being outside—in fact, it was more pleasant outdoors, with breezes from the lake and the sounds of people talking in the street. What was left but to leave the house and look for people? So they all had stood in the street talking, repeating radio news to one another.

Their neighbors were not co-op people, Hal knew, and it was only yesterday at the lake and tonight that he really saw who any of them were. There were families next door and across the street, parents in their forties and children under ten. A few houses down, in a pale-blue Victorian with periwinkle trim, was the single woman with the silver ring. Her name turned out to be Laurel. She had joined the crew bearing a bouquet of flashlights, a sack of matches, and long thin tapers.

Now Hal tried to be discreet about looking back at Greta, whose hands were shoved in the pockets of her shorts. Her blond hair shone even in the dusk; she was nodding intently as Laurel gestured emphatically over some conversational point. Karin was looking back and forth between both Hal and Greta.

Will might be the only person unaffected by the blackout, or the only one unperturbed by it. He might already be passed out. He couldn't go anywhere without his car keys, at least, and while that left Hal feeling a bit unsavory, he was also greatly relieved. He thought, too, that Mrs. Bryant might be unaffected as well. She would be in the dark, of course, but she would go to bed early. She had food and candles. He had managed to get one thing done, at the very least. He'd been no help to Will, no help with the impossible task of filling that warehouse, but he could, at least, fill up one kitchen.

"Any word on phones where you were?" Gary asked Karin. The phones had begun to fail in the late afternoon. Now all their cell phones showed a signal but the lines seemed too overloaded to sustain calls.

Karin shook her head. "No phones? I was at a farm all day," she said. "I forgot about all of this."

Gary nodded gravely. He had a nimbus of coarse dark hair that rose taller than all of them, even Hal. His features were all as exaggerated as his height. Perhaps this happened to people at the far end of the normal-size spectrum: everything was too large; the nose wide at the base and pointed rather sharply, lips downturned and fleshy. He struck Hal as spectacularly ugly at first, but the more they spoke, the more his neighbor's looks were growing on him. Now he just seemed large and comforting when you stood in his shadow.

The others, too, all seemed to be edging their way to be near Gary, though no one wanted to be opposite him. The circle of conversation kept breaking as people sidled over to be adjacent to him, Hal noticed. It must be a fascinating display if you were watching from above. They kept forming a loose little arc and rotating unconsciously to hold the shape. He was looking forward to pointing this out to Greta.

"I don't know about the phones," Greta was saying. "I don't suppose any of us knows people who work for the phone company?" A flutter of head-shaking. "Me, neither. I don't know why both would be out now," she continued. "The phones were fine most of the day, right?" Nods.

The radio had said the phones were just overloaded. It sat on the ground near Gary's enormous work boot, nattering pointlessly into the twilight air.

"Anyone want something to drink?" Gary asked now. "We have a bunch of beer and wine still. It won't stay cold forever."

"I'll have one," Karin said.

Gary ran to his garage and returned a moment later with a cooler full of ice and bottles. Everyone reached in and grabbed something, comparing labels, brushing water off the glass. Karin set her box of eggs inside the cooler, perched safely above the bottles. The mood was more pessimistic than freeing, like the moment at a long party when one sensed the next day was ruined anyway.

"So why is everyone out here?" Karin asked.

"Just to meet up, see what's happening, I guess," said Gary.

Karin nodded and drank deeply from her beer. "Well," she said, "at least we're not stuck on a subway or something, right? I thought there'd been a bomb or something."

No one laughed.

"There was a kind of—a booming noise," said Greta. "Back around four."

The late-afternoon dimness had been alleviated by a sudden flash of power for less than a second, accompanied by a faint boom in the distance, a hollow, echoing kettle drum strike that then dissipated into the still air.

At the time Greta and Hal had been in Hal's room on the ground floor. When the hall light fizzed on and then out again and the boom sounded, the two of them had gone very still and stared at each other. Their faces were so close that Hal could see the ripples of Greta's irises. Her eyes were as pale as a cat's, he'd thought, and he had seen the moment her pupils flared to catch the lost light. Her skin, beneath his hand, had seemed to cool by ten degrees.

"Did you hear that?" Hal had said. "That booming sound?"

"Like fireworks or something," Greta had murmured, sitting up and looking around them. She had gone to the window and peered to the side of the curtain. Golden late-afternoon light streamed in as she moved the curtain, illuminating the curve of her neck, a ledge of collarbone, and the smooth slope of one small breast, the nipple still erect.

"I haven't heard anything to indicate it was a *bomb*," said Greta now. "It was more like a big drum getting one good thump."

"We heard it, too," Benjamin said. "And we have plenty of batteries and matches and candles, too, if you need them, by the way. At least we do for now. Anyhow, I jogged out and bought a couple extra flashlights just in case. We just came out here for a while to see what was up." He made a circular gesture in the direction of the other houses and the people standing outside them. "Be near people."

"We all did," said Marianne. "Sorry to converge on you like this," she added to Karin. "We've been sort of heading toward everyone new to see what they know, I guess. Where were you today?"

The question seemed to startle Karin, and Hal realized how odd it must be to come home and find them suddenly surrounded by interested neighbors who felt they knew their local hero. Karin barely knew who any of these people were.

"I was visiting a cheesemaker a couple hours away," she said, after a pause. "They're not affected, or they weren't when I left. How far does it reach, anyway?"

"All of Madison, Sun Prairie, Janesville, et cetera," Gary said. "Waukesha, Brookfield, pockets of Milwaukee and Chicago. It's regional so far. It isn't nationwide or anything."

"God," Karin replied. Her voice cracked. "I didn't even think to worry about the whole *nation*. What about the big cities? New York, L.A., all those?"

Everyone shrugged. "For once they're looking at us, I imagine," said Gary, and a round of satisfied nods coursed through the group.

"We don't know that, though," Karin said thoughtfully. "I mean, we have no idea really what they're all talking about. For all we know the whole country is just going on about its business." The image of a map with a darkening match-burn spreading outward from their little town seemed to hover in the air above them. Surely it wouldn't spread. Their town was so small in comparison to the great width of the whole country; how could it touch off the effect they were all imagining?

"A bunch of police cars blew past me just outside the city," she said. "And a jet. Anyone know where they were all headed?"

"Just peace-keeping, I guess," said Greta. "There was a weird power flash but it didn't stay on. Anyway, imagine those huge dorms downtown with no power for the second night in a row. The students are probably going nuts."

"I doubt they're that scared," said Hal mildly. "They're not children."

"They're not that grown- up, either," Greta said. "On my cam- pus they're freaked out."

"What does the radio say?" Karin asked.

"Very little now," Benjamin said.

Gary crossed his arms. "I guess there was some issue with overworked transformers," he said. "And then the heat and some out-of-date equipment. There's a lot of speculation but it didn't seem like much was decided. Then the goddamn phones died."

"I think the lines were overwhelmed."

"I think they should be built to handle that," Benjamin said.

"Well," Marianne said, tugging her braid, "I guess they aren't."

"You realize the power plant is just a couple miles from here," Benjamin said. He was looking off toward the other side of the isthmus: the power plant was right in the center of the land, a block away from the deserted Washington Avenue. "Don't you just want to go see what the hell they're doing over there? If they're doing anything?"

Now all of them turned in the same direction, as though they could see the plant from here. Hal could certainly picture it: it was a great two- or three-block structure surrounded by cyclone fencing and topped with a forest of floodlights. He knew what Benjamin was thinking the plant should be like, a pumping, steaming creature, alight and glowing. Maybe it was: maybe they would all be comforted if they went over and just looked. There would be utility trucks, and a full parking lot there—there had to be, didn't there?—a flurry of desperate activity to bring them back online.

"So go check it out," Marianne said. She tossed one hand in

the direction of the plant. "All day you keep wondering; go see what they're doing already."

Benjamin crossed his arms and the two glared at each other. "I certainly should," he said. "At least it's an action. We could also just stay here all night and know nothing. They've given up on even trying to explain! They're playing reruns of call-in shows, for God's sake. They think we don't even need to know."

"So, go and find out!" she said. "Then you'll know!"

Benjamin looked around the group, his expression somewhere between excited and fearful.

"There's not going to be much to see," Hal said softly. "They won't let you inside, and you can't see anything going on in there even when everything's fine. How often have you driven past it and barely even realized it? There isn't anything to see."

Benjamin seemed to lose an inch of height. He took a deep breath and shrugged. His wife pressed her lips together but didn't say anything further. Hal was just relieved Benjamin seemed willing to forget it. There might already be people at the plant; it might be a natural flashpoint if there was an angry, heated crowd. He didn't want to be in the news twice in one week.

In the silence they heard the radio broadcast sputtering. "Great," said Gary. "Again." He aimed a kick at it, knocking the radio onto its side.

"Just turn it off," said Laurel. "Look, no one is saying anything of substance anyway. Maybe it's like a watched pot."

"Maybe none of the energy companies are talking because there's nothing to say. Or they don't know what to say," Gary said.

"Or there's no one left in there to say it," Hal said. He was trying for lightness, but the comment silenced all of them. They all looked up and down the street for signs of life. They crossed their arms, looked off down the street and avoided eye contact, tugged sandal straps into place, and shoved hands into pockets.

Finally, Karin rubbed her hands over the scratches on her arms and said, "That can't be. We would know."

"Eventually," Benjamin agreed. "If the newspapers came back."

"There were newspapers before electricity," Greta pointed out.

"That isn't reassuring," Hal said.

"My point is that we'll figure all this out one way or another. Next topic. Come on."

"Fine," said Karin. "What have you guys been doing all afternoon?" Hal felt Greta tense slightly next to him, her arm shifting against his. Hal could think of nothing to say.

"Just this," Greta said finally. "We were home—Hal and I got off work early. When we heard that sound we got up and came outside."

Karin stopped rubbing her arms. "You got *up*," she said.

"From the couch," Greta said coolly. Hal looked away.

Karin eyed them closely. Hal thought he might be blushing.

"Maybe I should have called," Karin said, "but I guess you might not have heard anyway." She took a breath, and then said, "I had a strange day."

Everyone nodded, refocusing their emotion on Karin. It seemed to help them all to have her be the uninformed newcomer. Now they had a chance to extend comfort, and it seemed to soothe the group into a murmur. Any response was acceptable, they seemed to say, on such a day.

Another round of drinks came out of the dripping cooler, and now the taut circle of neighbors began to loosen. There might be nothing new to know, they decided, and so the burden began to fall from them. Now they could only chat, sip beer, and gaze up and down the street.

Hal began to relax. The phones were gone, and perversely this was a relief. He could not be expected to reach his father now. His uncle Randy had probably already been there, had fried fish and baked potatoes with his father, and driven home. He must have tried to call Hal and couldn't get through.

Gary's twins were outside now, bearing a basketball and a baseball. Marianne disappeared into her house and came back with bags of chips. Hal helped himself to a handful. Good God, they were incredible. They weren't organic chips, either: they were Doritos and potato chips, pure salt and fat and genetically modified corn. He could have eaten the whole bag himself.

Everyone was looser, brushing potato-chip crumbs from their hands, and settling into the grass and crossing their legs. Hal glanced behind him at their co-op, its pink Victorian facade and waving curtains, and it seemed so cloistered to him all of the sudden. How had he managed to hide inside it for so long?

A game of basketball was taking hold next door. Karin crossed the lawn ahead of them, and Greta fell into step beside Hal. "Should we talk about today?"

"If you want to," Hal said cautiously. He'd been eyeing her all evening, wondering what the next step was, if there was a next step. To his own surprise, Hal kind of hoped there was. It was unlikely, he knew, and anyone would tell him Greta was not a good bet. Hal could just see what Wes would have to say, which made him smile to himself. Greta would mop the floor with Wes. It had been so long since Hal had slept with someone, several months, and being with Greta had felt like a return to his own body and a welcome shutdown of the brain. Afterward, he had felt creaturely and content, a pure sleepy warmth.

"I don't know if we really need to," she said. Her voice sounded serene. He could see her profile in the dusk, the tendrils of hair that puffed over her forehead, the fine stubborn point of her chin. "Let's leave it, shall we? No need to talk it to death."

"Okay." He couldn't keep the disappointment out of his voice.

Greta glanced at him. "Thank you for trying with Will."

"I wasn't very successful," he said.

"No one is. Thank you, anyway." She paused at the edge of the driveway, a hand on his shoulder, but she was only removing her shoes. Hal looked up and saw Karin standing near the basketball hoop, watching them. Greta didn't seem to notice. She kicked her shoes into the grass and joined the fray.

By now it was close to dark. Hal watched the players: skin disappearing, ghostly, between the flash of white shirts and pale socks. Greta's hair was silvery, flopping over her forehead as she caught the ball. She dribbled once, then took aim and sank a jump shot that barely moved the net. The sound of whoops and encouragement came from the corners of the crowd, impossible to tell who'd said what.

Hal closed his eyes: it could have been summer thirty years ago. The basketball's rhythm on the pavement sounded different in the semi-darkness. The sound was less playful than it would be in full sunlight, a drum-like echoing.

He opened his eyes in time to see Karin try a lay-up. He'd never realized he lived with a couple of athletes. Karin was a runner, but that didn't account for the grace with which her feet leaped and landed, the arc of her wrist. Greta clapped her gleefully on the shoulder. Karin gave her the briefest glance in reply.

There wasn't going to be anything ongoing with Greta. That was clear. Hal committed the afternoon to memory instead. Her body showed its age, just a bit, in that she was slender but not taut. The gentle downward curve of her buttocks, the wrinkles of her elbows, the nascent lines on her neck. He'd had a moment there, right in the middle, when he'd looked down at both of them and understood that neither of them was young anymore: his pudding belly, the slack drop of his bicep, Greta's small breasts pressed against his chest. The thought of their ages, of how long it must have been since Greta was with someone other than Will, made Hal understand that this was a way of breaking loose for her. But for him it was the opposite; it tethered Hal to something once again. He hadn't realized how solitary he'd been, for months, and the longer they went on the more mere contact seemed momentous. She'd wrapped her arms around his back and squeezed the breath from his lungs. She'd run the flats of her hands over his arms, his chest, his back, his legs. In the silence of the afternoon their breathing was loud, the friction magnified. He'd let his mind shut down and had been grateful for a moment in which he didn't wonder why his father had been silent for months, or if Will was still alive, or if any of the Swiff clients would get enough food this week. He just slid inside her and thought idly—not even *thought*; just let it wash through him— that women didn't even know themselves as men knew them. Right then, he knew Greta, knew her literally inside out, but afterward the gap between bodies would be unbridgeable. Sometimes you sensed that gap before the sex was even concluded, that already you were reaching across a distance that would only grow. Her skin tasted faintly metallic, electric, salty. Before they left his room, she had kissed him so gently he took it as an apology. That was it, then.

"Oh, pretty shot," Gary called to Benjamin. "You guys see how she did that?" The twins assented. Karin snatched the rebound from the air and retreated halfway down the driveway, dribbling and observing the formation of the players. Hal tried to figure out who was on whose team: Gary approached Karin, slightly bent at the waist, arms loose and held out from his body, ready to snap forward if her attention lapsed. Benjamin was darting around near the basket, waving his arms in the air for a pass. Guarding Laurel, Greta stayed light on her feet and whipped her head around to keep an eye on Karin.

Karin took a step forward, and now there was a surge of motion and a crescendo of voices. The whole crew seemed to converge on each other at once. Hal saw the orb of the basketball soar into the air in a low pass and saw Greta's hand rise to block it—how amazing that he could pick hers out among the crowd, but it was true, her slender arm and that delicate bone at her wrist were known to him already—and she batted the basketball back toward the earth. He had an impression of heads turning to follow the ball as it zoomed back toward Karin, who was glancing to one side, her mouth opening to say something in Marianne's direction just as the basketball collided with her. Karin's ponytail jerked upon impact, her head made a startling rebound off her shoulder.

Karin swayed but stood, her arms out before her as if for balance. The playful voices died.

Greta emerged from the cluster of people and ran toward Karin, calling *I'm so sorry, my God*. Karin looked at her quizzically, then took a step forward and reached out one arm. Her hand was splayed on Greta's sternum for a moment, and then her muscle convulsed and she pushed Greta back so hard the crowd had to stop her from falling.

The rest of the group swarmed backward. Hal was so shocked he barely kept a hold of his beer. "Goddamn it, Greta!" Karin shouted. She was standing over Greta, a scarlet blotch visible at her temple. "What is the *matter* with you? Do you do anything that normal people do? Can't you just play a game and relax, for once?"

Greta seemed to take a shallow breath and spit it out again. She barely looked up at Karin, her chin tipped downward. "You know it was an accident," she said.

"Right. You don't mean to do anything. You just pop in and fuck up my house but it's all an accident." Karin rubbed her head where the ball had hit, then turned and looked around. Hal took a step forward, realizing it was his place to do something—he knew Karin better than anyone else there. But she wasn't looking for him; she saw the basketball and stalked over and picked it up. Then she walked slowly back to Greta, who was shaking off their neighbors and watching Karin as if she expected another push.

"You need to get a hold of yourself," Greta told Karin. "You better take a breath and regain control. I'm not going to talk about this with you till you do."

Karin very deliberately handed the ball to Gary, who tucked it under one arm. She looked up at Hal, her dark eyes aglow. "Hal? Anything to add? Maybe you and Greta share opinions now, too."

Hal swallowed, understanding. How did women do it? They read the body language in an instant. Perhaps that was why Hal's sisters and his mother had experienced such contention, so much more aggravation and hurt feelings than Hal and his dad: they had been communicating on a whole different level, in a whole other, more complex language. "Not out here, not right now," he said. "We'll all talk. We can go talk right now if you want."

Suddenly the twilight had seeped very close to full darkness. The last of the sun was low and red over the horizon.

"I'm sorry," Karin said evenly. She looked around at everyone. "I apologize."

The group surrounded them, more cautiously now, patting both women's shoulders at once as if to connect them again. They were all on edge, people said. It could be anyone. But Karin's eyes flashed in Hal's direction, and he knew it really couldn't be anyone—it could be only them. He felt his stomach hollow out in famishment, the flooding of his muscles with exhaustion.

Why hadn't they all eaten? They'd been sweating and drinking and tense, and now everyone was sagging all at once. Gary picked up one of the twins as easily as if he were a flower stem, his palm reaching down to cover the back of the other boy's skull. Benjamin and Marianne were turning back toward their own house, hands at one another's shoulder blades. Laurel was speaking intently to Greta and Karin, gesturing.

But then they all began to shift, turning eastward. Hal saw Karin take a step and then stop. Everyone was peering down the street, in the direction of the park. From between the houses, from out on the lake, Hal could see a flashing light.

Now they began to move in the direction of the red and blue lights, though Gary set down his son and gestured to the twins to stay back. Hal paused as Greta and Karin approached him. Wordlessly, all three looked at each other and then began to walk. At the edge of the lake, they looked out over the water. Flags still bobbed in the waves. Hal made out the shape of the boats, which were the source of the bright circling light. Why, they've been there all day, he thought, and now he heard the sound of splashing and of voices magnified by the expanse of the lake, a creaking of chains and pulleys as something was lifted from the water.

CHAPTER FIFTEEN

Karin woke up that night to the sound of voices on the lawn. Her first thought was that Greta's husband had returned: he had come back, he had brought someone with him, he was talking to Greta. But the voices were soft and numerous; she guessed there were more than two people.

She sat up in bed, heart pounding, wishing now that it was Greta's husband. Let him come back and beg for her. At least Will seemed fairly harmless. And Hal was down there—now she heard his feet heading toward the front of the house, a voice at the door, and then Hal's voice in reply. The voice spoke briefly, bluff and now too loud for the time of night and this peculiar darkness, and then she heard the door close, the click of the lock, and the sound of the voices moving.

Out her window she saw they were men. Three of them, in pale clothing, light-colored jeans, white T-shirts.

She found their outfits reassuring; no one was trying to blend in with the darkness. They headed next door to the neighbor, to Gary's house, lingered briefly—in the stillness she heard that door as well—and then the sounds continued on down the street as they moved along like carolers, checking in house by house.

Karin listened to the room on the other side of the wall, for Greta to move or to get out of bed, but there was nothing. Maybe Greta was down in Hal's room, anyway.

Karin sat up and rubbed her eyes, realizing she felt alert, as if she'd never really actually slept. Maybe she hadn't; maybe she had simply dropped into a state of fatigue and half-dreaming, too embarrassed and shaken to relax at all. Maybe this was the direction she was headed in: this disconnection between her body and her head. It was like the sensation of observing her own self swimming into a lake while her mind still thought it over, or like the great explosion of tingling heat through her whole body, surging toward the palm of her hand where it touched the warm damp cotton of Greta's shirt.

They had watched the boat sail off in the other direction until the light began to wink out in the distance. Then all of them, the co-op members, their neighbors, the people drawn from their houses by the lights, had found themselves standing in a silent half circle. Karin could tell she was not the only one whose adrenaline had deserted her: the weariness was visible. Hal had taken her hand, said, "Come on." Everyone lifted their hands in farewell and walked home. Karin had lagged behind Greta and Hal, pausing to retrieve her box of eggs from the cooler. At home, she'd tucked them in the refrigerator, hoping the melting ice would keep them cold enough.

Hal and Greta were sitting there in the darkened kitchen, silent when she entered the room. They'd watched her place the box in the fridge, and Hal seemed about to speak, but then she'd shaken her head and said something inconsequential about sleep and had gone upstairs. In her room, she sat on her bed and listened through the floorboards to the murmur of Hal's and Greta's voices. Just like childhood: she'd sent herself to bed and wondered what they'd do with her now.

Now she decided to get up, but felt odd as soon as she stood. Her body loomed, elongated and sensitive at the fingertips. On her way downstairs she ran her hands along the walls; the paint felt pocked and pointed, extraordinarily textured.

Hal was sitting on the couch, arms crossed, staring in the direction of the window. She stopped at the bottom of the stairs, her hands on the smooth, cool banister, until he turned toward her. "Who was it?"

"Some neighbors," he said quietly, not quite a whisper. "Going around, for some reason, just making rounds, I guess. Checking on people."

"I'm sorry I made them think we needed checking on," Karin said.

"They're going to everyone's house," Hal answered. "You think you're the only person to lose it this week?" He rested his face in the palms of his hands. "I think they'd been up drinking all night or something. They had that feel, you know, men out there with no idea what men in crisis do, so they just roam."

She sat down next to him. There was a full moon, or close to it, but she had to crane her neck to see it. The living room had cooled slightly now, but she was still too hot in her short robe.

She propped her feet on the coffee table and crossed her arms. The couch's upholstery was rough and tweedy, unwelcoming.

"I wonder if there'll be a newspaper tomorrow," she said. "Or anything in it about the lake. Don't they have generators? I wonder if *our* paper's printer has a generator."

"I think the big ones do. But Laurel was saying they're all formatted on computers, and the blackout may have screwed that up even if the generators still had juice. They might just lose too much time before tomorrow." Hal breathed deeply. "At least we won't be in it again. They'll just want to find out who it was."

"I still don't understand why he'd take the dog with him. Why not just leave it at home?"

"How would you know anyone would come feed it?" Hal asked.

"I'd write a letter, I guess," Karin said. "Something that would reach someone after it was done, and they could go check on the dog, take care of it."

"But then you have to mail the letter, right, and you have to go through with it then. What if you wanted to change your mind but you knew someone was going to get this letter and be all upset, and then there you'd be, at home, watching football?"

"I think if you wanted to change your mind, you would." Karin closed her eyes.

"Are you going to work tomorrow?" Hal asked.

"I guess so," she said. "We have to go sometime. We can write longhand and be prepared."

"Maybe the power will be back."

"It won't be," she said. "Don't you feel like this could go on forever?"

"I feel very odd," Hal said. "Do me a favor and just move closer, please. Just a little."

She hesitated, but then he turned to look at her and Karin felt ridiculous for doubting it; his eyes seemed huge and damp. This was Hal. She knew him so well it was impossible to believe it had only been a year. They'd dated other people without impinging on their own friendship—why had she been so upset? She believed suddenly that things could remain just as they'd been, Greta or no Greta. She thought of Helen, who lived with a whole crew of people and children and noise: there was room for absorption.

She slid over. Hal uncrossed his arms and laid one over her

shoulder. His arm was heavy, faintly damp, yet the sensation was tranquil and rather sweet, like mammals huddling together for warmth. She had visions of a full-on Co-op-wide Cuddle. They could once a week get up from dinner and all go wrap their arms around each other on someone's big double bed. That could be where they talked out problems. They could say, "Please wipe the counter around the sink after you put in your contacts. I would very much appreciate your consideration," and then a little squeeze.

"That stupid knock on the door really freaked me out," Hal said, breaking through her concentration. "I want more men in this co-op. I hate being the only one among women. I'm a shitty protector."

"You don't need to be protecting anyone," she said. She added, "Everyone here is an adult. There aren't any babies here."

"Thank God."

Karin rubbed her eyes and said nothing. Hal's skin felt hot to her, but he kept shivering. "Are you going to kick me out?" Karin asked. She meant it a little playfully. She thought they were okay.

"I don't know," he said. "It's not my place to say."

Silence. Karin heard the sound of her own throat swallowing loudly in the darkness, a timid bubbling in her intestines.

"You were in the wrong and you know it."

"I know. I told her I was sorry."

Hal shook his head. "I don't even want to think about it, okay? I don't know what's going on, and I don't want to spend all my time mediating some ridiculous fight. I have other things to concentrate on." He shifted his weight and her skin cooled where it was no longer touching him.

"Maybe I should go," Karin said, but now Hal just shook his head impatiently.

"No, no," he said. "Forget it. You don't want to go. There's no reason to go. We'll be okay. Greta's tough." He gave a fond, prideful laugh.

Karin sat very still. That laugh—intimate, amused, pleased—moved through her like a brush fire; she felt very warm. Her own body, once again, had leaped ahead to the worst-case scenario, and it was always correct. She thought of that cave again, as she had throughout the drive, throughout the afternoon. The body always knew, and the mind dallied along the path like a nitwit.

She was frightened now. She had lived more vulnerably than she had realized. Now she was going to be shut out of her own home. She had no patch that belonged to her, or family that could surround her in a crisis. She wished she were Elaine, dead husband and all, because Elaine had cast out roots. Elaine had not fled her family but had entrenched herself among them in that protected, guarded space. Yet here was Karin's life, no land, just things: shards of clay, tatters of silk. Bent spoons and cups and useless things.

The two of them leaned against each other and watched the darkness outside the window. They were still watching when they saw a man's form climb the steps and walk slowly to the porch swing. Hal tensed, leaning forward and about to stand up, until he saw Will's profile.

"It's just Greta's husband," Karin said.

"I know," he answered. Hal leaned back against her. So Will had made his way back here somehow. Outside, Will sat down on the swing. He didn't even try to peer into the window. Hal and Karin listened to the creaking on the other side of the wall, the chains straining slightly as the swing moved back and forth.

"I guess we'll get used to having him here," Karin said. She sighed. "I'm not going to kick him out. Maybe Greta needs him for a while."

Hal nodded. She was right. Greta was tied to Will, though she was clearly trying not to be. No wonder Greta always seemed so distracted—she had been attuned to Will the whole time, one ear cocked in his direction. "I'll let him in if he wants to come in then," he said.

Karin nodded. "I feel terrible," she said. "I think I just want to sleep."

Hal waited until Karin was back upstairs. Then he opened the front door and peered out. Will had changed into shorts and a T-shirt, and he was stretched out on the swing with one leg propped on the armrest and the other foot on the ground. His face was in shadow; Hal couldn't tell if he was awake or not.

"Hi," Will said.

"Hey," Hal replied. He took a step out onto the porch. "It's not too bad out here tonight. The weather, I mean."

Will shrugged. He sat up, with some difficulty, and rubbed his eyes. "It's okay," he conceded.

"Come in anyway," Hal said. "That swing isn't that comfortable. You can sleep on the couch."

"I think I want to be out here," Will said. "Thanks, though. I don't know if Greta wants to come downstairs and find me there again."

Hal flushed in the darkness. No, better not to have Will inside, hearing whatever Greta or Karin said without knowing he was there.

"I'm sorry about today," Hal said. For a moment Hal considered telling Will what had happened that afternoon. But there was no point to that; Greta had already left Will. She could do as she pleased, technically.

"For what?" said Will.

Hal gave up and just shook his head. "I was just kind of an asshole today. I got pissy with you, in case you don't remember."

Will just nodded. "Anyway. You weren't the most pleasant person to be around this morning, but still."

"I'm told that a lot," said Will. "I'm working on it."

"Oh," said Hal. "Okay." There was a long silence. "Well, I'm going in now. You sure you won't come in? Or take a pillow?"

Will said, "I could use a pillow." Hal took a few off the couch and brought them out. "Thanks," said Will, settling himself against the pillow. "Well. Good night."

Hal lifted a hand to say good night. Inside, he listened to the faint, slow creak of the swing, and then he went into his bedroom and closed the door. He checked the regular phone line, which was dead, and then his cell phone. Its signal was low but usable. All you had to do was make your phone calls at two in the morning.

After a while, an unanswered phone sounded hostile. Hal paced, letting it ring. His father could ignore it all he wanted during the daytime, but he couldn't be out hunting or fishing now. He could answer the phone, or Hal would be calling every night in the middle of the night until he did.

"Hello." His father's voice seemed hoarse and unused, softer than Hal ever recalled hearing it. The quietness took some of the anger out of him.

"Dad," Hal said.

"Hal? Is this Hal?"

"Yeah, it's me."

"Cripes." Hal heard the rustle of fabric shifting. His father grunted slightly as he moved. "It's the middle of the night. Are your sisters all right? Are you?"

"Everyone is fine. We're all in the dark down here, you may have heard."

"Well, it's, what, two in the morning, son."

"I mean the *power outage*," said Hal. "The southern portion of the state, parts of Illinois, all without power? Mostly without phones? Are you avoiding newspapers, too, or just me? Did Uncle Randy come by?"

Hal could hear a scraping sound like a rough hand over whiskers. "Right," his father said. "Right. Give me a second." There was a pause, during which his father breathed deeply several times. "Okay. Randy mentioned you guys have that blackout. I meant to call you, I just didn't think so much of it."

"Well, you should have," Hal said.

"Look, they happen, son. Power company's run by humans like everything else."

"This doesn't feel like your average outage," Hal said. "If you were picking up the phone you'd know that." His father began to speak but Hal spoke over him. "So how is the life of a retired Huck Finn these days?"

"Hal." His father's voice was flat. "Why don't you take a moment."

"I just want to know where you've been." Hal sat on the edge of his bed. "I've been calling forever. Rennie and Jane are worried, too."

"Well," his father sighed. "I'm up here now, Hal. I don't live down there. I came up here to quiet things down. You kids are settled and grown up, and you don't need to hear about—what, about my sciatica. Or largemouth bass. I'm sorry it upset you. I really am."

"Don't be sorry for my entirely normal response," Hal said. "Be sorry for your actions, okay, but not for me doing what normal people do."

There was a long silence. "Okay," said his father. "You could be a little more respectful in your tone, I guess, but you have a point. I don't know, though, Hal; I can only offer so much—when you were little it was clearer, I suppose. Long as you were fed and warm and not playing in the streets. But you all made it.

You're all grown. You're thinking about another generation, you see? Looking forward, and you should be." He cleared his throat, and Hal heard the phone shifting. When his father spoke again his voice was slowed. "Your mother was good at that. With the grandchildren and all. Without her I'm not so good at it."

Hal was having a hard time maintaining his indignation. It was so much easier while his father was a distant cipher, but now Hal softened. His dad's voice was roughened and vulnerable in that clogged, middle-of-the-night way—Hal realized he had awakened a seventy-year-old man at two A.M. "She was good at it," Hal agreed.

His father chuckled. "She wasn't always. These things move in cycles. What doesn't, right? When you kids were young, I dragged her out a lot, just to remind her of life outside the house—she used to be down on herself a lot, and I was out in the world, working, seeing people. I thought she needed the same thing. I'd say I was right. Then later on, she sort of stood a little straighter. She seemed sort of—energized. And she blew right past me. You kids were gone by then, busy with your own lives."

His father took a drink of something, and Hal listened to the reassuring sound of routine. His father had a kept a glass of water on his bedside table all his life.

"I don't know how much I really noticed of anything," Hal admitted.

"Kids aren't supposed to spend all their time and energy observing their parents," his father said with surprising emphasis. "You're supposed to feel secure enough to turn your attention to the next thing. That was how we raised you three. It was on purpose."

"Well," Hal said. He stopped. All his anger had leaked out of him. "I think you're taking that approach a bit too militantly, Dad. You never even write to anybody."

"Has it been that long? Oh. Well, okay. I get it." There was another break while his father sipped water. Hal could almost hear him pondering through the telephone wires. "Nothing up here feels like it does down there. I don't know how much a blackout would even bother me. It's turkey season now, you know. I had some good ice fishing this winter, too. And got some good deer. Your mother wouldn't have agreed to come here in a million years, I guess, but I think she'd have liked it more than she expected."

Hal considered that. It seemed unlikely that his mother, who had taken great pleasure in the basic amenities of suburban life, would have found herself at home in the northern Wisconsin woods.

"Well, I'm glad you're enjoying it up there, I guess," said Hal.

"Yeah." His father yawned. "Hal—" he began, but Hal interrupted.

"You can't just hang up and forget we talked, though, Dad. You have to at least keep in contact so we know you're alive."

"I hear you. But I mean it: It's time for you to be with your sisters. Time for you to be thinking about maybe having your own family, or just being with theirs. It's time for you all to take it up, you understand?"

Hal's ears seemed to buzz. "I don't," he said.

"You're a grown man. Your mother's gone, I'll be gone sooner rather than later. I can't be down there playing Dad forever. At some point, the next generation takes over and you need each other. You don't need me."

"Of course we do," Hal said. "Are you depressed? What is so onerous about being part of a family? Just come down once a year for something, for whatever."

"I'll try," his father said. His voice was fading. "I'm sure things would be different if your mother was around, but she's just not. And I live up here now. You be with your sisters. Don't be worrying about me. You're a good man, Hal. In the morning this will all feel better. It always happens that way."

He hung up.

Hal stared at the phone as if it had more to say. He watched its screen go dark, then set it on the bedside table.

You never heard about this, really—of a father just removing himself from the game before death forced him to. Who did such a thing? Hal breathed shallowly, trying to name the emotions. He'd learned the exercise years ago, in some seminar: pause, enumerate the feelings, separate them all out. Naming them gave you a little time and distance before you leaped up and acted, before you phoned your father up again and railed at him for attempting to opt out. So: Anger. Disbelief. Frustration. Grief. Hurt. He tried to see each emotion as something he could put away in a box, but the exercise wasn't working.

He tried to lie back in bed, waiting for adrenaline to dissipate and sleep to return. He felt a strong urge to get up and go find the group of men who'd been patrolling, or whatever they were doing. He wanted to stalk quickly around the streets, to survey the land and take in each change to decide what response it required, then mete it out.

He got as far as standing, then thought he might go up to Greta's room. Greta would have something to say. He could never really be certain what her response would be to anything. Maybe she'd have something to say that would settle it all down again.

At his bedroom door, he remembered that Will was just outside. He couldn't go up to Greta's room with her husband right out there. Somehow he'd not really taken that in yet, that she was married, that he knew her husband and had spent a whole day with the man, seeing why they were separated. His stomach tightened up. They weren't together, it was true, and Greta had wanted to sleep with him for reasons of her own, which she hadn't shared, but nevertheless Hal saw their actions in a fresh ugly light. Faced with a sick man, this was what he'd done. And Greta seemed healed by the whole thing—she'd gone out and joined the neighbors on the street as if she was ready to be delighted by everyone, ask them all to barbecues. Even Karin's outburst hadn't upset her too much. She seemed to have expected it, and her attitude seemed to indicate this was a relief, to get beyond what was coming. She'd transferred all that turmoil to him, as if he'd put on an item of her clothing.

He sat back down on his bed, all his energy draining out of his limbs. His father was gone—not without love, or some powerless affection, but at a distance, nevertheless—and Hal's house was in disarray, everything was darkened.

Hopefully Karin was done being angry. He'd been shocked at her response, but he knew he shouldn't have been. Karin hadn't lived in co-ops for as many years as he had. She couldn't be expected to know that this was part of it: the splitting off and regrouping, the natural alliances that formed and reformed. Perhaps he and his father had this in common, the habit of trying to see the world from a clarifying remove. From far enough away, even the slow and painful transformation of Hal's own family seemed less wrenching. He tried to see it as clusters of cells that merged and split and sloughed away, the relentless motion of growth and loss.

WEDNESDAY

CHAPTER SIXTEEN

Greta dreamed of people at the door, of people roaming the neighborhood, and of the sounds of the lake water rising, sloshing onto the sidewalks. When her eyes opened she lay there for a long time, hungry and still tired.

After a while she sat up and looked out her window. The street was wet. There must have been rain overnight. The sun was hard and bright though it was barely past six. She got out of bed and tried her light switch, just in case. No.

Downstairs was still empty and quiet. She put water on to boil and opened the warm freezer for coffee. There was no ground coffee left, just several containers of fair trade beans, oily and glossy, black as beetle shells inside their moisture-beaded bags. She hefted one, the bag's condensation running down her fingers, and looked around the kitchen.

Two pans, she finally decided. A wide aluminum sauté pan and a slightly narrower cast-iron pan. She dumped the beans into the aluminum pan and then placed the iron one over the top. Crushed coffee would slop all over. She got a plastic bag and wrapped the whole thing in that. Then she decided to go out to the front porch to smash them, to keep the noise away from the others.

Greta unlocked the front door and stepped out, hoping for a breeze and getting only more of the same dry-smelling heat that filled the kitchen. There was no newspaper by the door today.

Then she glanced down the length of the porch and saw, with a shock, that Will was there on the swing.

He was rocking the swing gently, looking her way with an expression of anticipation. He was dressed in shorts and a white T-shirt. His belly strained at the shirt, over the too-tight waistband of the shorts. She couldn't recall when he'd bought them, only that most of his clothes were too small now, the collars of his shirts gray with strain, the pants painfully nipped at the waist. He was vivid and solid. Here he was. Yesterday she'd managed to push him so far from her mind that to be reminded he could still occupy space right there next to her gave her an uneasy feeling. She'd acted as if he didn't exist. That was all she'd done. She'd acted as if they were already divorced. But it didn't really matter—separated, divorced. Will might not even care.

"Why do you have a bag of pans?" he asked.

She stood there, silent, and tried to decide what felt different about him. Will turned to face her, bending one leg to bring his foot up to the swing, the other foot braced and rocking on the floor. His eyes seemed clear and steady.

"I have to crush up some coffee," she said. "We don't have any ground."

Will held out a hand for the pans, and she gave them to him, careful not to let the beans fall out of the lower pan. He got up from the swing and paused, looking at the contraption, and started to smile. It was a bit sad, she saw: baggy plastic and two different handles, like some Depression-era stop-gap.

"You could just use a pepper grinder," Will said.

He looked around the porch, then came toward her, passed her, and went down the front steps. There he crouched on the sidewalk, set the pans on the steps before him, and, bracing his hands on either side of the pan, he ground it down onto the beans. Greta stood just above him, looking down at his neck, shaved clean and neat, at the soft velvety backs of his ears. The cords in his arms stood out as he worked. When Greta had first met him he'd been working at a factory to pay for college, and his arms had bulged ridiculously, hard-edged and veined, from hours of daily labor. Muscle-bound men had never particularly attracted her, but now she missed that earlier body, its strength, its physical largesse. He used to eat bowls of ice cream with peanut butter and chocolate chips on top, a snack so childish and rich she'd started laughing when she first saw it, but it never showed up on his body. She suspected it still would not—it was just the alcohol that swelled him up this way, so that his chin, tipped downward, was padded in a bubble of flesh.

"If I use a pepper grinder," she said, "I end up with spicy coffee."

He nodded in agreement and kept grinding at the pans. Sweat began to stand out on his face, darkening his white shirt in patches. The scent of coffee became very strong on the porch. Will grasped the cast-iron pan in its plastic bag and moved the pan from side to side, pushed down so hard she saw the redness deepening in his palms along the edges of the pan.

"When did you get here?" she asked.

He wiped his forehead with his arm and leaned back on his heels. His arm trembled when he lifted it, shaking unmistakably, but he kept his balance.

"Maybe a few hours ago," he said. "I started walking last night, or last evening, I guess, and I kind of took a long time about it. I made a stop or two."

She raised an eyebrow.

"Not what you're thinking, though."

"No? Where'd you stop, then," she said. She looked away from him to see if their neighbors were around.

"I just sat for a while to see what people were doing," he said. He didn't look up at her.

"Where, in a bar?"

"No," he said. "I stopped in that little park and looked around for a while, and I just walked, I guess." He glanced over at her. "Your friend Charlie came by."

"Charles."

"Right. Anyway. I guess he was there. He left a note that made it seem we had a quick conversation or something."

Greta nodded. "He offered to stop by, I said okay."

"Really?" Will's eyebrows rose. "I wouldn't have thought you would."

"Oh, come off it," Greta said. "If you'd been sentient for any of the past week you'd realize that everyone knows. I finally got it that they've all known forever, in fact. He did a nice thing for you, Will. Everyone does nice things for you and you suck us all dry and just take it as your due, have you noticed that?"

Will was quiet. Then he nodded. "You're right," he said. He raised his chin in the direction of the porch swing. "I brought you that from our neighbors. My neighbors."

A paper parcel was on the porch below the chair—a bottle, it turned out. Before she could say anything, Will added, "You know they make that homemade wine? The people with the huge garden, who spend the whole summer outdoors having barbecues? Anyway, the guy waved me over sometime, I can't remember when, and gave me that. I thought you'd like it." Will was grinding the coffee again. "If I drink it," he said, breathing hard, "I won't even enjoy it. I'll just gulp it down and be done. Seems rude. I have a feeling I may have had dinner over there or something. When he gave me the wine I introduced myself, because I certainly have no idea what their names are, and the guy was just like, "I know your name," and he didn't tell me his. And all the rest of his family was waving very familiarly. I think I probably headed over there completely drunk one night and just hung out with them."

"You walked all the way over here?" Greta asked. She felt as if she were talking to a familiar stranger, someone she had known in grade school, who had kept track of her without her knowledge and now knew her far better than she knew him.

Will stopped grinding now, breathing hard, and bashed the pans lightly against each other. "I just wandered."

"Did you stop at the little dive on the corner?"

Will shook his head. "The East Side Inn, my God. That's exactly the kind of dump I've been trying to avoid by drinking in the broom closet." He smiled to himself, a tight, hopeful little smile, and only looked up at her when she laughed. He opened up the plastic bag and removed the heavy iron pan to see what lay beneath it. The coffee beans were well crushed—not as fine as a grinder would do, but fragrant and sticky and coarse.

"I just came to see you," he said. "I think I must be pretty sober by now. I feel like shit, if that's any indication. And I'm shaking like a leaf."

"How do you feel, exactly?" she asked. He had never discussed this with her before. He'd always disappeared, cranky, to the basement or the car and returned a reliable zombie.

Will sat down on the porch steps and ran his hands over his face. "I feel like I might have a panic attack or something. Restless, really nervous. I started walking to try and get rid of it, and I've been sitting out here trying to meditate or something to make myself calm down."

"It's withdrawal. You can't meditate it away. This is dangerous, Will. You could have a seizure."

"I know that. Believe me, I know withdrawal. Now my heart is racing. I might want to go to the emergency room."

"Okay."

"Or I might need to sit for a while. The grinding didn't help. I'm sorry. I thought I'd just show up and be helpful and see you— I haven't seen you in a really long time."

"You were just here," she said, but he was already shaking his head.

"Actually seen you, like not being in a haze."

"There was Christmas," Greta said. "There were a couple months."

"A few," he corrected. She nodded. "Anyway, I know I was here and spent some time with that guy who lives here and his friend, this old woman, but to be honest I don't remember much after a certain point." He paused, a look of confusion and then dawning moving over his face. "They were doing something crazy on campus last night. Let me think—" He clapped a hand on his knee. "Ogg Hall! They're tearing it down, right?"

"Yeah," Greta said. "Replacing it with a newer dorm is all."

Will nodded. "I went past it. I don't remember when. Late. And they were there, these military people, bursting in and tearing it up."

Greta stared at him. "You're wrong," she said. Her heart thrummed. She was looking around, up and down the street, where hardly anyone was even awake. It was insane to think there was some kind of military thing going on, but maybe the National Guard was here? Why would they be here?

Will grabbed her wrist. "Sit," he said. "I remember. It was a

SWAT team, they were in training, I guess. And since they were tearing down the building anyway, the university let them use it."

She took a breath. "In this kind of atmosphere," Greta said dryly, "when people are nervous and crazy?"

Will shrugged. "I can't quite recall the details. I asked someone. But yeah."

Greta sat down again. She wiped her palms over her face, trying to calm down. Her heart was slowing. "We heard a boom yesterday," she said. "Maybe that was it."

"Probably," Will said. When he raised a hand to his face she smelled coffee and iron, his fingers vibrating.

"Greta. What the hell is going on, anyway?" he said. "The stuff in the fridge is rotten, the house is like an inferno. Walking over here it looked like everything was totally dead and the gas prices are through the roof. How long have I been down for the count? I feel like the hell inside my head is just the way the world is now."

"I think it might be just a blackout," she said. "Or maybe it's more. They pulled someone out of the lake last night."

"Someone drowned?"

"I think so," she said. "I don't really know what happened. Did you hear about this dog that was out on the dock and drifting through the lake? We were there. My roommate got it out. Whoever left the dog there must have headed out with it, but I don't know if it was on purpose. He could have been, I don't know—fishing. Maybe just having too many beers and he fell."

"I wouldn't have been fishing," Will said. "I would have gone out there with a couple of bottles and waited till I felt strong enough. Maybe a plastic bag, too, or maybe tie my legs together. Or a knife. You could cut your wrists, jump in, make it so you can't change course."

Dizziness rose over her. At first she thought he might know about her dream—that plastic bag—but he was speaking of

himself. "Is this how you think?" She could have him committed, though she didn't know how. Will reached over and took
her hand. His was wet, hot from the plastic bag but chilled beneath. She felt it trembling, hard, as he squeezed her hand.

"Sometimes," he said. "I know you want me to tell you I never
feel this way but I do. I've come over here a few times thinking
about the lake. The other night I just came to your house instead." He swallowed hard and shook his head. After a second his
expression cleared. "I'm not going to do that," he added. "I think
I had to feel that bad before I knew I wouldn't do it."

Greta ran her fingers over his hand, touching the smooth
coolness of his fingernails.

"I don't want to drink that," he said, nodding at the wine
bottle, "but I feel like I might have a seizure if I don't. It happens. I can't remember if you get seizures from the drinking or
the withdrawal but I feel like I'm going to have one now. Feel the
back of my neck. It's all clenched." She touched it, and it, too, was
wet and cool, the muscles jumping in her hands.

"I'm just going to have some now, okay? I'm sorry. I brought it
to you and I really wanted you to have it. But please just go inside
the house now."

Greta watched him; she had watched him steadily for minutes. What misery this was. She should have done an intervention, she realized, she should have corralled his family and his
boss and caught him at a moment like this. Instead she had just
let him sink, hating him the whole time and wallowing in the
moments when she got to be enraged.

She knew she couldn't trust her own responses. She couldn't be
certain he was ever being honest. She was weeping now, but she
couldn't sort out why, whether it was in response to something
genuine or to simple manipulation, to despair and repetition.

"You're so stupid," she said softly. "Why is it so important to
you to be so stupid? This is why I had to get away from you."

"I know," he said. "Things didn't feel safe at home."

"They didn't," she agreed. "Sometimes I didn't know what you could do."

"I meant you," he said. Will looked at her, his eyes that calm pale green, and Greta felt a lurch inside her, her throat constricting around that same sore spot. So he did remember. It was an unfamiliar, cold-sweat kind of feeling: to be wrong and caught out, when you'd thought you had hidden enough to deal with your transgressions by yourself. She'd been unjustified. She knew that, of course. He knew it, too. Now she'd done even more, and maybe worse, and the shame was startling.

"I'm sorry," she said. Her voice emerged as a rasp.

Will nodded, still watching her. She expected him to say it was okay, that he'd pushed her to it—she knew she was wrong, but he owed her so much at this point—but he just clasped his hands tightly and watched them tremble.

"You're so much bigger than I am," she said. "I felt like nothing I did even registered. As long as I didn't, I don't know, really hurt you."

"Not for lack of trying," he said.

She drew a shaky breath. "No," she said. They stared at one another and then Greta looked away. Her face was flushed, she could feel it.

"Or lack of desire, for that matter."

"You could go to a detox right now," she said. "They'd give you something to calm you down. You'd feel a lot better."

"So, back to me now," Will said.

"What do you want me to say?" she exclaimed. "I *am* sorry. You know I am. I got myself away from you before I really did something crazy. You have to give me that."

"Okay," Will said. "I'll give you that. And they won't let you into a detox without a blood alcohol content. I've tried, but I keep fucking up and detoxing myself and going in when the withdrawal gets bad and they can't do anything if you aren't drunk right then."

She knew he was right. He'd told her before about people standing in the parking lot of the detox at the hospital, chugging six-packs to be allowed in. Greta rested her elbows on her knees and stared at the sidewalk between her bare feet. The shade of the porch was withdrawing, constricting as the sun got higher, and she was starting to squint in the glare.

She was supposed to give him the wine, she knew, and then he got it both ways—he got the credit for coming over here, for being sentient for a little while, but he still got to drink. He got to call her out on everything she'd done—and be correct about it, too—and then she couldn't be so righteous anymore. This used to happen all the time, these little knots that felt so baffling when really they were simple. Usually he got her to feel guilty about something she shouldn't even regret, but he really had her this time. Both of them were swimming in the same soup.

She understood all of this with a melancholy detachment, untouched by anger. She felt a little as a god is said to feel, saddened to see what the humans have done with their lot, how badly they've fucked it all up, but still never reaching in to nudge the gears back into line. What a surprise to find that she still loved him, a film that clung to her. She reached over and squeezed his hand. Her own body was never on her side. The mind kept surging forward while the body tried to pull you back.

"You just have to go back," she said. "If you're not drunk now, skip the detox and go straight back to the rehab. You know where it is. Call and make arrangements."

"I don't even know the number," he said. "You were the one who called."

Greta stood up, detaching her hand from his. She took the homemade wine, picked up the coffee pan. Will looked up at her. He didn't look like the skinny boy she'd known years ago, he looked round and pale and like a man who had drunk far too much and shut himself down for years at a time. But at least he was looking at her. That was how she knew she'd been living on nothing. Her husband looked her in the eye and she felt as grateful as if he'd breathed air into her lungs. "Sweetheart," she said. "You don't even have to figure anything out, you just have to get it going, and let yourself wind up in a rehab and figure it all out then. I'll take you. I don't know what you think is worse than this."

He looked up at her, squinting.

"Come on," she said. "You can make a call or two if the phones are up, and you can have breakfast with us till it's time to go. Do something normal. We have to eat before everything goes bad anyway."

Will shook his head and stood up. "I'm going to get some stuff done first," he said. "I'll come back later, okay?"

"You need to do it *now*," she told him. She was used to having no hope for him. Just a shred of it made her desperate. "You know that."

"I know. Listen, I've managed to put together a few hours of not drinking. That's more than I've done in a long time. I'll keep going for a while, maybe see if the lights ever come back on."

"They won't," Greta said morosely. "You'll end up in an ER running on some emergency generator, drinking vodka so they'll treat you."

Will acknowledged this with a shrug. "Hey. You know a couple of the guys at rehab had had seizures before, and I'm pretty sure they said it was different than this." He gave a shaky laugh and wiped sweat away from his forehead. "One guy swore he crawled into a liquor store during the seizure to get some vodka to stop it. And I remember thinking, now *that* guy has a problem."

Will tugged at the neck of his T-shirt and Greta saw that the shirt was damp with sweat now. He shook his head, and then seemed to give up on something—he cocked his head wryly to one side, as if to say there was no way around it, and reached down to pull her up next to him. He lifted her hand, covered her fingers and held them. "Remember when you visited me at rehab, and our life was pretty much in the toilet, and we felt okay anyway? We even had *fun*. I keep trying to remember that, because I drink and I just forget that none of this is new. It's kind of comforting to know it's just the same hell I unleashed on myself before. I can get through it. Just let me—I don't know. I'll come back. It's going to be okay, Greta."

Then he let her go and was heading back down the sidewalk, waving over his shoulder in her direction.

CHAPTER SEVENTEEN

No one was working today. No one had bothered. Karin knew this when she awakened for the first time, morning light bright but not too sharp yet, and heard none of the typical weekday sounds on the street and downstairs: no cars, no horns, no clatter in the kitchen. What day was it? Wednesday, she believed. She was fairly certain it was Wednesday, though it didn't matter. Wednesday, a name on paper, a set of marks soaked into fiber.

Her head felt heavy, her eyes swollen. She planned to get out of bed and see what was going on, but her limbs were jellied, dense and heavy. Clearly her limbs knew something she didn't, her eyelids swelling prophylactically closed, maybe for good.

She drifted. She heard Greta's voice now, and a male voice, not Hal's, and creaking on the porch. Then the front door closing and steps heading inside. The porch swing squeaked rhythmically and stopped. She thought about sitting on the couch with Hal, the warm fur beneath his arm. She strained to hear Greta's voice again, to see how she would respond to the sound of her. Karin had never lashed out that way in her life. Not at her parents, or at school as a child. And it was incredible at first, this empowering burst of electricity that propelled her forward. She'd never thought she could be such a person, prone to violence of even the briefest kind.

Some time later the room coalesced again, now hot and uncomfortable, the sheets damp and heavy. Her room got so much sun. She could probably grow plants in it. A window box of lettuces, things she could reach out, brush off, and eat, never leaving.

How tiring all of this was. She covered her eyes with a pillowcase and tried to summon the darkness and chill of the cheese cave, its complex moldy fragrance and the chthonic breezes that had blown up so strangely from the corner of the packed earth. That pregnant image on the wall, the velvety discs of milk. No one at that farm had had children. Where had that baby, that rounded belly on the cave wall, gone? Maybe Elaine had realized that even a place like that, as beautiful and rich as it seemed at first, was just inhospitable. Or maybe she had lost a pregnancy to something in the water, to some contaminant in the milk.

And maybe it had only been a wish all along. Not a portrait, just simple yearning, despite everything.

And all at once Karin understood. She'd never felt anything like it before, a rush of hormones moving through her, distinct as a vein full of soft, clicking pearls. She was a healthy, even beautiful, woman, the sort who ought to populate the earth if they were going to have any chance at all of survival. She was young, her hair was thick and gleaming and her skin smooth, and her teeth could tear whatever she gave them. As she thought about that cave it didn't seem so frightening anymore. It was an uncontrolled and gravid space, yes, where her hair had risen at the ends and the electric currents pulsed through the wrap of darkness. If Karin concentrated hard she could almost hear the striving of cells, reaching blindly to extend themselves and grab hold, just as any living thing would try to do, especially in so frightening a place. Maybe her parents had felt this, too—the need to make more beings like themselves, surround oneself with allies, and defy whatever was coming. She still supposed it was a selfish impulse, to bring a child into the darkening world, but maybe it was necessary in the end. Even brave. Karin couldn't help but understand, now that her own body was so hungry and softened, in a strange mix of plenitude and desire. So this was how it felt, to be a hopeful creature like any other.

Greta poured her coffee crumbs into boiling water, then poured the whole mess through a strainer and into a fresh pan. The coffee grounds seemed too valuable to throw away. Maybe she was being pessimistic, but maybe they would want them again. Better terrible coffee than none. She set the colander on a plate and put it in the refrigerator next to Karin's little box of eggs. The fridge was definitely room temperature now, the ice Hal had bought yesterday just bags of water. The cheese, the butter, and the yogurt all got tossed into the garbage can, though Greta did pause over a handful of rubbery carrots and liquefying greens. Compost, of course. They'd get the worm box going. Greta suspected they would need a garden, like World War II victory gardens. The CSA box had been so sparse.

The rest of the house was calm. Everyone must still be asleep. Greta went upstairs to get dressed, but then paused as she padded past Karin's door. Silence inside. Greta stood still, wondering whether to go in and see her. They lived together; as far as Greta knew they would live together indefinitely. They would have to sort things out. And Karin had seemed so weary and de-spairing the night before. She'd seemed old.

She put on shorts and an old cotton button-down and went back downstairs. Greta peered out the window at the front porch. Will was gone. Hal still had Will's keys, and Greta's car remained on the street, so he must have walked. The bottle of homemade wine remained in the kitchen where she'd placed it.

She pictured Will moving quickly past the capitol, through the campus, toward the remains of the dorm that must now be hanging open in tatters. He would be sweating, trembling still. He might have stopped at a liquor store; she felt it unlikely he had managed not to do so. But maybe this time he hadn't. He had gone this long—even just a few hours counted. He could still be walking.

In the garage she found a hoe, a shovel, and a garden rake, and dragged them all out back to the garden.

This did not seem the time to feel hopeful: the wheels were coming off the city; everyone seemed to scamper back and forth on foot and on bikes, trying to find out what was going on. The heat was stifling, and the kitchen smelled of cooking oil and stale spices and sour milk. She would have to keep busy.

She had not yet turned on the radio, or checked the phones. No one would be working today; she wouldn't even try.

She imagined Will, still walking toward their house, his shirt soaked through with moisture. She knew he felt horrific; she knew he would be panicky and chilled, heart pounding and nerves alight, but for him, feeling bad was good. The worse he felt, the more likely he was to change his life. He'd gone to a rehab once, and maybe now he would go again. Maybe she just had to wait him out for one more day, a few more hours. The last and most impor-tant shift—from that endless, animated coma to a necessary misery—could come at any time. Perhaps it had already begun.

At the back of the yard, the one-time garden was edged by a

rectangle of railroad lumber. She thought it through: turn the soil over, rake it around to break it up. It didn't seem like rocket science. She began to overturn shovels of earth, the metal scoop slicing into the garden, cutting through the weeds. Soon her hands began to blister. She kept shoveling, unconcerned. Her hands could heal.

She had become used to Will's befuddlement, to his flailings in the general direction of conversation. It had made her wild with anger that he couldn't even listen and respond logically. Even when she told him she was moving out, his distress seemed generalized and fearful. She wasn't sure he'd understood. She'd assumed he would get it when he saw her things gone, when she did not come home again.

She suspected it was embarrassment and pride that had kept him from returning to the rehab, even though he'd relapsed a full five months ago. She'd known, or she would have if she allowed herself, that even at the rehab and during the few dry months after it, that he would not stay sober that time. She hadn't wanted to think so, even though everyone warned you how many crises it might take. Greta had seen him herding men around, patting shoulders and speaking earnestly at meetings, and she'd felt that vein of self-awareness in him, the pleasure in AA platitudes and in being the one who helped them all. He'd been so pleased to be admired again, to be listened to and to wield a bit of influence. She sympathized—it must have hurt to realize you were a joke among your family and friends—but she had known that it boded badly for him. For a time after he first relapsed, she'd wondered if she resented him so much that she disliked any sign of confidence on his part, and that she wanted to see him miserable, because how else would he see how low he'd fallen? But before that, when she visited him in rehab, she had known then, too. She had sat with him in the big cafeteria, watching him eat a cherry turnover and drink weak coffee, briefly clasping hands with people passing the table, and it was clear to her even then that this was not the time.

The garden was looking gardenlike now: she had mixed the dampened topsoil with the rest of the dry earth. She poked at the dirt with her shovel and wondered if last night's rain would be enough to do more than dampen a few inches of earth. Before that it hadn't rained in weeks—another thing to fear. Another loosened gear flying off into the road and left behind.

Greta heard a sound from the kitchen. Turning, she saw Hal's shape in the window, a wave in her direction. At least when you lived with someone you didn't have to wonder when the awkward next encounter would arise. You could just plan for it.

That power flash the day before had been like the lights coming up in a theater. She and Hal had broken apart and looked around the room, and for a second Greta had been stunned and disoriented. The sheets were blue and white striped, the pillowcases navy blue, the walls a drab beige-yellow. Piles of clothing spilled out of a hamper next to the maple dresser, and a photo of a man next to an elk head stood framed upon it. Next to it, a photo of Hal among women: an older one who must be his mother, and two younger ones who looked a bit like Hal in their bright dark eyes and wispy hair. *Whose room was she in?* she'd thought. The deep unfamiliarity of her own home was what had struck her then. She didn't know where she was.

Then the lights disappeared and the music flashed off again, that boom resounded in the distance, and they both stayed resolutely still until the vibrato had shimmered away. They had been startled into a sitting position, facing one another. She eyed Hal's chest, broad and lightly coarsened with curling dark hair, his hand still on her shoulder. Will had very little hair on his chest, she'd been thinking, and his hands were entirely different: broader, shorter. Greta's ears were still ringing.

She'd gone to the window and peered out onto the street. It

occurred to her now that Hal might have found this insulting, but she didn't think so. At another time anyone would have, but now—normalcy had come and gone, disappeared with a thunderclap. Outside, people had been poking their heads out of doors, glancing up and down the streets.

She'd looked back at Hal, who was lounging on the bed like a sultan, watching her calmly. She bit her lip, undecided: all those people coming outside—she'd wanted to join them. Even if they knew nothing, she wanted just to talk. But she'd started this thing with Hal, and so far it hadn't been transporting. "Transporting" was the point. There was no reason to do it unless they ended up feeling better than they had before. So she decided not to end it on a bad note. She'd see it through—she would just will this encounter into being good. It could be done sometimes: you could simply make yourself happy. So she'd let the curtain fall and returned to the bed.

Later, they got up to see what their neighbors thought. At the door they'd kissed, lightly, before reentering the world. She'd marveled a bit at how differently a kiss began and how it ended an hour or two later—from cool and firm to heated and softened, like worked clay.

Greta pushed her hair off her forehead and sliced the shovel through the soil. She glanced back to the kitchen, but Hal seemed to be gone. Maybe he'd gone to check on Will. Or maybe now he never would—she'd probably ruined that.

Now she could see the last few years as a kind of paralyzed disaster. Maybe it felt different to Will—maybe his life was one of continually resurfacing and reaching for her before he disappeared again, but she couldn't experience that with him.

The night Will came home from the rehab they'd treated each other as if it were a first date. She'd driven out to get him and in the car they chatted about nothing, about insurance and gossip about the other men in the rehab, and Will seemed nervous and on edge as they neared their house. They'd eaten dinner—a basic, regular dinner of chicken broth with Chinese noodles and greens, rounds of scallion floating at the top alongside pools of orange chili oil. Will unpacked, moving slowly through their bedroom from the suitcase to the dresser and the closet. They'd had tea, read books on either side of the couch, now and again smiling uncertainly in the other's direction, until it was time for bed.

She thought maybe most couples came home and fell into bed, after a full month away. Or maybe not. People didn't go off to rehab because their relationships had been so happy just before. She and Will didn't discuss it. They just got into bed and burrowed in.

This was in October, the weather already chilly and stinging. Greta had run her fingertips over his back and sides, surprised to find him unchanged. His skin was still silky at the hips and waist, his legs, wrapped around her, wiry with dark hair. She didn't want sex. She would have refused, but he didn't ask. He'd been looking at her so intently, his expression grave in the light from the neighbor's window (and now the idea of such generous, wandering light seemed quaint and lost) that she didn't want him to close his eyes and concentrate on something else. She had said nothing, hadn't moved a muscle. She felt as if she hadn't seen him in years.

CHAPTER EIGHTEEN

And then Karin's eyes were open. She struggled to sit up and realized she'd been roused by a knock, which now came again. Greta peered around the edge of her door. "May I?" she said. She raised one hand to show she was carrying a glass of water, which she held out in Karin's direction. Karin nodded and wiped sleep from her eyes.

Greta perched at the edge of her bed. Karin took the glass and drank deeply; even tepid water felt luxurious and generous. Greta's eyes looked as if she'd been crying, but she smiled and asked, "How are you feeling?"

"Okay," Karin heard herself croak. She finished the water and then had no idea what to say. They sat in an awkward silence, and Karin was conscious of the dirty clothes on her floor, the desiccated plant by the window, a fairy-ring of dead leaves below it on the carpet.

"Sorry for my room," Karin said, but Greta didn't seem to hear her.

Instead she stood and said, "Want to come somewhere with me? I know we all have to think about what to do at some point, but honestly, I don't think there's a rush. I think the whole city is moving really slowly so far."

Karin tried to wake up enough to figure out what Greta was talking about. "How do you know? Is there a paper?"

"Not today. I went over to Laurel's house a few minutes ago, and she had the radio on. Listen, they identified the person in the lake. I guess his name was Terry Dodd."

"Terry Dodd? I didn't know him."

"Me, neither."

"Was he from here?"

Greta shook her head. "He drove in from DeForest. His wife had been calling their local police and it took them some time to connect."

Karin stared into her glass. "I never pictured him married," she said. "I wasn't really picturing a 'him' all the time, either." Greta nodded, raised one shoulder and dropped it. "Why drive here?"

Greta said, "Maybe to have time, so no one would see him and know him."

Karin's first impulse was toward a platitude, to say, "How sad," or "What a terrible thing," and so she chose to say nothing. She was trying to assimilate this new image, and was surprised to find she was angry, now that she knew who it was and what he'd done in her lake, so near her cozy house. She felt targeted—why would someone come specifically to their street? But, of course, she had no proof he had chosen them. He might just have followed the Yahara and parked his car where he first caught a glimpse of the water.

She imagined him—Terry, she should think of him by name—

getting out of his car and walking across the grass. She saw him climbing onto the dock and clapping to call the dog, heard the metal scrape as the dock separated. He might have rowed out as far as he could, and when he judged it far enough, he simply dropped the oar into the water. And maybe he sat in the chair then, stroking the dog's head and beneath its jaws. For the first time Karin wondered if he had only intended the dog as company. But she didn't have to conjecture this: whatever he had once intended, in the end he had left the dog safely on the dock, and for that Karin felt a little surge of gratitude.

But then he jumped. Once in the water, how had he circumvented the urge to swim? The dive would be the easy part. But a body in water will right itself and try to float and this is what shook her, that his chin would have been lifted by the current and by the motion of his arms. He would have been forced to see what he was leaving. She knew she couldn't have done it. That last view would have forced her to change her mind, Karin knew, and she would have tried to take it back. She would have begun to swim, to climb the clouded green tunnel to the sun.

Hal was hesitant. What he really wanted was to get to work. He and Greta and Karin stood on the porch, discussing what to do. Karin appeared relieved and tentative, clearly trying to get footing in what seemed to be a calmer day. Greta was serene—as far as she was concerned they were going.

"Look, you guys have jobs you can sort of pause," he said. "I did that yesterday and it was enough. It was too much. I feel like I should be there already."

Greta looked at her watch. "It's not even eight," she said. "The phones are still in and out, so you won't be able to call many people today—and anyway they won't be in till later."

The previous day felt as if it had lasted a week. The meager supplies Hal had left in the Swiff warehouse might be only dust and crumbs by now.

"People don't just offer you these," Greta continued. "She was probably flustered because it was hot and dark and she'd had to save my life, but I'm taking advantage of it no matter what. We are. I really want us to." She swallowed. "Please."

Finally Hal had said, "Look, if I get enough done today I *may* be able to have some food for people tomorrow. I don't even know if any volunteers will make it in. Can we be back fast? An hour or two?" The sooner he got to work, the sooner he'd know if Diana would let him stay. Nevertheless, even Hal had to admit that they had time.

"Sure," Greta said. "We can come right back."

"Cool," Hal said, surprised at how easily they both agreed. They must have reached some sort of truce. "Thanks."

"We should drop off the mushrooms anyway," Karin said. "And if you're short on volunteers we'll just come in with you."

Here Hal hesitated, touched that they planned to help out, but also wondering if they'd see him be fired on the spot. He'd been able to handle having Will there the day before, since Will seemed unlikely internalize and recall much of what he witnessed. But Diana would either accept him or tell him to get out, and Hal didn't know which. He didn't like imagining his roommates, their hands clasped behind their backs, bouncing on their toes, while they listened to his dismissal.

Greta was tying her tennis shoes. "What's wrong?" she said. "Do you need more people?"

"Maybe," Hal said. "Today might be a strange day."

"Tell me about it," Karin said.

"No, I know that, but I may not exactly be welcomed back."

Greta and Karin nodded. He'd hoped irrationally that they would protest, but neither did, of course, and this made him feel strangely better—not comforted, but somehow aligned with them. Flanked by them. He'd forgotten this, somehow, but his housemates were practical people.

"We want dead trees," Hal said. "They like them dead. Or burned, if you see any of those."

"I don't see anything that was burned," Karin said. "Maybe dying."

"That one looks a little crappy," said Greta. She pointed to a tree with spindly branches and frayed leaves.

Hal shook his head. "No, like dead and even knocked over. But then again they might be all over a perfectly healthy elm or an ash. Everyone know what those look like?"

Karin nodded and Greta shook her head. Karin said, "I think you want alternate branching and an unequal leaf base."

"I don't think that's always true," Hal interjected.

Greta looked over her shoulder at the house behind them. From the open windows they could hear a tentative violin. Julie Voltsheim was learning to play. "Look, we can start walking or we can talk about it for*ever*. I told her we'd only be here a couple hours at most. Let's hit it."

The three of them began to walk, the sound of the violin dimming until finally it disappeared all together. Greta listened to the brushing sounds of their feet moving through the wet grass. Julie's house wasn't the monstrosity she'd imagined: it was a neat farmhouse with silvery cedar shingles, plus two sheds and a garage. Julie had led them through the house, which had so many windows the lack of power wasn't noticeable, and out the back. She'd pointed eastward, past a grape arbor newly tendriled with vines. "Try in that direction," she said. "We've had some luck there. But honestly, who knows? It rained last night. They could have popped up anywhere."

The woods edged the house and its yard in a neat oval. Once

they reached the edge of the trees, Greta smelled damp earth and live wood, pine sap, and a pleasant, fecund whiff of rot. She began to walk very slowly, letting her eyes unfocus just a little and take in the ground. Her feet, in a pair of old tennis shoes, moved in and out of the frame of her vision. She watched green shoots bend in the breeze, loose leaves tumble over the twigs. The ground was a mix of mud and loam. Little paths wound through the trees in all directions. Bronze needles blanketed the earth below the conifers.

She paused near an old tree trunk that was lying on its side. It was ridged with white ruffled fungus on one side but nothing else. Greta touched it carefully; the fungus was meaty and moist beneath each shelf.

She glanced up to see where the others were. Karin was a few feet away, her head turning slow arcs as she eyed the earth. She was in jeans and a white tank top beneath an opened sweatshirt and she carried a couple paper bags. Her hair was pulled up in a bun at the base of her neck. Sometimes one hand drifted over her belly, tapping at the cavern of her navel beneath the thin cotton. She didn't seem to be aware of the gesture.

Hal was just behind them, walking with a slowness that was almost majestic. His hands were in his pockets, a couple canvas bags dangling from one wrist. The cuffs of his pants were dark from the wet grass. He looked very comfortable in the woods, which surprised her. She realized she knew almost nothing about Hal's background, if indeed he had spent his whole childhood in places like this.

They fanned out as they moved farther in. Karin turned eastward, her form flickering between the trees and shadows. Hal charted a loose westward arc, moving back and forth across it. Greta went due north.

The woods became darker as the leaf cover thickened. Out in the sun it was hot, but back here the air was damp and cool, the chatter of animals muted. Even the birds were quiet. Greta saw the paper of an old snakeskin mashed into the earth, May apples with heart-shaped flat leaves bent protectively over their stems. She slowed and slowed, and let her eyes pick out the details on the ground before her, patiently awaiting the right one.

Karin didn't see the mushrooms so much as understand that she'd been looking at them for several moments. A little clutch of three on the forest floor to her right. She crouched down to touch the honeycomb of their brainy, ghostly heads. Their hollowness made them feel that much more magical, as if they would be revealed as illusions if you turned them the wrong way. Each one reached out from a joined center in its own direction, as if toward a shaft of sun or a particular tree. Two of them came loose with a gentle pop, brown earth staining the ring at their bases. She peered inside them and placed them gently in her bag.

Karin stood up. She had left the third mushroom untouched, so more would sprout. Then she moved along, her eyes sweeping purposefully back and forth. There were more. The forest was full of them.

Hal was allowing the floor of the woods to unfurl before him: the key was not to tromp into it but to follow it. He wasn't used to being in the woods so late in the morning. When hunting, you went out well before light, when the forest was unwelcoming and stark, and every step broadcasted your intrusion. But it was peaceful once you settled into a tree stand. His father had taught all three of his children how to let go, to be relaxed, to be alert, but to sink into the woods. Spring was turkey season, Hal remembered. His father was most likely doing just what Hal was: he was out among the trees, searching.

Maybe he could get his father to give Hal some wild turkeys on the sly. It was illegal to sell hunted meat, but you could donate deer. Why not turkey? It hadn't come up before, because a deer fed so many and turkey only a few, so no one bothered. Perhaps Hal could get a few hunters together and they would donate what they bagged. He would just call until his father answered, assuming the phones became reliable again. Or he'd write. People wrote letters well before electricity, and Hal could do it again. He'd just send a letter a week, and add some coupons and clippings about grandchildren or muskie.

His father wasn't dead; the man had to communicate sometime. One of these days grief would lift and he would wonder what his kids were doing.

Hal decided he wouldn't waste time roasting whole birds. He'd cut them up and eke it out with noodles or rice and get twice the yield. Someone would give them some noodles. A few carrots for color.

Hal had awakened that morning from the sounds of Greta moving through the house and the murmur of voices from the porch. When he got up, the world outside was so quiet it frightened him. Without the television it had been all too easy to believe the world had settled into sleep outside their little isthmus. He knew, objectively, that the world continued, just as he knew that farther east, Mrs. Bryant was sleeping dreamlessly, her curio cabinet packed with rolled twenties; that somewhere else Will might well be drinking martini after martini; and that Wes was planning something, some gathering or uprising or another, and making lists of supplies and people.

Hal knelt to check out a tree stump, but it was simply crumbly and soft, with only a light carpet of green leaves around it. He poked a few leaves aside and found nothing, so he kept strolling and looked at his watch.

Luckily Greta had woken him early. There would be so much

to do today: already Diana must be looking for a generator. She'd have to hurry before the stores and restaurants got them. Actually, stores might not even bother to shell out for generators—they might find it more expedient to clear out anything perishable before it went bad, so they could start afresh. Imagine how much they'd have to get rid of.

Hal stopped walking. How neatly it would sync up. Businesses had been operating on little or no surplus and so had nothing to donate. But a blackout like this created a great wave of surplus if you could grab it fast enough. The Swiffies could gather up the perishables before they all turned and they could extend them: cooking loaves of meat, baking the butter and eggs into cake or rich breads, buying a little time with flour and sugar. He could get days of food out of this if he handled it right.

Now he began moving more attentively. His perceptions seemed to open up; Hal felt himself become porous. The individual sounds of the woods jumped forward. He moved left, then right, incrementally forward, and when he saw a little crescent of elms he let himself gravitate toward it, but he didn't rush. He moved methodically in its direction, until, just as he'd been certain he would, he saw the dark gold morel at its base. Once he saw it he couldn't imagine how he'd ever miss one again—they leaped into focus, scattered all around him.

The mushroom at the base of the elm was all precise formation and bright color. Its stem was a creamy ivory and its long cap was a dark goldenrod hue, the tip folded over like an elf-cap. Hal laughed aloud. They were so frankly phallic it was like a little cosmic joke—you were meant to laugh.

On her third downed tree trunk, Greta found the mother lode. The mossy old wood was spiked with them, in cool gray and brownish black and light yellow. At one end was a patch of tiny morels the size of her thumb. They might have sprouted up just since the rain that morning, they were so petite. A great tall one hid behind it, and several more yellow mushrooms sprouted in circles nearby. She reached to detach the big one, thinking how she'd cook it. She would leave it whole and fry it, maybe.

She looked the morel over as she went to place it in her bag, peering into the folds of its body. Inside it was a slug. The strange part was that she felt no revulsion at all, and normally she would have thrown it away from her as uncontrollably as a convulsion. But now she studied the slug, which was a glistening half-inch long, dotted with reptilian spots. It was really rather gorgeous against the yellow flesh. How had it gotten inside a closed space like the hollow of the morel? It hadn't even left a hole where it might have chewed through. Maybe the mushroom had somehow grown up and over it. However the slug had managed to get there, now she'd torn open its cocoon. She watched the dark gray body move in pulses, the slug unperturbed that she had opened up its pleasant cavern, until she put the mushroom on its side, back in the dirt. She'd stop on her way back and pick it up again, to see if the slug had given up its altered habitat or decided to adapt.

CHAPTER NINETEEN

First, Will would get a haircut. Then he'd get ice.

Will was walking down Willy Street in the direction of the capitol. He'd find a place for a haircut somewhere there, if he just walked long enough. There was a little hipster salon downtown he'd wandered into once. He could go there.

The walk was longer than he'd expected it to be, the streets empty and quiet, the buildings dark. The salon wouldn't be open this early, so Will stopped and ate breakfast in a little diner just off the square. He found a seat by the window and ordered an omelet and toast and coffee, but he couldn't drink the coffee. It smelled good at first, but then he took a sip and it made him feel more nervous and high strung, and suddenly the aroma was too much— too dark and too heavy. He thought it would eat right through him. He ate his spinach omelet instead, trying to go slowly and methodically and to think about nutrition. Drinkers forgot to eat. That was why the rehab gave them so much food, snacks, and extra carbs and fruit. Will had developed a love for the gooey cherry turnovers they set out each evening alongside weak coffee and tea. He was looking forward to one of those pastries.

He couldn't finish the omelet—the coffee scent had begun to bother him so much that Will finally just set money on the table and left for the salon, waving to the lone waitress.

At the salon he found two workers sitting in the adjustable chairs, spinning and chatting. They looked up at him, startled, when he walked in.

"Are you open yet?" Will asked. His voice sounded high to him, hopeful.

They were, barely, and some discussion ensued about where they should work: down by the chairs themselves it was quite dark, but perhaps the other employee would get some flashlights and hold them up, or maybe that was wasting batteries. Maybe they should improvise something up near the windows.

Will was enjoying the whole conversation, suggesting this and that, being accommodating about possibly sitting on the couches by the window, whatever worked for them. The point was not the haircut. He didn't even need a haircut. He was happy to be talking to people who didn't seem to find him embarrassing or pathetic, who knew nothing about him. The only thing they'd ever know about him was that he was apparently fastidious about regular haircuts.

He reached up and touched the back of his neck: sweaty and tense, but smooth. In the corner of his vision he thought he saw a yellow star burst and disappear. He tossed his head, shook the light away.

Finally a decision was made and a chair was dragged over near the best light. They propped a mirror on the couch before them.

"I'm still not sure we shouldn't just take it outside," the stylist said. "But you probably don't want to be on display." Her hand patted his shoulder. She shook out a plastic cape to wrap him in, then, humming, checked out his hair. She ran her fingers through it, tested the texture. Will let his eyes close. She rested both hands on his shoulders while they talked about how he wore it, what he wanted. He pretended to care about both, but really, he just wanted a little trimming. Nothing that would make it hard for him to get another haircut soon.

Every week he went to different places. He'd gone to the barbershops on State Street and Monroe Street, and suburban places on the far west side—loud, pricey salons and hushed ones with the sound of water falling. He went on Mondays, usually. He could get through a weekend that way. It didn't matter to him who the barber was, man or woman, good or bad. It was just a relief to feel someone's hands in his hair, all the offhand warmth of someone's fingers at the ears, the cheek, the neck. Otherwise he'd forget what contact felt like. Even then it could startle him, the coolness or heat of someone's hands, the untroubled way they all had of cupping his shoulders.

Now Will sat there, blinking into the mirror, while the stylist trimmed away, and he tried to think of ways to prolong it. He got more upset the closer it was to being finished.

When she began to brush off his neck and ears with an air of finality, he had to push down panic. He cleared his throat. "Would you mind trimming my eyebrows?" he asked. "I'll pay, of course."

"Don't be silly," said the woman, and she came around the front and lifted his face with a finger beneath his chin. He let her comb through his brow and saw the tiny clippings fall past his vision.

The temptation was to come up with something else, to prolong it: ask her to trim his ears, or to invent a slight unevenness at

the sideburns. But Will limited himself to one request. He had
to come back to them soon. He didn't want to be a nuisance.

After the haircut, he headed back toward Greta's. He'd find ice;
that was the next plan. No one had asked him to get some—
people rarely bothered to ask him for anything anymore—but
Will had seen Greta peer into the refrigerator and lift a dripping
package from it, grimacing at the water moisture. Surely ice
would be useful. And it gave him something to think about as he
walked through her neighborhood, something to concentrate
on. Ice: cold little circles growing brittle in the mouth and breaking apart. The crack through the center as a cube warmed up,
splintered and clouded from inside. The trick was to think only
about ice, not ice in vodka or ice packed around beer bottles. Ice,
alone.

Will was very thirsty. His T-shirt was damp but his mouth
was thready from dryness. He ought to have asked Greta for
some water. She would have given him that. But she had gone
inside the house and he'd watched the pale circle of her head
darkening through the screen door as she headed toward the
back, and he'd decided not to follow her.

He felt oversensitized and irritated. He could feel each hair
on his arms and his skull, every follicle shifting in the wind and
trailing across his skin like a spider web. He scratched his skull
and rubbed his neck and arms. He was damp and slick all over.
He watched his feet moving beneath him on the pavement, the
flashing progress of them, the streak of the pavement. In the
back of his head he felt a tightness, a gathering pain that made
his scalp tingle.

This didn't feel like Greta's kind of neighborhood. They'd always thought of the east side as a little hippieish and rough
around the edges. Then you wake up one day and your wife is liv-

ing across town with a couple of people you've never met and neither has she. When he'd found the house the other night he'd sat in his car and looked at it for a long time, sipping at a bottle of vodka. They came home one by one: a girl in a khaki skirt, long-sleeved white shirt, and a long brown ponytail. Young, very pretty, she'd slammed her car door and jogged up the front walk. Then Greta, in her usual pale summer clothes, sunglasses still on as she entered the house. He had waited for a while for more roommates, but it was just these two until the guy came home. The house seemed a little stale and sad to him—the fading bright paint on the trim, the saggy couch where he'd woken up. Couldn't Greta have found a more vibrant co-op if that was what she wanted? This one seemed to be limping along. It couldn't be that much better than living with him.

Having Hal in Will's own house hadn't been a proud moment, either. He knew the house smelled old and musty and hot; he had not cleaned in weeks. He meant to. He went out for food or to work and thought each day that he really had to clean. But then time just took these leaps, and the days were over before he'd done a thing.

Greta had taken the bottle of homemade wine with her. There in the house, no doubt, would be bottles of vodka and gin, cold white wine in the fridge, dewy bottles of beer.

But then nothing was very cold right then. Warm beer. Tepid wine. Gin, hot and musty in a dark cedar cabinet. He tried to think about water instead. About ice. When he got the ice he might keep a bag for himself. It would give him something to eat, piece by piece. That might take up a good hour. He could worry about the next hour when this one was done.

He knew he'd been inside Greta's new house but the actual memory was fuzzy, so it had the sensation of a place you'd been in childhood, or in a dream. A lot of things felt this way to him, these flashes of brightness when he realized he had seen something or someone before. The whole neighborhood felt altered but familiar. There were more people on bikes than he recalled there ever being. Strangely dressed people, as far as people on bicycles went: in suits and skirts, with baskets strapped to the handlebars. Will slowed down and gazed at one woman in her front yard, in white linen pants and a blue sleeveless blouse, bending over a yellow bicycle with a basket at the handlebars. The basket—and it was a real basket, woven out of wood or something that looked like it—was strapped on to the handlebars with a thin leather belt. He saw her tug at the belt to test it, pick up a notebook and some folders from the sidewalk beside her, and place them in the basket. She flipped her long brown braid over her shoulder and climbed onto the bike. As she pushed off with one sandaled foot, the bike wobbled dangerously, her braid twitching and her posture growing straight and tense. Then she pumped her legs and the bike surged forward, down her driveway and onto the sidewalk. He caught a glimpse of her face as she checked the street: the eyebrows dark and raised in alertness, the mouth clenched in concentration.

He looked up and down the street. He'd forgotten to watch where he was going and had gone west of Williamson Street, which was where he would have found ice if there was any to be had. Or he could keep heading west across the isthmus, toward East Wash. He could keep going past Washington and hit the other lake on the other side of the isthmus. Plenty of water around.

He'd been headed toward the lake the other night, actually. He was almost there when he realized how close he was to Greta's new house, so he'd gone there instead, thinking he might go to the lake afterward.

These lakes weren't the oceanic Great Lakes, but they were big enough to be treacherous. People sailed on them in bad weather and drowned. Drunk students got confused and swam

out too far. Will had thought about it, too: swim out to the center, where around him there would mostly be blackness, the
lights of the city too far to reach. And then a few nights ago he'd
thought the blackness was a nudge to try it, to swim out far and
hope to sink, unencumbered by the sparkling bracelet of city
light around the water.

This other man had done it, floated out on the dock and just
jumped right off, leaving his dog to float or swim to shore. Will
hadn't considered that particular solution before, but he understood. People liked to act so confused by these things, but he
understood.

Or at least he had. Now the idea no longer seemed like the
right one. Something had shifted, though he wasn't sure just
what. He kept thinking of the odd group of three he'd been part
of yesterday, a stranger in a stranger's house. Generally when he
ended up in some place like that, some place that wasn't his, it
went badly. But that hadn't been so terrible. He must have annoyed them; there was no way he hadn't. Neverthless, some
stranger had picked him up and hauled him around. For whatever the reason.

Now Will turned around. Another bicycle whooshed past
him—no, not a bike. A man on one of those reclining vehicles,
leaning on his back, legs pumping madly, head propped forward
to see where he was going. It looked far less comfortable than
any typical bicycle. Were people really doing this now, unwilling
to even admit they were ambulatory? Jesus. Will stood still and
watched the man recline out of sight.

He would buy the ice, take it back to Greta, and fill the cooler.
He would ask her for some water. He would drink a glass, with a
lot of ice. That would take him through the next half hour or so.
Maybe more if he stretched it out. That left the rest of the day,
and an entire night. He would need something else to concentrate on, but for now he'd get ice.

He held up a hand, experimentally. It shook. He let it fall again.

The worst part of all of this had been the precise moment last night when Will came back to himself. It was never as bad if he simply woke up on the couch, or in bed. He might be fully clothed, shoes and all, but being in his own house was close enough to normal that it didn't alarm him. This time, however, he'd come to while walking. It had never stopped frightening him, no matter how many times it happened, to become aware of himself in motion, even mid-speech, the world dawning in a flash and rushing by as he hurtled through it. He'd learned not to stop and show shock or surprise. He just barreled through, kept talking to his wife or his boss or kept walking, it didn't matter. The key was always to get through the immediate moment unscathed. Get to the next thing.

Last night it had happened as he stumbled, midstride, in his own neighborhood. He was dressed, yes, he was wearing normal clothes and shoes, so instinct or habit had carried him that far. The darkness was a shock: every house dark, the streets in total blackness. He'd stopped and looked around until he understood that he was seeing light inside the houses, moving in cones and beams, fuzzy dandelions of candlelight floating past the curtains. It was so dark he didn't worry about standing and gaping. No one could see him.

His first thought in those moments, when he first felt awake again, was usually of his wife. How mad was Greta now? He often awoke and assessed his situation piece by piece: if he was in bed, this was good. If Greta was in bed next to him, he was close to all right. If she was in the guest room, he was in bad shape. When he awoke alone in bed he usually raced through a shower and ran out the door to work before she could talk to him. He never wanted to know what had happened the night before, but she always wanted to tell him. She had an endless store of things to tell him. Greta's greatest fear seemed to be that he would forget a single facet of his general failure. He couldn't really blame her for that.

He was back at Willy Street now. He peered up and down the block. No cars. The BP station looked empty. He decided to turn around yet again and go toward Washington Avenue.

He knew he'd been making her crazy but he'd never felt he had any real say in the matter. If she chose to go crazy over whatever Will did, then he couldn't stop her, nor could he blame her. This was how he'd done it—he'd watched their lives carry on without him for the past few years. After a while you just didn't want to know.

But then, last night, he'd begun walking, heading east instead of toward home, even though he knew he should check on their house. It was possible he'd left the front door open, the car running in the driveway—no. That man had driven it. Hal. Greta's roommate. Anyway, he just didn't go in that direction. He went back toward Greta's new house, on the lake, but this time he didn't intend to go all the way to the water.

Will paused and rubbed his face, his hands smelling of coffee, and found himself remembering a woman's face. An old woman, her hair a dull white halo and her eyes showing the white below the iris, a pouch of skin beneath. Mrs. Bryant. He hadn't been in such bad shape when they'd gotten there. He didn't recall leaving. He certainly didn't recall why he had gone in the first place. Sometimes he did things like that: he sought out people when he shouldn't. Which he never should. He wasn't really welcome to anyone that he could think of.

He suspected he had not been to work in a few days. Why wasn't Greta at work? He thought it was a weekday. Obviously some people were heading to work, but there were a lot more just standing around in their yards, talking in groups across fences. They nodded in his direction as he passed.

He nodded back but it all felt fake to him, everything always did. In a way, the walk through a blacked-out campus last night, the neighborhoods spooky with darkness and reckless whoops from parties, was a relief. It was better than waking up and being miserable, knowing your life was a mountain of fuck-ups from start to finish, and then watching people act normally and expect you to do the same. The lightlessness, the empty streets, had felt almost natural to him, as if he had been awaiting it for a long time. When he'd come across the dorm being torn apart by people in uniform, he'd thought, *Well, here we go, it's here.* They looked like high-school kids, and maybe they practically were, being hollered at by a group of striding helmeted people before they all hunched over and raced into the black building. He'd approached a kid leaning against the open back of a truck, drinking a cup of water.

"We're SWAT," the kid had said, turning to him. It was a girl, freckled, deep-voiced, but definitely a girl. "In training," she admitted. "The school's letting us use the building for practice since it's being demolished."

"That's insane," he'd said.

"It's fucking amazing," she exclaimed. "We'll be down to the skeleton soon. We keep finding leftover shit from the students, you know. They're so lazy they forgot half their stuff. Clothes, jackets, books. I heard someone found an iPod."

Now another little sizzle crossed Will's vision, like a pop from a flashbulb. He stopped, but it seemed to be gone. He swished what little saliva he could muster around his mouth and swallowed it. His teeth were the worst. A faintly magnetized, acidic feeling, an ache both deep and surface. He felt his mouth as something metallic and soft-fleshed, swollen with nerves. Ice would either feel good or be unbearable. A bottle of vodka would take most of the ache away, certainly it would quiet his hands and calm down his nerves. He knew he ought to drink some-

thing or else go to a hospital, but he wanted very much to put together twenty-four hours without a drink. Then he would go. He
would prove that he could keep from drinking, then he'd go back
in time for cherry turnovers.

He passed one gas station, which was closed, and now he
approached another. Someone around here must be selling ice.
Someone must have a generator or a cool basement. What was
going on in the larger world? It couldn't be that everyone lacked
power. He should have asked Greta. Maybe she knew. Maybe her
roommate knew.

He wanted to stay outside today, if he could. It was best to be
in fresh air, able to see a little of the larger world. There was
something frightening to him now about being walled off and
hidden. Not frightening to be inside, but frightening to return to
the outdoors, to see what had happened while you were away.
He'd gone inside after work, lost track of a couple days, and now
look at them all. His wife in a half-empty, shabby house on Lake
Monona. The city baffled and dark. No electricity, the cars useless as dead animals.

Or that was how it seemed. It wasn't truly possible that no
one anywhere had gas. Plenty of people had hybrids, they could
afford a little gas. They could rent out rides. Maybe he even had
a full tank at home; he didn't know. He could drive it up to the
rehab, if he went, and after a month he might find that anything
at all had happened—maybe he would drive back to town and all
would be normal again.

Because, some mornings, everything worked out. He would
wake up and Greta would be in bed next to him, sleeping on her
side, the comforter between her knees and a hand flung out toward the wall, her face blank and restful. He'd get up and make
coffee, try not to shake too hard, and when she awoke she would
be calm and happy. She'd open the newspaper and chat about a
book review, some new bit of legislation. He could never figure

out how this happened, but sometimes it did. He assumed he must have gotten through one or two nights, every now and then, without ruining something. On those mornings he could nearly convince himself that this was normal life.

A man in a light gray suit passed him, riding a jazzy neon orange bike. Madison was a biking town, but had this many people just had bicycles in reserve? Will hadn't been on a bike in twenty years at least. He certainly didn't own one. These people must have kids, and had taken their bikes. Maybe the ones without bikes were just sitting at home, stranded, eking another day out of work. The sidewalks were no longer as deserted, either. People were walking here and there, jaywalking lazily, but still this was not a normal day's volume of people in transit. The streets still felt somnolent and sparse.

On the block ahead he saw a gas station. Someone was moving inside it, he was certain. Will walked a little more quickly, worried he'd miss out. He couldn't be the only one looking for ice.

Another bicycle. This time a child. Just a child on a bike, the most normal thing in the world. He was just a man taking a walk. He and his wife were separated, yes, but that happened. This, too, was normal.

It suddenly seemed possible that people were jumping the gun. Was there truly any reason to think that power would not be restored, and future crises averted? Will couldn't quite convince himself that the world would just drop the reins so instantaneously. In fact, what if this was all the silliest thing—a woodchuck had wandered into the grid somewhere, a switch thrown incorrectly? And there was Greta and her co-op full of roommates, tetchy and frightened. An old headline from *The Onion* returned to him: IN RETROSPECT, PERHAPS WE RESORTED TO CANNIBALISM TOO SOON. Will chuckled. Maybe at the power plant someone was right there playing solitaire, waiting for the boss to show.

There was no way to know. If you were just a man—a man who needed to drink and was trying not to, who felt tense and shaky and whose entire plan for the future consisted of getting two bags of ice, but still, just a man walking down the street in the hot sun—you could never know where they all were in the cycle. The rise of a new crest or the long descent? The first morning or the last? Will didn't know. He was reduced to basics: a person in search of ice.

And here was the gas station. To the left of the front door was the same oddly shaped silver ice bin they all had. He headed over to it, across the empty parking lot to the cooler, anticipating the cold burst of fog and the frosted silver interior. He opened the door and reached in—but the bin was empty and warm.

Will kept his hand inside the ice bin anyway, feeling around as if he would find the pocket of coldness somewhere. He was unable to accept that, of course, the ice was long gone, and, of course, the freezer was dead. He squeezed his eyes shut and gripped the cooler door, just for a second, to calm himself. Then he closed the door to the bin and went inside the gas station.

There was only one guy inside the dim store, eating a bag of chips and reading an old *Us Weekly* in the light from the window.

"I don't mean to ask a dumb question here," Will began, "but is there any chance you have ice anywhere?"

The guy smiled. "You'd be amazed how many people have asked," he said. "And the answer is yes and no. I don't have any right here on the premises, but I know where you can get some."

Will sighed. "Then tell me," he said. "And how much?"

"Twenty per bag."

"Fine." But Will wasn't certain how much money he had left. He reached back to his wallet and flipped it open casually, glancing at the bills. He still had a few twenties. It would do for now.

Banks would have to open without ATMs; they couldn't just close and wait for the power to return. He could afford this for now. "So, where's your ice?"

The guy tossed the magazine down and came out from behind the counter, glancing around as he opened the gas station door. He was young, in his twenties, with warm brown eyes and lank dark hair around a round-cheeked face. "No one's coming anyway," he said, and gestured for Will to follow.

They began to walk across the parking lot. Will was expecting to go behind the building for some reason, but the gas station attendant crossed the lot and then turned down a side street, continuing down the sidewalk. He looked to be sure Will was following, but Will had slowed down. The attendant paused, hands on his hips. "I realize this feels a little freaky, but it's not. My buddy lives on Dayton. He has a basement and a fridge down there, and we put the fridge on its back like a cooler, took as much ice over as we could and bought a ton of gel packs and just packed it in. When those go, we're going to call around and see if anyone has sawdust. That's how they used to do it, you know. Sawdust."

"Are you serious?" Will asked. It was either preposterous, or else this attendant was much smarter than he seemed. "Look. I'm not going into some stranger's house."

"It's right down there. That green one." The attendant gestured one pale arm toward a moss-colored bungalow with a red pickup truck parked in the drive. Will turned to walk away. He felt like shit, he was nervous and sweating and he kept seeing misplaced light in his vision, and all he wanted was coldness, and moisture, and not to think about a drink. Or maybe only to think about a drink, which would make everything else unnecessary.

"Jesus, fine," the guy said. "You try to help somebody, right? Look, you wait here. Go have a seat in the shade. How many bags you want?"

"One. Two."

"Two?" He took a step toward the house. "Okay, two. Seriously, go sit in the shade. You look pretty bad. I'll be right back."

And the attendant set off jogging down the sidewalk, a set of keys jangling in his khaki shorts, holding his baseball cap onto his head with one hand. He went behind the pickup truck and knocked on the door. The door opened—Will couldn't see by whom—and the attendant spoke, pointing in Will's direction. A dark head peeked out from behind the door. The person waved. Will raised one hand in reply, and both people disappeared inside the house.

Will moved off the sidewalk and into someone's yard, beneath a tree, hoping no one would see him. The shade was a relief; the attendant was right. Out of concern for the attendant, he kept an eye on the gas station, in case a customer showed up, but no one came. He wondered how long he should wait before leaving—because already the whole idea seemed ludicrous. How was he going to tell Greta he'd thought he'd get ice from some tattooed kid in a gas station and his buddy around the corner? But then again, how much respect for him could Greta really lose by now? It probably made no difference at all. He was just standing up, thinking he should leave, maybe find a store and save his money for something important, like gin, when he heard the slapping sound of jogging feet and a jangling of keys. The attendant was back, heading toward him, a dripping bag of ice in each hand.

"You never thought I'd come back, did you!" he cried.

Will met him on the sidewalk, desperate now to get his hands on that ice. Just to feel the coldness of it—there was no refreshment anywhere else. He fumbled getting out the twenties, not caring if he was being cheated, but then he didn't see anyone else with any ice. He shoved the bills into the kid's hand.

"You have no idea how much I need this," Will said.

The kid tucked the twenties into his pocket. "Thanks, man. And be cool about who you tell, okay? I didn't really mention it to my bosses. They just think it all melted."

He waved and began walking back toward the gas station.

Will bent down and picked up the bags. They were a little more slushy than a bag of ice should be, but you couldn't have everything. They were chilly and substantial, the plastic wet.

He began the walk back to Greta's. The bags were heavy and dripping, leaving little water trails down his legs where they brushed against him. His headache was intensifying now. His vision seemed to tremble and reset itself.

Withdrawal from other drugs was unpleasant but not dangerous, but alcohol was a different story. At the rehab they'd hammered that home. He was in danger, in danger, in danger. The words stopped meaning much if you said it enough. The old trope was that you didn't have to go all the way to the bottom—but really, you did. Everyone did, but only addicts knew to expect it. All these other people were shocked to find themselves down here.

The fact was, you'd never know you were done till your feet touched the silt. He thought he'd hit that point once before, but this was different. This sensation had turned out to be a relief. All the machinations and rationalizations he'd spent years trying to work out—it was actually very demanding not just to drink the way he did but to try and justify it, too—had fallen away. It was all so simple.

Deep down, Will felt it was unlikely that this was really it for them, for a culture that adored its structures and complexity, adored being moved and transported. Then again, it was also such a half-assed culture in so many ways—he could imagine them having created a vast, flimsy infrastructure that was only good for fifty or sixty years, forever assuming someone else would renew and replace it.

Maybe cars would become a luxury again. Who knew? Will himself always came in on the aftermath—he only realized his wife was done with him when she moved out; he understood there was a problem not when she went out of town and he spent the entire time drinking alone in his house, but only when she came home and her eyes widened in shock when she saw how swollen his whole face had become. It took a certain kind of talent, genius even, to perceive a shift at the moment it occurred: to understand what would arise by allowing two computers to communicate, to hook the energy of an explosion to metal and gears, to harness an electrical impulse and follow its racing path from wire to wire.

Still, you had to wonder where all that energy would go now. Everyone learned the same thing in grade school: energy never died, it simply shape-shifted.

He had the ice, which made him feel both accomplishment and dread. There was one less task to occupy him now, endless minutes now to fill with something else.

Why did everyone act so shocked by the man who'd gone out on the lake? Will could understand; he could see what that morning might have been like as easily as if he'd been there himself: the linoleum on the kitchen floor scrubbed clean, the dog's nails clicking, the smell of lemon detergent and cigarettes. He would have cleaned. He would have left vacuum tracks on the carpet and gleaming surfaces in the kitchen, every book in its place, every bottle bundled into a trash bag.

At the little park, the dock was back in place. Kids were playing in the grass and on the playground toys. The lost man was already forgotten.

Will sat down at a picnic bench and tore open one of the bags. He let the ice dissolve on his tongue, hoping the headache would go away. He should go to the hospital—anyone would say so. He knew it was true. He was afraid to get up and run, however, not knowing what the exertion would do to him. He felt a profound need to stay still, so he tried to heed it, and hoped the kids nearby would notice if anything happened to him. People still tried to help one another: he was out here getting ice for Greta, after all, and he was the least helpful person he knew. But he was trying to offer her a little relief. One useful thing, at least.

He could feel the seizure, for that was what it must be, skulking at the outer edges of his vision. Like a ripple in the grass. He reassured himself that people lived through them all the time. Many didn't remember a thing. He closed his eyes and tried to relax, but he seemed to be clenching painfully all over, a strange dissolving sensation filtering through his muscles and out through his skin. His skin, too, was thinning, the wind tearing away cell after cell as it moved over him, numbing him.

He opened his eyes, just to see if he could. The shapes around him were looming and smoky at the edges: a whirling merry-go-round, its colors blurring; the trunk of a tree that seemed to grow higher. In the water, the dock creaked softly. A shape approached him from the street, leaping forward in flashes, or else he was shutting his eyes and opening them again. He wasn't sure. The shape was dark and many-faceted, its parts able to move independently of one another. He was marveling at this as it drew nearer and then began to dissolve, and now the connected thing separated into three. He almost laughed, finally realizing it was only Greta and her roommates, leaning over him and mercifully blocking out the glare of the sun. They carried sacks that smelled of something earthy and fresh. Someone took the bags of ice from him and he let go.

He opened his eyes again, long enough to see Greta's white teeth, the golden down on her jaw when she turned to speak over her shoulder. Then he gave up and closed them. Even so, there was so much to see! For now his skull surged with brightness, a magnesium flash of sifting white light. The flash seemed to uncrumple at his mind's center and crackle outward, through him and beyond him, toward the swollen sun. Will tried to concentrate on the ice in his mouth and the hand he was gripping in his own, on the sound of the water that now seemed to surround him so intimately. The membrane that separated him from the world had turned out to be so sheer; the film between them stretched until the light began to burst through it. How long had the man stayed on the dock before he finally stood up and took a step? Perhaps the lost man hadn't waited long enough. The urge might have passed. He might have sat down again, let the dog rest its head on his lap, and rowed back.